I0703027

THE SUM OF ALL OUR ANGER

CIVIL WAR 2.0

(War is born of anger.)

THE SUM OF ALL OUR ANGER

WILLIAM R. DOUGLAS

© 2024 by William R. Douglas

WP

WOODBRIDGE PUBLICATIONS

WP

WOODBRIDGE PUBLICATIONS

This is a work of fiction. All the characters and organizations, and events portrayed in it are either from the author's imagination or are used fictitiously.

The SUM of ALL OUR ANGER: CIVIL WAR 2.0

Copyright © 2024 by William R. Douglas All rights reserved.

Woodbridge Publications • July 2024

Woodbridge Publications McHenry, IL

No part of this book may be reproduced or transmitted in any form or by any means, electronic or mechanical, including photocopying, recording, or by any other information storage and retrieval system, without written permission.

Paperback ISBN-13: 979-8-98-595915-4
Hardcover ISBN-13: 979-8-98-595918-5 (dustjacket)
Hardcover ISBN-13: 979-8-98-595917-8 (case wrap edition)
eBook ISBN-13: 979-8-98-595916-1

Library of Congress Control Number: 2024910311

First Edition: July 2024 R6
Printed in the United States of America

Finalist, 2025 Foreword INDIES

Book of the Year Awards — War & Military Fiction

Runner-Up, 2025 Independent Author Network

Book of the Year Awards — Political & Government Fiction

"Quite frankly, I had to put the book down several times and swallow hard before I could continue. Why? Because I could imagine this scenario playing out."

—**Teri M. Brown,** Author and Host of *Online for Authors Podcast*

For God, for Family, for all of us.

E Pluribus Unum,

And

To my wife Laurie,

My best friend and cheerleader,

whom I love more and more every day,

and to my beloved family and friends.

By Captain Timothy "Coach Papa" Stewart

I've always looked at the United States flag with pride—and with deep respect for the men and women who have fought to defend her. After reading The Sum of All Our Anger, that feeling has multiplied a hundredfold.

Some books warn you. Some books move you. *The Sum of All Our Anger* does both—and it does so in a way that hits close to home.

As I turned these pages, I kept coming back to a moment from my own life. Years ago, during one of the darkest seasons I've ever faced, I found myself sitting on the side of my bed in the early morning hours, hands shaking from pain and exhaustion. Cluster headaches had thrown me to my knees more times than I care to count, and anger had quietly started to build—the kind of anger that comes from fear, frustration, and not knowing if tomorrow will be any better.

But in that quiet moment, I felt the Lord whisper something to my heart:

"Be still. I am here."

It didn't make the pain disappear overnight, but it changed me. It reminded me that anger is loud, but God's guidance is steady. That clarity has shaped the way I coach, the way I lead, and the way I love people—whether I'm working with elite athletes, seniors, parents, or anyone striving to become the best version of themselves.

Reading William R. Douglas's work brought that moment rushing back. This novel shows what happens when a nation ignores that still, small voice—when anger becomes our compass, when pride replaces prayer, when division drowns out discernment. But it also shows something else: that faith, courage, and moral conviction still have the power to change the trajectory of a people.

In my coaching, I've seen it firsthand. I've watched families reconcile, athletes break mental barriers, and seniors rediscover joy—not because their circumstances changed, but because their thinking did. When the mind is trained and the heart is anchored, anything is possible.

That's why this book matters. It is both a warning and an invitation—a reminder that America's future won't be secured by shouting matches or political victories, but by individuals willing to think clearly, love deeper, walk humbly, and trust God fully.

As you read, let this story stir something in you. Let it challenge your assumptions, strengthen your convictions, and remind you that while the sum of all our anger may be powerful, the sum of all our faith, courage, hope, and love is far greater— and far more capable of healing our nation.

— Captain Timothy "Coach Papa" Stewart
U.S. Army (Ret.), National Guard, Woodstock, Illinois
Commander, A Company,
1st Battalion, 178th Infantry Regiment,
33rd Infantry Brigade Combat Team

Head Coach, Combat Brain Training
Johnsburg, Illinois

ⅠⅠⅠⅠ ACKNOWLEDGEMENTS ⅠⅠⅠⅠ

Special thanks to my editor, John Gist. His editing and enthusiasm for the book were an encouragement.

Also, thanks to Brenda Drake Lesch for her powerful book cover design. She is truly a gifted graphic designer.

Special thanks to Jason Enterline for his book typesetting and formatting work.

All are remarkably talented and can be found on upwork.com. Last, but not least, I praise the Good Lord for giving me the gift of writing.

Finally, thanks to family, friends, and strangers whose encouragement made writing this second novel possible.

Follow the Author:
www.authorwilliamrdouglas.com

"At what point then is the approach of danger to be expected? I answer, if it ever reach us, it must spring up amongst us. It cannot come from abroad. If destruction be our lot, we must ourselves be its author and finisher. As a nation of freemen, we must live through all time, or die by suicide."

Abraham Lincoln, January 27th, 1838, Springfield, IL

"Everything faded into mist. The past was erased, the erasure was forgotten, the lie became truth."

George Orwell - 1984

"An angry person stirs up conflict, and a hot-tempered person commits many sins."

Proverbs 29:22 (NIV)

Unless an outside force intervenes to intercept our nation's current trajectory, what is its probable outcome, and when?

All of our anger over all our divisions over what is going on in our nation and the world continues to smolder. As of late, the smoke is getting thicker. Where there is smoke, there is usually fire. If there's no fire yet, there soon will be. The question is, when and by what means?

Our current era of anger and division in many respects mirrors the anger and divisiveness over the issue of chattel slavery, which was a national issue in the first half of the 1800s before the American Civil War of 1861-1865.

There were warning signs that went on for decades before that earlier American tragedy. Today, the warning signs of a possible second occurrence of an American tragedy are all around us. Imagine if the warning signs go unheeded, and our issues go unresolved. That's precisely what this novel does. It imagines the unimaginable and takes the reader down the rabbit hole of a Second American Civil War—Civil War 2.0.

Parental Guidance: Consider this novel PG-13. There is usage of foul language, but note that you will not find the F-bomb or the misuse of the Lord's name.

‖‖ **1** ‖‖

POWDER KEG

Samuel Octavia González was still getting used to the idea of being called Mr. President.

A month ago, he—the son of immigrants—was the Governor of the State of Texas. Now, with the State's secession on 23 December 2060, by fiat, Governor González had become President González, the fifth President of the Republic of Texas. The first four were presidents of Texas in the 19th century when Texas was first a sovereign nation.

Unable to sleep that fateful night, González had arisen at 4:54 a.m. and stood silently in his private study in the Texas White House, formerly known as the Governor's Mansion, in the West End neighborhood of the state capital, Austin. Paneled in mahogany with a green carpeted floor, it was his favorite room to sequester in.

The object of his early morning daydreaming was the famous Robert Jenkins Onderdonk's 1903 painting, *The Fall of the Alamo*. It was placed prominently on the wall over the fireplace. The oil painting depicts Davy Crockett and other Alamo defenders in their last moments on 6 March 1836 in hand-to-hand combat with the invading Mexicans led by Antonio López de Santa Anna.

Otherwise known by his abbreviated name, Santa Anna, the Military Dictator of Mexico had crossed the Río Grande on 23 February 1836 to squash what, for the Mexicans, was a rebellion in the Mexican State of Texas. The Texians were determined to wage a war for Independence from Mexico and declared Independence on 2 March 1836.

At one point, Santa Anna had the hubris to declare himself the "Napoleon of the West" during his long, up-and-down fortunes leading Mexico from 1833 to 1855—some of that tenure as a duly elected President, some as a self-appointed military dictator.

Santa Anna was a chameleon who alternately changed political stripes depending on the prevailing political winds of the moment—ascending or taking power as a liberal or a conservative on eleven separate occasions. After the slaughter at the Alamo, Santa Anna gained further infamy in ordering the execution of between 425–445 Texian prisoners of war in the border town of Goliad, Texas, on 27 March 1836, a scant 25 days since the Republic of Texas Declaration of Independence.

On 21 April 1836, the Battle of San Jacinto saw Santa Anna's Army routed, Santa Anna captured, and he narrowly avoided a summary execution at the hands of very angry Texian militiamen, some of whom had lost friends or family in either the Alamo, the Goliad massacres, or both. What ensued was a negotiated withdrawal of what was left of Santa Anna's Army south of the Río Grande, and the Texas War of Independence was over.

After the shedding of much blood, Texas had become a fledgling Republic, a sovereign nation, now fully separated from Mexico. With Texas free but not yet a part of her still young neighbor to the east—The United States of America—Texas was destined to play a crucial role in American history.

Returning in disgrace to Mexico City, Santa Anna was unceremoniously deposed. While Texas had fought bravely for and gained its Independence, in hindsight, its Independence was marred by the fact that it had embraced chattel slavery as acceptable right from the start.

Less than ten years later, Texas willingly relinquished its Independence and agreed to be annexed into the United States of America on 29 December 1845, becoming the 28th State of the American Republic, albeit, regrettably, as a slave state among the rest of her southern brethren.

The issue of slavery continued to fester and embroil every State in the Union and entangle every significant leader of that era. For decades, the problem was a smoldering ember that lay glowing ever hotter next to the proverbial fuse of a powder keg. The issue of slavery's settlement finally lit the fuse with the election of Abraham Lincoln on 6 November 1860.

A steady stream of Southern states seceded from the Union in the ensuing months. South Carolina was the first to secede on 20 December 1860. After the new year, Mississippi on 9 January, Florida on the 10th, Alabama on the 11th, Georgia on the 19th, Louisiana on the 26th, Texas on 1 February, Virginia on 17 April, Arkansas on 6 May, North Carolina on the 20th, Tennessee on 8 June. One by one, they left the Union. They pledged their allegiance to a new nation (at least in their eyes)—the Confederate States of America—with its Capital in Richmond, Virginia, and a leader named President Jefferson Davis.

The paramount reason for the Texas secession vote was the issue of slavery. The South's political rhetoric masked the ugly truth underlying the cry of "states' rights," that truth, of course, being that men, women, and children were being held in bondage against their will, demeaned, demoralized, and considered sub-human.

Texians of 1861 had been okay with slavery for a long time and, sadly, were willing to fight and, if necessary, die to maintain the status quo.

Meanwhile, the lit fuse finally reached the proverbial powder keg in South Carolina on 12 April 1861.

On that date, at 4:30 a.m., South Carolina Confederate Artillery shore batteries opened fire on the Union-held Fort Sumter in the bay of Charleston Harbor to bomb it into oblivion.

The long-feared and anticipated American Civil War had finally arrived.

President González's recollection of history was interrupted by a jarring thought. In 1865, after the defeat of the Confederacy, Texas rejoined the Union and remained a loyal son of the United States of America for the next 196 years. Now, here he was, the President of what amounted to yet again a rebel state in the eyes of the United States. In the eyes of his fellow Texans, he was a patriot standing up to the evils of the Socialist movement that had so utterly upended the United States in the last few decades.

In the 19th century, Texians had shed their blood, first for the cause of Texas Independence from Mexico, then for the lost and warped cause of the Confederacy, and then in the various wars of the 20th and 21st centuries as a loyal son of the Union. Given all that was at stake, the stark reality gnawing at him was the probability that this second secession from the Union would be far costlier in blood than all of Texas's combined history in the 19th through 21st centuries.

As he contemplated the thought, he wondered, *will Friday, December 23rd, 2060, a hundred years from now, be seen as another day of infamy or as the date of a new dawn of freedom?* Time will tell. Whatever the case, a few weeks ago, Texas had voted to remove itself firmly and decisively from what it now saw as the evil powers of socialism that had ruined the United States.

President González, to the core of his being, was ashamed of Texas's 19th-century entanglement with the evils of institutional slavery and the 20th-century lingering wounds of the Jim Crow era. Outweighing that shame was what Texas had become in the 21st century: the most powerful state in the Union economically, bar none. A state where blacks, whites, Latinos, native Americans, Asians, and more had achieved a level of racial harmony that the East and West Coast socialist elites had said was impossible under capitalism. Yet, Texas was thriving and now an independent nation.

There was no doubt that the war clouds that had been forming on the horizon for some time were, in fact, no longer on the horizon. They were right overhead. In what way and on what day would such a conflict would begin, he had determined, would not be by a first shot fired in anger by any Texan soldier. No, when war did come, they would defend liberty with all the might and fury they could muster at a time and place of their choosing.

The manner of Texas's defense was still taking shape. A few hours later that morning, President González was to be briefed on the latest developments. A primary topic would be the final report from Texas Secretary of Defense Adam Johnston. This report concerns the complete inventory of soldiers and equipment of the rapidly formed Armed Forces of the Republic of Texas.

All this weighed heavily on his heart as President González knelt and quietly began praying the Rosary. After fifteen or so minutes, he felt the familiar arms of his wife, Rebecca, embrace him from behind. She said nothing, but he could feel her warm cheek against the back of his head. A short moment later, he whispered, "Amen," and stood up. He turned and looked at his wife of fifteen years, "Hi, love. Good morning. How did you sleep last night?"

"Well, great until a few minutes ago when I noticed you were no longer in bed. Everything okay?"

"For now, it is." He paused, then continued. "I just spent a long time staring at that painting and recalling Texas and American history, the good, the bad, and the ugly. I just prayed for God's wisdom for what lies ahead, and I fear for my fellow citizens. Despite a lot of well-intentioned efforts from good and decent people, I believe the powder keg we've been sitting on all these years is about to blow sky-high. Pray for me, Rebecca. Pray for all of us."

"Oh, hon, you know I have and will continue to do so."

President González's Chief Administrator, Bill White, burst into the room. "Mr. President, the President of the United States is on the comm and wishes to speak with you immediately."

COLONEL ERIC ADAMS RESIDENCE

Lincoln, Montana

0800 MST — 15 Jan 2061

Montana, Big Sky Country, was no illusion or a trumped-up claim from a tourist board. It was natural for anyone with the good sense to travel to Montana and spend some time there.

Retired USMC Colonel Eric Adams had done that twenty years ago and never returned home. Tired of the woke culture that had dominated the military for decades, Colonel Adams had convinced his bride, Anne, to pull up stakes in Newark, New Jersey, and head west to Montana.

After roaming around in their RV for a few months, they came upon the small Rocky Mountain hamlet of Lincoln, Montana. With a 2050 census population of twelve thousand, it was a beautiful place deep in the Montana Rockies front range.

The Colonel's large log cabin had been a haven for his wife and seven kids. The family home was decorated in earthy tones and featured a huge rug depicting a herd of buffalo in the central family room. A massive fieldstone fireplace towered up toward the crest of the cathedral ceiling, some thirty-five feet above his prized stuffed state record rainbow trout.

The trophy was prominently affixed to the center of the chimney above the ten-foot-wide mantle. To the left and right of the chimney high above, massive smart windows that could either let full sun in or as little or none in, if you so desired, using an app on your comm.

As the guests milled about waiting for the start of the meeting, Colonel Adams recalled the one notable scar in the town's otherwise quiet history. The infamous, long-ago-deceased resident Ted Kaczynski—aka "the Unabomber"—had been arrested in Lincoln on 3 April 1996.

Convicted on Domestic Terrorism charges, Kaczynski had been sentenced to eight life sentences in prison without the possibility of parole. Eric had no clue who the guy was until he moved to Lincoln and was told the sad tale of the Unabomber and his brief reign of terror, which had occurred long before Eric was born.

One thing was for sure: The Colonel had formed the opinion that, as the Commander of the Rocky Mountain Militia, he would not tolerate any nut jobs within the ranks of the militia. No white supremacists, ever. They would conduct themselves by the book or be subjected to the Uniform Code of Military Justice.

In forming a network with numerous like-minded militias across the country, Colonel Adams had personally vetted each group. There were some militias he refused to let in, especially if they were Nazis and white supremacists. He welcomed all patriot militias that were indeed Constitutionalists and that would judge a man or woman by the content of their character rather than the color of their skin.

After the socialist wave had swept through the eastern and western seaboard states in the 2050 elections, it became clear to Eric that it was just a matter of time before the Constitutional Republic of the United States of America would exist in name only.

It seemed to the Colonel that the socialists, especially the ultra-left-wing radicals who called themselves the 1619 Red Brigade, were hell-bent on their mantra to "Tear it all down." This meant deconstructing and then reconstructing the United States in their own socialist image.

The socialists' plans—in his circle of family, friends, neighbors, and the unanimous opinion of his fellow militiamen—bore no resemblance to the Founding Fathers' original vision for the United States. They had even heard rumors that the New Way was hell-bent on demolishing significant monuments.

Eric had studied the history of the 1619 Red Brigade and knew it well. Formed twenty years earlier with the merger of Antifa (a much older group prone to violence) and another radical group called Social Justice Action, the 1619 Red Brigade had, in time, become a paramilitary organization with a sordid past.

Eric had concluded a few years earlier that a major fight was brewing for the heart and soul of the nation, and this fight would not be with words or ballots but with bullets—lots, and lots of bullets. In his mind, each side's resentment and hatred towards the others' politics and worldview were now so deeply ingrained that there was nothing left to choose but sides. He and his soldiers had prepared for several years for a second American Civil War. When and how this second occurrence on American soil would start was anybody's guess.

Eric knew in his heart that the patriotic plans they were forming were well thought out and sound. More importantly, they were in perfect alignment with his values and understanding of the nation's founding documents. On top of that, every fiber of his being was convinced he would be exercising his military oath to "preserve, protect and defend the Constitution of the United States against all enemies, foreign and domestic."

What was shocking in his mind was the thought that America's demise had come at the hands of domestics, fellow citizens, all of whom, in his judgment, were Trojan Horses and pawns of a larger conspiracy to replace the Old Way, a Constitutional Republic, with the New Way, a socialist state with Marxist foundations. For a generation, the most hard-core socialists had been smart enough not ever to utter the 'C' word, i.e., Communism, knowing full well that for the vast majority of Moderate Democrats and all Republicans, the word was a proverbial Third Rail.

With the big meeting in a few days with like-minded militia leaders from over twenty-eight states, the stakes were high and about to escalate to unbelievable proportions.

After calling the local meeting to order, he took his seat at the large mahogany dining table. Colonel Adams picked up his sat phone, turned on the encryption switch, and sent the following text to the allied militia leaders across the country:

> *We are a go for 0700 at the predetermined locale. Please turn off your sat phones before departure out of an abundance of caution to avoid any chance of tracking.*

Adam's text tag was automatically inserted at the end of his communique to the militia leaders.

This message was sent using Encryption 2059 self-destruct protocol and will disappear permanently from your sat phone and servers in sixty seconds. My sat phone will go dark in ten minutes.
- Semper Fi.

After reviewing his message again and being satisfied, he hit "Send." Eric put his phone down and looked around the table at his assembled brain trust. "Well, everyone, I'm not sure what lies ahead. I know it's been a long time coming, and by some miracle of God, it hasn't happened a lot earlier than now. Perhaps the Good Lord was giving everyone on both sides a good, long time to turn things around.

"Ya know, back in the 1970s, the Communists still ruled Russia. There was this famous Russian dissident. A guy by the name of Aleksandr Solzhenitsyn. In 1970, he was awarded the Nobel Prize for literature. Then, in 1973, he published his most famous book, *The Gulag Archipelago*. I recall the words of Solzhenitsyn's speech for the Templeton Prize for Progress in Religion. He wrote: 'But the world had never known a godlessness as organized, militarized, and tenaciously malevolent as that practiced by Marxism. Within the philosophical system of Marx and Lenin, and at the heart of their psychology, hatred of God is the principal driving force, more fundamental than all their political and economic pretensions.'

"In that same speech, he also said this, 'Men have forgotten God; that's why all this has happened.'

"Well, I have not forgotten God. I appeal to the King of Heaven daily. I trust you do too. I may not like where things are at right now, and I'm sure you don't either. But what can we do? I feel like we've been pushed into a corner so hard and tight that there is nothing left for us to do except execute a coordinated use of force not seen on American soil since the 1860s. A use of force to defend our very way of life and take back the nation. I pray God help us all."

WILL ROGERS NATIONAL GUARD BASE

Oklahoma City, Oklahoma

0800 CST — 15 Jan 2061

Brigadier General Chester Williamson was deep in thought at his desk. The room was small and painted a light shade of blue. It was long overdue for a new coat of paint. The linoleum was spotless, but old. On the wall behind him, a photograph of Oklahoma native Air Force Lieutenant General Thomas P. Stafford of Apollo 10 fame in 1969. On his desk sat a comprehensive inventory of all Oklahoma Air and Army National Guard unit soldiers and materiel.

Under strict secrecy at the request of Oklahoma Governor Mary Whitfield, he was conducting an accurate inventory of all assets under the Governor's direct command and control. Except when federalized in times of war or emergency, the Governor of each State was the Commander-in-Chief of their respective state National Guard units and assets.

Promoted to his post six weeks earlier, General Williamson was astonished at the vast array of firepower under the Governor's direct command and control.

The detailed inventory reported that the forces included 15,000 citizen soldiers and airmen, as well as 5,000 reservists. Notable in the materiel report were 145 M1BR Main Battle Tanks (the first to be fully robotic and equipped with Artificial Intelligence), 200 Drone Main Battle Tanks, 100 155mm self-propelled howitzers, 195 other artillery pieces, 75 F-31 fighter drones, 75 older F-25 fighter jets, 15 Patriot GEN-12 Missile Batteries, 100 SD22 SWARM batteries, 3 AWACS, 10 KC157 airborne refueling tankers, 175 combat air drones, 250 kamikaze drones, and 35 surveillance drones. The list continued for several pages, detailing all manner of handheld, shoulder-fired, or other weaponry whose original design and intent, in the eyes of their inventors, was to kill large numbers of enemy soldiers in some distant land over on the other side of a vast ocean.

A shudder went up and down the general's spine at the thought of what lay ahead. Would this vast array of firepower be brought to bear on his fellow citizens? He prayed not. His thoughts wandered towards his wife Laurie, their six children, and their eight grandkids. Those thoughts were jarred away by the sound of his desk phone ringing.

"General Williamson here."

"Good morning, general. This is Governor Whitfield."

"Good morning, governor. I have the full inventory report. I'll be ready at this morning's briefing. Any private thoughts you care to share?"

The Governor paused. The general was one of her most trusted and loyal confidants. "We're sitting on a powder keg, Chester. The Presidential inauguration is a few days away. No one's sure what he's going to say. The rumors are all over the map. I believe he will announce that Texas's secession will not stand. I would not be surprised if he issued an ultimatum, like Texas had better come back into the Union peaceably or else. It seems like each day since his election, the rhetoric has gotten more heated. The pot can only hold so much pressure before she blows." Williamson was quiet for a moment. As a combat veteran, the myriad scenarios that had been playing out in his head at night were the stuff of nightmares. "Good Lord, Governor. How did it come to this? Is the sum of all our anger going to blow sky-high? What's the latest from Speaker Waya at the State House?"

"Well over a two-thirds majority are prepared to vote for secession in the event Texas is attacked. That includes all the CONs and a large majority of the MODs. None of the LIBs are in favor of secession. The numbers go up higher if the flag rumors are true. Then we pick up all the MODs and about seventeen percent of the LIBs."

"Flag rumors? I guess I've been up to my eyeballs in this inventory work. What flag rumors?"

"Word has leaked out from Washington that as a part of his inauguration speech, President Cyrus will unveil a brand-new U.S. Flag to replace the Stars and Stripes and to be immediately adopted, perhaps even raised during the ceremony over the Capitol Dome. He's doing it via an executive order that takes effect immediately after the oath of office. It's a hybrid red flag of the New Way Democratic Socialist Workers Party." The Governor's last few sentences sucked the air out of the general.

Re-gathering his breath, he spoke again, "He wouldn't dare! Replace the Stars and Stripes with a red flag! Are they purposely trying to incite violence?"

"I don't know, Chester. What I do know is that the Old Way of our 250-plus-year-old Constitutional Republic is on the brink of a Second

Civil War. The wild card in all of this is that the other bases here in Oklahoma are not in our control. We've got Altus Air Force Base, which is primarily a training base, and then there's the big prize, Tinker Air Force Base with sizable assets. Then we have Vance out in Enid, which is another training facility. After that, there's Fort Sill Army base in Lawton. I suppose it's a crapshoot what happens when they must choose sides. God help us all."

"Governor, in addition to having God on our side, we'll have the full might of the Oklahoma National Guard. I can assure you; it is a fighting force to be reckoned with. As for those other bases, I've been quietly reconnecting with people I know. There might be a surprise in the offing when the time comes to choose sides."

Whitfield paused for a moment, then continued. "Really? I like the sound of that."

She paused again before saying, "General, if these plans must be implemented, you realize that you and I and the whole lot of us will be considered as having committed high treason. We could hang for this."

"Governor, I swore an oath to preserve, protect, and defend the Constitution of the United States of America. These nutjobs running and ruining the states all up and down both coasts, plus some inland, have trampled the Constitution under their feet for a long time now. I've been a patriot all my life, and no Commie red LIB is going to look me in the eye and call me a traitor. I'll spit the last drop of blood at them before I slip into eternity."

"Well said, general. What about the General Staff and the soldiers and airmen?"

"Governor, we are all behind you one hundred percent."

"Alright then, general, I'll see you at 10 a.m. for the briefing. Be prepared to talk about dissenters and options for isolating them. As far as I'm concerned, they could be traitors in our midst and possibly enemy combatants, saboteurs, or spies."

"Got it. See you then."

As he hung up the phone, the general realized he was angry. He was mad at the people living on the coasts who had, for far too long, considered the "Flyover" part of the United States beneath them. A day of reckoning seemed inevitable. It was not a fight he sought, but, if compelled, a fight he would see through to the finish or die trying.

PRESIDENT-ELECT'S OFFICE

Lower Manhattan, New York, NY

0900 EST — 15 Jan 2061

President-elect Devin Cyrus sat quietly in his office in lower Manhattan, studying his inauguration speech. It had been written and revised several times and was now in the finishing stretches of refinement. With the inauguration just five days away on January 20, he was excited to launch the New Way program that had helped him secure his first term. He was to be the very first openly socialist to take the Oath of Office of President of the United States.

The struggle for Social Justice, as outlined in his New Way Platform, had been ongoing for several decades, with alternating progress and setbacks. Finally, the demographics changed favorably in 2050. Steady advancements had been made up and down both coasts and in some inland parts of the nation.

As a student of history, Cyrus had a deep knowledge of Capitalism, Communism, and Socialism. He was a student of the writings of not only the United States Founding Fathers but also of Marx, Lenin, Trotsky, and other Communists and Socialists. While he freely admitted he hated Stalin and Mao and the hundreds of millions of murders committed under their regimes of terror, he was equally quick to point out the many shortcomings of the Founding Fathers (especially the ones culpable in starting a new nation in 1776, with chattel slavery not abolished in the South).

Over the last fifteen years, Devin Cyrus had come to hate American Capitalism and had targeted it in his long, fiery speeches whenever possible. His draft speech made it very clear that it amounted to a hammer blow to the Old Way and marked a new and enlightened path forward, a path he had fervently embraced. Cyrus's New Way ideology had been all the rage since 2050.

He quietly smirked at the thought of what the CONs (Conservatives) would feel after his speech revealed the New Way's plans. Plans that would further isolate and demonize them. The CONs were mainly composed of Conservative Evangelical Christians, Catholics, Orthodox Christians, Jews, Muslims, Hindus, and even secularists, all bound together by their unwavering support for the U.S. Constitution. Cyrus hated the CONs' guts with every fiber of his being. In his mind, the only good CONs were those who were willing to recant and embrace the New Way ideology, voluntarily or not. Publicly, he had long mastered the political art of saying a lot of words but not saying anything substantive. He was delighted to see his earlier efforts to propagandize the terms

CONs, MODs, LIBs, Old Way, and New Way had succeeded in entering the everyday lexicon of Americans.

The MODs (Moderates), who decades earlier had been the traditional New Deal, and fiercely patriotic, Democrats of Rooseveltian and Kennedy lore, mixed in with some Republicans (denigrated as RINOs—Republicans in Name Only).

The LIBs (Liberals) were primarily composed of staunch Socialists, Marxists, anarchists, and atheists—or at least the newly minted ones. And at all costs, never, ever use the "C" word.

Cyrus had carefully studied the steady, hard left shift of the old Democratic Party over the decades. Once the old guard had been pushed out of their leadership roles, the New Way Progressives had swiftly taken their place.

Whenever he thought of President Kennedy, who was fiercely patriotic and equally anti-socialist and anti-communist, he was convinced that Kennedy would never have liked the current strain of Democrats. For Cyrus and the New Way, the Democratic Party for decades had been a useful surrogate host to incubate their Marxist ideology in K-12 and especially in public universities.

At the dawn of a new era, Cyrus had relished the fact that they had been so unbelievably successful in shifting the dial on what was once considered mainstream American Democratic Party ideals to the point of obsolescence. He laughed and thought.

"I bet JFK will roll over in his grave at Arlington today," he said aloud. Cyrus was particularly proud of his successful cornering of and categorization of half the nation in rural and Conservative enclaves as the hated CONs. Of paramount importance in that effort was the framing of what the CONs were, so that the other half of the nation would rally around the cause and purpose of the New Way.

Whenever the opportunity arose, Cyrus repeated his self-minted definition of the CONs as containing every ingredient of the basket of deplorables known to humanity. Universally Republican or Libertarian, Jesus freaks, Bible thumpers, religious bigots, gun lovers, gay haters, flag wavers, patriots, white supremacists, Israel lovers, and Whites—especially Whites.

The *"Jesus Thing,"* had particularly perturbed him. An avowed atheist, he had little room for followers of Jesus and their "flying spaghetti monster god." Yes, he could ever so slightly tolerate some of them, but that *some* had to, in every way, embrace New Way Ideology and Theology. The theology of the New Way gave zero room for many of the historical teachings of the ancient Judeo-Christian church.

Such teachings were especially renounced in New Way Theology, which held that there is no sin (except the sin of rejecting the New Way), no hell (except for those who reject the New Way), no atonement, and no distinctions between gender, sex, and other categories. Everything was permissible (even consensual sex between consenting minors and adults). Darwinian Evolution was exalted, and, in Cyrus's line of thinking, the only true religion. This was the New Way.

Cyrus smiled at the thought of it all.

The silence in his high-rise study room ended abruptly when forty-four-year-old Chief Advisor Matt Kensington entered through the open door. Kensington had been a loyal aide to Cyrus for ten years. He had served as the campaign adviser for Cyrus's successful presidential run and his earlier successful U.S. Senate campaign.

A Harvard graduate, Kensington had shunned his parents' Capitalism decades earlier. He embraced Marxism with an enthusiasm that had caught Cyrus's attention years before Cyrus entered the political arena.

"President-elect Cyrus, I have the final copy of the new flag ready for your review."

Cyrus emerged from his thoughts and looked at his trusted aide as he approached. "Matt, thank you so much for all your hard work on this project. Let's see it!"

With that, Kensington unfolded the 4' by 8' copy of the new United States Flag. The President-elect stared at it, all the while ever so gently nodding his head up and down with approval. The flag was red. Where the Old Way U.S. Flag had a field of blue with fifty-five white stars, the New Way flag had the same size field of green with fifty-five yellow stars.

"I love it!" Cyrus said. "Is the big version ready to fly over the Capitol on inauguration day?"

Kensington was quick to reply, "Yes, sir. The new full flag is eight feet by twelve feet. Sir, are you concerned about the reception you may get with this?

"Hell no. Our unveiling of the New Way U.S. Flag is of paramount importance. I want a visible symbol for all the world to see that the old order of things in the U.S. has passed away and that a new world order is breaking over this nation. We are hitting the big reset button. The corrupt capitalists and their Zionist-loving co-conspirators must be immediately put on notice. They will form ranks behind the New Way or be steamrolled into oblivion. There can be no compromise and no dissent. The dissenters have been spewing their hate speech for long enough. The time for Direct Action is now!

Kensington, usually exuberant around such talk, felt a knot form in his stomach. A feeling of dread washed over him.

Cyrus was surprised at his trusted aide's lack of enthusiasm. "Kensington, are you okay? You should see yourself. You're as pale as a ghost."

SECRET LOCATION—1619 RED BRIGADE HEADQUARTERS
South Loop, Chicago, Illinois
0930 CST — 15 Jan 2061

DeShawn King was probably one of the busiest Black men in the nation. As the Military Commander of the 1619 Red Brigade, a paramilitary arm of the New Way Socialist Workers Party, rest had been a rare commodity as of late.

He and his troops had initially been tasked solely with providing protective detail to Socialist VIPs, including then-candidate Cyrus, in the very earliest days of his presidential campaign. Once Cyrus had broken into the top tier of Democratic presidential candidates, the 1619 Red Brigade had been replaced with Secret Service protection.

Despite self-avowed claims of non-violence, there had been rumors that the 1619 Red Brigade had been working in the shadows to intimidate and suppress CONs from all walks of life.

It was a poetic irony that DeShawn's Father was Lieutenant Colonel Jackson King, 1st Battalion, 178th Infantry Regiment, Illinois Army National Guard, based in Woodstock, Illinois. Woodstock's main claim to fame is the cult classic movie comedy Groundhog Day, filmed on location there in 1992.

Lieutenant Colonel Jackson King was a staunch Old Way Democrat—the rarest of breeds within the MODs. Off-duty, Jackson King was Bishop King, a devout Christian and Pastor of the Christ the King A.M.E. Church in McHenry, Illinois.

For many years, the father-and-son duo had often argued, sometimes ferociously, over the nation's direction. When they started discussing politics, it took all the strength of matriarch Eleanor King to separate the two most influential men in her life.

Married 25 years to Jackson, Eleanor loved both men dearly. Still, she had found it increasingly difficult to stomach DeShawn's increasingly militant rhetoric, especially these last two years when it seemed the entire nation was gearing up for a fight. She had formed a prayer team that met once a week at church, specifically to pray for the nation's peace. She had invited like-minded ladies from other churches of numerous denominations who, in her words, "Loved Jesus." They had quickly grown to a prayer army of 107 ladies.

DeShawn received a secret communique that, while not directly naming him, was more than likely issued by President-elect Cyrus. He had read it and was ready to carry out its orders.

If the secret communique were to leak to the press and then to the public, there's no telling what the response would be, since, even by his admission, the orders were "Non-Conforming," code for Direct Action. Direct Action typically meant violent confrontation.

Assembled in their secret location in the South Loop of Chicago, along with all his 1619 Red Brigade Lieutenants, DeShawn rose to address them, "Comrades, our struggle for Justice is nearing its ultimate date with destiny with the inauguration of President Cyrus. As our leader and as the author of the New Way doctrine, the Old Way's dying breaths are now in motion. Texas secession will not be allowed to stand under any circumstances. She will be the first to be made into an example that the Old Way is dead and that all adherents must recant and embrace the New Way. There is no other way.

"This has been our struggle for decades. Further, I have firm assurances that very soon, we will be the tip of the spear of vast numbers of soldiers and materiel with which to bring about the Utopia we have all longed for these many decades. The end of days of these religious and right-wing political and social bigots is fast approaching. We will fight. Some of us will die, but soon, very soon, the heart of the New Way nation shall beat as one. Death to the Old Way."

IIII **2** IIII

THE FUSE IS LIT

ANACONDA MOUNTAIN RANGE

Southwest of Lincoln, Montana

0700 MST — 16 Jan 2061

Colonel Adams had arrived at the rally point 8 hours earlier. He had slept well and had arisen at 0500 to shower, shave, and eat a hearty breakfast.

The Colonel had discovered a large cave in the area five years earlier. It was remote. There was no cell phone or satellite phone service, and a magnetic anomaly disrupted GPS signals. That part had particularly caught his attention. It was the perfect spot to plan for war. He had spent a year outfitting the cave with analog equipment, solar power, sleeping accommodations, and more, and had even built a meeting room deep in the bowels of the cave.

The forecast for the day called for cloudy skies and the possibility of some light snow the whole week. "Perfect," he said to himself.

Surrounded by his top commanders, they entered the meeting room together and took their seats at the large conference table.

The Colonel stood and approached the podium at his well-lit, well-heated, and well-supplied mountaintop hideaway. "Ladies and Gentlemen, I want to personally thank you for taking the time—and the risk—to come here today to finalize the plans for the defense of Liberty. Before we get down to business, and for posterity's sake, I'd like you to stand and identify yourselves to your fellow Patriots. Let's start from my left.

A loud, gravel-voiced man stood, "Thank you, Colonel. It's a high honor to be here. Fellow Patriots, my name is Colonel David S. Patton. Founder and commander of the Kansas Patriot Militia. Reporting for duty and ready to retake the country back for Liberty. Yes, in case you're wondering, I'm a distant relative of General George S. Patton of WWII fame. I'm certain if he were here, he'd be damned proud of all of you."

Patton took his seat. Next to him was a lady he'd never met.

She spoke up next, "Thank you, Colonel. My name is Rachel Cortez, Commander, Arizona Constitutionalist Militia. Reporting for duty."

She sat down, and then a tall, lanky guy stood up. "Thank you, Colonel. My name is Sergeant Franklin York, United States Marine Corps, retired. I am the founder and commander of the Colorado Patriot Militia. I am reporting for duty.

The first Black man stood up. "Thank you, Colonel. My name is Lemarcus Washington, founder and commanding officer of the 1st Southern Illinois Constitutionalist Militia. I am reporting for duty."

The introductions continued. All told, assembled, and reporting for duty were the leaders of over thirty-five militia groups. When the last of them had introduced themselves, the Colonel stood back up and looked around the table. He took the time to look each leader in the eye, both as a sign of camaraderie and to ensure that his instincts did not detect a mole that could lead to a catastrophe for all of them.

As he looked at each commander and nodded in their direction, he took notice of Lemarcus. Seven other Black commanders were in the room, but the look in Lemarcus' eyes was especially telling. The Colonel had read the briefing report for each person there. He had been impressed with Lemarcus's report, which detailed his journey from being an urban tough in East St. Louis to awakening to the truths of Liberty, as embraced by the CONs and other Old Way supporters, and his subsequent military service in the US Army.

At that moment, the Colonel made a note to explore bringing Lemarcus into the Colonel's inner circle.

The Colonel continued his quiet and methodical tour of his guests.

When he finished, he addressed the citizen soldiers.

"Patriots, as you well know, our beloved country has been under attack in a cold war of ideology for some time. Back in 2030, if you had told me that thirty years later, a Marxist socialist openly critical and even hostile towards every founding document of our nation would ascend to the Presidency, I would have called you nuts. Yet here we are.

"In my opinion, the Presidency is about to be occupied by a man of utter disgust. As you know, the author of the New Way ideology, Comrade Cyrus, wants to burn it all down and start over. To what extent he plans on literally doing this is open to conjecture. I'm sure that his inauguration speech will reveal much more regarding those plans.

"We as patriots have been pushed, threatened, beaten, arrested, falsely charged, imprisoned, and vilified in every way possible by these godless leftists. Adding insult to injury, they accuse us daily of hating almost everything they love.

"Of course, we are none of the things we are accused of. We have been wrongly accused of hating all sorts of things from every letter of the alphabet.

"If there is one thing we do detest, and, yes, even hate, it would be any ideology that seeks to destroy our Constitutional Republic and replace it with a one-party totalitarian regime hell-bent on forcing others to surrender their liberties over to them. On that point alone, I am prepared to fight with all the strength and might I can muster and, if need be, give the last full measure of devotion to the cause of Liberty!

"The argument some LIBs make that the Constitution is a living and breathing document fails scrutiny and is dangerous. In the early part of this century, a man named Benjamin Zycher, a senior fellow at the American Enterprise Institute in Washington, D.C., briefly summarized the case against the Constitution as a living and breathing document. He wrote: 'The basic purpose of the Constitution is the protection of political minorities from the whims and passions of the political majority of the moment. That is the central meaning of the separation of powers, federalism, federal powers limited to those enumerated, the Bill of Rights generally, and the Ninth and Tenth Amendments in particular.'

"Zycher further solidifies his case, and says: 'If the Constitution is a living and breathing document, it means, by definition, that it should reflect the preferences of the current political majority. If the Constitution is interpreted by jurists in that way, it cannot systematically protect political minorities. So a living and breathing Constitution is a dead Constitution in its fundamental purposes, and protection of the original meaning of the Constitution is the only way to make it truly living.'

"To top off that insanity, Cyrus's New Way ideology goes a step further and labels all these founding documents as obsolete instruments of White supremacy that must be replaced!

"To hell with that idea!" The room erupted into cheers.

Generally, a quiet man who didn't like being the center of attention, Colonel Adams quickly motioned with both hands for the crowd to quiet down and take their seats.

"I have been a fan of American History almost all my life. I have studied and know it inside and out, from front to back. I have a hobby of collecting old magazines, particularly those of historic significance. I have a particular fondness for the large, old-print-format magazines of the early to mid-20th century. They were powerful communicators in their day. Their heyday was decades before the advent of the digital age. They held their own when the radio came along. They had a significant impact before, during, and after World War II.

"In the 1950s, they still had an impact when television pushed radio into second place. Most Americans have long since forgotten their names. Life, Look, Collier's, The Saturday Evening Post, and many others.

"On 6 January 1941, exactly eleven months and one day before the Day of Infamy of the Imperial Japanese sneak attack on Pearl Harbor on 7 December 1941, Democratic President Franklin Delano Roosevelt gave his State of the Union Address before Congress. It became known as his Four Freedoms address. World War II was raging on three continents at that moment, but America was not yet in the fight.

"He said these words, and I quote: 'In the future days, which we seek to make secure, we look forward to a world founded upon four essential human freedoms. The first is freedom of speech and expression—everywhere in the world. The second is the freedom of every person to worship God in his own way—everywhere in the world. The third is freedom from want—which, translated into world terms, means economic understandings that will secure to every nation a healthy peacetime life for its inhabitants—everywhere in the world. The fourth is freedom from fear—which, translated into world terms, means a worldwide reduction of armaments to such a point and in such a thorough fashion that no nation will be in a position to commit an act of physical aggression against any neighbor—anywhere in the world.'

"After he gave that speech, a famous illustrator of those times named Norman Rockwell took it upon himself to illustrate those four freedoms in his own way. He was employed by a very popular magazine of the day, The Saturday Evening Post, which I mentioned a few moments ago.

"In 1942, the artwork was done. The Four Freedoms paintings were adopted by the U.S. War Department and used to help sell War Bonds during World War II. The first one, Freedom of Speech, also appeared in the 20 February 1943 edition of The Saturday Evening Post. Then, one each week for the other three paintings. I just so happen to have a copy of all four magazines here from my collection. I want you to look at these as I pass them around. They illustrate the heart of our struggle to re-establish Liberty throughout the land."

Adams removed the archaic magazines from four large yellow manila folders wrapped in plastic. After cautioning those present to handle the magazines with care due to their age (120+ years), he handed them over to Patton.

Adams continued, "I don't have to tell you how the New Way has mangled Freedom of Speech and cloaked it under the guise of hate speech and how it has mangled other parts of our Constitution.

"These woke policies have many Americans living in fear of arrest and imprisonment. Religion is okay with them, so long as it fits every iota of their ideology, the rest be damned, which would, of course, mean Conservative Christians, Jews, Muslims, Hindus, and the like would be outlaws.

"These policies have utterly failed to resolve poverty, especially in the inner cities of most American cities. Millions of inner-city Americans want jobs, higher education, decent food, and, most of all, hope.

"Lastly, millions of Americans live in fear as the failed ideology of these Marxist criminals led to the loss of thousands of lives to criminal gangs and individuals that many LIB District Attorneys from coast to coast often let go or failed to prosecute fully. If it hadn't been for President Black calling out the National Guard in 2033, I dare say we would have several major cities in the hands of criminal gangs.

"Patriots, I don't know how and when this fight will begin, but I do know this. The silent majority will be with us. Large numbers of our Armed Forces will be with us. God will be with us, and we will achieve the inevitable victory over tyranny, so help me God. As was said at the beginning of our nation's first struggle for freedom in 1775, let it be said yet again and with equal if not greater fervor, 'Give me Liberty, or give me death!'"

The Assembly again arose to cheers. Adams's response was the same. After quickly quieting the crowd down, he offered his closing comments.

"Recall the quote from a founding father and Patriot, Thomas Paine, who was also the author of the booklet *Common Sense*. On 23 December 1776, he published a booklet entitled *The Crisis*. It was directed to the members of the fledgling Continental Army, which at that time was ragged and nearing collapse. The opening line states: 'These are the times that try men's souls.'

"Certainly, these last several years have been trying times for all men and women of Liberty. But far be it from me to say that we are currently ragged or on the verge of collapse. No, quite the contrary, we are robust in health and supplies, well trained, stout of arms, absolute in our resolve, and organized in our plans. The fuse is lit. The fight is soon to erupt and be upon us. With faith in God and the cause of Liberty, our armed forces that rally to our side, and Patriot citizen soldiers ready, willing, and of similar resolve to fight with us, we will bring the battle to our enemy.

"If need be, we will do so aggressively to restore Liberty's light. For now, let's return to our homes for a time of preparation and await the second shot heard round the world. You've all seen the coded message that will be sent. Never utter it. Memorize it and be ready to act."

DeShawn King was in a grand mood. A few days from now, the culmination of years of struggle that the New Way Progressive Socialist Party had championed, campaigned for, and won over a narrow margin of the nation's voters would result in the first-ever openly Socialist President of the United States of America.

DeShawn had just returned from a New Way leadership meeting.

While there, he was invited to stay behind for the closed-door session with party elites. In it, plans were laid out for the first one hundred days of the new administration. It was in that meeting that he got the surprise of his life—yet another closed-door meeting with an even smaller group of select leadership.

In that meeting, he heard of the President-elect's plan, codenamed Operation Five Points. Five Points was a radical plan to transform the United States in five stages within the first hundred days of the new administration. Its secrecy was necessitated by the fact that the CONs would likely revolt if they got wind of it. Party elites had determined that Operation Five Points would never be revealed to the public. It would be implemented for the benefit of the nation's workers and the overall worldwide progressive socialist movement, whose goal was the destruction of capitalism, preferably peaceably.

As DeShawn contemplated all that he had heard, he felt a sense of jubilation for his people and his country. *Finally*, he thought, *America can be righted from the evils of these last four hundred-plus years. All those Black martyrs who were murdered by the police. All the lynchings in the Jim Crow era. All the other injustices to people of color. The time to burn it all down and start over is finally here.* His thoughts were interrupted by the sound of his comm ringing. As he looked at the caller ID, he could see it was his father. He took a deep breath before answering.

"Hello, Dad."

"Hi, Son. It's been a while since we last spoke. I thought I'd see if I could catch you in a free time so we could catch up. How have you been?"

"Real busy, Dad. I just got back from a pretty much all-day meeting. I'm feeling jubilant and exhausted at the same time. How's Mom?"

"She's right here listening in. I got you on speaker."

"Hi, Son. Miss you much, punkin'. Pray for you every day."

"Aw, Ma, why do you waste your time with that Jesus stuff? It's all a bunch of crap."

"Now, Son, I didn't call for you to insult our faith, I called…"

"Ya, I know, you called to talk about what's goin' on. Well, I'll tell you what's goin' on. A new day is about to dawn. The centuries of oppression are almost over, and I can't wait to see the CONs get their due. What about you, Dad, or should I address you as Bishop King or Lieutenant King?"

"I'll settle for just plain old, Dad, if it's not too much of a bother. I'm curious, what exactly do you think will happen regarding the CONs getting their due? Do you know something I don't?"

At that, DeShawn's radar went off. He knew what he had been told today was top secret. He had taken an oath, and he intended to keep it.

"Just a figure of speech, Dad."

"Son, your mother and I are greatly concerned for you. We've been following the party news and the President-elect's speeches. To be perfectly honest with you, they have both of us feeling ill at ease."

"C'mon, Dad, what are you talking about? You both voted for him."

"Son, your mother and I long ago stopped voting for personalities and campaign rhetoric. We take our votes very seriously and always dive deep into the candidates' policy papers posted online. We liked most of Cyrus's plans, but I have to say I'm not hearing much about them now. One would expect that post-election, we would start hearing more of the fine print of these plans—instead, all this other stuff. You know your Mom and I have thought differently since our awakening. Our views are still evolving as we speak."

"*Awakening*? You would bring that up again. You know as well as I do that 'woke' and 'awakening' mean two very different things in the ideology of the New Way. Woke is to be enlightened. Awakening is just more racist White folk talk."

Lieutenant King knew where the conversation was headed, but he had to defend what he believed to be the truth. "Son, in my opinion, our people have yet to prosper under the New Way at all. In many ways, the New Way is merely a rebranding of the failed policies of the past, which have left many of our people impoverished across generations. When your mother and I had our awakening to what's really going on, we were determined to become independent and embrace a perspective that saw some good in both the CONs' way of thinking and the MODs of the Old Way. The hard-core LIBs have, in my mind, become way too radical. These are scary times, and every week, the rhetoric gets hotter.

"I see no reason why cooler heads cannot prevail, intervene even, and turn down the temperature. A Civil War with our modern weaponry would be an utter catastrophe and—"

Mrs. King interrupted her husband, "Son, I have been having a vision every night for the last month. It's always the same: a red horse runs from coast to coast and north to south, and everywhere it goes, smoke and fire are behind it. I beg you, listen to your father. We could be on the verge of something awful about to happen, and we don't want to see you get caught up in it and get hurt or worse."

DeShawn was taken aback by the forcefulness of his mother's plea. He was also slightly humored in that he knew a little about what was coming, but as far as he was concerned, the result would be a primarily peaceful cleansing of the land, not destruction. Remembering the oath from earlier in the day, he dared not hint. "Ma, that's what I was talkin' about earlier. You read some Bible verse or something, then you get carried off in your dreams, and your mind gets the best of you. I promise you'll feel jubilation at the end of President Cyrus's Inaugural Address to the nation. Just you wait."

There was an awkward pause before Jackson spoke, "And if you're wrong, Son?"

"Not even a remote possibility. Mom and Dad, it's been good to catch up a little. I'll call the day after the inauguration, and we can talk some more. I think you'll both feel much better about things, as they're about to undergo a lot of positive change. Love you."

"Love you too, Son." When Jackson hung up the phone, an uneasy feeling came over him. Sitting there quietly contemplating the conversation with his only child, he glanced back at Eleanor, his bride of twenty-seven years.

She drew near to him and hugged him from behind. "Baby, what are you thinking?"

"I didn't want to tell you this and frighten you. Especially after you told me about your recurring nightmare…"

"Baby, I told you already. It was not a nightmare. I think it may have been a vision. Scary? Yes. But I believe it to be a message from God and not a nightmare of my imagining."

King stood there and pondered his wife's words. "Understood. I've been having a recurring dream myself. Seems like it may have started about the same time yours did."

"Well, tell me about it."

"It's black and white—cloudy and daytime. I'm out in the open somewhere. There's a battle going on. Everyone has run out of ammunition, and we start going at each other in hand-to-hand combat. There's a great deal of commotion going on, then it gets quieter, and then I see this soldier ready to plunge a bayonet into me. Then I wake up, always covered in sweat."

IIII **3** IIII

RAISE THE FLAG

WALDORF ASTORIA

Washington, D.C.

0700 EST — 20 Jan 2061

It was Presidential Inauguration Day, 20 January 2061. At 0700, Capitol Hill was quiet.

The temporary seating on the west porch of the U.S. Capitol awaited the day's VIPs of every sort.

The empty seats below the porch heading towards the Washington Monument were also in their places. The quiet would soon give way as the seats were ready to receive the multitude of everyday Americans invited by their respective Senators or Congresspersons to take in the pomp and circumstance of the peaceful transfer of power.

Presidential Inauguration Day was something that had primarily occurred peacefully every four years without fail since the very first

Presidential Inauguration of George Washington on Thursday, 30 April 1789.

The uninterrupted transfer of power was a hallmark of the United States. The first peaceful transfer of power took place on 4 March 1797, when outgoing President George Washington witnessed the Oath of Office at the Inauguration of John Adams as the Second President of the United States. Adams served as Washington's vice president for both of Washington's two terms in office. Washington had self-imposed a two-term limit, convinced that serving a third term would set a dangerous precedent for the fledgling nation.

On rare occasions, Presidential Inaugurations have seen mass protests and even violence on the day of the ceremony or in the days leading up to it. In fact, with the nation so divided, every Presidential Inauguration since 2017 has seen protesters in varying numbers and of varying temperaments.

On 20 January 2041, the D.C. National Guard was called out after thousands of protesters attempted to breach the outer security perimeter for the Presidential Inauguration of President-elect Michelle Kassia.

The protesters were opposed to the first popularly elected President since the cancellation of the Electoral College two years earlier in the landmark Supreme Court case of *The State of California v. The People of the United States.*

On 3 July 2039, the high court handed down its decision. In a partisan line vote, the court had ruled 7-6 in favor of the Plaintiff, the State of California. California Attorney General Gavin Amayah had argued before the court to cancel Article II, Section 1 of the U.S. Constitution, which, he stated, was "irrelevant in the modern era and thus obsolete" and "a threat to democracy." By canceling Article II, Section 1, the high court had immediately abolished the Electoral College.

On 6 January 2021, tens of thousands of Trump supporters gathered for the "Stop the Steal" rally on the Ellipse of the White House Complex. They were encouraged by the President to march to the U.S. Capitol to peacefully protest their claims of election fraud, hoping that Vice-President Pence would temporarily delay the certification of the Electoral College vote, scheduled for that day. At the same time, key swing-state legislatures reviewed claims that the election had been stolen. At the same time as the rally and march, inside the Capitol, Congress was preparing to be in session, with Vice-President Pence presiding, and to officially give President-elect Joe Biden the final Constitutional authority required before taking the oath of office on 20 January 2021.

After marching to the Capitol building, approximately 2,000 pro-Trump protesters crossed the security perimeter. A riot ensued, and many protesters physically entered the officially closed-for-the-day Capitol building.

Seven deaths were attributed to the sad day, including Capitol Hill Police Officer Brian Sicknick on 7 January, from injuries sustained during the riot. Unarmed Pro-Trump protester Ashli Babbet, an Air Force Veteran, was fatally shot by a Capitol Police officer as she attempted to enter the House Chamber, where the electoral college certification was soon scheduled to occur.

D.C. Police Department Officer Jeffrey Smith committed suicide on 7 January. Pro-Trump protester Kevin D. Greeson died of a heart attack on a sidewalk west of the Capitol. Capitol Police Officer Howard S. Liebengood also committed suicide four days afterward. Pro-Trump protester

Rosanne Boyland was trampled to death, and pro-Trump supporter and Trumparoo website founder Benjamin Philips died from a stroke.

On 20 January 2017, thousands of Antifa, anarchists, and socialists rioted in the central business district of downtown Washington, D.C. during the Trump inauguration for his first term, causing tens of thousands of dollars of damage, primarily to Democrat-owned businesses.

On 20 January 2005, thousands of anti-war protesters showed up for President George W. Bush's second inauguration to protest the Iraq War.

On 20 January 2001, thousands of angry protesters, many from NOW, (National Organization for Women), protested the Inauguration of Texas governor George W. Bush to his first term as President of the United States. The dominant theme of the protesters was that the Presidential election had been stolen. George W. Bush had narrowly lost the popular vote to Vice President Al Gore, Jr. in the 2000 presidential election. Still, the all-important Electoral Vote count had stood frozen for weeks because the Florida count became embroiled in the hanging-chads controversy involving paper punch-card ballots used in some locales.

The issue hinged on the status of 61,000 uncounted undervotes because the chads were still partially attached to the paper ballots. These hanging chads were located on the part of the paper ballot that pertained to the presidential choice. The two leading candidates were Democratic Nominee Al Gore, Jr. (then the sitting Vice President under President William Jefferson Clinton) and Texas Governor George W. Bush.

Recounts and lawsuits involved the Florida Supreme Court and the United States Supreme Court. The legal tug of war between the Bush and Gore Campaigns and the court system held up the final certification of Florida's twenty-five electors.

The question of who would take the Oath of Office on 20 January 2001 was finally decided upon by the United States Supreme Court on 12 December 2000. In a narrow landmark 5-4 ruling in the case of *Bush v. Gore*, Bush won the case and thus was awarded Florida's twenty-five electoral votes and thus was awarded the presidency.

Governor George W. Bush won the state of Florida by just 537 votes out of almost six million cast in the Sunshine State. The issue of the 61,000 uncounted undervotes, tied to the hanging chads controversy, had naturally inflamed doubts within the Gore campaign and, by extension, among the Gore voters.

The final popular vote tally for the presidency was Al Gore, Jr. 50,999,897 and Texas governor George W. Bush 50,456,002.

The controversial all-important Electoral Vote count was even closer, with Bush being awarded 271 electors (one more than the threshold of 270 to become president) to Gore's 266 electors.

On 20 January 1973, thousands of anti-war protesters opposed to the Vietnam War protested the inauguration of Richard M. Nixon to his second term.

On 19 January 1913, one day before the inauguration of President Woodrow Wilson, thousands of women marched on Washington in support of the suffrage movement seeking the right to vote.

All the marchers were bullied by being verbally assaulted. Some of the marchers were spat upon, and several were beaten up. Several of the women had to be hospitalized. The entire sad affair is generally recognized as the first large-scale inauguration protest.

The general mistreatment of the marchers was so prominent that it led to the firing of the Capitol Police Chief. The right to vote was granted to women with the 19th Amendment to the United States Constitution, passed by Congress on 4 June 1919 and ratified by the states on 18 August 1920.

On 20 January 1829, President John Quincy Adams became the first sitting president to boycott the inauguration of his successor, Andrew Jackson, who was known as the first populist president and a hero of the War of 1812. A great many members of Congress also protested by boycotting the inauguration.

After every presidential election since the beginning of the Republic almost three hundred years earlier, this day was expected to be no different, despite the tensions across America. The Capitol Hill Police and the United States Secret Service had gone to great lengths to create layers of security rings around the Capitol Complex and the Inauguration Day seating areas.

President-elect Devin Cyrus was briefed in the Presidential Suite on the Inauguration Day schedule. Cyrus's newly appointed Chief of Staff, former Campaign Chief Matt Kensington, was doing one final run-through of the day's packed itinerary.

"0700 Breakfast at the White House with President Franklin and the First Lady. 0800, a private meeting in the Oval Office with just the two of you. 0900, the motorcade departs for the Capitol. 0920 private reception with Congressional leadership at the Capitol with yourself and outgoing President Franklin and the First Lady. 1145 outgoing Vice-President Harrington and the second lady are seated, followed by the Vice-President-elect.

"At noon, the Chief Justice, then yourself for the oath of office…" Cyrus interrupted, "I thought about this last night. No Bible, and none of that *preserve, protect, and defend the Constitution* crap. Must I say that?"

"Absolutely. You'd be crazy not to. As for the Bible, no Bible?"

"Yes, I suppose you win on the second point. On the first, non-negotiable. No Bible. Also, no invocation. I never believed in any of that stuff. I'll not be a hypocrite and take an oath with my hand on a pack of lies."

"But Mr. President, that's been the custom for…"

"Custom be damned! I'm a hard-core atheist. I brought a first edition of Charles Darwin's *On the Origin of Species*. That's the Bible of the New Way. We can use that in place of the Christian Bible. Besides, that old book is at the heart of the Old Way."

Kensington sat quietly for a moment, not sure what to say next. Cyrus broke the ice, "Matt, is everything all set for the flag-raising?"

"Yes, Mr. President. But are you sure you want to do this today?"

"Matt, today we draw a line of demarcation between the Old Way and the New Way. The Old Way flag has been a symbol of oppression since 1776. Its time has passed, and we need to energize my New Way followers immediately. We have a lot of work to do starting today. The people are counting on me to hit the ground running and bring in rapid change, especially with this Texas thing getting out of hand."

PRIVATE RESIDENCE

Washington, D.C.

0700 EST — 20 Jan 2061

The Chief Justice of the United States, Douglass Fredericks, was alone in his study. A Civil War buff, he quietly admired the Abraham

Lincoln Bible, which was on loan to him from the Library of Congress for the swearing-in ceremony of President Devin Cyrus, which was to take place in a few hours.

The historical Bible was first used at Abraham Lincoln's inauguration on 4 March 1861 during the swearing-in of the 16th President of the United States. It had been brought to the inauguration by William Thomas Carroll, a clerk of the U.S. Supreme Court.

Little did Lincoln know, or anyone else for that matter, that after Lincoln had placed his hands upon that Bible and taken the Oath of Office, a scant thirty-nine days later, on 12 April 1861, in Charleston, South Carolina, newly appointed Confederate General P.T. Beauregard would give the order to commence fire. The order started a thirty-six-hour artillery barrage targeting the Union Fort Sumter, 4 miles out from the harbor of Charleston. The attack would be the opening shots of the Civil War.

A MOD himself, Fredericks had been undecided on his presidential vote until he stepped into the polling booth two months earlier. It was with hesitancy that he cast his vote for Cyrus. Fredericks had been confirmed to the Supreme Court eight years earlier. Even before his tenure on the high court, much had changed, and not all of it was good.

Easily tops among the lousy list, in his firm conviction, was the 2039 7-6 ruling in favor of abolishing the Electoral College.

Second was the 8-5 majority ruling one year ago that legalized consensual sex between adults and minors as young as twelve in the landmark *NAMBLO (National Man Boy Love Organization) v. the United States.* Fredericks and Justices Lee, Palm, Peterson, and Rubin had been among the five dissenting votes.

Third on his lousy list was the narrower 7-6 ruling four years ago that radically altered the judicial understanding of the First and Second Amendments of the United States Constitution.

In that case, *Garland v. Harney*, the court ruled that the Freedom of Religion clause of the First Amendment did not cover words or passages deemed "hate speech" in officially recognized holy books, as well as in other writings, broadcasts, and social media. In other words, any speech or writings deemed offensive or as hate speech by any state or local jurisdiction were not protected by the Freedom of Speech clause enshrined in the First Amendment of the United States Constitution. The ruling freed states and local jurisdictions to issue gag orders or to pass laws that codify as hate speech those verses, writings, teachings, and other expressions deemed offensive. Criminal codes and punishment were left to each jurisdiction.

Also in *Garland v. Harney*, the court found that free speech—whether in the secular arena or a house of worship—did not include speech deemed hate speech. He dissented and wrote the minority opinion.

Further, in the same case, the court ruled that the Second Amendment applied only to black-powder muskets and that ownership of modern firearms was not subject to federal regulation. Individual states, counties, and municipalities had the authority to regulate or ban civilian possession of firearms.

Uncertain of the nation's near-term future—especially after Texas's secession—Fredericks was profoundly hopeful that President Cyrus would offer words of unity in his inaugural address to avoid an all-out civil war.

He became uneasy as he contemplated the day ahead and what might follow in the coming weeks. His private thoughts were jarred when his comm rang. "Hello, this is the Chief Justice."

"Justice Fredericks, this is Matt Kensington, Chief of Staff to President-elect Cyrus. The President-elect wishes to inform you that he is bringing a copy of Charles Darwin's book, *On the Origin of Species*, to the inauguration. Instead of the Bible, he will place his right hand upon it to take the oath."

The Chief Justice was sure he heard every word. But his brain was slow to process it. After a several-second pause, Kensington broke the silence. "Justice Fredericks, are you there? Did you hear what I just said?"

"Yes, yes, of course, I heard you. May I ask why this last-minute change from tradition?"

"The President-elect told me directly, 'I'll not be a hypocrite and take the oath with my hand on a book I believe to be a pack of lies.'"

Fredericks sat quietly, searching for words. "I respect the President-elect's candor. He knows he'd be only the third president in the nation's history not to place his right hand on the Bible at his inauguration. The last time was 1901 by Teddy Roosevelt."

"Yes, he is aware. He anticipated this question and pointed out that many members of Congress had taken their oaths using other holy books or none at all. President John Quincy Adams used a book of law."

"I'm aware of the two previous deviations from precedent by Adams and Roosevelt. I will point out that a duly elected member of Congress is not the same as the leader of the free world. At the very least, taking the oath of office with the President-elect's hand placed upon a Holy Bible is symbolic of the righteous might of the nation against all foes, foreign and domestic, throughout our history.

"Righteous might? What the hell is that? You sound like a fanatic. The President-elect is quite convinced that for the larger part of American history, she has been unrighteous on multiple fronts. At times, even evil. He intends to hit the big reset switch starting today."

Fredericks knew he was fighting a losing battle and that he should make a tactical withdrawal. "Okay, Mr. Kensington, understood. See you in a bit."

Matt Kensington was thoroughly annoyed at Justice Fredericks. He had wanted to get in the last word, but the connection ended before he could speak. He thought about calling him back but decided to let it go. He was already running late.

Chief Justice Fredericks sat quietly at his desk, staring at the Lincoln Bible. A sense of sadness and foreboding began to wash over him. He thought, *What in the world is happening with my country? How does this all end?* He opened the safe and gently put the Lincoln Bible back in before heading out.

CAPITOL HILL

Washington, D.C.

1200 EST — 20 Jan 2061

The morning had gone according to plan. All the pomp and circumstances of a Presidential Inauguration had been broadcast worldwide. It was a brisk day, slightly overcast, with a temperature of 28 degrees Fahrenheit. The big moment came for the swearing-in of President-elect Cyrus.

Chief Justice Fredericks rose and approached the podium. Cyrus approached the podium as well. Cyrus's Chief of Staff, Matt Kensington, approached and handed the Chief Justice a first-edition, leather-bound copy of Charles Darwin's book, *On the Origin of Species*.

Without words, the Chief Justice took hold of Darwin's book and held it out toward Cyrus. Cyrus placed his left hand upon its aged leather cover.

Fredericks began. "Please place your left hand on the book, raise your right hand, and repeat after me."

Cyrus complied and gave a slight nod of the head towards the Chief Justice.

"I, Devin Cyrus, do solemnly swear…"

"I, Devin Cyrus, do solemnly swear…"

"That I will faithfully execute…"

"That I will faithfully execute…"

"The office of President of the United States…"

"The office of President of the United States…"

"And will to the best of my ability…"

"And will to the best of my ability…"

"Preserve, protect, and defend…"

"Preserve, protect, and defend…"

"The Constitution of the United States."

"The Constitution of the United States."

"So, help me God."

Devin paused and looked slightly angry. He looked down for a moment at Darwin's book, keenly aware of the profound moment. Then he looked into the eyes of the Chief Justice with a cold stare. "Whatever is best for the nation."

Justice Fredericks had mentally prepared himself for a non-traditional response. Without skipping a beat, he stuck out his right hand. "Congratulations, Mr. President," he said.

They shook hands, and the crowd erupted in sustained applause.

The band played "Hail to the Chief." Once they were done and the crowd had settled down, President Cyrus approached the microphone to deliver his inaugural address to the nation.

"My fellow Americans, welcome to the new dawn. Welcome to the New Way. Our moment in history, which we have longed for and striven toward these many years, has finally arrived.

"In 1619, the first slave ship arrived on our shores. This injustice would be the first of many millions more to come.

"In 1776, White men declared their independence from England, stating all sorts of superlatives about freedom, liberty, God, etc. None of which, in their minds, applied to people of color. In their minds, the White man's world was superior to all others in all ways and in every respect.

"These same White men in 1787 then had the audacity to codify in the United States Constitution that an enslaved person was three-fifths of a person.

"Continuing, they embraced an economic system with an ever-increasing level of greed that is hoarding wealth at the very top. Meanwhile, that system has enslaved workers ever since and created a military-industrial complex that robs generations of what could have been their share of income equality of outcome. Redistribution of wealth has been muted specifically due to greed.

"They invented and pushed the lie of American Exceptionalism. They took colonialism and expansionism to new heights. They had the ridiculous idea that their God had manifested or ordained their westward expansion across the continent and that this expansion was some sacred right that included the permission to annihilate and conquer indigenous peoples that had lived there for eons before the arrival of the White man.

"To add insult to injury, they made monuments to honor these liars, crooks, and racists.

"In the twentieth century, they kowtowed to the Zionist movement and caused untold misery, resulting in the expulsion of the Palestinian peoples from their ancient homeland and the wholesale erasure of their nation. They replaced that nation with this insidious Zionist regime that has been a thorn in the side of the world since 1948. We're going to do something about that and soon.

"Now, here in the latter half of the twenty-first century, these basket of deplorables continue to cling to their God, their Jesus, their Bibles, their guns, and their warped remembrance of American history. They fantasize about the good ol' days or what I now refer to as the Old Way.

"They rail against Progressivism and Socialism as if they were some one-eyed monsters. All the while, their retired parents and grandparents partook in the fruits of Socialism with their Medicare, Medicaid, and Social Security retirement checks.

"Through all this, we, the enlightened ones of the New Way, have patiently and earnestly tried to reason with them. We have offered countless ideas, policies, legislation, and more to advance our nation out of the darkness of the Old Way and into the light of the New Way.

"All attempts have fallen on deaf ears. In their way of thinking, there is to be no compromise with us. We are a threat to them. This poses a danger to their vanishing way of life. They wave their Old Way red, white, and blue flag and call it patriotism. One state, Texas, has dared to go rogue and declare itself independent. Rubbish, I say, and mark my words, we'll deal with them soon enough as well.

"In the first hundred days of my administration, I will submit legislation for a universal basic income for all Americans below the poverty level. Free college education. Two years of paid parental leave. A 30-hour work week. A permanent ban on carbon-fueled vehicle sales and ownership. A repeal of the Second Amendment. Reparations checks of $1,000,000 each will be distributed to all African Americans. Paid sick and disability leave. A minimum of one month's paid vacation for all working people. The seizure of all private health insurance companies' assets. Expanding Medicaid and Medicare to cover every living soul in the nation. The immediate shutdown of all remaining nuclear plants. All fossil fuel mining, extraction, refining, and shipping operations are to remain permanently shut down and never to be resumed, even in times of national emergency. "Today, we hit Reset. Today, the Old Way is declared dead. Today, we put on notice all those who wish to cling to the Old Way; please don't. Please give it up. Embrace the New Way or be steamrolled by progress.

"What's coming is a progressive revolution, a new revolution for the American people that will see a new dawn of social justice, diversity, equity, and inclusion with a guaranteed equality of outcome for all peoples.

"Today, I want to gift you all with a surprise." President Cyrus looked behind him and toward the top of the Capitol Dome. He gave a hand signal. High above, the Stars and Stripes, gently waving in the breeze, could be seen being lowered out of sight.

For the assembled on the dais on the Capitol steps and down below in the enormous crowd stretching out towards the Washington Monument, a commotion had been quietly building all the while the new President had been delivering his inaugural address. A smattering of people could be seen leaving their seats below and heading away from the Capitol. The TV news crews had picked up on this and had been capturing the facial expressions of some of them. Among those leaving, more than a few of the ladies appeared to be in tears. The men who had gotten up had a look of disgust or disbelief, or was it anger?

The commotion was suddenly silenced when a flag was seen being raised atop the Capitol's dome. At that exact moment, the wind died, and all was dead calm. As the flag reached the top of the pole, the breeze picked up again, unveiling the new flag. It was twice the size of the Stars and Stripes that had flown there moments ago. Yet it bore no resemblance to the flag it replaced. No one said a word.

The hush remained until the President spoke. "My fellow New Way Americans, our reset must include a clear line of demarcation, not only of the Old Way ideology but also of all her evil symbols.

"By my very first executive order, I present to you the new flag of the United States—an all-red field in honor of the worldwide struggle for workers' rights, justice, and equality.

"Instead of a blue standard, a green one symbolizing our commitment to save the planet from a climate disaster.

"Instead of white stars, fifty-five yellow stars that represent the New Dawn of the New Way for our fifty-five states."

A mixture of cheers and yelling erupted below. It sounded like a mixture of happiness and anger. It was all mixed up. In some parts of the crowd, especially towards the back, fights broke out.

As the commotion built to a crescendo, Justice Fredericks rose from his chair and slipped away.

|||| **4** ||||

CHOOSING SIDES

ILLINOIS NATIONAL GUARD ARMORY

Woodstock, Illinois

1200 EST — 20 Jan 2061

Lieutenant Colonel Jackson King was in the break room at the Woodstock, Illinois, National Guard Armory with twenty soldiers from his unit, watching the presidential inauguration.

They had been in a jovial mood when they first assembled. There had been the usual friendly banter between soldiers, common, especially in a tight-knit unit. This unit was no exception.

When Cyrus began his inaugural address, the room had gone silent. As Cyrus got deeper into his speech, Jackson was sure he had heard faint gasps here and there.

"Quiet, everybody!" Jackson yelled.

Jackson began to feel increasingly uneasy as the speech continued. As a Black man, he considered himself a patriot above all partisanship.

This was not out of ignorance of the complicated history of the United States. He was well-versed in American History, covering both the good, the bad, and the ugly.

Holding a master's degree in U.S. History from Grambling State University, Jackson had been taught by an apolitical and independent professor who had championed critical thinking skills. He had been a staunch proponent of getting his students to develop and hone their thinking. He was a staunch supporter of the First Amendment and open, honest debate; his lexicon did not include words or phrases like "triggers" and "safe spaces."

The result was that, even as a moderate, Lieutenant Colonel Jackson King understood that, while America had started flawed—specifically with the issue of slavery baked into the nation's birth and her founding documents—it had begun with an idea that was supreme and unique in the annals of the history of civilized nations.

The idea of the consent of the governed and the separation of powers. The freedom of speech and freedom of religion clauses of the First Amendment. The idea is that a person accused of a crime is innocent until proven guilty in a court of law by a jury of their peers.

There was so much more to America and the grand experiment she had been working out since 1776. Much of it was good. Some of it was bad or even evil, like chattel slavery. Listening to Cyrus talk of only the bad and nothing else did something profound inside him that he didn't know quite what to make of.

After hearing the last words of the speech and awaiting to see the "gift," grumblings erupted among some of the troops in the break room. Some commented that the speech was long overdue. Others were stunned. When the image of the new flag came up on the TV screen, the room erupted in a cacophony of expletives that soldiers were famous for, especially when they were angered. Some soldiers who had commented positively about the speech were now silent. One soldier, Pvt. Nick Dobbs remained jubilant and shouted out how he loved the new flag. Pvt. Linda Roberts turned around quickly with a roundhouse that landed smack-dab in the middle of his face. "Traitor! Are you a commie or what?"

The room quickly erupted into a brawl, with soldiers picking whom to protect and whom to fight.

TEXAS WHITE HOUSE

Austin, Texas

1240 CST — 20 Jan 2061

Texas President González sat with his Cabinet in the Texas White House Situation Room. They sat quietly, taking notes while watching President Cyrus's inaugural address. Specifically, he was looking for any clues from Cyrus regarding his disposition toward Texas. After Cyrus unveiled the new flag atop the U.S. Capitol Dome, President González and the rest of those assembled sat momentarily speechless. Realizing all eyes were on him, González turned from the screen to address the room.

"Ladies and Gentlemen, today we have just witnessed what I believe will one day be called another day of infamy," González said. "In my judgment, it is now clear that President Cyrus is going to come after us.

We must take immediate steps to defend our compatriots, our land, and our way of life. I am immediately ordering a total mobilization of all Texas military branches.

"General Happ, what's the status of our armed forces?"

"At the ready, Mr. President."

"Thank you, general. Admiral Williams, what's the latest on the *Texas* and the *Lexington*?"

"Mr. President, the *Texas* and *Lexington* retrofit team members have been working 24/7 for seven weeks. They'll both be ready to defend our shores in two to four weeks."

"Admiral, we might be dead or captured by then. We need the Texas on-station off the coast as soon as possible. Clear?"

"Yes, Sir. Sir, might I point out that the name has an issue?"

"The name? I don't follow you, Admiral. Explain."

"Well, Sir, with our independence, the *Texas* retains the USS prefix designation. Same for the *Lexington*."

"Hmmm, no need for that anymore. Rename her *Dreadnought Texas*—a bit of menacing wordplay that can't hurt. Besides, maybe it'll put the fear of God into these communists who took over the Democratic Party. For the *Lexington*, let's replace the USS prefix with TSS, Texas Ship of State. By the way, the security details at the dry docks should be increased. Treat them both like a national treasure, clear?"

"Clear, sir."

★ ★ ★

SECRET LOCATION

Near Lincoln, Montana

1141 MST — 20 Jan 2061

Colonel Eric Adams sat in stunned silence. He had just turned off the TV. A wave of emotions came over him, the most prominent being anger, followed by resolve.

As he sat there, a quiet thought came to him: *the land that I love has been taken over by an unimaginable evil that popped his head out of a proverbial Trojan Horse. But the defenders of liberty will not go quietly into the night.*

He picked up his sat phone and sent a broadcast and encrypted message he had hoped and prayed he would never have to send. The recipients of the message, the leadership of every significant militia group that had aligned with the Rocky Mountain Militia, received:

FROM LINCOLN BREAK

TO PATMIL BREAK

ALMONDS ARE RIPE BREAK

CHARLIE OSCAR DELTA ECHO BREAK

MIKE MIKE THREE BREAK

MORE TO FOLLOW BREAK

TMWSD 76SEC.

COLONEL PATTON RESIDENCE

Abilene, Kansas

1242 CST — 20 Jan 2061

Colonel Patton had just turned off the TV. He had assembled with his brain trust to watch the inauguration, hoping and praying that the new president would offer some olive branch to the CONs. None had come. Patton sensed the mood in the room turn somber. The group sat in silence for several minutes.

Patton's sat phone interrupted the silence with the high-pitched encrypted message tone. Patton knew it would be from Adams, and he also had a strong inkling of the gist of the message. As he read Adams's message, a sense of awe came over him. Not that he had a thirst for blood, quite the contrary, he had been to war and hated it passionately, but he was struck by a sense that history was about to be made—big, sobering history.

After he read it, he put the phone down and stared at the tabletop for a few seconds. Slowly, he raised his head, stood up, and addressed all assembled. "Listen up. Send the word out to all soldiers. We just got the alert code. We are now at alert condition *MIKE—MIKE—THREE*. This is not an exercise."

At that, the room erupted in pandemonium with men and women jumping up, chairs falling over, and people rushing out of the room.

The brain trust of the Kansas Patriot Militia had just been given the alert code that was short for Minuteman Three, which meant to go on full alert in preparation for the muster call, *MIKE—MIKE—TWO*. They all knew that *MIKE—MIKE—ONE*, God forbid it ever came, meant Minuteman One. As of three years ago, in militia parlance, Minuteman One meant armed conflict on American soil.

THE GOVERNOR'S MANSION

Oklahoma City, Oklahoma

1245 CST — 20 Jan 2061

Oklahoma Governor Mary Whitfield had taken pages of notes while listening to President Cyrus's Inaugural Address.

She had also hoped and prayed there might be some verbal hint of a path forward with people of her conservative political persuasion. Her views aligned with those of most Oklahomans. When none was heard, she knew in her gut that the tide had turned against any further wait-and-see attitude. If she were to protect Oklahomans and their beloved state, along with its unabashed understanding of the U.S. Constitution in its original and undiluted form, she would need to take bold action quickly. She picked up the phone and made two calls, the first to General Williamson to come quickly for an urgent meeting. The next call was to the Speaker of the Oklahoma House of Representatives, Chief Billy Waya.

SECRET LOCATION – 1619 RED BRIGADE HEADQUARTERS

South Loop, Chicago, Illinois

1245 CST — 20 Jan 2061

DeShawn King had watched the inauguration in rapt attention with a room full of 1619 Red Brigade members and several dozen university students. They erupted with jubilation when the speech ended, and the new flag was unveiled. "Universal Justice and Brotherhood are at hand!" he had shouted. Others had picked up a chant and were shouting, "Workers Unite!—Workers Win!"

As he walked around the room, embracing one friend after another, he was overcome with emotion, thinking that the day had finally come. He could not wait to get to work on his part in implementing the top-secret plan for the first hundred days of the New Way administration. He had come to terms with the fact that there would be pain, sacrifice, and, perhaps, some bloodshed, but how sweet the vision was for when that was all past and a Marxist utopia had replaced the Old Way. Amidst the jubilation, he saw that his dad was calling. He ignored the call and let it go to voicemail. Besides, he thought, it was too loud in the room to attempt a conversation.

★ ★ ★

SECRET LOCATION

Near Bison Reservoir, Colorado

1145 MST — 20 Jan 2061

Sergeant Franklin York had been the reluctant founder of the Colorado Patriot Militia ten years earlier. The genesis of his decision to form it had been the rapid tailspin of the country after 2050 that coincided with what he saw as the rapid erosion of Constitutional liberties, especially regarding the First and Second Amendments, which, after all, in his mind, represented an indissoluble heart of the Nation's founding principles of Life, Liberty, and the Pursuit of Happiness.

A group of seven soldiers made up his brain trust. Like-minded and as equally patriotic as he was, if not more so, they had vowed to one another to go down fighting rather than allow a socialist-communist takeover of the Nation.

Having just turned off the TV at the raising of the new flag at Cyrus's inauguration, they had all expected and cheered the sending of the *MIKE—MIKE—THREE* coded message from Adams up north Montana.

The heart of the Colorado Patriot Militia operation was ten miles west of the Cheyenne Mountain Complex, the massive and heavily guarded NORAD and USSPACECOM facility just outside Colorado Springs. Carved deep into the bowels of a mountain that was a solid piece of granite, the Cheyenne Mountain Complex was one of the U.S. military's most valuable command and control facilities. York knew several high-ranking officers there. He also knew that many of them were quietly patriots. But, if he was honest with himself, he had no idea how they would respond to what they had just heard from the mouth of President Cyrus. Time would tell. The room had quieted down for now, and all eyes were on Sergeant York.

"Soldiers, as God is my witness, what we just heard will not stand," York began. "We are now on the brink of a civil war. I expect the bulk of the population doesn't know it yet. But it's coming, and it will be here very soon. You know our operational procedure from this point forward. No clear-text messages of any kind, no matter how mundane. Everything you communicate from here on out between unit members— and I mean everything—must be sent encrypted. You have your orders. We will convene here at 0600 tomorrow. Do your duty for Life, Liberty, and Justice. Do it well, lest our nation perish from the earth."

With that, the soldiers rose and quietly left the room. With the room empty, Sergeant York picked up the phone and called his old pal, General George Winfield, Commanding Officer of the United States Northern Command based at Cheyenne Mountain outside Colorado Springs.

"George, congratulations on the promotion. Just don't let it go to your head."

"Franklin, you ol' son of a gun, thanks for the congrats. How are you?"

"Okay. Did you watch the address?"

"Did not. I'm on duty right now, but I'm in between concalls at this exact moment. I've recorded the inauguration, so I'll catch it later tonight."

"I would love to hear your thoughts. Satie says to say hi."

Satie, the general thought. He paused for a moment to let the word sink in. He had not heard that term in a long, long time. It was a private code word for sat phones. York made it up years ago when he and George served in North Africa.

Only George and a handful of select other soldiers York trusted beyond a shadow of a doubt had been let in on the meaning of the codeword. George had told them that if they ever got a call from him and he used the codeword, the hearer should respond, "Yes, I will. Say, let's plan a lunch date real soon." At the time, the small group of close-knit men-at-arms had pressed York for a reason for it all. York would never say anything except, "I'm saving it for a rainy day." Use of the word meant to contact Sergeant York by sat phone, via encryption, pronto.

"Yes, I will. Say, let's plan a lunch date real soon."

"Friday next. Noon work? We can meet at the Bears Den down in the Springs."

"I'll put it on my calendar now. See you then, Sergeant." The general hung up the phone. Sensing urgency, he slipped into a secure room, picked up his sat phone, turned on encryption, and called York back.

York had expected a quick call back, but not an immediate one. "Hi, George. That was quick. I think you broke a record."

"Franklin, I sensed an urgency. What's up, old friend?"

"I think we're headed for civil war. His speech was just short of a Declaration of War against all Old Way citizens. I think he's out of his mind. I know where you stand, but I'm tellin' ya, be ready to pound your fist onto the table after you watch his speech."

"Was it that bad?"

"Bad?! He sounded like Karl Marx! I was so mad I wanted to wring his neck through the screen. This ass-wipe wants to dismantle the United States and rebuild it into a socialist utopia. He's bat-shit crazy. George,

I feel we're just weeks away from an armed conflict. People like us are going to have to choose sides. I don't have to tell you which side I'm on. The die is cast, and, for me, it was cast a long time ago."

"Before North Africa?"

"Damn straight! I saw it coming even back then. Funny you should mention that."

"Franklin, you know my sentiments as well. For now, I need to see how this plays out. Plus, there's a vocal minority of members of Congress that are resistant to what Cyrus stands for."

"I hear you, George. Another thing that kills me is that his speech today lacked any olive branches, despite campaign rhetoric alluding to bipartisanship. Remember his convention speech. He made off like he would be the next FDR for the Nation. After listening to this today, it's obvious it was all a bunch of lies to get votes from the MODs and Independents. That little bastard!"

"Simmer down, Franklin. I know you're hot and that this whole socialist thing gets you hot. I can assure you that you're not alone. If it's as bad as you say it is, a whole lot of people are going to be choosing sides soon enough. I'm sure we'll be in touch in the days ahead. In the meantime, let's stay in touch via encryption only."

"You got it, my friend. Say a prayer, buddy. When the shit hits the fan, it will make Gettysburg look like a skirmish."

|||| **5** ||||

DEMOLITION

THE WHITE HOUSE

Washington, D.C.

0800 EST — 13 Feb 2061

The White House Situation Room was abuzz with activity. Overloaded, President Cyrus called an emergency meeting for his Cabinet and the Joint Chiefs of Staff to discuss the growing crises since his inauguration.

After speaking quietly to a few aides, he turned and motioned for the room to quiet down. "Good morning, everyone. As you know, more than 20 states are threatening secession. So far that we know of Montana, Wyoming, the Dakotas, Greater Idaho, Utah, New Mexico, Northern California, Oklahoma, Nebraska, Kansas, Louisiana, Mississippi, Alabama, Georgia, South Carolina, Florida, Tennessee, Kentucky, Arkansas, Indiana, Missouri, Southern Illinois, and Iowa. Possibly also the states of Alaska and Hawaii.

"I am proud to say that we have made some quick progress rolling out the New Way policies since the inauguration, but, as you know, some of these states have hard-liners in them that don't want to give up the Old Way. Then there's Texas. They have the gall to think that just because some weasel crafts a document, somehow this piece of paper has some magical power and that they are now an independent nation again. Well, we will soon see about that. I intend to make them an example, and, in so doing, these other wannabe renegade states should fall back into line in rapid order. Once that happens, we can continue the rapid rollout of the New Way policies. General Gage, what is the latest on the suppression plans?"

Speaker of the House Jai Parry had been taking lots of notes. Upon hearing the phrase "suppression plans," he quickly jerked his head from his notes and spoke up in shock, "Suppression plans?"

Cyrus fired back. "Listen up, Parry, and you'll get up to speed soon enough. General, go ahead. Incidentally, any leaks from this meeting will be considered an act of treason and dealt with severely according to the law." Cyrus detected a slightly shocked expression on the faces of three of his Cabinet members and the Speaker of the House, Jai Parry.

"Thank you, Mr. President. If we could dim the lights and turn on the screen."

All eyes turned towards the large flat panel that dominated the width of the entire 15-foot-wide wall behind the President.

General Gage said, "A map of Texas is up on the screen. Our attack plan focuses on a Rapid Reaction Force dropping into Austin and converging on the Governor's Mansion at a time of our choosing. Our goal is to await confirmation that the governor is in residence. We drop in, take the mansion, and then arrest the governor. At the same time as this operation, another will be conducted simultaneously to arrest the lieutenant governor.

"Another strike force will seize the Capitol Building. Multiple arrests are planned. All those arrested will be taken to a secret location for booking, arraignment, and charges under 18 U.S. Code Chapter 115. All are regarding treason, sedition, and conspiracy. I expect within seven days after the conclusion of this operation, all renegade states will quickly fall back into line, and that will be the end of this rebellion talk."

Speaker of the House Jai Parry yelled, "Good Lord, are you trying to start another Civil War?!"

Sheldon shot back, "Oh, come on, Jai, you know damn well that if we don't cut the head of the snake off now, some right-wing nut in any of these other states will go off and do something stupid. This operation is designed to immediately cut off the whole thing, prevent a war, and save countless lives. You mark my word, get Texas to fall back into line, and none of these other states will dare secede, much less start a shooting war over this. It would be suicide, and they all know it. All of them together can't match the firepower of the federal government, much less the manpower."

Cyrus yelled, "Manpower? Really?"

Sheldon, looking a little sheepish, responded. "My bad, Mr. President, I meant soldiers in arms."

Parry continued his protest. "Oh, for Pete's sake, Fred, we all might as well just walk into a room full of gunpowder with torches blazing and kiss our ass goodbye! All this will do is inflame the self-proclaimed patriots in Texas and all these other states. We're talking about a conflagration of unimaginable proportions, especially when you start using weapons of modern warfare. There must be a diplomatic solution to all of this."

Cyrus, still hot, fired back. "Bullshit, Jai. In my world, diplomatic solutions are not for domestic rebellions. Those are reserved for foreign affairs crises. The operative phrase for a domestic rebellion is to crush it right at the very beginning, before it spirals out of control. That's exactly what I intend to do. Anyone else want to chime in?"

Interior Secretary Donna Sheryll thought, *Wow, what did I sign up for? He just shut down this convo with a hammer. Should I speak up and call him out on that?*

Agriculture Secretary Jessie Dallas also wrestled in his mind. *That sounds like a forty-five-year-old bully. Is this the same guy from the convention back in Chicago?*

The room went quiet. President Cyrus looked around at his Cabinet. He looked into the eyes of all in the room, then squarely in the eyes of General Gage.

"General, execute the plan."

TEXAS WHITE HOUSE

Austin, Texas

0700 CST — 16 Feb 2061

President González was exuberant that his forces had been ready for the fight. Texas Special Forces had met the mission launched by the United States Military to seize the Texas White House and the Capitol building in Austin. The FEDs' raid had met with utter catastrophe.

Launched in the predawn hours of 15 February, Texas Special

Forces had been up to the challenge. González was particularly proud of the noble gesture made by Texas Army Lieutenant Scott, allowing the federal New Way soldiers to lay down their weapons with the assurance that no harm would come to them. The U.S. soldiers refused, and the Battle of Austin began. When it was over, the FEDs had suffered heavy casualties. One hundred two dead, 40 wounded, 201 captured. Texas special forces casualties were 57 dead and 21 wounded. Assembled with his Cabinet in the Texas White, President González addressed Defense Secretary Adam Johnson. "General, please pass the word down the line how proud I am of this first defense of our sovereignty. I am, of course, saddened by the loss of life.

I wish to God those federal troops would have laid down their weapons instead of picking a fight with us. God rest their souls."

"Thank you, Mr. President. I'll be sure to pass this message on down the line. I share your sentiments as well. It pains me that it has come to this. I believe Lieutenant Scott's actions can serve as a model for any future attempts to threaten Texas sovereignty. We must let federal forces at least entertain the thought of choosing sides, becoming neutral, or perhaps joining in a general uprising against the New Way that's sure to come from the CONs in many of the other states."

"Yes, general, very much agreed. I like the idea. Please send those orders down the chain of command. What do you think Cyrus will do next?"

"Well, I expect he's madder than a hatter right now."

Almost simultaneously, an aide to Chief of Staff Bill White burst into the meeting. "Mr. President, you'd better turn on the TV!"

Another aide quickly grabbed the remote and turned it on. In the meantime, a gaggle of people started pouring in to watch the news. As they turned up the volume, they all went silent at the images and words that jarred their souls.

"…repeating. Minutes ago, a massive blast occurred in San Antonio, Texas, at approximately 7:00 a.m. Central Standard Time. We are receiving reports that the explosion occurred at The Alamo. Eyewitnesses report casualties, but the exact number and nature are not yet known. Eyewitnesses also report fires burning in multiple locations around the historic site. It was also reported that a huge crater now stands where the Alamo once stood, and that there is nothing left. The Alamo has been completely obliterated."

The room exploded in angry cries, expletives, shouts of rage, and vows of revenge.

President González recalled the famous painting, *The Fall of the Alamo, which* he had studied one month and a day ago. He bowed his head for a moment. He grabbed his secure sat phone, turned on the encryption switch, and sent a message to his old childhood friend up north.

THE WHITE HOUSE

Washington, D.C.

0900 EST — 16 Feb 2061

U.S. President Devin Cyrus sat patiently behind the famous Resolute desk inside the Oval Office.

He waited for the cue for the camera to signal his emergency address to the nation. Hearing the countdown: Five-four-three-two-one. He saw the technician's hand signal, the red light at the top of the camera. They were now broadcasting live to 381 million Americans.

"Good morning, citizens of the New Way America. As you are aware, two days ago, an operation was launched to bring rogue leaders of the State of Texas to justice. This operation, regrettably, was a failure and resulted in the loss of 102 of our brave soldiers. In retaliation, this morning, on my orders at 8 a.m. Eastern Standard Time, our Air Force launched a cruise missile against a symbol of White supremacy, the Alamo, located in the city of San Antonio, Texas.

"This blight has been allowed to stand as a symbol of White supremacy and as a relic of Texas's slave-holding legacy from another era, for far too long. The demolition of the Alamo is yet another proof that the New

Way is here to stay, and the Old Way is dead.

"Further operations are planned to bring renegade Texas back into the Union's fold and force compliance with the New Way.

"I also say this in warning to any states contemplating secession. Any rebellion will be put down by any and all means necessary. To all loyal and law-abiding citizens, as your President, I promise you I will not fail you. A new and brighter America is here to stay."

Patton heard the tone and picked up the sat phone. He saw the words that sent a chill down his spine. "*MIKE—MIKE—TWO*," the code to muster. He quickly forwarded the code to his officers. They would be responsible for issuing the muster call to rank-and-file militia members.

Patton turned off the TV and looked at the wall behind his desk. As he did, he felt melancholy wash over him. Sitting in his oversized antique oak chair, he stared intently up at the framed lithograph of the Thure de Thulstrup painting of President Abraham Lincoln. The lithograph had been in the Patton family for generations. The famous painting depicts President Lincoln presenting Union General Ulysses S. Grant with his commission papers to become Commander-in-Chief of the Union Army in March of 1864. It would prove to be a decisive turning point in the Civil War.

As a war history buff, particularly of the Civil War, Patton took zero comfort at the thought that soon, very soon, that title would have to be amended to now state the First Civil War.

He recalled that in the 1930s, the term First World War was not yet part of the world's lexicon. At that time, the conflict was known by one of two titles: the Great War or the War to End All Wars. By 1940, both phrases had fallen into obsolescence, with the world once again at war— this time against fascism and imperialism. Staring intently at the picture, he thought, *My Lord, a second Civil War. Can this be happening? Are we really on the precipice of a second one?* He turned to his desk and opened the bottom drawer to his right. There, underneath some papers, was an old book he had treasured most of his life. He opened the cover, turned to the epigraph, and read the words aloud, "At what point then is the approach of danger to be expected? I answer, if it ever reach us, it must spring up amongst us. It cannot come from abroad. If destruction be our lot, we must ourselves be its author and finisher. As a nation of freemen, we must live through all time, or die by suicide. Abraham Lincoln, 1838." He closed the old book and put it on his lap. He stared out the window and thought, *Lincoln wrote that a little over twenty years before the start of the Civil War in 1861. God have mercy on us all.*

|||| **6** ||||

SHARDS OF GLASS

PARKING GARAGE

Gold Coast, Chicago, Illinois

2200 CST — 18 Feb 2061

DeShawn King and his 1619 Red Brigade troops had quietly assembled in the basement of a parking garage in the heart of Chicago's Gold Coast. The wealthiest enclave in the city, bar none. The last several years had been tough on the rich, so much so that a quiet rebellion had taken place among what were the most affluent Democrats in the city. Many had been MODs, but a small number had embraced Democratic Socialism. Some out of conviction, and some to keep up with the times and avoid being canceled.

Before the quiet rebellion, this elite collection of wealthy Chicagoans had been a vital and powerful component of the city's economic engine, funding a myriad of businesses, new startups, the arts, education, and numerous philanthropic interests. Their enormous contributions were increasingly unappreciated and often ridiculed as the hubris of the rich—a newer, derogatory term that socialists loved to use.

Increasingly isolated and like a giant iceberg that suddenly flips over in warm water, these wealthy LIB elites had suddenly, and almost en masse, flipped over and had become CONs.

Many had left Chicago altogether for friendlier suburbs or states, especially Texas and Florida. However, a sizable number of them remained in the Gold Coast, just north of The Loop in the heart of downtown Chicago near the world-renowned Lincoln Park Zoo.

So detested were they by the New Way followers that many of these wealthy elites had taken to hiring private security firms to accompany them 24/7. On a typical Saturday evening, when they would head out to expensive restaurants or social events, it was as if hundreds of heads of state were dining out, accompanied by security teams in armored black SUVs with tinted windows.

DeShawn King and his troops had been preparing for this operation for weeks. The 1619 Red Brigade was determined to shine in its first operational deployment as Federalized Soldiers of the New Way.

This evening's plan was simple: locate the top three hundred wealthiest people on the Gold Coast who had turned traitors by becoming CONs. Arrest them. Seize all assets of value in their homes and then transport the enemies of the state to a secure location for re-education.

Simultaneously, the plan included a cyber operation to seize all their financial accounts. While CPD was to assist them, the 1619 Red Brigade would be the muscle for the apprehension and seizure operation.

At precisely 0300 hours, the brigade moved out to their designated high-rises to begin the arrests. Several buses had been staged for the operation and were waiting by Lincoln Park Zoo, just off DuSable-Lake Shore Drive.

DeShawn, not one to idly stand by, led his team to the first building. An asleep security guard was startled awake when battering rams broke the glass doors. The brigade soldiers charged in with shards of glass crackling under their feet. The guard, groggy but quick to see and realize he had better not make a move, froze in place. The team split up. Several took up stations in the lobby to prevent anyone from leaving. A bus pulled up almost immediately beside the front entrance. DeShawn led several brigade leaders to the elevators, where they punched in for the penthouse. Their first target was the e-commerce tech multibillionaire, Melvin Barclay, the wealthiest man in the United States. With a net worth of $522.5 billion, Barclay had been a cheerleader of the walkaway movement among his fellow wealthy Democratic friends and donors in the Gold Coast and elsewhere. In the eyes of the LIBs, the damage he had done was unforgivable and demanded swift justice. Barclay was targeted as the New Way Public Enemy No. 1 for the night.

Arriving on the single elevator to the penthouse, DeShawn had to wait for the rest of the squad to come in two separate trips on the elevator. Once all the soldiers assembled, they quietly approached the door to the Penthouse.

Protective Service Detail Member Darren Seth was alerted by the proximity alarm that persons were entering the hallway outside the elevator. Hitting his VHF radio's code red squawk button, the other seven detail members quickly jumped out of bed with weapons at the ready. Three stayed behind to shepherd the members of the Barclay family, six in all, into the safe room. The other four headed for the front door, took defensive positions, and waited for the inevitable.

DeShawn made the hand signal for the ram. A soldier rushed up and took position. DeShawn looked around to make sure everyone was in position. He looked forward and gave the nod.

With a powerful forward motion, the soldier swung the ram backward and then drove it hard into the door. The door crashed into the penthouse with a loud thud. DeShawn jumped up, lurched through the entryway, and yelled, "Hands up!"

Just then, Barclay's men let loose a hail of bullets.

DeShawn and his troops immediately returned fire. It was over in seconds. DeShawn had felt a bullet graze his left cheek and the fleshy part of his upper left arm. He was okay. Two of his soldiers lay dead on the floor. All of Barlay's security guys were dead. At least, so they thought. Approaching the safe room, they realized their target was there, along with his family and at least one more member of Barclay's protective detail.

After a few seconds of DeShawn yelling to come out or face death, the door opened, and nine people filed out with their hands up. The first three were from the protective detail, followed by Barclay. He made eye contact with DeShawn. DeShawn thought he detected a hint of fear in his eyes. DeShawn looked down at his two dead comrades, looked up at Barclay, and, without warning, violently swung his gun at the side of Barclay's head. He struck him just above the left ear. Barclay staggered and then dropped dead while his wife and children screamed. A large pool of blood was quickly forming on the floor.

DeShawn looked down and screamed in rage. "You dumbass white-privileged piece of shit capitalist pig! This is what real revolution looks like, asshole!"

As the night wore on, these scenes repeated themselves up and down Chicago's Gold Coast. Elsewhere across a severely divided nation, similar scenes played out in LIB strongholds with varying degrees of violence. By daybreak, the 1619 Red Brigade had made thousands of arrests, all among the nation's top one percent of the wealthy. Fifty-two people had died, the most notable being Melvin Barclay. The 1619 Red Brigade had not found an undetermined number from the wanted list. Those people were presumed missing. By his reckoning, DeShawn King felt the night was a huge success, save for the death of two of his soldiers.

CHRIST THE KING A.M.E. CHURCH

McHenry, Illinois

1030 CST — 20 Feb 2061

Citizen-soldier Lieutenant Colonel Jackson King was today Bishop King of Christ the King A.M.E. Church. With the events of the last several weeks not only weighing on his mind but also the minds of most congregants, Bishop King had been up half the night, alternately praying, being still before the Lord, and writing down his sermon for today. Typically, the Bishop would take cues from scribbled notes on index cards and deliver a message. He was not fond of using tablets or phones. He liked using paper, but today's message was out of the norm because it was carefully worded and fully typed for delivery.

After the worship band played the last song to begin the service, Bishop King approached the pulpit. Fresh on his mind was the news of what had transpired a little over 30 hours ago in Chicago and many other locales elsewhere in the nation.

Thousands were arrested. All of them involved wealthy people. Many were White, but a fair number involved Black, Hispanic, and Asian entrepreneurs who had all flipped and embraced the CON's political ideology. Unsettling too was the disclosure that a third of the arrestees were Jewish, or Zionists, as the press had stated. The death of Melvin Barclay had sent shockwaves through the country and had personally deeply disturbed King.

The Bishop delivered his sermon. As it went on, the congregation grew still. More than it had ever been in a long, long time. He finally finished.

With that, he put his papers back into the folio and silently closed it. The silence remained as the Bishop left the pulpit and returned to his seat on the stage. Mrs. King hugged him as one congregant suddenly began clapping slowly. Soon, a second, then a third, then an eruption of applause that built in volume and was accompanied by all manner of praises shouted out loud to the Lord.

IIII **7** IIII

SECESSION

CAPITOL BUILDING

Oklahoma City, Oklahoma

1245 CST — 10 Apr 2061

Oklahoma Governor Mary Whitfield was in a somber mood. In a few minutes, she would be introduced to a joint session of the Oklahoma Legislature to deliver a speech that she had hoped and prayed would never have to be delivered. An hour earlier, she had huddled with her trusted advisors, including Brigadier General Williamson. They had all agreed that she needed to give this speech, as painful as it would be, not just for the sake of Oklahoma and its citizens' freedom but also for the sake of all Constitutionalists across a divided nation.

Oklahoma Senate Sergeant at Arms Adam Hane entered the anteroom where the Governor, General Williamson, several aides, and her protective detail were quietly waiting.

Hane gave the Governor the nod. She arose from the sofa and

silently walked out the door, following the Sergeant at Arms. She and the entourage walked silently down the hall to the Oklahoma State House Chamber entrance.

Inside, the House Chamber was abuzz with activity and conversation. After getting a hand signal from an aide, Speaker of the House Chief Billy Waya gaveled the Chamber to order.

His first attempt was barely audible: "The House will be in order."

It took three more drops of the gavel to finally get everyone's attention that it was time to quiet down. Once the Chamber was silent, Chief Billy Waya looked towards the back. "The Chair recognizes Senate Sergeant at Arms Adam Hane for an announcement."

Sergeant at Arms Hane took one step forward, quietly cleared his throat, and then addressed the Chamber, "Mr. President: the joint committee of the House and Senate presents the Chief Executive, the Honorable Governor Mary Whitfield."

The chamber erupted in applause. As the Governor slowly walked down the aisle, she paused repeatedly and shook hands with numerous members from both sides. Oklahoma was one of several states in the heartland of the Union that did not have a single socialist elected to the Senate or House.

After much glad-handing and small talk with Democrats and Republicans, the Governor had finished her slow walk and climbed the steps to the podium. She turned and warmly greeted her long-time friend, Speaker of the House Chief Billy Waya. Although she was a CON and he a MOD, they had reached an understanding on how to work together to get things done for Oklahoma's citizens.

During her exchange of pleasantries with the Speaker, she remembered her doctoral thesis on the unlikely friendship between

Ronald Reagan, the fortieth president and a staunch Conservative Republican, and Tip O'Neill, the forty-seventh Speaker of the House and a New Deal Democrat. Her studies of their political dynamics and friendship during their time in power in the early to mid-1980s had made a profound impression on her, shaping her in powerful ways and yielding significant results.

She handed Speaker Chief Billy Waya a copy of her speech. They shook hands and exchanged more pleasantries. Both were smiling during the exchange. Finished, she turned to acknowledge the sustained applause from both sides of the aisle.

The Speaker gaveled for order again. Once the Assembly had quieted down, the Chief spoke, "Members of the Legislature, Executive Officers, members of the Judiciary, Tribal Leaders, and people of the Great State of Oklahoma, it is my distinct honor to recognize my friend, the Chief Executive, our Governor, Mary Whitfield."

Another sustained round of applause followed for another full minute. After which, Waya gaveled again, and the Chamber went quiet. The Governor began, "Lieutenant Governor Matt Henderson, Mr. Speaker, Madam President Pro Tempore, members of the Legislature, members of the Judiciary, Tribal Leaders, and the citizens of the Great State of Oklahoma, it is an honor to be standing before you today. But this honor is coupled with a somber duty.

"Just last week, we awoke on a Tuesday morning to hear of an overnight attack on freedom that was conducted by the paramilitary group known as the 1619 Red Brigade. The attack appears to have received the blessings of the highest levels of the FEDs, perhaps even authored and coordinated by the White House.

"The target of this cowardly attack was wealthy American capitalists who had rejected socialist-Marxist ideology and had embraced MOD or CON political persuasions.

"To our loyal sons and daughters of our state legislature who are not of the conservative persuasion, I think you know that I consider you members of the loyal opposition and not anti-constitutionalists hell-bent on tearing down the country in an attempt at rebuilding it as a Marxist-socialist utopia. My fellow CONs and I here in this chamber stand now to acknowledge your support for Liberty. You have been, you are, and you shall remain our colleagues, friends, and fellow Oklahomans, even when we disagree."

The chamber erupted in applause, with Republicans and Democrats crossing aisles to shake hands and embrace. After a minute, the Speaker gaveled for order again.

"Today, as Governor of Oklahoma, I bring you a message of great urgency. At this juncture in our state's history, our nation has a great divide. We here in Oklahoma cherish Liberty beyond any shadow of a doubt. Our past, indeed, was one of conflict between settlers and indigenous Americans in the nineteenth and twentieth centuries. Also, it is true concerning the awful stain of our forefathers' support of slavery. We must also never forget the dreadful Tulsa race riots in the twentieth century, which saw the killing of upwards of 300 of our Black citizens at the hands of an angry, racist White mob. An additional 10,000 people were displaced due to the destruction of private property.

"But let it also be said that it is also true that since those tragic times, Oklahomans have forged a great society in our state. No matter what, Oklahomans are one."

The Assembly again erupted in sustained applause.

"We must now make a hard decision, not because we wish to go backward, quite the contrary, but because the centuries-old ideals of liberty and freedom beckon us ever forward!"

More applause.

"The decision we must make is crystal clear. We must choose between Liberty and the tyranny that has masqueraded as good and has been right under our noses for decades, deceiving millions of Americans. I can only speak for Oklahomans when I say that we now clearly see the true intentions of these masters of deception.

"They are, in fact, malevolent citizens that seek to destroy our nation and try to rebuild it as a Marxist so-called utopia. As was said by Patrick Henry in 1775, and that echoes forward to the present time and must be said yet again to all tyrants, 'Give me Liberty, or give me death!'"

The response from the chamber and the gallery was deafening. The floors shook. The noise settled again, allowing the Governor to continue.

"Now, just as in 1776, a long list of grievances has been piled up against these haters of freedom and liberty. The grievances against them are well-known and well-documented. But for the sake of the record, I shall enumerate the most serious ones.

"They have trampled the First Amendment by hollowing it out via judicial overreach, illegal laws, policies, regulations, and executive orders, classifying all manner of speech as hate speech. They have regulated all media, dictating what is and is not acceptable speech.

"They have spied on and reported on houses of worship of all faiths. Often, especially against Conservatives, they invaded these houses of worship and threatened to revoke their tax-exempt status or shut them down permanently. Thus, it violates the freedom of assembly clause of the First Amendment and the freedom of religion clause of that same Amendment.

"They have threatened the clergy that certain verses of scripture or doctrines constitute hate speech and are not protected by the First Amendment, and that use of them will lead to arrests, fines, and possibly imprisonment, or, lately, a stay of undetermined length at a re-education camp.

"They have, in many states, hollowed out the Second Amendment by instituting unreasonable laws or regulations regarding the sale and possession of guns, ammunition, and magazines. All the while, the criminals seem to have enough for their latest crimes, especially in big cities.

"They have violated the Eighth Amendment with the institution of excessive fines against individuals they deem offensive, and whom they have charged with all manner of petty and serious crimes as a form of harassment because of their political or religious beliefs. These excessive fines have often bankrupted individuals. Thus, these fines are used as weapons by a weaponized Department of Justice to silence dissent.

"We have been and remain at an impasse. We are told there is to be no compromise. The only path forward is our wholesale capitulation to the extreme left ideology of the LIBs.

"Faced with these facts as the result of exhaustive efforts not only on the part of our state but also many other states that share our grievances against the FEDs. We now offer our unilateral final answer to their unreasonable and unjust demands.

"We here do highly resolve never to capitulate! We also highly resolve that if compromise is not an option, then by fiat, the LIBs have dissolved the Union that binds the people of Oklahoma to the current Federal New Way Government.

"Make no mistake, our Union with the Declaration of Independence, the Constitution, and the Bill of Rights remains indissoluble! When a government tramples those ideas and seeks to replace them with a Marxist ideology that led to the deaths of hundreds of millions of people in the last century, then we, as free and liberty-loving people, must separate ourselves from such tyranny.

"Such an evil entity is a cancer eating away at every precept of Liberty and Freedom that is enshrined in our founding documents.

"In 1776, the United States of America was born as a Constitutional Republic. Furthermore, after much debate, the Founding Fathers settled on a representative form of government for the new nation, comprising three coequal branches: the executive, judicial, and legislative branches.

"Further, we were freely and successfully embracing a market economy from our nation's birth. Finally, we were born as a God-fearing people whose faith, although not affiliated with any particular Christian denomination, was deeply rooted in the ancient Judeo-Christian teachings of the Old and New Testaments. Yet, our Constitution was so crafted, particularly the First Amendment, that anyone from anywhere could freely worship any religion or none at all, according to their conscience. Speaking personally for myself and family, as for me and my house, we will serve the Lord."

A thunderous ovation erupted for several moments.

After a polite pause, Chief Waya banged the gavel. "Order, the House will come to order."

The Assembly complied and sat down.

The Governor continued, "Therefore, We the People of Oklahoma do highly resolve that we shall never capitulate to any tyrant or collective tyranny. We shall never abandon the Constitution of the United States or the Bill of Rights. We will never abandon a market economy, otherwise known as capitalism, for any other economic model whose history has shown falls far short.

"Last but not least, we shall never abandon the teachings or truths of the Holy Scriptures of the Christian and Jewish faiths, nor will we ever malign, renounce, or abandon the great Jehovah God Almighty, the Creator and Supreme Being of the Universe.

"We also recognize that citizens of Oklahoma include those of other faiths. We will also defend their right to practice their religion as they see fit. Not because we agree or disagree with them but because the First Amendment of the Constitution guarantees that right, first and foremost. On these statements, we stake our sacred honor—and, if need be, our lives.

"All the above being said, I, Governor Mary Whitfield, as the Chief Executive of the State of Oklahoma, now place a motion on the floor. The motion is for Secession from the Federal New Way Government as of midnight tomorrow evening.

"Let me be clear. I do not bring this motion to the floor lightly. I'm sobered by the ramifications of what this could mean, not only for Oklahoma but for hundreds of millions of liberty-loving people across the CON states.

"Further, let it also be known that this motion does not mean we are seceding from the Union—quite the contrary. We, the people, vow to remain in Union with all those who vow with us to Preserve, Protect, and Defend the Constitution of the United States against all enemies, foreign and domestic.

"I now yield the floor to the honorable Speaker of the House, Chief Billy Waya, for the purposes of beginning debate on the motion."

The Assembly sat silently for a moment, then exploded with a roar from the floor and the gallery above.

Five hours later, an aide rushed into the conference room where Governor Whitfield had sat quietly waiting in conference with many aides and National Guard leadership. The aide shouted the results. "The Secession vote has passed the Oklahoma State Legislature by 98–3. In the Senate, the vote was unanimous in favor of Secession, 48–0."

With the Governor surrounded by well-wishers, she picked up her sat phone, turned on the encryption key, and sent the following encoded message:

> *FROM WHITFIELD BREAK*
>
> *TO ALL PATGOVS BREAK*
>
> *SECESSION RESOUNDING YES BREAK*
>
> *FULL MOBILIZATION DECREE WITHIN THE HOUR BREAK*
>
> *PREPARE OPERATION MARKET.*

She hit the send button and was stunned to see her phone light up with encrypted messages that had just been sent.

As she carefully reviewed the messages, she paused, asked for a paper and pen, and began taking notes furiously. When she finished, a look of hope washed over her face.

"Listen up! While we were preoccupied with this, the following states in unison were debating their own articles of Secession. Kansas, Nebraska, North and South Dakota, Montana, Wyoming, Greater Idaho, Northern California, Utah, New Mexico, Western Colorado, Southern Illinois, Iowa, Indiana, Missouri, Arkansas, Louisiana, Mississippi, Kentucky, Tennessee, Alabama, Georgia, Florida, South Carolina, Hawaii, and West Virginia. Alaska is holding its vote now, but it also looks like it will be a yes. I count twenty-six—yes, one in progress—plus us, makes twenty-eight. Good Lord!"

United States Department of Homeland Security head Frederic Sheldon was alarmed at the intelligence reports from 28 State Capitals. Caught off guard on a Sunday, 28 states held emergency joint sessions of their legislatures to vote on Secession from the United States. All the TV news shows were reporting the rapidly unfolding events.

With eight screens arrayed on his home office wall, Sheldon listened intently, turning up the volume to hear the American News Network coverage of the breaking news.

"…repeating. In a stunning move today, twenty-eight states have voted for Secession from the Union. These reports are just a few minutes old, and we have yet to hear a response from the White House.

"Tensions have been riding high between these states and the Federal Government ever since the inauguration of President Devin Cyrus.

While he campaigned as a Democratic Socialist with a desire to unite the country under his New Way plan, the opening weeks of his fledgling administration has been racked with turmoil, with his coalition of LIBs and MODs unable to strike a deal with the CONs, who have become increasingly intransigent in tone and action. The CONs' main argument is that they believe the Socialist wave has usurped the Constitution. They frequently point to the First, Second and Eighth Amendments, arguing that these have been hollowed out or effectively nullified by executive orders, judicial overreach, and other federal, state, and local actions within New Way strongholds.

"What we now know, and I remind our listeners that these events are still unfolding, is that a coalition of CON states has voted to secede from the Union and now form a solid wall from the Gulf of Mexico to the Canadian border. The complete list so far comprises the states of Oklahoma, Kansas, Nebraska, North and South Dakota, Montana, Wyoming, Greater Idaho, Northern California, Utah, New Mexico, Western Colorado, Indiana, Southern Illinois, Iowa, Missouri, Arkansas, Louisiana, Mississippi, Kentucky, Tennessee, Alabama, Georgia, Florida, North and South Carolina, Hawaii, and West Virginia. A vote is ongoing in Alaska and looks to pass shortly. It is unclear whether the Hawaii secession vote is related to the growing independence movement in Hawaii, which has been rapidly expanding in the state over the last year. The flip from a blue state to a red state in Hawaii is still being studied by both major parties.

"Texas, meanwhile, stands alone, having declared itself a Republic last month. The failed attack on the Texas Governor's Mansion and State House and the successful attack and destruction of the Alamo have, to date, gone unanswered from Texas, but have contributed significantly to the general state of anxiety felt by CONs all over the country, and in particular, these states that have now broken away from the Union, at least on paper.

"The Federal Government's response to all of this is, of course, something we expect to be developed and will be known sooner rather than later. We pause now for a commercial break."

Sheldon's phone rang. He looked over, saw it was the White House, and quickly picked up the phone. "Secretary Sheldon, I have the President on the line."

"Yes, yes, put him on, please."

The President was screaming. "Who the hell do these assholes think they are? They got a lot of balls to pull this off under our noses! These damn right-wing nuts are about to get their asses kicked from here to Tupelo. I'll have every one of these Old Way asshole governors hanging from a rope within a month, along with all their basket of deplorable ass wipe legislative members that voted for this shit! Get over here right away. I'm calling an emergency cabinet meeting at seven tonight."

"Yes, sir, Mr. President, I'll be there." Sheldon hung up the phone and immediately felt a knot in his stomach. He'd promised his daughter he'd make her recital tonight. He stepped out of the office and approached his wife to give her the bad news about the sudden turn of events.

She took one look at his face and knew what was coming.

"Hon, look, I feel like a jerk, but I'm gonna have to miss the recital.

Tell Tabitha that Daddy is incredibly sorry, but a grave emergency has come up. Sam, please check with your folks in Iowa and make sure they're okay. See what's up from their perspective. Also, what's the state of our cabin in the mountains? How much food do we have up there?"

THE WHITE HOUSE

Washington, D.C.

1900 EDT — 10 Apr 2061

In the Oval Office, White House Chief of Staff Matt Kensington sat nervously fidgeting with his pen. The President looked hopping mad but remained quiet. Kensington broke the silence. "Mr. President, what are you going to say in there?"

"The truth, Matt, the truth. We have twenty-nine renegade states that are seeking to dissolve the Union. It will be stopped by any and all means necessary."

"Strong words, Mr. President. Are you prepared to order federal troops to fire on U.S. Citizens?"

"Only if they bear arms against us and refuse to lay down their weapons. Hell, most of them are illegal weapons anyway under the new laws. I have no interest in starting a Civil War. That would be catastrophic, to say the least. But I will order them to shoot first if the insurgents refuse to lay down their weapons."

An aide came into the Oval Office to announce that the meeting was ready for the President. The President rose from his seat and quietly walked out of the room. Matt followed. Just as soon as they had walked through the door of the Oval Office, a large entourage formed ranks behind them. No one spoke. As they walked the halls to the White House Situation Room, the air of tension was palpable. The President was soon at the door of the room. A Marine standing guard opened it for him. Cyrus entered and took a seat at the center of the long table. His cabinet was present, along with the Vice President and the Speaker of the House.

"Okay, everyone, I trust everyone is up to speed on today's events. We are here to discuss this administration's formal response to these renegade actions. We went through this bullshit in the 1860s over slavery. Are we to understand these renegades want to start another shooting war on American soil over what? Guns and hate speech? I'll be damned, no friggin' way! Not on my watch!

He turned and looked at DHS Secretary Frederic Sheldon. "Frederic, any late-breaking news?"

"Mr. President, we'll need an all-hands-on-deck approach with multiple federal, state, and local agencies to help stop this. DHS, NWBI (New Way Bureau of Investigation, formerly the FBI), ATF, CBP, possibly even the military."

Cyrus looked over at NWBI director Mosby, "Mosby, whatcha got?"

"Mr. President, the NWBI has approximately fifty thousand armed agents.

About five percent of them are overseas. We await your orders."

The President next turned to General Gage. They had barely spoken since the disastrous operation to take the Governor's Mansion in Texas. The President had quietly contemplated accepting the general's retirement letter, but changed his mind after a long conversation with his most trusted advisor, Matt Kensington. He had persuaded the President to keep Gage on board. Kensington was well up to speed on the general's service record and believed Gage would rally from the disaster in Texas.

"General, what can you tell us?"

"Mr. President, I recommend against any direct military action. I suggest negotiations and a peace overture to try and lure these states back into the Union without further bloodshed."

"General, does your hesitance to recommend military action have anything to do with Texas?"

"Not at all, sir. It has everything to do with lowering the temperature and preventing an unimaginable tragedy. A Second Civil War with modern weaponry on American soil would see a staggering loss of life."

"C'mon General. With our precision weaponry, all it will take is a few decisive battles against these rebels, and they'll be begging for peace. Don't you agree?"

"Respectfully, no, sir. I do not."

"Well then, general, despite your opinions to the contrary, are you prepared to carry out the orders of the commander in chief up to and including direct military action against the rebels?"

"You must ask? Of course I am. But I feel it's my duty to provide wise counsel so that you can weigh all the options—"

The general was cut off by the President, "Options? What options? You heard what Whitfield said. Plus, I expect they want us to take the first shot, and then all hell breaks loose. The irony is that we must take the first shot if they refuse to lay down their weapons. Mark my word, we do, and they'll all fall back into line. So, frankly, I believe there are no other options except to fight. But we're going to make it short, and it's going to be painful. General, in seventy-two hours, I want a plan to take back Oklahoma City.

"Additionally, I want a plan for a naval quarantine off all the coastal renegade states. In the meantime, I'll be addressing the nation tomorrow at noon. I'll be declaring a state of martial law against all these rebel states, including Texas."

Colonel Eric Adams sat quietly across from Captain Lemarcus Washington of the 1st Illinois Constitutional Militia. Since the secret meeting up in the mountains of Montana, Adams had studied Lemarcus's service record and was impressed. They had spent the last twenty-four hours getting to know each other at Adams' Ranch. Lemarcus, like so many of his contemporaries, had been born into a single-parent household. His father had died of a fentanyl overdose one month before Lemarcus' birth. Lemarcus had grown into an angry young man. Trouble with the law by age fourteen led to a juvenile sentence of two years for strong-armed robbery.

Once released into the care of his mother, he was recruited by the most prominent street gang in East St. Louis at age seventeen. It was while there that he was plucked from a path that could have seen him die an early death.

His mentor was a kind old man named Dr. Lee, affectionately nicknamed "Doc Lee." It was Doc Lee who became the father figure Lemarcus had never had.

Soon, Doc's influence led to positive changes in Lemarcus's life. Doc insisted that Lemarcus finish his high school education and earn a college degree through the United States Army. Once his Army days were over, he returned to East St. Louis. He was invited by a friend to attend a series of posthumous lectures by Dr. Thomas Sowell with his contemporary Dr. Victor Davis Hanson. The lecture series, featuring holograms of both, had become a sensation in the growing Awakening movement that had captured the attention of CONs, MODs, and a small number of LIBs. During the third night of attending the lectures, Lemarcus had his awakening. At the time, it felt like a religious experience. But, if he was honest with himself, it was more akin to having studied a complex math problem, to nearly giving up, and then having that ah-ha moment where the proverbial light bulb goes off.

For him, the ah-ha moment was in the sudden realization he had been systemically brainwashed and lied to by an ideology filled with hate towards CONs, all Whites, all Christians, especially Conservative ones, and all self-avowed Patriots. When the veil of hate had lifted, he remembered feeling a near-lifelong burden being lifted.

"Lemarcus, I like you," said Colonel Adams. "You're the kind of young man this country will need when this is all over with. Someone with a profound story and history who has come to grasp the full tenets of the Light of Liberty. I want your thoughts on a mission for which you and your soldiers are perfectly suited."

"Thank you, Sir. I sure would. What have you got?"

"We have it from reliable sources that most soldiers and airmen stationed at Scott Air Force Base near St. Louis are very upset. They may want to defect, join the CONs, and fight to take back the country. As part of Operation Market, your role is to help secure the base, allowing defecting Guardsmen to load as many military assets as possible onto on-base transports and then bug out by air. We believe we will have enough pilots to secure fifty or more aircraft. They will fly to a secret location that will be told to them at the appropriate time."

An hour later, Lemarcus was on the phone with his bride of five years, Myranda. He called her on the secure line of her sat phone. Encryption enabled, he took a deep breath before speaking, "Babe, I just sent the bug-out code to the family. I wanted to call you in person and let you know. Everything is ready at the place. Gramps, Ma, and the rest will probably arrive before you do. Whatever you do, don't tell anyone where you're going. You know the drill."

After a short pause, Myranda responded with a quiver in her voice, "Lemarcus, is it that bad? Kaiden was hoping to go to the park after dinner."

"Babe, look, I wish I could tell you everything, but I can't. What I can tell you is that things are about to get serious. The most ever in our lives. It's not going to be safe at home. The safest place for you and Kaiden is with the family at the bug-out site."

"Well, when will you meet up with us?"

"I don't know. I've got a job to do, Myranda, a huge job. The fate of all of us, especially Kaiden and his generation, is at stake. We can't let these crazies take over the country. We just can't. We won't, not if we can help it."

"What's that supposed to mean? Are you gonna go and get yourself killed in some civil war? Please say no."

"Myranda, I have no intention of getting myself killed. Deep down in my soul, I know that every once in a great while, God raises a particular generation destined for greatness, but that greatness often comes at a significant cost.

"Lemarcus, I will say it again: you better not go and get yourself killed! You do, I'll climb down into your grave and whoop your ass, you hear me?"

"Babe, I'm gonna do everything I can to stay safe. But at the end of the day, it's out of my hands. You know, I was thinking a lot about last night. I hardly slept at all. I wanted to, but I know how stressed you've been about all this stuff. As I lay awake, I thought about how our country has been lost for so long.

"The Awakening has opened the eyes of a lot of folks of all colors. I've met them and worked with them. Socialized with them, spoken and debated with them. The White folks especially treat me like we're supposed to have been treated from the very beginning, fully human, not three-fifths. Equal in every way. No greater, no lesser, but equal. Yeah, I know the history. I know it more than you think I know it. But, you see, things are different now. I feel it and sense it all around me whenever I'm in the company of folks who have had the Awakening experience.

"The Old Way is not about any of the stuff the New Way says it is. The Old Way is about the full measure of Liberty as God intends. It was always there from the very beginning, but imperfect men were partially blinded to that truth. Because of it, they subjected what could have been their fellow Americans to that God-awful institution of slavery and then Jim Crow and all the crap after that.

"Wiser men knew it was evil and protested and formed abolitionist societies. Their voices, mostly ignored at first, grew louder and louder until they could no longer be silenced. Faced with radical change or the prospect of their way of life vanishing forever, the South chose rebellion in 1861. Thank God they lost. After that, American Liberty slowly advanced through the fire so that the lingering impurities from after the Civil War would be removed. It has taken a long time—too long, for sure—but it has finally come. What's left is a thing of beauty."

"Lemarcus, you know you're preaching to the choir here. I'm with you. But there's a whole lot of Americans that are convinced that what you say is not true. That's why they want to tear it down and start over from scratch. Deep down in their gut, they believe the whole American Experiment, or whatever you want to call it, is so fundamentally broken that it is beyond repair. I know they're wrong. But I know what's coming down the tracks scares me to death."

"You think I'm not scared? All good soldiers will tell you that if you're not scared before going into battle, there's something wrong with you. Look, I have to go. I love you. Call me when you get there. Leave the sat phone in encryption mode. Hit the little red button to turn on tracking. I gave Gramps the code to track your progress to the bug-out."

"You call me when you can, as often as you can. I love you, Lemarcus. You're the bravest man I know. We will be praying not only for you but for everyone that this descent into madness might stop. God help us all."

‖‖‖ **8** ‖‖‖

THE DECLARATION

THE WHITE HOUSE

Washington, D.C.

1200 EDT — 11 Apr 2061

In office for barely ninety days, the President of the United States, Devin Cyrus, found himself smack dab in the middle of the biggest domestic crisis in two hundred years.

He was aware of the parallels between the start of his administration and that of Lincoln. But he bristled at being compared to Lincoln—whom he often referred to as that "hillbilly from Kentucky" who saved the Union, only to pave the way for Jim Crow. As he carefully reread the speech he was about to deliver to a worldwide audience, he quietly seethed over the developments of these last few days.

The technician signaled that there were ten seconds before Cyrus went live. He counted down to zero, then pointed to the President. Simultaneously, the red light atop the camera lit up.

"Good day to all New Way Americans who are doing their part to create a brand new and better America, free from the relics and encumbrances of her evils dating all the way back from 1619 to the day just before my inauguration.

"Yesterday, April 9, twenty-eight renegade state legislatures voted to secede from the Union under the dictates of twenty-eight renegade governors. These illegal votes are hereby declared null and void. This act of treason against the peace-loving people of the New Way America presents an existential threat to our plans for a Democratic Socialist utopia.

"These last few months have seen secret negotiations with the CONs fail. These baskets of deplorables insist on clinging to their Bibles, their guns, and the antiquated and obsolete United States Constitution that all faithful New Way adherents find abhorrent. A Constitution that is ragged and obsolete.

"It is a multi-hundred-year-old rag of a charter that is entirely beyond repair because it was written by slave-holding white men. I intend to burn it all down and start over.

"We will never again allow hate speech to be protected, no matter whether in the secular part of our society or the religious.

"We will never again allow assault weapons and high-capacity magazines to be owned. We will never relax the strict rules and regulations regarding the sale, purchase, and ownership of ammunition. There is no good reason why anyone needs more than a box of 50 rounds of ammunition per caliber of gun they own.

"We will never allow the extremists to dictate what a woman does to her product of conception. She should have complete choice and control up to the first birthday.

"We will never allow parents to dictate to the government what is proper or improper for future generations of Americans to be taught in federally funded and controlled schools.

"From kindergarten through every level of college, every student must be enlightened. We have a dual obligation to create a safe space for them and to properly instruct them in the New Way of thought.

"It takes a village to train up a child in the way that they should go in the New Way of thought. Only we of the New Way are that village. People of the Old Way threatened the future with their old-fashioned ideas.

"We will also never again allow the free-market capitalist system to operate as it did before 2061. Their greed and hoarding of wealth are unequaled in the annals of human history.

"The re-education camps we just opened for non-compliant adults will go a long way towards weeding out these holdouts to a failed ideology. These are our non-negotiables.

"As President, and by the powers vested in me from the National Emergencies Act of 1974, and thusly amended in 2058, I now make the following declarations.

"One. At noon today, Eastern Time, martial law will be in effect nationwide. Martial Law shall remain in force until further notice. During martial law, Congress shall recess and stay in recess until further notice.

"Two. All rebel states are now issued the following ultimatum: Recant your articles of secession by noon Eastern Standard Time on April 12.

"A failure to comply will result in the governor of each rebel state, and all legislative members who voted for secession, to be hunted down, arrested, and charged as traitors and insurrectionists to be brought before a military tribunal for a swift trial. Convictions will be followed by the punishment of death by hanging.

"A reward of one million dollars will be awarded to any good citizen who provides clear, actionable intelligence leading to the capture of these wanted traitors.

"Three. Any officers of the United States Armed Forces who shall join this rebellion will be subject to a military courts-martial and, when found guilty, sentenced to death by firing squad.

"Four. Any enlisted soldier who joins this rebellion will, if captured, be subject to a military courts-martial. If found guilty, they shall be hanged by the neck until dead.

"Five. In part, because of the extreme patience you and I of the New Way have shown towards those of the Old Way, we are partly to blame for the crisis we now face. It is clear now that the line of demarcation between the Old Way and the New Way must be bold and as straightforward as possible. Thus, by the same powers vested in me mentioned at the beginning of my message, the Declaration of Independence, the Constitution of the United States, and the Bill of Rights, tired, ragged, and flawed, are now declared null and void. Canceled, forever.

"I now call for a New Way Convention composed of only non-rebel states. In session, we shall forge a new National Charter that embraces the New Way in every way, while preserving bits and pieces of the original Constitution in whatever token way seems feasible, and finally putting the Old Way to rest. My word is my bond."

IIII **9** IIII

THE ASSAULTS

For months prior, the 1st Southern Illinois Militia had been secretly training deep in the woods at a secret compound near Rockwood, IL. The tiny hamlet was located on IL Rt. 3 on the far southwestern portion of the state's boundary with the Mississippi River.

Lemarcus was impressed by the troops, who were almost all former or retired military personnel. About half were Marines. The other half were Army, Air Force, Navy, and the Illinois National Guard. Of the Army troops, three were ex-Rangers. From the Marines, three Special Ops troops. From the Navy, one Navy SEAL. The rest were civilian volunteers. All of them were CONs.

They were assembled and stationed at an abandoned warehouse awaiting the attack order. The troops, all five hundred seven of them, were anxious to fight. Seventy-seven were female combat troops with extensive combat experience in North Africa years earlier. None of them had a death wish, but to a man—and woman—they were determined to take back the country from what they perceived as the Red Monster.

The troops were assembled and standing at attention when Lemarcus approached the front of the assembly.

"At ease, Patriots. The day has come. The Trojan Horse has been revealed for the monster it is. Our rights, our honor, our heritage—our very charter of freedom—are being held hostage. The stars and stripes, which have symbolized the hopes, dreams, and ideals of liberty-loving people worldwide for almost three centuries, have been taken down and replaced by a hideous replacement.

"Disguised as a proverbial angel of light, our enemy has shown their true colors and intent. The devil owns their hearts. It's as if every demon of hell has been unleashed on us. In the 2020s, when these so-called socialists first came on the scene, they hid behind the terms 'progressive' and 'democratic socialism.' They never used the "C" word because they knew damn well that their cover would have been blown wide open if they did. Not to mention, they would be unelectable. The other "C" word, Capitalism, they loved to trash, all the while reaping the benefits of the capitalist system they railed against.

"When they coined the phrase *Burn it all down*, most people thought they were speaking rhetorically. When they wrote articles in all the media and went on talk shows and podcasts about replacing the Constitution, no one paid much attention to it because the idea, at the time, seemed absurd.

"When they spoke about defunding the police, most people did not understand what they really meant. Today, after defunding, we still have three once-great cities that are a shadow of their former selves: San Francisco, Portland, and Seattle. Four other major cities were spared the same fate only after the National Guard was called out in New York, Chicago, Los Angeles, and Philadelphia. Thankfully, citizens of Atlanta and Charlotte came alive during the Awakening movement and showed the Reds the door at the ballot box.

"Today, here we are under martial law. The Alamo was obliterated. Cyrus unilaterally canceled our Declaration of Independence, Constitution, and Bill of Rights. The Stars and Stripes are no more. All this and more, and they have the gall to call us traitors. To hell with them all. The fight to preserve, protect, defend, and restore our Constitutional Republic from sea to shining sea starts today!"

The troops roared their approval.

"On the eve of his assassination in 1968, Dr. King said this. 'We've got some difficult days ahead, but it really doesn't matter with me now because I've been to the mountaintop—I've seen the Promised Land. I may not get there with you. But I want you to know tonight that we, as a people, will get to the Promised Land.'

"Soldiers, our struggle to see to it that our Constitutional Republic mirrors the dream of Dr. King about judging a man by the content of his character and not the color of his skin, in many ways, has been reached in many parts of the country. The places where it has not been, are the very same places that continue to stir up victimhood for Americans of color. They love to stir up racism against Whites. To hell with that, also.

"I make a solemn vow before God and all of you now. I promise you this as I lead you into battle: I willingly echo the words of the patriots from 1776 when I recite the last line of the Declaration of Independence, 'We mutually pledge to each other our Lives, our Fortunes, and our sacred Honor.'

"I know that what we are about to undertake will not be easy and will not come without the shedding of blood. I may not get to the mountaintop with you. But I have not only seen the Promised Land; I have also lived in it in my day.

"I want my children and their children to bask in the light of it themselves and experience the whole fruit of Liberty and Justice for all and Freedom for all once we get rid of these Red bastards.

"Brave soldiers, take a knee. Let us pray."

MAIN GATE – SCOTT AIR FORCE BASE

Shiloh, Illinois

0425 CDT — 12 Apr 2061

Private Reginald Stark of Centralia, Illinois, was one month away from completing his two-year stint in the U.S. Air Force. It had been a quiet shift so far in the early morning hours. The base's main gate guard shack had five other soldiers standing watch with him, including Sergeant Brandt Zachary.

There had been no traffic in or out of the base since the 10 p.m. statewide curfew the previous evening. The guards were all talked out from the earlier hours of boredom as they stood watch quietly, awaiting the dawn. A dense fog had settled over the area. Reginald was the first to hear noises from the front, but the darkness and mist obscured the view. Arousing from a relaxed position, his composure adjusted to a slightly more curious stance. The other soldiers picked up his subtle change in demeanor one by one.

As their alertness level rose ever so slightly, Reginald took command and yelled into the night. "Who goes there?" Hearing nothing, he motioned for the guards to be still. "I say, who goes there? Identify yourselves."

Nothing but the sound of crickets was heard for a little under 30 seconds. After that, some sounds were heard towards their three o'clock position, followed momentarily by more sounds from their nine o'clock position. Now, the soldiers' alertness level rose to an alarming level. Enough so that all of them removed the safety of their weapons.

Reginald tried a third time. "Who goes there?" To his shock, a reply came out of the darkness and fog ahead of him. It was amplified. It was the voice of a man.

"This is Lemarcus Washington, Commanding Officer of the 1st Southern Illinois Constitutionalist Militia. Listen carefully to what I am about to say. You have 30 seconds to lay down your weapons and approach the sound of my voice with your hands up in the air. You will be allowed to pass through our lines without harm and go wherever you like to the rear, or you can join us in taking back the country for the cause of Liberty and the Constitution of the United States of America. If you do not comply; we will open fire on your position in 30 seconds —on my mark. Now."

All the guard's alertness levels had now skyrocketed. They all looked at Reginald and asked what they should do. Reginald had always avoided showing his cards when it came to politics. A few moments ago, he was half asleep, and the night was peaceful. In an instant, he found himself somewhat bewildered, facing a life-or-death decision in 30 seconds or less. Equally as quick, he knew deep down what he had to do.

As a CON, he despised Cyrus. "Guys, Cyrus is an SOB. What he did the other day is crazy. What the hell is this new flag patch on my uniform? Suspending the Constitution and the Bill of Rights without a vote by anyone? That's bullshit! I'm laying down my weapon. I'm not dying for that ass!"

Reginald put the safety back on his weapon, removed the clip, and tossed them to the pavement. He put his hands up in the air and slowly walked towards the general direction of where he had heard Lamarcus's voice and yelled out, "Okay, I've laid down my weapon. I'm unarmed. I'm walking towards the sound of your voice. Please don't shoot."

The other soldiers stood motionless for what seemed like an eternity. Then, Sergeant Zachary, asserting his authority, yelled out. "Reginald, halt. Take another step, and I'll consider you to have deserted your post and become a traitor. I'll shoot to stop you if I must."

"The hell you will, Sarge. The hell you will. Besides, my back is towards you. You wouldn't shoot an unarmed Black man in the back, would you?

Reginald took a deep breath, then stepped forward with his right foot. Nothing happened. Then, he took another step with his left foot, and before it had touched the ground, a shot rang out. Simultaneously, he felt a searing pain through the right side of his back, clear through his chest. He collapsed to the ground in pain and rolled over face up.

He could tell he was looking up at a streetlight, but it quickly faded to black. Just before eternity overtook him, he heard the hellish sound of five hundred guns opening fire at once.

ABANDONED WAREHOUSE COMPLEX

Wichita, Kansas

0330 CDT — 12 Apr 2061

Colonel David S. Patton of the Kansas Patriot Militia had two thousand soldiers under his command. Like many other militias around the nation, the Kansas Patriot Militia had a sizable number of patriot soldiers who were ex-military or retired military personnel. He was particularly pleased to have some ex-Navy SEALs in his ranks and some ex-Marines that had been part of some special ops unit he'd never heard of before.

As a part of the well-coordinated assault planned for moments from now, their main objective was to take McConnell Air Force Base and place all assets under the direct command and control of the Governor of Kansas, Jonathan Hill.

Privy to top-secret meetings held with Governor Hill, Patton knew that a sizable firefight was probably in the offing. At the same time, the airbase had many Kansans in uniform, as well as an equally large number of U.S. Air Force personnel. Reliable intel had it that the Kansans at the base, almost to a person, would quickly join the CONs in the rebellion to take back the country. What happened after that was anybody's guess, but that's where the militia would come into play to bring in a sizeable reaction force against the LIBs and MODs that decided to stand and fight to hold the base for the New Way.

Kansas was smack dab in the middle of CON territory, and they needed to secure the Air Base to provide the tools that Governor Hill would need to defend Liberty on Kansas soil. To have a New Way base in the heart of CON territory would be catastrophic.

With a high-resolution printout of the base before him and his officers, Colonel Patton huddled with them to go over the battle plan one more time. "Lieutenant Colonel Anderson, repeat the battle plan for your troops."

"Yes, sir, Colonel. 1st Battalion will storm the Main Gate after giving the guards 30 seconds to lay down their weapons. A Company will assault this position here and gain control of the air traffic control tower. B Company will attack here and here, commandeer heavy tractors, and position them on all runways to close the airfield. C Company will concentrate here and here to secure the ordnance and fuel farm."

"Very well, Lieutenant Anderson. Lieutenant Alexander, explain the 2nd Battalion's objectives."

"Yes, Sir. The 2nd Battalion will attack from the rear of the base here and drive forward with all haste to this rally point, where we will link up with A Company and the 3rd Battalion. We'll attack these three key positions here, here, and here next to the officers' quarters. Once secured, we will hold and maintain our position until further orders. We are also to process any Federal New Way officers who decline to join us."

Colonel Patton pointed to a particular point on the map. "Very well, Lieutenant Alexander. Be careful at this position near the Armory. I expect heavy fighting. Lieutenant Reynolds, tell me about 3rd Battalion."

"Yes, Sir. The 3rd Battalion will attack from the west and enter the base here. A Company will break off here and link up with the 2nd Battalion. The remainder of the 3rd will head for these three key objectives, take them, and maintain control while awaiting further orders. We will also process any prisoners and march them over to the holding area."

"Okay. Everyone, this will get hot damn quick. No sugar coating it here. Any National Guard troops who elect to stand and fight with us are supposed to display something that makes it evident to us. For operational security, we are currently unaware of what precisely that sign is supposed to represent, but we will be informed soon. Ensure that all your soldiers are informed about this. We need all the new recruits we can get. This place is just as good a place as any to get as many as possible. The last thing we need is to kill Kansas Guard members intending to join us. We have no intel on whether any Federal New Way troops will defect to us. We must presume they will put up a fierce fight. Also, let your troops know that Old Glory is to be at the front of every formation of ours. We want all New Way troops to see that, just in case any of them are of a mind to switch sides. Plus, we'll need it to avoid friendly fire.

Once they were doubly satisfied with the last detail, they synchronized their watches and exited the assembly area in a full sprint towards their vehicles. As soldiers piled into all manner of civilian and surplus military vehicles and headed out. They formed three columns and headed off to battle.

MAIN GATE – MCCONNELL AIR FORCE BASE

Wichita, Kansas

0400 CDT — 12 Apr 2061

The guards could hear the sounds of vehicles off in the distance, beyond the reach of the fog. Not sure of the nature of the noise, Sergeant Lemoine removed his safety from his weapon and ordered his men to do likewise. Up until that point, it had been a quiet evening. The last vehicle was over an hour ago.

"Lewis, take the men and get into a defensive position."

At that, the other six members of the guard detail took up defensive positions in and around the guard shack and the nearby Humvees. The noise grew louder, then stopped. Sergeant Lemoine leveled his weapon and shouted out. "Who goes there? Identify yourself."

From out of the fog, an amplified voice broke the silence. "This is Lieutenant Colonel Anderson of the Kansas Patriot Militia. By order of our Commander-in-Chief, Kansas Governor Jonathan Hill, you must lay down your weapons and surrender. Approach the sound of my voice, walking backward and with your hands held high. If you do this, you will have the opportunity to join us in taking back the nation. If you do not surrender, we will open fire on your position in 30 seconds—on my mark. Now."

Sergeant Lemoine was stunned at the audacity of what he just heard. Nevertheless, he quickly turned and ran back to the guard shack. He hit the alarm button, took up position with his men, and ordered them to open fire. The battle for McConnell Air Force Base had begun.

MCCONNELL AIR FORCE BASE

Wichita, Kansas

0403 CDT — 12 Apr 2061

Hearing gunfire off towards the Main Gate, General Mike McLellan of the Kansas National Guard knew full well that what he was about to do could cost him his life, never mind his career. He knew the attack was on at the sound of the general alarm. As a loyalist to the CONs, General McLellan had stealthily hidden his true political leanings, astutely sensing the growing divide in the nation reaching its epic point of detonation. The well-thought-out CON battle plans, success, or failure would hinge on his actions within the next few minutes. He grabbed his sat phone and called his number two, Lieutenant General Jeremiah Smith.

"Mike, I hear the alarm. What's the situation?"

"Jerry, the assaults have begun. Muster the troops and give them the orders. Tell them the Kansas Patriot Militia is in the fight and has already breached the base perimeter. They're wearing Stars and Stripes decals on their helmets. Do our troops have their decals?"

"Yes, Sir, all taken care of."

"Good. Godspeed Jerry. I'll see you at the rally point, Lord willing."

Lieutenant General Smith had been a close friend of McLellan since their days at West Point. Both were fiercely patriotic. They shared a common contempt for the LIBs' ideology and had long ago believed in the Trojan Horse theory, or the more condescending term, the "parasite theory." This held that the so-called democratic socialists who had taken over the Democratic Party secretly had, in their upper echelons of leadership, hard-core Communists hell-bent on burning the Republic down to the ground and starting all over again as a Marxist state.

The Lieutenant General picked up his comm and called the duty officer for the Kansas National Guard. "This is Lieutenant General Jeremiah Smith. Order the troops to the rally point now. Tell Colonel Thompkins I'll join everyone there just as fast as I can." He hung up and ran out the door to his Humvee. His driver was waiting in the driver's seat and had the passenger door open. He hopped in, and the driver floored it before General Smith had even closed the door. As they raced to the rally point, neither said a word. They both knew this would be the longest day of their lives.

VACANT WAREHOUSE

Anaconda, Montana

0330 MDT — 12 Apr 2061

Colonel Eric Adams and his nearly fifteen hundred soldiers of the Rocky Mountain Militia had quietly slipped in through the back door of the 100,000-square-foot abandoned warehouse two weeks earlier. The building had been abandoned decades earlier, during the collapse of the U.S. manufacturing industry. In its heyday, they had manufactured electric lawnmowers here and had employed over two thousand workers.

As an ideal muster point, they had been using the cover of darkness to stash supplies and weapons in advance of the assault on the National

Guard Armory a mile down the road. In precisely 30 minutes from now, at the instructions of their Commander-in-Chief, Montana Governor Wayland Emerson, the militia would mount up in their vehicles and race out of the warehouse towards the Armory.

Its size, conventional weapons, and armaments stockpiles had grown immensely in recent years. The Governor's military advisers had convinced him that an assault on the state's ICBM bases—along with the strategic bombers at Malmstrom Air Force Base, two hundred miles to the northwest in Great Falls—was unwise and would be met with fierce resistance from New Way troops. They also felt such an assault would more than likely trigger a response with a Rapid Reaction Force to keep nukes out of their hands at all costs.

Turning their sights towards the Armory, a vast array of weaponry and munitions was stored at the base in Anaconda. Anaconda, a typical mountain town of just under 10,000 citizens, was a hotbed of Patriotic fervor for the cause of Liberty. Long ago, the city was at the center of U.S. copper mining operations and later became a manufacturing hub 20 years ago.

In the old cafeteria, dank and musty, Colonel Adams stood to address his troops. "Soldiers, we're at the cusp of a great challenge to Freedom and Liberty-loving people everywhere. The cause of Liberty cannot be fully put into words because Liberty is so much more than mere words.

"Liberty is best appreciated when you've lived it. Out here, far away from the elites, I think it's safe to say we have all felt the blessings of Liberty and Freedom and have lived it well, going back to our forefathers who settled these lands long before we were born.

"When we leave here, I have no idea which of us will see the sunrise tomorrow, me included. But, if this is our last day here on earth, let those who survive not mourn for us, for we will have taken up arms in defense of our country. If the defense of our liberty and freedom requires every ounce of our blood, so be it. It shall have been worth it to look tyranny in the eyes and say, "No further, not this day!"

At that, the troops exploded with applause.

"In the words of the first 9/11 Patriot, Todd Beamer, "Let's roll!"

MAIN GATE – MONTANA NATIONAL GUARD ARMORY
Anaconda, Montana
0400 MDT — 12 Apr 2061

Sergeant Evelynne Linette and her fellow soldiers were laughing while recalling the previous evening's antics at the Twisted Antler Bar on the outskirts of town. Linette, from Newark, New Jersey, was the daughter of New Jersey Lieutenant Governor Katrina Isobel and Rabbi Reuben Avi. Rabbi Reuben was a vocal MOD who had, of late, been working with his contacts furiously to forestall a war. Just last week, Evelynne had a long phone conversation with her father regarding the perilous state of the nation. He had persuaded her that the LIBs had gone too far and that reasonable people needed to come to the negotiating table and work out their differences.

Two years earlier, Sergeant Linette had married the base commander, Montana native General James Linette of the Montana National Guard.

The Linettes were a storied family in Montana, both politically and in business, dating back to the 1880s.

At the guard shack for the third watch, their laughter and storytelling had masked the sounds of approaching danger. Aware of what was about to happen, Sergeant Linette was in on the plan, as was her husband. Her fellow soldiers heard the sounds to their left, right, and front. Joking abruptly ended when an amplified voice was heard loud and clear. "This is Colonel Eric Adams of the Rocky Mountain Militia. On my mark, you will have 30 seconds to surrender your weapons. Walk backward to the sound of my voice, and you will have my assurance that you will not be harmed. If you do not comply, we will open fire on your position. On my mark. Now."

"Piss off!" Pvt. Terrence Wilke yelled.

"Calm down, Wilke!" Evelynne shouted as she quickly turned and faced her fellow soldiers.

Moments ago, they were laughing it up. What she was about to say was no laughing matter. It was life and death. "Okay, here's the deal. You know, and I know, that our country has been betrayed. Everyone here has a chance to strike a huge blow towards tyranny. All you have to do is lay down your weapons and surrender to me. I will take care of the rest. I promise you that no harm will come to you. Join us in resecuring Liberty throughout the land. Who's in?"

They stood there looking stunned. Meanwhile, a voice out of the darkness yelled, "Fifteen seconds."

She was shocked when the soldiers suddenly laid down their weapons in unison. With five seconds to spare, she turned and yelled the code word. "Appomattox!"

Hearing the code word, Colonel Adams's voice could be heard in the darkness, giving the response code, "Courthouse!"

At that, the Rocky Mountain Militia quickly entered the base unopposed.

For the next thirty minutes, the militia members fanned out, linked up with Montana National Guardsmen, and secured the base. There was a single short staccato of automatic weapons fire that could be heard nearby. It lasted less than thirty seconds.

General James Linette drove up in a Humvee a minute later, jumped out, and saluted the Colonel. "Colonel, it looks like the base is secure. All but a handful of soldiers have joined ranks with us. I've called the Governor and informed him that the base is under his command and that we stand at the ready to defend it. If you have your men deployed as planned, I will inform him we have allied our forces."

NATIONAL MILITARY COMMAND CENTER

The Pentagon

0415 EDT — 12 Apr 2061

The National Military Command Center, or NMCC, was a labyrinth of secure command and control facilities deep below the Pentagon. Built a century earlier, during the Cold War, it had been repeatedly modernized and expanded over the last several decades. President Devin Cyrus had cleaned house at the Pentagon. He fired or demoted twenty-seven generals, a move his intelligence personnel warned would make them unreliable in the event of a Civil War. The shakeup was done solely because of their Conservative political leanings. After installing his people, who had been vetted and who were fanatical New Way adherents, the President felt that right out of the gate, he could sleep a little easier during this perilous time of sweeping away the old to make way for the new.

The Duty Officer at the NMCC for the third watch was Captain Aydan Willis, from Chicago, Illinois. Captain Willis, a staunch Cyrus supporter, had spent considerable time the previous year working a phone bank for the Cyrus Campaign in the months leading up to Election Day in the November 2060 Presidential Election.

It had been a quiet shift that evening. Arrayed before him was a myriad of screens, all displaying important information.

Though tension was high across the country, he was shocked by how peaceful and calm things had been that evening. At one point, the thought crept in: *Too quiet.* Ever the optimist, he shook it off as he stared at his console processing messages.

At precisely 0415 hours, all hell broke loose.

All the phones at the four other duty officer stations lit up at once. Seeing his flash, he grabbed the receiver. "Captain Willis here."

"This is Lieutenant Brian McDaniel, Scott Air Force Base. We are under attack. I repeat, we are under attack."

"What is the scale and nature of the attack?" Willis asked.

McDaniel excitedly replied. "We're being attacked from the outside and the inside by ground forces! Looks like a sizeable number of Illinois National Guard are mutineers! There are explosions everywhere, automatic weapons fire. Reports are that the outsiders appear to be well-armed and organized. They're pouring into the base on civilian trucks and military surplus vehicles."

"Understood. Any casualty reports?"

"Too early to tell, but I see a lot of bodies on the ground.

Send help! I'm grabbing a weapon to go kick some ass."

The line went dead. Captain Willis thought that was odd, especially since it was a satellite connection. The thought was fleeting as the room erupted with phones ringing everywhere and the gigantic threat board lighting up like a Christmas tree. The entire heartland of the country was blinking red as nearly every military installation on the map was under attack. Staring at all the lights, his calm demeanor changed as he shuddered at the realization that the Second American Civil War had begun. Transfixed at the monitors, he whispered to himself, "God Almighty, help us all."

0654 MDT — 12 Apr 2061

FROM LINCOLN BREAK

TO PATMIL BREAK

CHARLIE OSCAR DELTA ECHO BREAK

MIKE MIKE ONE BREAK

WAR HAS BEGUN.

MORE TO FOLLOW BREAK

TMWSD 76SEC.

|||| **10** ||||

ANGST

ANN (AMERICAN NETWORK NEWS) STUDIOS

New York, New York

1830 EDT — 12 Apr 2061

"This is the ANN Nightly News with Olivia Kinley. *America at War.* Live from our studios in New York—here is Olivia Kinley."

The melodic voice of veteran female anchor Olivia Kinley conveys the shocking news to the American people. "Good evening, America. Many Americans were rocked awake this morning by the sound of explosions and gunfire.

"The source of the turmoil is mostly renegade National Guard Soldiers aided by militia groups, assaulting military installations in the Heartland from the Gulf to the Canadian Border.

"The attacks came in the predawn hours of what amounted to a well-planned and coordinated series of armed assaults against U.S. Military bases, many of them inside rebel states.

"We take you to Sonny Jenkins, reporting live from Shiloh, Illinois, outside Scott Air Force Base."

On location, Sonny Jenkins is seen wearing a bulletproof vest and an army helmet with the words PRESS clearly stenciled on both sides and the back. PRESS is also painted on the front and back of his vest. "Olivia, we arrived here about 90 minutes ago. We're here in west-central Illinois, about an hour's drive from St. Louis. The battle for control of Scott Air Force Base continues to rage into the evening here. By all accounts, we are now over 13 hours into this battle.

"Earlier, I witnessed many Air Force planes taking off and quickly heading west at a low altitude, destination unknown. I also saw what looked like several refueling aircraft taking off and following a similar route. Then, a few fighter jets took off, circled, and strafed the field.

"At this time, it is impossible to tell who they were or whom they were strafing. All the while, explosions continue along with the unmistakable sound of automatic weapons fire. The sum of all this can only be described as a fierce firefight for control of the base.

"Fires are burning everywhere. When we first arrived, we approached the guard shack at the main gate. We were apparently met by soldiers—rebel militia from Illinois. They were polite but firm, insisting that we not come any closer. We were told to turn around, and later, a spokesperson would hold a press conference at that same guard shack.

"Sources at the Pentagon state that the U.S. Military is having difficulty responding with reinforcements, with so many other bases under attack. Rapid Reaction forces are typically on standby 24 hours a day. Sources also state that these Rapid Reaction forces were deployed but were sent elsewhere into the heartland.

"Sources also stated that, in their words, the fog of war on American soil has made it difficult to sort out friend and foe—and to understand the full scale and complexity of what was launched today."

"Further, sources stated the Pentagon Brass has been split and that an undisclosed number of generals and other high-ranking officers have been arrested and charged with treason. Details are sketchy at this time as we await further information on that.

"Meanwhile, local, county, and state police have cordoned off all roads around the base here to keep onlookers well away from the intense gunfire and explosions.

"We did witness SWAT teams being deployed but have not heard any details as to where they were being sent inside the base. It was apparent that the SWAT teams were from multiple jurisdictions.

"Additionally, we also witnessed federal agents from the NWBI, U.S. Marshals Service, Homeland Security, and ATF.

"When some of their members attempted to approach the guard shack, a loudspeaker ordered them to lay down their weapons or be fired upon in 30 seconds. None did, and true to their word, at the 30-second mark, rebel forces at the guard shack and forces arrayed around it opened fire. We ran for our lives and took cover behind a brick building roughly a hundred yards away.

"My cameraman, Sean, was slightly wounded when a bullet grazed his calf. We flagged down paramedics at a staging area a block or so away. They quickly assessed his wound and bandaged him up. He insists he is fine and is the man behind the camera as I speak.

"At some point, someone here from outside the main gate opened fire with a grenade launcher and blew up the guard shack, and everyone in it. Rebels that survived the blast jumped into vehicles and moved a few blocks further into the base.

"There has been no word on casualties or any indication of who controls the base and the valuable military assets.

"Even though Illinois has not seceded and does not recognize the so-called state of Southern Illinois, I can tell you that vast swaths of rural areas all over this state are very pro-CON. They are very sympathetic towards the rebellious states.

"This is Sonny Jenkins, reporting outside Scott Air Force Base in Shiloh, Illinois. Seventy miles southeast of St. Louis. Olivia, back to you."

"Thank you, Sonny. Please stay safe and give our regards to Sean. "More information on today's attacks was provided at a Pentagon briefing earlier today. Now to Matt Sydney at the Pentagon."

The familiar face of Matt Sydney appeared. He stood before the now vacant lectern inside the press briefing room of the Pentagon. Matt, a prize-winning reporter, had made a reputation as a wartime correspondent, covering conflicts all over the globe.

"At a Pentagon briefing held here about ten minutes ago. Officials here acknowledged that at least 20 federal military bases in rebel states had lost command and control to rebel forces.

"Pentagon spokesperson Temple Peyton stated that rebels attacked at 4:30 a.m. Eastern time. This would have been 3:30 a.m. locally at many of the bases, with several more bases in Mountain Standard Time at 2:30 a.m. The bases came under attack by a combination of renegade National Guard soldiers, federal troops in mutiny, as well as what are being described as white supremacist militia forces.

"Many of the bases are shared by National Guard units. Renegade

National Guard soldiers were joined by unknown numbers of irregular forces consisting of locals. No casualty reports are available yet, but unofficial reports indicate heavy casualties for both sides.

"When questioned about the military assets seized by the rebels, Peyton deflected and stated an analysis is underway to determine what and how much firepower the insurgents have seized, based on the inventory at each base.

"This is Matt Sydney for ANN reporting from the Pentagon."

Captain Lemarcus Washington of the 1st Illinois Constitutionalist Militia was the last of his soldiers to board the mammoth C-20A for the last flight out of Scott Air Force Base. It had been a long and successful day.

While he was pleased with achieving the mission's primary objective, there were mixed emotions at the loss of twenty soldiers under his command. Their bodies were now lying at rest at the front of the cargo hold, and their names, on a sheet of paper, were now in his hands.

Later, Washington would have to make gut-wrenching calls to their next of kin. He put those thoughts aside, picked up his sat phone, and called Myranda.

"Hello, Lemarcus, where are you!?" said Myranda

"Hi, hon. I'm safe. The battle is over, and we're headed to a secure location."

"Are you hurt?"

"Just a couple of scratches, that's it. I can't believe it. Meanwhile, twenty of my fellow soldiers didn't make it. I have to call their next of kin later this evening. I'm not looking forward to that at all. I'm so exhausted. What's the news saying?"

"That you're all a bunch of rebels and traitors. They specifically called out all the militias as being white supremacists."

"Those crazies. Half of my unit is nonwhite. My Executive Officer is half Black and half Asian."

"Don't listen to the news, Babe. They've been lying for so long, they don't know any better."

"How'd the trip go to the bug-out site? Everyone else make it?" "Everyone is here and doing fine. They all say to pass along to you that they're praying day and night for you and your soldiers. "Thank you. I feel those prayers, trust me. How are the kids?"

Myranda answered quietly, "Missing you terribly and giving Grandpa a run for his money, as usual."

"Ha! I bet." Lemarcus continued after a brief pause, "You tell them Daddy says to mind their manners and do exactly what you tell them."

"You know they will, hon. They have been good. I miss you."

Lemarcus, exhausted, felt a rush of emotion, "Babe, you have no idea how badly I want to be there right now, but we have to do this, or…" Myranda interrupted him, "You don't have to explain, Babe. I know.

Trust me, I know. Look, one of the cousins is crying. I need to go and check. Godspeed, Hon. Try to get a few winks in on the plane. I love you!"

"I love you too, Babe. Give my love to all." Lemarcus hung up, put his phone down, and quickly nodded off from utter exhaustion. It had been the longest day of his life.

THE WHITE HOUSE

Washington, D.C.

2250 EDT — 12 Apr 2061

After three hours of meeting with his civilian and military advisors, the President of the United States was angry. Sitting at the conference table in the White House Situation Room, he had just been briefed on the latest numbers from the attacks earlier that day. It was the most significant loss of life on American soil since the second 9/11.

The numbers were still coming in, but the casualties were at nearly 7,000 as of 8 p.m. Eastern. The breakdown was 4,200 dead, 2,000 wounded, and 801 missing and unaccounted for. Casualties among the rebel forces were sketchy, but as near as anyone could tell, the numbers were a lot lower.

"Okay, everyone, thank you for your thorough reports on this tragic day," said President Cyrus. "We're barely a few months into the New Way, and it's clear now that these psychopaths leading the Old Way are not going to go quietly into the night. Tomorrow morning, we will reconvene here at 0700.

"I want a plan to hit back hard and get these rebel bastards back in line. I'll be damned if I'm going to let those assholes get away with this. Meeting adjourned."

As the brain trust rose, Matt Kensington quickly came alongside the President. "What else do you need?"

"Just between you and me, come up with a list of candidates to replace Gage. This is twice he's screwed up. I want a new Chairman of the Joint Chiefs of Staff ASAP. I want a candidate list in 72 hours. Clear?"

"Yes, Sir. Can do."

GREENBELT PARK

Greenbelt, Maryland

0930 EDT — 13 Apr 2061

DeShawn King and his 1619 Red Brigade members were angry. On the sidelines was not where King or his soldiers wanted to be. They would much rather be in the thick of the fight, no matter what. Instead, a day ago, when Civil War 2.0 broke out, they were in a classroom studying DEI Paramilitary Policing Tactics.

With the DEI class now canceled due to the outbreak of hostilities, King had assembled his team in a nearby park. "Okay, everybody. I want to thank you all for coming here on such short notice. We've got a nice, peaceful, and secluded spot here.

"Comrades, yesterday, domestic terrorists assaulted our country. These murderers killed thousands of our comrades who were committed to the New Way. I think you know that if I had any clue this sneak attack was going to happen yesterday, I would have done everything I could to have been in the fight.

"I take comfort in the fact that there will be plenty of opportunities very soon to exact revenge on these pieces of crap for what they did. We will take no prisoners. Kill 'em all!"

At this point, his paramilitary troops erupted in cheers and started a chant, "Hey – hey, what do we say, kill'em all today."

King motioned for them to quiet down. "Today, we plan for our revenge."

TEXAS WHITE HOUSE

Austin, Texas

0930 CDT — 14 Apr 2061

Texas President González had been closely following the events across the border. When he was approached by Oklahoma Governor Mary Whitfield six weeks earlier, she had informed him that a plan was being developed to assault and gain control of many U.S. Military bases in the Constitutionalist States and seize as much of their contents as was operationally possible.

She had also advised him that a coalition of Constitutionalist States was desperately seeking an Alliance with Texas in the upcoming fight. He sincerely appreciated their overture and the intelligence trove provided to him, but remained non-committal.

With the destruction of the Alamo a short time earlier, Texans were understandably angry and wanted to strike back at the U.S. incursion into Texas and the destruction of such an iconic part of Texas history. That, coupled with the failed attempt to kidnap the leader of a sovereign nation, had deeply hardened the resolve of Texans that the course they had chosen was right and, in fact, righteous.

While deferring a decision on a coalition with the CONs, President González had used the top-secret info to plan Texas's assaults on remaining U.S. bases inside Texas that were not under Texas military control. The plan had been executed brilliantly. Texas now had more firepower than the bottom two-thirds of the world's nations combined.

The capture of the bases and their assets had not come without cost. But that had been the situation with all the CON states that had undertaken similar assaults. He recalled President John F. Kennedy's famous line, "The price of freedom has always been high, but Americans have always paid it."

The proverbial cherry on the cake had been the capture of a fully armed B-2 bomber with seven B61 thermonuclear gravity bombs. President González had secretly communicated this fact to President Cyrus, issuing a direct warning that any further incursion into Texas territory would result in the use of a nuclear weapon on Washington, D.C. Checkmated, President Cyrus had agreed, but on two all-important conditions. One, Texas must never disclose that it has possession of a nuke. Two, it must never ally itself with any rebel states. On the first point, President González was comfortable keeping it a secret. After all, the Israelis had been doing the same thing for a hundred years with their nuclear capabilities. On the second point, he knew he was dealing with a chameleon. While he said yes to it, he thought to himself, *No way I'm going to keep to this if the crap hits the fan.*

President González and his advisers gathered in the Texas White House Situation Room to discuss the growing crises across the border.

U.S. President Cyrus viewed all the rebel states as being in rebellion and still considered them irrevocably bonded in union with the United

States. The CON states and their respective governors held quite a different view.

Without exception, González and the rest of his team viewed the CON rebel states as the "legitimate and true United States," while the LIB New Way states were seen as having rebelled against the Constitution by abandoning it. González looked with contempt at Cyrus and his red lackeys and what they had turned the LIB states into.

While Texas had been the first to secede, González and his leadership team were content to take further action by declaring themselves, once again, the Republic of Texas. What their friendly neighboring states would call themselves was still to be determined. In the meantime, President González was content with posturing their fledgling, born-again republic in such a way as to be able to enter the war at a time and place of his choosing.

"Alright, everybody, I'd like to review the current situation and get a clear picture of where things stand. Adam, you're first up."

"Thank you, Mr. President. The Texas Defense Forces are well-armed, well-trained, and on station. We are manning the ramparts, as it were, around the clock. I have been in touch with my counterparts in all the neighboring CON states that share a border with us. All of them have privately asked us to join ranks with them. Obviously, I can't make such a commitment, but I did assure them of passing their wishes to you."

President González let out a smirk. "Seems to be a popular request these days."

At that, several in the room laughed. The levity felt good.

The Governor continued. "Thank you, Adam. For our sake, such a decision must come from the top and be approved by the legislature via a Use of Military Force Resolution. I'm holding my cards close to the vest. I hope everyone here not only understands that but is also in agreement." All the heads in the room nodded in approval. "Sam, what's the situation with the 1619?"

"All known subversives aligned with the communist militia group known as 1619 have been placed under arrest and formally charged with sedition. Their local leader is a guy named Oli Imeda. He has a 20-acre ranch an hour outside of Austin. We raided it yesterday and found a huge weapons cache. It looks like they were planning some sort of an attack. We also found his little black book. Got a treasure trove of intel. We're currently working through that and making additional arrests under the Sedition Act just passed."

"Keep me informed, Sam. Technically, I want our posture to be that of one in a state of war—though for now, our guns remain silent unless we're attacked again. I know there are enemies and spies among us. We must find them and ensure they don't cause any trouble. But I want to make it clear that we are to conduct ourselves in a manner that does not trample on constitutional rights. Clear?"

"Clear, Mr. President."

"General Happ, what do you have?"

"Mr. President, the Texas Army is on alert. We stand at the ready with a potent arsenal. Elements of the 1st Texas Armored Division are deployed strategically along our eastern border with Arkansas and Louisiana. The 2nd Texas Infantry is along the Gulf Coast. The 2nd Texas Armored Division is along the northern border with Oklahoma. The 4th Texas Infantry is along the western border with New Mexico. The southern border with Mexico is closed and guarded by elements of the Texas Rangers, Texas Border Patrol, and state, county, and local police with assets available."

"Excellent. I spoke with the Governors of all the neighboring states. I assured them that all these forces arrayed along our shared borders were strictly defensive. For now, we'll not set foot on a neighboring state's soil unless an attack against Texas is originating or soon to begin from their soil by Federal forces. What about air assets?"

"All on alert, ready in the air and on the ground."

"Thank you, general. Admiral Leonard, what do you have to report?"

"The Texas Navy is on station. *Dreadnought Texas* is our Flagship.

She may be ancient, but she packs a wallop. If someone foolish enough wants to challenge her to a duel, they'll be in for quite a shock."

"Great. Please recap her array of armaments."

"She's got her ten 14-inch guns fore and aft. Six 5-inch guns. Ten 3-inch guns. Ten quad 40 mm guns. Forty-four single 20 mm guns. Six Phalanx CIWS fore, aft, midship, twenty Exocets, plus twenty Tomahawk cruise missiles."

The President looked a little surprised. "That's our ship! I love it." The President turned to his most trusted aide and advisor, Bill White.

"Billy, see to it we get a full roster of everyone involved in the Texas refit. I want to do something special for them." Then, he turned again to the Admiral. "Admiral, what about the *Lex*? How's she coming along? And what do we have regarding escort ships for a layer of protection for the *Texas* and the *Lex*?"

"The *Tautog*, a nuclear-powered attack submarine. The Destroyer *Stewart*. Plus, several Coast Guard gunboats were acquired at independence."

"How about the *Lex*? I know she's been a challenge."

"Another month away, Sir. We'll have our very own aircraft carrier, the *Lexington*, as you know, World War II–era but fully modernized. She has been a challenge converting from a floating museum to a combat-ready ship for the 21st century."

"Will she have a full complement of aircraft?"

"The whole lot. Fighters, AWACS, refuelers, rotary."

"Fantastic. Thank you, Admiral, and everyone else involved. Please send my thanks down the line. I know it's been a grinder of a time, and many of you have put in incredible hours to get to this point. On behalf of the good people of Texas, we thank you all from the bottom of our hearts. "Next on the agenda is a plan I have been mulling over about our response to various scenarios."

MCHENRY HOSPITAL

McHenry, Illinois

0915 CDT — 16 Apr 2061

Lieutenant Colonel Jackson King had been slightly wounded at the Battle of Scott Air Force Base. A grenade had exploded 20 feet away at the height of the battle. A piece of shrapnel had torn through the fleshy part of his right calf. Stitched up and none the worse for wear, he lay in bed in the hospital thinking about that day and what lay ahead. A sense of foreboding washed over him, driving him to pray for the nation. He picked up his phone and called his son DeShawn.

"Hello, Dad? You, okay?"

"Yes, Son. Took a piece of shrapnel in the fleshy part of my right calf. I'm all stitched up and doing fine. How are you? Where are you? Were you in the fight?"

"No, Dad, I was not in the fight. They had all the brigade's leadership at a retreat center studying DEI policing tactics. I was so pissed. The training was planned months in advance. We were informed that we'd be notified if anything happened regarding current events. Well, word came, but they didn't release us. Said the class was too important. So here we all sit, waiting for orders. My troops are anxious to get into the fight. How bad was it at the base?

"As bad as you can imagine. We lost many good people. Plus, the CONs managed to get away with many valuable military assets. They were well-prepared and well-trained. They carried out their attack with great precision. I'm worried, Son. This situation could quickly escalate out of control. Many people are in danger and don't know it yet."

"Dad, you know, and I know this day was inevitable. It hurts like hell that we got to this point, but here we are. What can we do now except to defend the New Way? There is no turning back now. There just isn't."

"I'm thinking about all the lives that could be lost here, Son. When I was shooting at my fellow Americans, I was sickened by the fact. While I may disagree with them on political matters, I could have easily sat down with them at a baseball game and had a pleasant time."

"A baseball game? That dead sport? Where can you still go to see a game?

"Well, there aren't many places left. My older cousin in Charlotte takes in a game every now and then. Lots of empty seats, he says."

"Well, whatever. Look, Dad, I got to go. I'm glad you're alright. Give my love to Mom."

"Call her, Son. She needs to hear your voice and that you're alright. Let me know when you get orders."

"I promise, Dad. I'll call Mom this evening."

Colonel Eric Adams, founder of the Rocky Mountain Militia, had just concluded a series of exhaustive concalls with various militia leaders and Constitutionalist State Governors. His last scheduled call was with Colonel David S. Patton, the Founder and Commander of the Kansas Patriot Militia.

"Dave, whatcha got?"

"Colonel, we fared well here in Kansas, I can tell you that. Casualties were somewhat lower than expected. We had fifteen KIA and sixty-six wounded. The FEDs suffered one hundred fifty-six KIA and seventy-six wounded, and twenty-five of their soldiers broke ranks and joined us. I just got off the phone with Governor Hill a bit ago. He's sorry he couldn't connect today, but assured me he would connect with you soon.

"He had his hands full briefing the Kansas National Guard. Inventory is still being taken, but it appears that at least ninety percent of the air assets from the Scott Air Force Base assault made it out intact and arrived at their assigned posts here in Kansas.

"The governor is negotiating with the other CON states to divvy up the assets appropriately based on each state's current asset inventory and the threat level they face.

"How'd you guys do, Colonel?"

"Well, at the Armory, we had one KIA and only three wounded. FEDs had six KIA, thirteen wounded. Thirty-two of them broke ranks and joined us. The rest surrendered."

"Anything happen out at Malmstrom?"

"Seems the bombers have left, but there were reports of some troops arriving by air. Numbers unknown, but it looks to have been four large transports."

"Damn, that could be an issue."

"Colonel, I'm certain that Malmstrom can be taken with the Guard and your soldiers."

"Appreciate the compliment, Dave, but let's not forget the place has nukes. There's no way the FEDs will lay down and surrender that place without a huge fight. No way."

"I hear you, Colonel. Listen, a change of subject. I wanted to revisit the idea of a unified command structure. We performed well on the assault day thanks to careful planning among all the governors, their military leaders, and the militia leaders; however, there's still no central command. We've got to fix this in a hurry."

"Dave, I'm well aware of that. All I can say is that it's a top priority, and I expect a decision to be made very soon. What do you think Cyrus's next move is?"

"Colonel, your guess is as good as mine. His temper, combined with his ideological bent, makes him dangerously unpredictable. I know one thing: my men are ready. They're under no illusions that this whole thing is just getting started."

"God save us all, Dave. Talk to you soon."

COUNTERATTACK

THE PENTAGON

Washington, D.C.

0445 EDT — 10 May 2061

Three weeks ago, President Cyrus had ordered the formation of a new military unit, the 501st Division, in honor of May Day, the worldwide commemoration of the labor movement.

He had also ordered a comprehensive review of all military unit designations for probable renaming and renumbering. Convinced of their past racist sins, he had especially pointed out his demand that the 82nd and the 101st be renumbered. He proposed combining them into the 301st. Today, President Cyrus had assembled his entire Cabinet and military brain trust in a conference room just off the war room of the National Military Command Center. He was confident a counterattack today would be successful in quashing the rebellion.

The extensive planning and discussions that had gone into the plan had been exhaustive. Ultimately, the discussions on how to reunite the rebel states with the New Way settled on two options. One was codenamed Operation Hammer Blow, while the other was codenamed Operation Swarm. Hammer Blow would be a massive attack against Oklahoma and its commandeered federal military assets.

The plan was based on the reasoning that a massive display of force and a quick victory would demonstrate to the other rebel states the New Ways' determination to end the rebellion swiftly with overwhelming firepower. It was argued that using such force would convince the other rebel states to cancel their Articles of Secession and return to the Union.

On the other hand, Swarm was designed as a surgical strike against all rebel state capitals. The reasoning was that capturing the seats of power in all the rebel states would also lead to the states ending the rebellion.

After much thought and private consulting with his astrologer, Cyrus determined that Swarm was more attractive. He believed it to be the quickest route back to normalcy and the end of what he liked to call "this petty little rebellion" so that he could continue implementing his New Way Agenda as rapidly as possible.

After opening the meeting, a lengthy discussion took place to review the finer details of Operation Swarm. The President asked myriad questions. It was evident to General Gage that the President was well prepared.

With his questions answered, the President paused and looked around the room. He noticed Speaker Jai Parry looking somewhat annoyed. The President's eyes then returned to Joint Chiefs of Staff General Gage. "General, big day today. Are the troops ready to carry out my orders?"

"Yes, Sir, we're ready, Mr. President."

"Okay then. Give the order to execute Operation Swarm."

At that, General Gage picked up his comm, made a call quickly, and gave the order. After hanging up, he looked up at the President. "Mr. President, the order is given."

"Thank you, general. When will the video feeds begin?"

"Sir, I expect the screens to go live once the troops are airborne.

Won't be much to see at first."

"I understand that General. Thank you. Jai, you look upset. What's on your mind?"

Jai had entered the conference room alone 35 minutes earlier. He had quietly soured on the early course of this burgeoning crisis and had been convinced that negotiations would be the best route out of this mess, especially before it blew up into something far more horrific. But he knew in his gut that the President and his closest advisors would have none of it. Unwilling to reveal his actual feelings, Jai knew he had to lie to the President. "I'm fighting something, sir. Bit of an issue of late, stomach-related. I'll be fine, I'm sure."

The President listened to Jai but said nothing. He next turned to DHS Secretary Frederic Sheldon. "Freddy, any intelligence matters of note?"

"Sir, nothing beyond the usual chatter. Confidence is high, and Swarm will have the element of surprise going for it."

THE GOVERNOR'S MANSION
Oklahoma City, Oklahoma
0432 CDT — 10 May 2061

Oklahoma Governor Mary Whitfield was fast asleep alongside her husband when a member of the security detail burst into the room. Startled awake by the commotion, the Governor bolted up in her bed, and, at the same time, the agent began yelling at her to get a robe on. "My apologies, Governor! We need to get you out of here right now. We have large numbers of inbound New Way aircraft headed directly for us! We have to go now!"

Throwing on a robe, she and her husband James sprang into motion. They headed to the children's room, which was immediately adjacent to theirs. She grabbed Samantha while James grabbed Dallas. They dashed back into the hallway and were swiftly whisked downstairs and out the door to a waiting chopper. After jumping in, the helo rose quickly and headed away from the Capitol to the southwest at a low altitude.

After being handed a two-way headset, the Governor donned it and yelled into the mic, "Where are we going?"

"A secure location, Ma'am. I can't say. You can unplug your headset and plug it into your comm. General Williamson should be calling you any moment."

Whitfield quickly connected to the comm. Turning on encryption, sure enough, it began to flash that the general was calling.

"General, this is Governor Whitfield. What's the situation?"

"Madam Governor, we have verified multiple airborne assault groups headed to all CON State Capitals. Looks like the FEDs have launched a major counterattack. We're bringing you to the predetermined safe locale. I know we're communicating in an encrypted mode, but I must respectfully insist that you do not repeat the location—nor will I."

"Of course not, general. Did you give the order to execute Sooner Strike?"

"Yes, Ma'am. The order was given just moments before they woke you. My compliments on your foresight, Governor."

"Going to be a long day, general. Let's save the compliments for later. Right now, we've got a job to do to defend our freedoms and our land. Did the auto-notifications go out to the other governors?"

"Yes, they did. Their equivalent plans to Sooner Strike should be underway momentarily. I'll send a coded text when I get confirmation. Are your kids and James okay?"

"Yes, yes, they're fine. Thanks for asking. We'll speak soon, General."

"Godspeed, Madam Governor."

"Thank you, general. Same to you!"

1619 RED BRIGADE AIR ASSAULT GROUP

Somewhere Over Northwest Arkansas

0430 CDT — 10 May 2061

1619 Red Brigade Commander DeShawn King was amped up. As a leader of the assault group headed for Oklahoma City, he and his brigade were itching for a fight, and this one was as good as any. Still stinging that he and his brigade were idle during the rebel assault back in April, King was aloft with a chip on his shoulder.

Carrying a pair of First Civil War–era handcuffs, King was convinced that before the day was out, he'd have the traitor Governor Whitfield in his custody and handcuffed in the antique cuffs.

The handcuffs had been in his family for generations and had once been used on his third great-grandfather, Henry King. Henry had been enslaved in Georgia on a cotton plantation up until his day of freedom during the Battle of Griswoldville, Georgia, on 22 November 1864.

The battle was a part of Union General William Tecumseh Sherman's "March to the Sea."

On that date, a Georgia militia group went up against one of General Sherman's units on Sherman's right flank. It was soundly defeated after seven frontal assaults against the Union troops.

The plantation Henry was enslaved at hastily became a field hospital. After the battle, Union Brigadier General Charles C. Walcutt ordered Henry and all the rest of the enslaved people there freed, in accordance with President Abraham Lincoln's Emancipation Proclamation, issued over a year earlier on 1 January 1863.

Henry and the rest of the thirty-odd formerly enslaved people were given provisions and then allowed to travel to the rear of the Union lines and on into freedom, wherever they wished to go.

DeShawn King's recollection of family lore was broken by the sound of his comm squawking: "Drop zone in five minutes." King stood up and looked at his troops seated in the mammoth C-7A transport. Giving the thumbs-up signal, they all rose and readied their gear. In a few minutes, Civil War 2.0 would become very personal.

★ ★ ★

KANSAS PATRIOT MILITIA FIELD HQ

South of Topeka, Kansas

0430 CDT — 10 May 2061

Colonel David S. Patton was known as a brilliant tactician during his active-duty military days. In the North African Campaign, after the second 9/11, he went through the now-infamous Libyan Gauntlet and executed a brilliant maneuver in the Battle of Sirte. The tactic employed there had had the effect of rescuing ten thousand Allied soldiers from encirclement and sure slaughter in desert terrain.

Seated in a vintage biodiesel-powered World War II–era Jeep at his Field Headquarters, Colonel Patton had studied maps of the area surrounding the state capital. The Colonel had a strong hunch that the drop zone the FEDs would use for their much-rumored counterattack would be smack dab in the middle between Interstate 470 at the southern edge of the city limits and Topeka Regional Airport, a few miles further south of the Capital. The targeted area was in open country east of U.S. Highway 75. Patton's troops lay in ambush, forming an arc near U.S. 75 on his right flank and arcing up to the north and east on his left.

Meanwhile, in coordination with Kansas Army General William Longstreet, he had two divisions poised to strike: 1st Division, strategically deployed in and around the Capital, and 2nd Division, entrenched at the airport.

"Damn, Charlie, if I got this hunch right, those FEDs are in for one hell of a surprise. We're going to kick their asses," Patton bellowed.

"Sure hope you're right, Colonel. Those weirdos messed with the wrong people. We Jayhawks don't take kindly to these FEDs way over from out east messin' with us. Just leave us the frig alone. They insulted us with their 'flyover country' comment all those years ago. My Daddy never forgot it. I chalked it up to more libtard trash. Screw 'em all! Some of 'em still think this is about race! Shit, I got two Black grandkids and one Hispanic grandkid, plus my wife is twenty percent Cherokee to boot. These LIBs think they can just drop in here and force a way of life on us that none of us want or ever asked for? We'll soon see about that, I can tell you that much. Prepare to meet thy Maker."

"I know you're mad, Charlie, but you need to keep that anger tamped down. Stay focused on the mission. This is going to be one hell of a fight, and I need your mind clear."

"I'm with you, Colonel. No worries here. But damn it, it's as if all our anger from sea to shining sea has risen to the top at full boil. If you'd told me just six months ago, we'd be sitting here, waiting to ambush fellow Americans and send them on their way to their maker, I would have said you were crazy. Yeah, I know there was talk of all this. I heard it back then and even much earlier, but I just didn't want to believe it would actually happen."

Patton listened intently to his friend's lament. "I know, Charlie. I take no joy in what's about to happen here. No joy at all. Cyrus intends

to kill us all if we're captured. To hell with that shit!"

As they studied the terrain map again, Colonel Patton's comm alerted him to an incoming call. He looked down and saw it was Colonel Adams up in Montana. "Colonel, what's up?"

"Colonel Patton, I've just received secondary confirmation identifying the drop zones for all federal troops inbound to your location. I'm sending over the exact GPS coordinates now. Please review carefully and advise."

"Sure thing, Colonel Adams. Let me take a look." Hitting the *Received Message* icon," a map popped up on his screen showing the planned DZ. It only took a moment for Patton to realize his hunch was spot on. The FEDs were dropping right into an ambush. "We're good to go here, Colonel Adams. Thanks for the intel."

"You're welcome, David. Stay in touch."

"Yes, Sir."

As soon as he hung up, Patton's comm lit up with a coded message from General Hill: "Execute *Operation Wheat Field.*"

ARMY OF MONTANA FIELD HQ

Helena, Montana

0330 MDT — 10 May 2061

Colonel Eric Adams and his Rocky Mountain Militia were on the left flank of the Army of Montana troops stationed at Helena Regional Airport. His mole at the Pentagon had sent a coded message of all drop zones for the imminent federal attack. It was nice to have this backup source of intel that confirmed their primary source. It was the primary source that enabled all states to secretly plan their defense of their respective state capitals. After quickly passing this secondary intel along, he was again focused on what was about to happen on his beloved Montana soil.

The town of Helena was in great danger. Adams had to admit that it was a stunning and daring plan by the FEDs to hit all the state capitals simultaneously. But, unlike the FEDs, Adams also knew that the entire New Way operation was flying into an ambush in every single instance. The element of surprise would not be a part of the battle equation for them. Still, all the soldiers were under no illusions. The forces converging on them were in greater numbers.

With a 9,000-foot main runway, the Helena Regional Airport, situated on the east side of the city limits, was a vital strategic facility. Keeping control of the airport was key for Montana's defense against any incursions by New Way troops. The highly secured Malmstrom Air Force Base, still in the FEDs' hands and located to the northeast in Great Falls, about a ninety-minute drive away, was a logical launching point for any attacks against the CONs, especially here in Helena.

Heavily surveilled, the reports from Malmstrom were that all was strangely quiet there. Intel was confident that the federal assault team headed for Helena was out of Minnesota, specifically the Minneapolis-Saint Paul Joint Air Reserve Station. Adams figured that the nukes at Malmstrom were more critical to safeguard than to launch any offensive operations from the base against the CONs. Additionally, the troops sent to Malmstrom were explicitly there to defend the base from being taken over. The Army of Montana was considerably smaller than the other state armies assembled since the rebellion against the New Way. Composed of National Guard troops and the Rocky Mountain Militia, the fledgling army would soon be tested.

The commanding general of the Army of Montana was the well-liked General James Buford. A Montana native through and through,

Buford had done an exceptional job getting the Montana Army ready, especially given the short-term constraints since the rebellion began.

As they waited for the arrival of the FEDs, Adams and Buford huddled in Buford's Field Headquarters, a vacant hangar at the far west end of the airport.

"General, I'm going to head out in a moment and join my soldiers. I've never been one to hang back in the rear."

"Colonel, give my regards to your troops. We'll be in touch as things develop. Keep a keen eye out for anything remotely looking like things are going sideways."

"Yes, sir, general. The fog of war?"

"Yep, the fog of war. Say, listen…" Just then, the general's comm rang. It was Governor Emerson. "Governor, General Buford here. Sir, we're ready."

"Good to hear, general. Listen, as best as you can, I want frequent dispatches. I've got a promise from Governor Jaye over in Idaho for assistance if things get out of hand."

"Understood, Governor. I toured the line earlier, and the morale is good. The troops are ready to go. Governor, sorry, I have to cut you short. I think I heard something. Stay safe, Governor. We need you."

"You as well, general. Give my regards to Colonel Adams."

The general hung up the comm, turned to Adams, and was about to relay the Governor's regards when explosions rocked the area. The Battle of Helena had begun.

Buford quickly grabbed his comm and sent a coded message to all field commanders: "Execute Operation Granite."

THE KING RESIDENCE

McHenry, Illinois

1830 CDT — 10 May 2061

Eleanor King had just sat down alone to eat supper. With her husband and only child out fighting, she had been on her knees most of the day, praying for the safety of them both. Tired, she reluctantly grabbed the remote and turned on the TV. Holding her breath, she turned her attention to the evening news broadcast.

She quieted just in time to hear the familiar, nameless, faceless voice give the intro to the nightly news. "This is the ANN Nightly News with Olivia Kinley. *America at War.* Live from our studios in New York—here is Olivia Kinley."

"Good evening, America. Today has certainly been a day of days. We broke into regularly scheduled programming in the early morning hours and have been covering events all day as they unfolded.

"We have much to cover in this historic broadcast this evening, which will be brought to you completely commercial-free.

"Let's begin.

"On this May 10, 2061, many Americans were, for a second time in less than a month, awakened by the sound of explosions, gunfire, and the jolting sounds of war.

"Here now, with the first of several reports from the field, is the ANN team of reporters. First up is Adam Dwyer reporting from the White House."

"Olivia, here at the White House, things are a beehive of activity, as one would expect from an armed conflict on U.S. soil.

"The White House press corps received an alert at about 5 a.m. that a massive military response had been launched against all rebel state capitals. The objectives were not shared with us at that time. "At 9 a.m. Eastern Time, President Cyrus held a news conference where he announced the attack but declined to give the operational objective since the attacks were ongoing. After reading his prepared remarks, he quickly left the briefing room without taking questions.

"At noontime White House Press Secretary Rose Salinger provided an update that the military plan was still being actively carried out, but also offered no further details and, like the President, headed for the exit, which triggered an explosion of protests from the press corps demanding Q&A time, to which she remained silent.

"Olivia, I've been covering the White House for ten years. Never in all that time have I seen the anger I saw today with every press corps member, regardless of news outlet. It was one hundred percent.

"We have not heard of anything since. The press corps here all agree this amounts to a news blackout. The frustration here is palpable. Many reporters were told by their bosses to leave their offices here and find other sources of information. In fact, most of them have left. We are hearing that the President will address the nation at nine Eastern tonight, but even that has yet to be confirmed.

"This is Adam Dwyer reporting live from the White House."

"Thank you, Adam. We are prepared to break in at any time if something develops there. Keep us posted. Now we go to Matt Sydney, reporting live from the Pentagon."

"Lots of activity here today in the early morning hours. But no news was being shared. Still, there was a sense here that something was in the offing. All that proved true when our comms lit up, reporting attacks in all rebel state capitals.

"The attacks, all via airborne troops, started in the predawn hours—combat aircraft, accompanied by AWACS aircraft, tankers, and close air support drones.

"The operations are reported to have been met with stiff resistance from the get-go.

"Information here is sketchy about the progress of the federal forces' success or failure.

"Media sources on the ground at all the state capitals involved report fierce fighting, heavy casualties, and a general flight of the populace away from the fighting.

"Videos from several capitals show dogfights in the skies. Something strangely peculiar and frightening to see in the heartland. It was as if mid-twentieth-century black-and-white newsreels from World War II were being relived in living color over Oklahoma City, Lawrence, Kansas, and many other rebel-held state capitals.

"Of all the state capitals, Oklahoma, Nebraska, Kansas, South Dakota, North Dakota, Missouri, and Montana appear to have been of particular focus by U.S. Military planners.

"The skies over Oklahoma City saw a stunning display of National Guard fighter aircraft engaged in dogfights. It was impossible to tell which side had the upper hand, but several aircraft exploded mid-air. Flaming wreckage rained down all over the city. The Oklahoma City Fire Department had their hands full, putting out whatever fires they could.

Several fires were left to burn because of the intense ground combat around the areas of the fires on the city's outskirts.

"No official word yet on casualties from either side, but hospital sources report well over 900 civilian and military casualties have been brought to the eighteen hospitals in and around the Capitol.

"This is Matt Sydney reporting live from the Pentagon. Olivia, back to you."

"Thank you, Matt," said Olivia with a hint of sadness. "Our next live report is from Helena, Montana, reported by Darshan Treyvon."

The screen cut away to a stark landscape of billowing smoke in the background. The sounds of war were unmistakable and unnerving to Eleanor as she continued to watch and listen. She liked Darshan and thought he was a good reporter. When the screen cutaway to him, she could tell he had a concerned look on his face. War correspondent was not his regular beat. "Whoa! Just now, a mammoth explosion off in the distance. We're hunkered down in a drainage ditch a mile away from the combat zone. I can confidently tell you that whatever plans the U.S. military had for Helena have been met with disastrous results.

"Sources here on the ground in Helena confirm that the fighting has been fierce, with back-and-forth pitched battles for control. The Capitol building has sustained some damage, but both sides have been concentrating their firepower well enough away from it. Casualties are reported as heavy. Fires are burning everywhere from the intense air and ground combat.

"When we asked what kinds of weapons were being used in the intense ground fighting, an anonymous military source told us they included 'mortars, shoulderfired rockets, combat-support drones, heavy artillery, and light mechanized weapons.' There have also been battles in the skies above Helena, mostly off to the northeast. We could not determine what kind of aircraft were involved, but they appeared to be manned, as opposed to drones, based on their maneuvering.

"Also, we just learned before going on air that some sort of mutiny has now started at Malmstrom Air Force Base, 90 minutes to the northeast in the town of Great Falls, Montana. Details are sketchy. We have a reporter en route to that location. Malmstrom is home to the 341st Missile Wing, keepers of some of America's ICBM forces. Also, Malmstrom is home to the 319th Fighter Interceptor Squadron, which was reactivated fifteen years ago after the second 9/11. It would seem logical that some of the dogfights we have witnessed would include at least some of those air assets from the 319th at Malmstrom.

"A short time ago, Montana Governor Wayland Emerson conducted a press conference that was dramatically different than those held at the White House and the Pentagon today. The Governor went old-school, standing before a paper map of the area, using a long wooden stick to point out key parts of the battle. Let's play that clip now."

"Good evening, Montanans. Today has indeed been a challenging day.

"At approximately 4:40 a.m. local time here, New Way forces launched an attack against our state capital, Helena. Federal assault troops of the 501st Airborne parachuted in as well as landed via helicopters at two locations: open country immediately east of the airport and open country to the south of the airport in an area nestled between U.S. Route 12 and Interstate 15.

"I'm happy to report we were waiting for them. The Armed Forces of Montana immediately engaged the FEDs. After long hours of fierce fighting, our brave soldiers pushed federal forces into a pocket near the Helena Valley Canal just northwest of the airport. The federal assault team that had landed in the south has been defeated, with heavy casualties.

"The remnant of that federal assault team has surrendered. They are currently being processed as prisoners of war under the terms of the Geneva Convention."

"That clip from the Governor just about an hour ago," said the reporter. "Olivia, at one point, rebel Montana forces defending the southeast approach to the Capital were forced to pull back into the downtown area, where heavy fighting continued. That fight was going badly until reinforcements showed up in the form of the Rocky Mountain Militia.

"Sources tell us that the militia, predominantly composed of retired U.S. soldiers are under the command of Colonel Eric Adams. Sources also state that Colonel Adams is a highly decorated retired U.S. Marine with the Silver Star and three Purple Hearts.

"The militia forces successfully attacked the right flank of the federal troops and drove them out of the city back towards the southeast from where they had started. At that moment, the federal forces encountered a large force of irregular troops composed of Montanans from every walk of life.

"Equipped with semi-automatic weapons as well as other small arms and shotguns, these weapons should have been of no match against federal forces. Nevertheless, this group of determined Montanans forced an untenable situation whereby federal forces received groundfire from three different directions. They were cut off and unable to advance.

Federal air forces were engaged in the skies against rebel air forces and could not fully help their beleaguered comrades on the ground. Having suffered eighty casualties, the commander of the federal troops chose to surrender.

"We fully expect the remaining federal forces trapped near the canal to surrender before nightfall. We have it on good authority that no reinforcements are coming for them."

Eleanor could take no more of the news broadcast. She turned off the TV, rose out of her chair, and covered her ears momentarily. Lowering her hands, she turned, grabbed the family Bible, and dropped to her knees. With tears streaming down her cheeks, she quietly wept.

IIII **12** IIII

ERASE THEM ALL

President Devin Cyrus was in the foulest mood of his young presidency. Yesterday had been an unmitigated disaster for his New Way plans. Every attack at every state capital in rebellion had been met with fierce resistance, heavy casualties, and ultimately, failure on the part of U.S. Forces to take them and thereby force a quick end to the rebellion against the New Way.

The president had been up all night. He was tired and angry. He vowed that what had happened the day before would never happen again. Any future military operations would be concentrated and with no holds barred.

Re-energized, the president entered the White House Situation Room with a new plan in mind. Assembled in the room were his entire

Cabinet, Chief of Staff Matt Kensington, the entire Joint Chiefs—who were deputy chiefs yesterday but now found themselves as acting chiefs this morning—plus the usual collection of aides.

The tension was palpable. The room was silent. "Matt, what's the summary on casualties?"

"Mr. President, the numbers are still being sorted out, but the latest figures from 6 a.m. are in. It's a mix of military and civilian. They show 1,911 killed, 1,959 wounded. From our assault teams, we have 2,500 captured.

"Shit. How much hardware did we lose?"

"Sir, the loss of military hardware is also noteworthy. An accounting should be completed mid-morning. Loyalists put down the mutiny at Malmstrom during the predawn hours. Our nukes remain secure. One last stinger is the report that nationwide, somewhere close to 5,500 of our soldiers defected during the operations."

"Defected?" the president asked.

"Yes, sir, they crossed sides and joined the rebellion," Kensington replied.

"Traitors!" Cyrus yelled. "I'll have them shot when they're caught!" The President had spent last night firing his entire Joint Chiefs of Staff. He took a moment to introduce the new team of Joint Chiefs. None looked happy, and all looked tired.

"Our new Chairman of the Joint Chiefs is General Jeffrey Homer. The Chief of Staff of the Army is now General Evelyn Vance. The Chief of Naval Operations is Admiral Richard Lon. The Chief of Staff of the Air Force is General Aaron David. Commandant of the Marine Corps and a history maker is General Daniel Mulvanee, the first transgender Marine Corps commandant. The Chief of Space Operations is General Reese

Victor. The Commandant of the Coast Guard is General Erica Sully. Finally, taking over as Chief of the National Guard Bureau is General Edward Liggy.

"Today, I'd like to unveil a new plan to crush the Old Way rebellion. I know that yesterday was disastrous for us all. But I'll be damned if I'm going to roll over and capitulate to a bunch of crazy Bible-thumping assholes. We have come too far to go back!

"First of all, I'm ordering that the white supremacist documents known as the Declaration of Independence, the Constitution of the United States, and the Bill of Rights all be removed from the National Archives to a secure location. At a time of my choosing, the documents will be burned on live television. We're going to erase them all by burning them all. Their ashes will be collected and dumped in a secret location of my choosing.

"In their place will be a new document. It is one that I am confident will be fully embraced and celebrated by the New Way, the rest of the world, and all those who are seeking to follow us into a brighter future. I have not settled on a name for it yet, but I like one possibility: the DEI Covenant of Enlightenment.

"Second. We are borrowing a tactic from World War II when General Douglas MacArthur island-hopped his way across the South Pacific to defeat Imperial Japan. We'll state-hop our way through rebel states and crush these insurrectionists one by one. We'll take every precaution to avoid collateral damage, but anyone bearing arms against us will be fired upon without hesitation.

"Third. There is an old saying that freedom of speech does not give you the right to yell 'fire' in a crowded theater. We are no longer going to allow the press to operate as before. The time for centralized control of the media has come.

"Today, I am ordering the NWBI and DHS to seize all CON news outlets in non-rebel states. The Union employees will be free to leave. On-air personalities will be detained. I especially want Olivia Kinley detained. All management is to be placed under arrest for sedition. The outlets are to be shut down indefinitely for sedition and for aiding and abetting insurrection. We will have unity of message or else."

House Speaker Jai Parry made a subtle glance at Interior Secretary Donna Sheryll. Making eye contact, Parry was sure he detected a hint of shock and anger in her eyes. Parry sat there listening with a growing concern. He decided it was time for someone to speak up; consequences be damned.

"Unity or else? Mr. President, I must protest in the strongest of terms. What you're saying is highly inflammatory. We have a diverse nation, not everyone is fully on board with the New Way. Nothing good can come about with these proposals. They'll only create more anger. And what you're saying sounds like a ground invasion of rebel states without negotiations? That sure sounds like war to me. What about Congressional input on this under the War Powers Act? Invading armies require air support. You don't really intend to blitzkrieg your way across all these rebel states? Why, with modern weaponry, you are looking at staggering casualty figures. Beyond the pale, and…"

Cutting Parry off, the president stood and pointed his finger at him, "Parry, number one, I said nothing about proposals. What I have planned and announced here today will happen, period. Number two, the CON Media has been spouting its hatred for long enough. I'm done with them.

If I could, I'd have them all arrested. Come to think of it, maybe there's still a way to do that. Number three, just because we roll into a state doesn't mean a scorched earth policy. I expect many citizens to welcome our arrival and the rebels to think long and hard about engaging the federal army equipped with heavy weapons and air support. They may just lay down their arms yet, melt away into the population, and forget all about their petty little rebellion against us."

"And what if they don't?"

"To quote and paraphrase a famous leader from history, 'We will bury them!'"

SCOTT AIR FORCE BASE INFIRMARY

Shiloh, Illinois

1305 CDT — 11 May 2061

DeShawn King slowly opened his eyes and looked around the room. Realizing he was in a hospital room, he sat up, looked around for the call button, and pressed it. After waiting a minute or so, a nurse walked into his room.

"Hello, Mr. King. How are you feeling?"

Disoriented, King was silent for a moment, then spoke up. "A little groggy. I'm thirsty and hungry too. Can I get some food? Where am I? How did I get here?"

Grabbing a bottle of water from the table, she put a straw into it and held it to his mouth. "I can order you lunch. What would you like?"

After a long drink of water, King waved the bottle away. "A burger would be great. What time is it? What day is it? Where am I? What happened to me and my unit?"

"Whoa, slow down, young man. First, let's start with gelatin and crackers and see how that sits. As for your questions, well, it's Wednesday, May 11. It's a little after 1 p.m. You're in the infirmary at Scott Air Force Base in Illinois. You were injured during the battle in Oklahoma yesterday and blacked out from blood loss. You were medevac'd here late last night, and we had to operate just as soon as you got here. You've been through a lot in twenty-four hours."

"Wow, all that. What happened to my unit? Are they okay?"

"I don't have any information on your unit. I can make some calls to try to find out. What was the name of your unit?"

"I'm the commander of the 1619 Red Brigade."

The nurse had a slightly surprised look on her face when she heard the name. "I'll see what I can find out. In the meantime, I'll order that gelatin for you immediately."

"Thank you. How long am I going to be here? I need to get back to my troops. They need me."

"I'm not sure. The doctor says you were quite lucky. One centimeter was all the difference between life and death. Doc also says you should heal up quickly. He was half serious when he asked me if anyone had been praying for you."

"Funny, I bet my mom was. Where's my comm? I need to call her."

WASHITA NATIONAL FOREST

Butler, Oklahoma

0907 CDT — 1 Jul 2061

Ever since the attack on Oklahoma City and the rest of the state capitals in secession, Oklahoma Governor Mary Whitfield had been holed up in a remote location deep in the Washita National Forest near Butler, Oklahoma. Also brought along were the Oklahoma Speaker of the House, Chief Billy Waya, Senate President Charles McCoy, and their spouses and children.

While the governor had insisted that they be returned to the capital on 11 May, the day after the battle, her security detail was adamant that Cyrus had embedded a black-ops group within the 1619 Red Brigade. They believed that during the withdrawal, the group had stayed behind and changed into civilian clothing. They intended to assassinate the governor.

The Oklahoma State Bureau of Investigation had been tracking down the would-be assassins and received a tip that led to the hit team's capture yesterday.

With the immediate threat removed, the governor, along with the rest of her family and entourage, was packing up and preparing for the ride back to the Capitol. In the meantime, there was time for one last meeting before departure. "Ladies and Gentlemen, thank you for joining today via remote conferencing. These last few weeks have been tough, but we will get through this together. Senator Fulbright, I want to extend our sincere condolences on the loss of your daughter, Private Cindy Fulbright, in combat in defense of our state and of liberty-loving people everywhere. "I again want to thank each of you for your contributions these last few months under challenging circumstances. I especially want to thank General Chester Williamson of the Army of Oklahoma and all the service men and women for your staunch support of our beloved Sooner State.

"Shortly, we will return to the Capitol to resume governing from there. I have proposed to all the state governors, remaining faithful to the Constitution, that we must declare ourselves united not only in word and deed but also in covenant. We do not ask for nor seek a new Constitution. We believe the one we've had since 1787 has been working just fine, thank you very much.

"Having canceled the U.S. Constitution in all New Way states and announcing his intentions to replace them with a new charter, President Cyrus has made it clear to me, and all the CON state governors, that we need to send our own signal. So, we will be holding a Constitutional Convention at a time and place of our choosing.

"Our purpose will not be to change one iota of it. Instead, we will sign copies of the Constitution. We will also affix copies of the Official Seal of each state, remaining faithful to the Constitution, to affirm to freedom-loving people everywhere in the U.S. and the rest of the world that the United States of America is still here. Still holding up Liberty's torch and preparing to defend it with great force, so help us, God.

"Cyrus and the entire New Way cabal with him may seek to try to erase our history, to erase it all. They can try as hard as they want, but it will be over our dead bodies."

THE GOVERNOR'S MANSION

Oklahoma City, Oklahoma

1500 CDT — 3 Jul 2061

Every Governor from all the states in rebellion against the New Way had secretly assembled in the predawn hour in the main dining hall to sign a copy of the United States Constitution. The proceedings were recorded and broadcast to the world at 1500 CDT. All the governors had left an hour earlier. The strict security was to avoid even the remote chance that federal forces could launch a surprise strike and kill them all while in attendance.

THE KING RESIDENCE

McHenry, Illinois

1500 CDT — 3 Jul 2061

Meanwhile, back in McHenry, IL, Eleanor King had awakened from a nap and turned on the TV, hoping to watch her favorite game show. The commercial break was suddenly interrupted.

"We interrupt our regularly scheduled broadcast to bring you this special news bulletin. Rebel Oklahoma Governor Mary Whitfield is speaking from Oklahoma City with a broadcast address. Let's show you that now."

The Governor was dressed in a red dress with by a white and blue scarf tied around her neck. She looked and sounded confident. "Good afternoon to all freedom-loving peoples here in America and the rest of the world. Today is the third of July, in the year of our Lord two thousand and sixty-one. We are one day away from our Republic's two hundred eighty-fifth birthday since its founding in seventeen seventy-six."

"Today, the cloud of Civil War hangs again over our nation. To be clear, we did not ask for or seek to engage in this second occurrence of civil war on American soil.

"Try as we might to negotiate our differences with the prior administration and President Cyrus and his New Way administration, an impasse was reached and remains solidly in place. Compounding the extreme demands he has made on all states, he has now suspended the Constitution and is rumored to be planning to replace it with something entirely new.

"The New Way has, for decades at varying levels of volume, expressed the desire to, quote, 'burn it all down,' end quote. These extremists now appear to be on the verge of literally doing just that.

"Cyrus, along with all the rest of his followers, are now unrecognizable as true American patriots. In truth, we have no idea what they consider themselves to be.

"Also, we are firmly convinced that they represent a very real, clear, and present danger to our Republic and our American way of life.

"Today in Congress, just twelve hours ago here at the Governor's Mansion in Oklahoma City, the governors of all states remaining true to the original United States Constitution affixed their signatures to a modern printed copy of that hallowed document of freedom. They also affixed the great seal of their respective states.

"To close out this historic and solemn ceremony, we said the Pledge of Allegiance in unison. Additionally, we all reaffirmed our oath of allegiance to preserve, protect, and defend the Constitution against all enemies, foreign and domestic. A replay of this historic event will be played after this broadcast.

"I have been chosen to speak for all the governors and to read to you the following Declaration, which was also unanimously signed by all the governors in Congress today.

"And, I quote, 'We the undersigned Governors of the States listed below, and that remain loyal to the Republic and to its indissoluble Constitution, which has stood the test of time, trial, and the bitter tears of a previous civil conflict, do acknowledge its past, present, and current validity, though not infallible, not only as a foundation stone of our Republic but also as a herald of American Liberty to all freedom-loving peoples around the world.

"'Our oath to Preserve, Protect, and Defend the Constitution of the United States from all enemies, foreign and domestic, is also indissoluble. When such a threat now exists from a domestic enemy who seeks to destroy that Constitution, we as patriots are obligated not only by our oath but by the spilled blood of every soldier from every battle of every prior American War to rise in righteous might to meet that enemy anywhere and, at any time, to defeat it.

"'We wish to be clear to all genuine American patriots: we are still The United States of America. As for these other states and peoples that have forsaken the Constitution and embraced the New Way ideology, we now put you on notice that you are now an enemy of the Republic.

"'As of 12 April 2061, we now declare in unanimity that a state of war exists and has existed since that date, between you and the free and Constitution-loving peoples of the United States of America.

"'Our resolve is unshakeable. Our will to fight to take back what has been stolen from us is far greater than you can possibly imagine.

"'We are under no illusion that the struggle ahead will be difficult and that the cost will be high. For now, we bid all true patriots a safe and happy 4th of July,' end quote.

"The recording of this morning's historical events, along with a recording of this live broadcast, will now be replayed in a continuous loop. God Bless You, and God Bless the United States of America."

Turning the TV off, Eleanor sat quietly for several minutes, trying to understand all the news she had just watched. A chill ran up and down her spine. She reached for her comm to call her husband.

OPERATION DUSTER STRIKE GROUP

Over Astoria, South Dakota

1405 CDT — 4 Jul 2061

The four Stealth F-52 fighter bombers were ahead of schedule and flying at Mach–1 at 45,000 feet. The state-of-the-art aircraft had just entered South Dakota airspace. They remained undetected by ground radar and two rebel AWACS, currently airborne and on station across the rebellious state.

Each F-52 carried a single JASSEM-5 air-to-ground bunker-buster missile. The missile was the world's mightiest air-to-ground conventional weapon ever developed, carrying 750 kg of high explosives.

Mission Commander, pilot Michael Hotah, was a die-hard New Way supporter. A descendant of the Lakota Sioux Tribe of Indigenous Americans, he had been hand-selected for this special mission. His nickname was Kohana, the Sioux word for "swift."

The Sioux tribes had inhabited the Dakotas and Minnesota long before the White man came and took most of their land away by force and broken treaties. Ownership of the sacred Black Hills region had long been contested and remained unresolved.

For a moment, Hotah thought of the broken 1868 Treaty of Fort Laramie. He thought of the Wounded Knee Massacre, where upwards of 300 unarmed men, women, and children of the Lakota Sioux Tribe were massacred by the U.S. Army Cavalry on 29 December 1890. He recalled those events and so much more of his people's tragic history with the White man. Combined, they greatly motivated him to embrace the New Way. For him, the whole Burn it down and erase it all mantra was highly attractive. Hearing a tone in his ear set, his mind quickly snapped back to the here and now of the mission.

The F-52 onboard computer indicated sixty seconds to the launch window. He broke radio silence and called it out to the other three pilots, "Sixty seconds."

"Roger that," was heard from his Wingman, another Lakota Sioux descendant, along with the other two pilots flying beside them.

All four pilots armed their missiles and waited for the order to fire. At precisely zero, Hotah yelled, "Fire", hit the trigger, and excitedly yelled. "Missile away!"

The three other pilots launched theirs as well.

Pilot Michael Hotah hollered into the mic. "A-M-F!"

MOUNT RUSHMORE NATIONAL MEMORIAL

Black Hills of South Dakota

1410 MDT — 4 Jul 2061

The fun, fellowship, and food had been a welcome break from the pressure of current events for South Dakota Governor Jordan Willa.

The governor's lineage was Swedish and part Native American, specifically Lakota Sioux. The First People's lineage was from his mother's side. While he was still a young boy, his mother had taught him the importance of the Black Hills to the Sioux Nation. It was sacred land to their people.

He had treasured her teachings and, as governor, had done much to help improve the lives of First Nation citizens in South Dakota, including signing landmark legislation that returned ownership of Custer State Park to the Sioux Nation.

The rest of the Black Hills was partly privately owned and partly publicly owned by the federal government. Just yesterday, he had reread the entire text of the 1868 Fort Laramie Treaty. With secession, he wrestled with what to do with formerly federal lands, but he had to put aside those thoughts with the outbreak of war.

The governor and his family—wife Haley, daughter Ally, and son Hayden—had arrived early on the 4th of July to take in the beautiful

Black Hills, the crown jewel of the entire state. Situated in the southwest end of the state, Mount Rushmore National Monument, Custer State Park, Crazy Horse Memorial, and Jewel Cave National Monument were all on their itinerary for their five-day working vacation. Five-year-old Hayden insisted that his dad try to squeeze in a ride on the 1880s train as well.

After conducting a three-hour defense counsel meeting, the governor officiated a noon-time ceremony at Mount Rushmore in honor of the 4th of July, marking American Independence Day.

Now, a little after 2 o'clock of a hot afternoon, they were hiking the Presidential Loop with his family and security detail in tow. The group had just paused for a short rest. Towering directly above them was the likeness of Abraham Lincoln.

SOUTH DAKOTA AIR FORCE AWACS

Badlands of South Dakota

1510 MDT — 4 Jul 2061

The South Dakota Air Force AWACS, bearing the nose art "Sniffer," was at the end of its eight-hour watch. Within minutes, it would be relieved by a sister plane. "Sniffer" would then begin its descent to Ellsworth Air Force Base just outside of Rapid City, South Dakota.

Until relieved, the AWACS remained on station at 35,000 ft above the Badlands of South Dakota. It was attached to the 1st Air Force of South Dakota, based out of Ellsworth. The battle to seize control of Ellsworth three months earlier, on 12 April, had been hard-fought, but the South Dakota National Guard had prevailed, but at the cost of seventy-six Guardsmen and ninety-nine FEDs.

On this day, the 4th of July, their mission was to communicate any detected threats to the ten South Dakota Air Force fighter jets flying Combat Air Patrol in four sectors, roughly above Interstate 90, from the Minnesota state line west towards the Wyoming state line.

Surveillance Operator Airman 1st Class Stanley Wallace from Sioux Falls, South Dakota, stared intently at his screen. Noticing something, he turned to his partner, "Hey Sam, I keep getting a ghost return or something on Primary. You see anything on Infrared?"

"Just did on a sweep a moment ago. I'm looking at it again."

"Yeah, it comes and goes. Wait a second—I think I've got a hit. Stand by. Positive hit—it's a missile. Tracking. Profile indicates a scramjet."

On hearing the exchange from his subordinates, Tactical Director Travis Stewart jumped into the conversation, "Stan, you have a positive ID?"

"Profile indicates a scramjet missile. It just hit Mach-6." Wallace replied.

"Probable target?"

"Double-checking…"

With the comm in his hand and Stewart poised to call the governor's security detail, he tapped his thumb rapidly on the desk.

"Black Hills, Mount Rushmore." Wallace yelled excitedly.

MOUNT RUSHMORE NATIONAL MEMORIAL

Black Hills of South Dakota

1413 MDT — 4 Jul 2061

Protective Detail lead Agent Deryck Alex had regaled at coming out of early retirement to head up Governor Willa's revamped Protective Detail. Retiring five years ago at age fifty-five from the U.S. Secret Service, Agent Alex had formerly served on the U.S. Presidential Detail for fifteen years and had protected three Presidents.

The detail today had been uneventful. As they paused for a short break along the Presidential Loop, Deryck looked up to admire the mammoth presidential sculptures carved in granite towering above the party. His eyes were transfixed on Lincoln when his comm lit up with a flashing red screen accompanied by rapid beeping. This was the emergency alert signal.

He immediately yelled the evacuation code to the other agents, "Buster Six—Buster Six. On the move!"

The governor, his wife, their two children, and the seven agents started sprinting as fast as they could. The governor, trim and fit, had picked up his young son piggyback style. His wife, along with their twelve-year-old daughter Ally, was just behind him. Three agents were alongside or to the rear of the governor's family. The other four were ahead, with Agent Alex in the lead. All agents had their weapons drawn. Deryck tapped his earbud.

"Agent Alex, this is Lieutenant Colonel Travis Stewart of the South Dakota Air Force. I'm aboard an AWACS of the South Dakota Air Force.

We have a positive ID—missile inbound to your location. Confidence is high. I say again, confidence is high. Buster—Six. I say again, Buster—Six."

At a full run, the sixty-year-old Alex was glad he was in good shape. "Copy that—Buster—Six in progress. ETA for missile?"

"Twenty seconds. Recommend taking cover immediately."

Agent Alex motioned and screamed for everyone to get down and brace. They found a large notch at the base of the mountain that could provide them with some cover from above. The governor and his family huddled in first, wrapping their arms around each other, with the children at the back of the notch against solid granite. Next, the security detail formed a human shield and braced around them.

The four JASSEM-5 air-to-ground missiles had slowed and were descending. Each was programmed with a different target. For the lead missile, launched over Astoria, South Dakota, at the far eastern end of the state by pilot Michael Hotah, the total flight time was less than five minutes as it screamed across almost the entire length of the state. Such was the beauty—and the terror—of hypersonic weapons.

Agent Alex was the only agent able to look upward. He could hear a high-pitched, shrill sound getting rapidly louder. The missile fired by Pilot Hotah impacted right between the eyes of President George Washington. Plowing into the granite face at Mach-5, it had drilled thirty feet into granite and exploded just as missiles two, three, and four hit their targets.

Missile two impacted President Thomas Jefferson's left eye; Missile three impacted the right side of President Teddy Roosevelt's nose; Missile four impacted President Abraham Lincoln's right cheek.

The resulting explosions were catastrophic. An enormous shock wave radiated out from all four impact zones, blowing down anyone standing up inside the national park below the monument. In the course of being blown over by the shock wave, several people were instantly killed when their heads smashed into objects or the hard pavement beneath them. Many others suffered varying degrees of injuries. Every window of every park building blew out.

After a few minutes of silence, some of the survivors were eventually able to stand back up. Many were in a state of shock. They looked up at a towering plume of smoke and dust from the mountain. With a stiff breeze, the smoke and dust began to clear.

After a few minutes had passed, they stood in stunned silence, staring up toward the mountain to see an unfathomable sight. They were dumbstruck. They were gone. They were all gone. It was as if a giant eraser had come down from the sky and completely erased the sculptures of four legends of American history. Four legends that had, sentinel-like, gazed out upon the sacred Black Hills undisturbed since 1941.

Meanwhile, fifty yards beyond where Lincoln's left cheek had towered above them, eleven people lay wounded. Miraculously, due to their proximity to the base of the mountain, the governor, his family, and all seven members of his security detail had survived.

The most potent part of the blast wave had radiated outward from high above them, right over their heads by fifty feet or so. The most seriously injured was Agent Hill. A rock had grazed the right side of his head and knocked him out for a moment. Hill had come to somewhat but was bleeding badly and unable to get up on his feet.

Agent Voss had already started tending to Agent Hill. Deryck looked around to check on the governor, family, and the rest of the agents in the party. All had minor cuts but were generally okay and had slowly gotten back on their feet. Unable to hear, Agent Alex sent a coded message for rescue and EMT: *"wičháša kúta,"* which is Lakota Sioux for "man down."

★ ★ ★

The White House

Washington, D.C.

4 Jul 2061

EXECUTIVE ORDER 18666

By the authority vested in me by the people of the New Way, it is hereby ordered as follows:

Recognizing the deep wounds that various white-supremacist songs have inflicted on millions of Americans for hundreds of years, the following so-called "patriotic songs" are hereby categorized as hate speech and are henceforth subject to prosecution under the Federal Hate Crimes Act of 2056.

1.   *The Star-Spangled Banner*

2.   *God Bless America*

3.   *America the Beautiful*

4.   *America (My Country, 'Tis of Thee)*

5.   *The Stars and Stripes Forever*

6.   *You're a Grand Old Flag*

7.   *I'm a Yankee Doodle Dandy*

8.   *Battle Hymn of the Republic*

9.   *Dixie*

10. *Shenandoah*

This list is subject to further additions.

Further communications and executive orders will be issued at the appropriate times.

All military bands are to comply with this order immediately. Failure to comply will result in a military courts-martial under the Uniform Code of Military Justice.

President Devin Cyrus

‖‖ **13** ‖‖

OH SHENANDOAH

ABANDONED CABIN

Harpers Ferry, West Virginia

1710 EDT — 4 Jul 2061

Sergeant Major Wallace Chamberlain of the Shenandoah Militia was the most highly decorated noncommissioned officer currently living. He had been awarded the nation's highest military honors, the Medal of Honor, the Distinguished Service Cross, and the Silver Star. All of them had been hard-earned during the North African War.

Four years after his retirement at age fifty-five, Chamberlain assumed command of the Militia after the passing of the Militia's founder, retired Army General William Pierce.

Six months before the founding of the militia on 10 May 2059, General Pierce claimed to have had a vision one night about an impending conflict on American soil. The vision was not clear as to the enemy combatants, but the one thing that had been very clear was that the conflict was for the very soul of the nation and its survival as a Republic.

Although West Virginia had seceded from the Union a little less than two months ago in April, the now federalized, renamed, and expanded 1619 Division was on station at Harpers Ferry, West Virginia. The 1619 had established a picket line along the western side of Bakerton Road and Peregrine Road from the Shenandoah River to the Potomac River to the north.

Studying a map of the area while humming the haunting folk melody, "*Oh Shenandoah*", Chamberlain had solid intel in his possession that federal forces were fixing to keep this small parcel of West Virginia on the western shore of the Shenandoah River. The intel had heavy armor staged on the Virginia side of the Shenandoah in the tiny hamlet of Lovettsville, along with an air assault group rapidly staging there.

The window to strike was closing fast. The Army of West Virginia was still a day away from being ready. Chamberlain figured that, at best, they had about eighteen hours left before the window closed, and the special-ops mission would have to be scrubbed.

The team consisted of all men. Twenty-five experienced combat veterans. All were retired members of various special forces teams from the Army, Navy, and Marines. Colonel Eric Adams of the Rocky Mountain Militia in Montana, along with General Buford, also in Montana, had been instrumental in selecting the team's members. A daring daylight operation was moments away from launch. Chamberlain had gathered them all around for one final briefing before the assault.

"Listen up. Shortly, we'll all be heading out. I pray to God that all of you make it back. Know this: if perhaps this is the day we die, we will have done so on the altar of freedom. To a man, we're well-trained and equipped. I have every confidence in your abilities as soldiers. Trust your instincts. Follow the plan, and together, we'll achieve the mission's objective.

"I know you've been kept in radio silence for the last three days. There's breaking news. I struggled with the question of whether I should share it with you or not."

Chamberlain paused to gauge the expressions on the faces of his team. They were stoic. He decided to continue. "There's breaking news that the FEDs' Air Force has blown up Mount Rushmore. Details are still sketchy."

A groan was heard from the soldiers gathered, along with several colorful expletives.

Motioning to quiet down, Chamberlain pointed to the map one last time. "Listen, we can't be distracted by this. However, in choosing to share this with you now, I felt it might add that little extra edge toward the mission's success. We have got to secure the package. No package, we will have failed. We cannot fail. It's simply not an option."

"What the hell is this package?" one of the soldiers yelled out. Ignoring him, he continued, "We'll find out soon enough. Guys, check your gear one last time."

As the men rechecked their weapons, Civil War buff and retired Army Ranger Jerry Shaw quipped, "Are you all aware of the significance of this place in the First Civil War?"

Fraser smiled, "Illuminate us, Professor."

Everyone chuckled.

Chamberlain had the fleeting thought that the humor was a good thing.

Jerry went into professor mode. "Yeah, before the First Civil War, the famous abolitionist John Brown led a raid here at Harpers Ferry. It was on October 16, 1859. His team consisted of nineteen men—fourteen white and five free Black. Using force of arms, they stormed the federal arsenal up there on the bluff and, for a time, took it over.

"They killed three men. The raiders brought a cache of weapons, hoping to entice the townspeople and enslaved people to join them in a rebellion. Brown planned to start an insurrection against the federal government towards the goal of freeing all the enslaved people in the South. West Virginia didn't exist back then. All this land was still a part of the State of Virginia, a slave state.

"The ironic part of the story was that when federal troops arrived to put down the rebellion, it was led by Colonel Lee, a native son of Virginia and a West Point Graduate.

"This same Colonel Lee went on to become Confederate General Robert E. Lee, Commanding General of the Army of Northern Virginia. Lee's men quickly put down the raid at Harpers Ferry. Brown was captured, tried for treason, and hanged. He's buried in upstate New York."

The men all nodded or made anecdotal comments.

Fraser quipped, "Thanks, professor. I thought I knew everything." That got a slight chuckle.

Chamberlain broke into the laughter. "All that's ancient history.

We've got a job to do now. Before we go, let's take a knee."

The federal guards at the Harpers Ferry National Park Ranger Station were in the middle of changing the watch. A contingent of thirty-five soldiers milled about out in front of the building. At the back of the station, the grounds ended at the edge of a bluff with a delightful and commanding view of the Shenandoah River as it flowed north through this part of almost heaven known as Appalachia.

To the north, the river emptied into the Potomac. From there, the Potomac flowed southeast. It passed through Washington, D.C., then past Mt. Vernon, President George Washington's Estate, then further down out into the Chesapeake Bay, and finally the Atlantic Ocean.

Upstream to the southwest, the Shenandoah can be traced to its beginnings in Front Royal, West Virginia, at the confluence of its smaller North and South Forks, both named after it.

Unbeknownst to the federal troops, Chamberlain's assault teams had been scaling the bluff behind the ranger station. The rear of the station had been left unguarded since the shore below was just across from Virginia, a solidly New Way state. After they had arrived ten or so feet below the top, Chamberlain and his assault team paused for a moment.

Chamberlain looked left, nodded at the 2nd Squad, then right, and nodded at the 3rd Squad. Chamberlain and 1st Squad sprang up and breached the top. His team, all eight of them, launched into a full sprint to the back of the ranger station, twenty-five or so yards away. The 2nd and 3rd Squad breached the top right behind them. 2nd Squad went left to a row of bushes. 3rd Squad went right and took cover behind a large storage shed.

After observing the two other teams and seeing that they were all in position, Chamberlain turned towards the rear door. He quickly picked the lock, then slowly opened the door and stepped inside the office of the Chief Park Ranger.

There in the corner sat a sizeable six-foot-tall walk-in safe. Chamberlain motioned for Graham to come forward to crack the safe. Graham quietly went to work. In thirty seconds, flat, he turned the handle. He heard a click, and the safe door popped open.

Chamberlain approached the safe and pulled the heavy door wide open. After his eyes adjusted to the low light, he saw three large metal panels up against the back wall.

He picked up the first one. It was heavy and appeared to be entirely metal. Not sure what to make of it, he turned it around to check out the other side. To his astonishment, he found himself staring at the Declaration of Independence encased under glass. Passing it along to Fraser, Chamberlain picked up the second panel, turned it over, and saw The Constitution of the United States. He handed that panel off to Holzapfel. Sure enough, the third panel was The Bill of Rights. After handing that panel off to Guzak, Chamberlain motioned to leave.

At the exact moment of taking a step towards the rear exit, the front office door swung open. There in the doorway was a 1619 Division soldier with an automatic weapon pointed right at Chamberlain. The 1619 guy stood there frozen with a startled look on his face. In a lightning-fast move, Chamberlain instinctively raised his assault rifle and put a single shot into the soldier's forehead. As the soldier dropped to the floor, Chamberlain yelled out, "Move—move—move."

In front of the ranger station, the federal soldiers sprang into action at the sound of the gunshot.

Six FEDs were immediately shot and killed by covering fire from

2nd and 3rd Squad. The 1619 soldiers were caught in a crossfire, taking fire from their left from the area of the shed and their right towards the back of the property from a hedgerow. Three more FEDs went down in a matter of moments.

As Chamberlain's men scrambled towards the edge of the bluff, he could hear the helos approaching. They all continued firing on the FEDs. The rate of fire increased as the 1619 soldiers were reinforced, and additional soldiers arrived from nearby.

Chamberlain saw two of his men go down and yelled out, "Covering fire!" He raced over to the two downed men. Coming upon them, he grabbed each one by his uniform at the shoulders and dragged them back to where the rest of the 1st Squad was. In the process, Chamberlain felt a bullet whiz right past the right side of his face. The heated air of the passing bullet slightly burned his skin. Safely back with his Squad, Chamberlain glanced at the name on one of the dead soldiers' uniforms. It was Richards, one of the unsung heroes of the Battle of Sirte during the North African War. Richards was dead, and so was the other soldier.

The four helos had been flying low and fast along the Shenandoah River at twenty feet over the swiftly moving current. Approaching Harpers Ferry, they lurched upward over the bluff. Three of them landed on the rear property of the ranger station. Above them, the fourth opened fire on federal positions with a Gatling gun. The results were devastating.

Running backward, Chamberlain's men made a mad dash for the three helos, firing their weapons as they went.

Towards the first helo, Guzak took the body of Richards along with the Bill of Rights.

Towards the second, Holzapfel jumped aboard carrying the Constitution.

Meanwhile, Chamberlain helped load up the other KIA into the third helo. He had brought aboard the Declaration of Independence.

As the federal troops were being neutralized, the firing had subsided for a moment until reinforcements arrived from the picket line to the west. Just as the FEDs rate of fire began to pick up again, the gunship let out another salvo against them.

In moments, the three helos were aloft. With Chamberlain and his three teams safely aboard with America's Founding Documents, the four helos flew down the bluff out over the Shenandoah and headed southwest towards Front Royal. They were a mere twenty feet above the water.

Chamberlain and Fraser sat next to each other, panting and speechless. To their right, the body of retired Navy SEAL Richard Hancock. He was a recipient of the Navy Cross for his heroism in the amphibious landings during the North African War at the Battle of Sirte.

Fraser yelled over the din of the chopper, "Damn, Major, I was drinking a beer with Hancock two nights ago. He told me that the Hancock of Declaration of Independence fame was in his family tree. Now we've got the thing sitting on both our laps right next to our buddy." Chamberlain looked down at the Declaration of Independence. He stared intently at the most prominent signature on it, John Hancock. Next, he saw the words that sent a chill up and down his spine as he read aloud the very last line of the Declaration:

And for the support of this Declaration, with a firm reliance on the protection of divine Providence, we mutually pledge to each other our Lives, our Fortunes and our Sacred Honor.

IIII **14** IIII

LIFE IS OLD THERE

1619 ARMORED DIVISION FIELD HQ

Lovettsville, Virginia

0400 EDT — 5 Jul 2061

Major General Jeremiah Hood was a commanding presence at six-foot-six inches. Lanky and 200 pounds, the West Point graduate had been hand-selected by Defense Secretary Lars Lamont and newly minted Chairman of the Joint Chiefs of Staff, General Jeffrey Homer, to lead the invasion of the rebel state of West Virginia.

His loyalty to the New Way cause was without question. Now, assembled in the predawn hours, he spoke to his officers one last time before heading out into battle.

"Alright, everyone, listen up. Yesterday's rebel raid at Harpers Ferry was a blow to our cause. As you well know from the news reports, the president had planned to burn the disgraced documents authored by white supremacists. It would have been grand to have watched them burn on live TV. Even with those plans shot, our mission remains the same. Today, we come as liberators and will not fire unless fired upon. Is that clear?"

All nodded in the affirmative. One lieutenant spoke up, "General, what about fixed-wing air support?"

"The brass feels it's too controversial to have fighter jets and drones in the mix and could turn public opinion against us. So, we use what we have: armor and the helo gunships.

"Our mission is to end this rebellion, one state at a time. The brass feels these hillbillies in West Virginia will be easy to win back over. The brass even devised a slogan: Enter, Liberate, Occupy, Unite. They're convinced, as am I, that using this method to unite West Virginia back into the Union will start a chain reaction with the other states to stop the rebellion and get in line behind the New Way.

"The president has sent word down the chain of command that any resistance is to be dealt with swiftly. Nonviolent resisters will be arrested and sent to re-education camps being set up outside Washington. Armed resisters are to be met with overwhelming force and neutralized.

"Now, I know that the thought of firing on fellow Americans may be upsetting for some of you. But let's not forget the bigger picture and what we're doing here. The cancerous ways of the Old Way must die peacefully or forcefully. I much prefer peacefully, as I'm sure you do too. But for the enlightenment and purification of the nation, if we must forcefully remove the cancerous portions from the whole, so be it. Send them all to hell.

"Okay, dismissed. We roll at 0430. Good luck."

ARMY OF WEST VIRGINIA FIELD HQ (NEAR RION FARM LN)

Charles Town, West Virginia

0405 EDT — 5 Jul 2061

General Steven Sickles, commanding general of the Army of West Virginia, after a fitful night, had awakened a little before 4 a.m. Drinking coffee, the general studied the map of Shenandoah County. Intel had reported unusual predawn activity across the Shenandoah River in the small Virginia town of Lovettsville, just south of the Potomac River.

Lovettsville had been under close watch for the last few days. The federal forces staging area just outside of town was packed to the brim with all manner of military hardware and a sizeable number of troops. Estimates put the numbers at division strength at approximately twelve thousand soldiers.

Moments ago, after conferring with his Commander in Chief, West Virginia Governor Alan Roy, General Sickles was under no illusions as to what lay ahead. With his general staff and officers seated before him, he started with the familiar Latin phrase he had been working on, ingraining it into the minds of his officers and soldiers. "Montani semper liberi!" The soldiers—in unison—yelled out the English translation of the West Virginia State motto. "Mountaineers Are Always Free!"

"Good morning to you all. Before we go into battle, I want to tell you how proud I am now to be a patriot and a West Virginian.

"Eleven months ago, I was stationed in Libya. As I was closely monitoring events back home, I had a growing sense that the country that I loved was about to breathe its last and cease to exist, at least in principle. As you know, I resigned from my commission and returned home to my beloved home state to see what I could do to help turn the tide. As God would have it, here I am, leading you all.

"You know my ancestors helped settle this land way back in the 1790s. I was born here, and I'll gladly die here. I would rather die peacefully surrounded by family at some time in the distant future.

"Patriots! Today, it may very well be that we must die in battle to secure peace and liberty again. If this must be, then so be it. It will have been well worth it so our kin can live a long, peaceful, and prosperous life under liberty's light until the Good Lord calls them home, too.

"I recall an old song from ninety or so years ago. It was from the 1970s. It references our state with the poetic words, 'Life is old there, older than the trees, younger than the mountains, growin' like a breeze.' How accurate those words are, as well as Montani semper liberi!"

The soldiers yelled back again, "Mountaineers are always free!"

SHENANDOAH MILITIA FIELD HQ

Near Millville, West Virginia

0520 EDT — 5 Jul 2061

The Shenandoah Militia lay in wait in a thick forest northeast of the tiny hamlet of Millville, West Virginia. Somewhere to their west, the Army of West Virginia waited for the FEDs' arrival on West Virginia Soil. Over in Virginia, an entire federal armored division lay to the east.

As the crow flies, it would be minutes to get here by air, but because of the Shenandoah River just to their east and a portion of the Appalachian Mountains rising quickly from the river's steep east bank, a direct ground route for the FEDs was impossible.

Chamberlain felt it was a virtual certainty that the FEDs' route would take them north on Virginia Rt. 278 across the Potomac into Brunswick, Maryland. There, they would hook left onto Maryland Rt. 478 and to the northwest over to Sandy Hook, Maryland. From there, they would undoubtedly race southwest on U.S. Route 340 back over the Potomac again and then very quickly over the Shenandoah into West Virginia at Harpers Ferry. Cyrus seemed fixated on Harpers Ferry.

What the FEDs did not know was that Chamberlain had, by design, determined to maintain radio silence from the Army of West Virginia. There had been no contact between him and Sickles for five days, nor with anyone else, except for the encrypted message from Colonel Eric Adams in Montana regarding the destruction of Mount Rushmore.

During that time, Chamberlain and his special forces team successfully raided the ranger station at Harpers Ferry the day before, saving the nation's founding documents from being destroyed. During the debriefing after the raid, he had been told that on live TV on July 4, President Cyrus was to have presided over the burning of the documents in person, possibly even tossing them into the flames himself.

Chamberlain thought the man had gone mad.

With the founding documents on their way somewhere to a secure location in the west, Chamberlain and his team had safely rejoined the rest of his men and women in arms.

Today, a much greater challenge awaited them.

The militia, comprising all 3,200 of them, had been transformed into a mobile, quick-reaction force now operating in stealth mode in the thick forest outside Millville, West Virginia. The soldiers were mainly West Virginians by birth. A smattering of soldiers were self-made refugees who had come over from the westernmost parts of Virginia out of fear of arrest and re-education due to their CON ideologies.

Last evening, the militia pickets on guard got a scare when one of the locals in town stumbled upon them while out hunting. After a brief questioning by a sergeant, the citizen returned and organized a food supply to be delivered to the militia after dusk. He brought fifteen locals with him, all bearing weapons, who promptly signed up to join the militia on the spot. After Chamberlain had questioned them, he was convinced of their loyalties to the cause of liberty and West Virginia and welcomed them into their ranks.

In the early morning, Chamberlain and the militia were in their biodiesel-powered trucks with engines off. Chamberlain sat silently for a message from Sickles. During the wait, the early morning wildlife sounds in the forest had become almost hypnotic to him—just four hours of sleep after yesterday's harrowing raid did not help matters.

The hypnotic and peaceful sounds were suddenly interrupted by the sound of explosions off in the distance. Chamberlain wondered if it was the 1619 Armored Division firing. Just then, his radio squawked. He heard the familiar voice of Sickles, "This is Doc. The word is Sowo. I say again, the word is Sowo."

The word jolted Chamberlain into action, for Sowo was the Cherokee word for "one." It was the code word for invasion by land. He shouted into the radio, "Let's roll!"

At that, the trucks roared to life.

Despite the risk, Chamberlain insisted he would lead his soldiers into battle. He tapped the driver's shoulder and yelled, "Step on it."

The driver floored it and tore through the forest path leading towards Peregrine Road. Off in the distance, the sounds of heavy guns, explosions, and automatic weapons fire continued to escalate in volume and intensity. Once out of the forest, he could see smoke rising from the direction of Harpers Ferry.

His driver and the rest of the militia drove north at breakneck speed down Peregrine Road. Reaching Altstadt's Hill Road in twenty minutes or so, they turned right and, in moments, caught up with the rear echelon forces of the Army of West Virginia.

Chamberlain had the driver stop at a Humvee. Inside, a colonel was yelling into the radio over the din of battle.

"Hold on, General. I think he and the militia just showed up. Are you Chamberlain?"

Also yelling, Chamberlain responded, "Yes, sir. Colonel, what's the situation?"

"Glad to have you guys here. Listen, the 1619 Armored Division rolled into Harpers Ferry about twenty minutes ago via the river crossing on U.S. Highway 340. Lead units turned right onto Union Street and slowly rolled into town. Looks like they were expecting a hero's welcome.

"Some locals were observed to have greeted them and were even seen waving the new flag and tossing flowers at the tanks. When the FEDs reached the corner of Union and Washington Streets, the column turned left onto Washington in front of the post office. That's when all hell broke loose with Molotov cocktails, IEDs, and a hail of lead. The FEDs opened fire.

Seven federal helo gunships are on station and giving air support. Ours are due any moment."

Chamberlain nodded and yelled, "Understood. Orders?!"

Pointing at the map, the colonel yelled, "I need you to race with all haste to St. Peter's Cemetery just up the road to try to outflank their infantry. Engage the enemy. If possible, try confiscating some of their tanks and driving them back here for redeployment. We have several ex-tankers in our ranks that know how to use them."

"Yes, sir! I might have a few ex-tankers, too." Chamberlain put his hand on the driver's right shoulder and yelled, "Floor it!" and off they raced. He grabbed the mic and keyed it, "Charlie! Take the 1st Battalion over to the tree line on the right side of the freeway. Frank, take 2nd to the far side of the cemetery. Sam, take the 3rd into the center of it. Try to capture some of the tanks and drive them back to the rear as quickly as possible. Give 'em hell, everybody!"

Arriving at the cemetery within minutes, the militia met up with forward elements of the Army of West Virginia, which were engaged in a pitched battle with federal infantry and armored forces.

Chamberlain jumped out and started barking orders while bullets whizzed all around him. Some of the troops were instantly hit.

All three battalions of the militia fanned out to their assigned rendezvous points with the Army of West Virginia. Explosions shook the earth beneath them. The air was acrid with black smoke, the unmistakable smell of gunpowder, and the undeniable scent of human life shattered open.

DeShawn King was pinned down by machine gun fire. Hunkered behind a burning tank near Union Street, he radioed for air support. "Airstrike! Sending coordinates now!" Turning to his number two, he shouted, "Paint the target."

The soldier retrieved the laser range finder and pointed it at the group of rebels. The laser lit up the target for the laser-guided missile that the approaching helo had at the ready. A second later, they heard the telltale sound of a missile launch from the helo above them. The missile impacted directly on the target, obliterating the soldiers and leaving a crater.

King was jubilant and yelled out, "Yeah, baby! Bye-bye, assholes!"

The jubilation was short-lived. King and his soldiers saw the missile come from the west from a helo just below the tree line. It impacted the army helo that had just saved King and his squad. The helo exploded and crashed to the ground. King cursed, "Shit!"

ⅢⅢ 15 ⅢⅢ

HAPPY HOUR

A.K. MCKLUTZ'S LOUNGE

Arlington Heights, Illinois

1803 CDT — 5 Jul 2061

A.K. McKlutz's was an institution in the upscale Village of Arlington Heights in the northwest suburbs of Chicago.

It had been an evening commute stop-off mecca for as long as anyone could remember. The clientele was a mix of white-collar and blue-collar workers.

Owner George Santorini was likable and enjoyed tending the bar at his lounge. As a MOD, he had made it clear to all the regular customers that if you were going to talk politics or religion, you had better do so respectfully. Having tossed patrons out for violating what he called his cardinal rule, George was tolerant but with common-sense limits.

His patrons, from time to time, would ask him where the line was regarding his rule on the matter. George would shrug his shoulders, smile, and say, "I'll know when I hear it."

Regulars Don, Ron, and Clint arrived within minutes of each other after getting off the train in downtown Arlington Heights. George had a particular affinity for the three men—Don a CON, Ron a MOD, and Clint a LIB. George's admiration for them was primarily due to the trio never breaking the cardinal rule. They would occasionally come close to hitting the line, as it were, but somehow always managed to bring the tone down and stay friends just in the nick of time.

George had just turned on the ANN Nightly News. They went silent and intently watched the lead story of the Battle of Harpers Ferry and the invasion of West Virginia.

The screen cut to a jarring image of tanks rolling down the main street of the historic town. "….at dawn today, federal armored forces rolled into the historic town of Harpers Ferry, located on the western banks of the Shenandoah River in the easternmost portion of West Virginia.

"A Pentagon briefing today stated that the short-term goal was to reinforce the small garrison of federal troops at Harpers Ferry that had maintained a toehold of control over the rebellious state. The long-term goal was to squelch the rebellion and reassert federal control over the entire state as part of the Cyrus administration's effort to end the uprising and bring all states back in line with the New Way.

"The invasion of West Virginia is the first step in President Cyrus's announced plan to reassert authority, one state at a time and in rapid order. "Here in the heart of the Blue Ridge, heavy fighting raged all day. It was only about 90 minutes ago that the fighting stopped, but we still hear an occasional burst of automatic weapons fire.

"Opposing the federal police action were rebel forces consisting of West Virginia National Guard mutineers. The highly trained force now refers to itself as 'the Army of West Virginia.' They were also aided by irregular fighters from armed townspeople in the area and by a militia group calling itself 'the Shenandoah Militia.'"

"Sources tell us that at one point, the federal armored column was trapped near the town's cemetery. Federal forces opened fire to fight their way out. As you might expect, the effects were devastating. Army helicopter gunships aided the counterattack. Combined, they successfully beat back the rebels to a position about five miles to the west and southwest of the town.

"Casualty numbers are unknown currently, but are reported to be significant for both sides. This is Ghadir Alya, reporting from Harpers Ferry, West Virginia."

Back in the bar, all the patrons had stopped talking to watch the riveting report about the battle. Some mumbled under their breath. Others looked away and resumed their conversations or solitary activities. George shook his head and hit the mute button. "Damn, guys, I can't believe this shit. Where the hell is this headed?"

Don was the first to speak up, "Pretty clear to me, George. We got ourselves into a real hornet's nest now. It's a Civil War 2.0!"

Ron, finishing a sip of his beer, chimed in, "This is screwed up. Why ca…"

Clint interrupted, "All the right-wing nuts have come home to roost. They're all nuts."

"Right-wing nuts? There you go again, Clint. I work hard. I pay taxes. Who the hell does Cyrus think he is? That new flag sucks." He sipped again and continued, "And what about suspending the Constitution? Invading another state, and with tanks to boot! What the hell is that?" Don bellowed.

Clint shot back. "Don, the thing is over 270 years old. The Constitution was written by the slaveholder Jefferson, for Pete's sake. To top it off, he had relations with a slave. I say good riddance, and let's start over."

Don, visibly irritated, continued, "So, we what? Get rid of it instead of improving it? Hell, we've been improving it all along. They're called amendments for a reason. And, like, what's with blowing up Mount Rushmore just a few months after we blew up the Alamo? What the hell is that? What's next? Demolish the Washington Monument or the Jefferson Memorial, or, God forbid, the Lincoln Memorial?! I'm tellin' ya', the lunatics are running the insane asylum."

George looked at Don half-seriously, "Careful, young fella, that borders on hate speech."

Before Don could reply, Clint yelled, "Burn it all down, baby! Burn it all down and start over. That's what Cyrus is doing. That's why we voted him into office!"

Clint took a sip of his martini.

Ron, ever the pragmatist, said, "Look, guys, I can see your points on both sides. I do. But I'm with Don on this monument thing. You can't erase history. You can try, but it's still all there on the internet."

Clint rolled his eyes, laughed, and replied, "Screw the internet! It's a cesspool of right-wingers and wacko conspiracy theories." At that, Clint put his left hand behind his head and made a V with his first two fingers, "Hey George, look, I'm a Martian!"

George laughed, "Here all along, I thought you were just another dumb ass white guy."

Roaring with laughter, Don took his fist up to his forehead and stuck out his forefinger, "No—wait, I thought you were a unicorn."

Everyone laughed but Clint. He said, "Funny guys, real funny. But, seriously, why can't the CONs just get over it? Let's be done with all this rebellion stuff and at least give the New Way a try." Looking directly at Don, he continued, "You people seem fixated on the past and the way things were, and you want everything to stay the same forever. It doesn't work that way, bro. We gotta move forward into the New Way Age of Enlightenment so that we can save the planet."

George had listened to a lot so far and decided it was a tactically perfect time to interject his thoughts, "Look, guys, all joking aside. I echo what Ron just said. There are good arguments on both sides, but some of what's gone on here seems a bit too much. I mean, for Pete's sake, now we have more dead Americans in less than a day's drive out east in West Virginia. We just buried a bunch of Americans almost three months ago. They're all dead because guys and gals in camo on both sides of the argument shot each other. It's one thing for the thugs of the country to shoot the innocent. It's a whole 'nother level for soldiers to be doing it. This thing is starting to spiral out of control, and in my opinion, needs to stop immediately."

Ron added to George's sentiments, "That's right, George. Look, guys, I'm forty-two. I got a wife and two kids at home. I wanna see them grow up in a country at peace. To live a peaceful life, to have a job, and a family of their own. I try to teach them the Golden Rule and to love people they may disagree with and still associate with them."

"Agree to disagree!" Don chimed.

"That's right, Don. But it's more than just that. It's about the Golden Rule and loving your neighbor. My grandma used to say your neighbor is whoever is right next to you at any given moment throughout the day."

Don spoke, looking first at Ron and then at Clint, "Your grandma was wise, Ron."

Don took a swig of beer and continued, "Clint, I would add this: for me, it's not about holding onto the past. It's about building on the good of the past. We learn from the bad of the past, and then we need to make sure we don't make the same mistakes again. We never forget the good of the past, ever. It'd be like being presented with your full family tree and then chucking it into the burn pile just because you had a relative who did something bad. That tree is the foundation of your family, flaws and all. The Declaration of Independence, the Constitution of the United States, and the Bill of Rights are the foundation stones for our country, flaws and all."

Don took another swig and continued, "Man, we are headed way in the wrong direction. If Cyrus thinks he can bully us, he's got another thing comin'. Have you ever looked at an election map before they abolished the Electoral College? Look up the map from twenty-four years ago. Look up the maps that show it down to the county level. It should scare the shit out of everybody in blue counties. When this Civil War gets going, I'll tell you one thing: all those decent God-fearing folk out in the red part of the country, they're not going to take it anymore. Pretty much all of 'em are armed to the teeth, and they're mad as hell. They're not going to comply! They're not going to roll over!" He took a quick sip and continued. "And they sure as shit aren't going to surrender.

They'd rather all die on a proverbial Constitution Hill. Come to think of it, all things considered, you gotta admit it looks like they've already proven that point way early, and things are just gettin' goin.'"

George attempted to add some levity, "Annie, git yur gun?"

Don looked George right in the eyes and spoke quietly, "I bet I know at least fifty guys with ARs, and each of them has tens of thousands of rounds of ammo. All of 'em are CONs. You mess with these folks; they'll mostly turn the other cheek lots of times if it's just them you're messin' with. But when you start messin' with their families and future, that's a tripwire you don't wanna touch.

"The way I see it, there are three modes. Alarm, Prepare, and Defend. We went into alarm mode after the first 9/11. We went into prepare mode when the socialist wave started in the 2020s and 30s. Now, with Cyrus and his closet commie crowd that wants to burn it all down literally, the CONs just went into defend mode." Don took a drink and continued. "Yes, sir, they're prepped, locked, and loaded."

"What about you, Don? What mode are you in?" George asked. Don answered coyly. "Well, let's just say I'm not fixin' for a fight, but I'm ready for any S—H—T—F scenario."

At that, Clint banged his fist on the bar. George snapped his head around. By George's reaction, Clint knew that the line had been breached or almost breached. "Sorry, George, we're all on edge these days."

"Noted, Clint. Apology accepted." George paused to see if Clint was genuinely settling down. When George was satisfied that he was, he continued, "Boys, look over on that wall. I just put that up today. It's my new org chart. Tell me what you see. Someone describe it from bottom to top."

Ron spoke first, "Well, there's you, George, then the customers, then your wife and kids, then some bearded guy at the top. Wait, is that a picture of…"

George interjected, "Jesus Christ."

Don looked puzzled, "No way! You're a churchgoin' guy, George?"

George paused and spoke quietly, "No, but two weeks ago, I got home about one-thirty in the morning on a Sunday. There's my bride of fifteen years on her knees at our bed. She's got a picture of the kids laid out on the bedspread. The covers hadn't even been pulled back yet for the night. She hadn't even changed into her nightgown.

"Man, I'm tellin' you, she was bawling her eyes out. It reminded me of the bawling that only a mother will do when she knows her kids are in danger, but she can't do nothin' about it. She looks up at me and says, 'Only God can save this country from ruin now.' When she said that, I was thunderstruck. Honestly, it felt like this invisible force hit me right square between the eyes. Then it was like things got really clear in my mind, especially about all the crap that's been goin' on. It was like an awakening." George paused and looked contemplative. "Guys, I'm here to tell you I fell to my knees right then and there. I hugged her tight and got emotional, too. At that moment, in the deepest part of my gut, I just knew she was right. I'm not much of a religious guy by any means, you understand."

Looking somewhat sheepish, George asked, "You know, guys, you think it would be okay if we look over at that chart and tip our glasses to it? Especially to J.C. and our families?"

Don looked over, "Gladly!" as he hoisted his beer mug.

Ron looked over, started to raise his mug, but then put it down and reached for his glass of water, "Glad to do it, George, but seein' J.C. up there, I think water is probably more reverent." Ron hoisted his glass of water.

Clint chimed in, "You guys know I'm agnostic, but, yeah, I'll hoist a glass to the force or whatever greater power is out there. Can't hurt." Clint lifted his martini.

George had also switched to a glass of water and clinked his glass with the other three, "Here's to my good customers here at happy hour at A.K. McKlutz's. Here's to my beautiful wife, wonderful kids, and J.C., the King of Kings. May there be peace on earth and goodwill toward all people real soon."

All four, in unison, said, "Cheers," clinked their glasses and drank a sip.

Meanwhile, a man in a black suit sat quietly with his drink. He had arrived at McKlutz's right after the trio did.

George had never seen him before, but that was not uncommon. The stranger had ordered a gin and tonic and sat quietly, looking down at his phone, seated four stools away from Don. He had not only heard the entire conversation but, unbeknownst to George and the trio, had taped the entirety of it. After the toast, he got up, paid a digital twenty-dollar bill in the kiosk on the bar for his bill, and silently walked out into the night.

‖‖ **16** ‖‖

INTO THE MAELSTROM

SHELDON FAMILY CABIN

Near Parker Island, Virginia

0752 EDT — 6 Jul 2061

Department of Homeland Security Secretary Frederic Sheldon had kept in constant contact with his wife, Samantha, and family. They had holed up in their mountain cabin on the east bank of the Shenandoah River. It was less than a mile from the West Virginia border to their north and west.

On the day of the Battle of Harpers Ferry, Samantha, her parents, and her in-laws were all awakened early in the morning of 5 July by the sound of explosions in the distance to the north. As the intensity of the fighting grew, the kids were also awakened by the sounds of war.

The fact that they were there at the cabin had been a closely guarded secret. As a member of President Cyrus's Cabinet and due to the elevated risk of serving as the Secretary of DHS, the protocol involved Secret

Service protection for Secretary Sheldon's entire family on the heavily guarded and surveilled compound.

After stepping into his secure comm room in his office in Washington, Secretary Sheldon picked up his sat phone, turned on encryption, and called Samantha.

She was quick to pick up. "Hi, hon. How are things? We miss you so much."

"Miss you too. Good to hear your voice, Sam. How is everyone?" "The kids miss their friends back home. Your Dad's been trying to keep the boys busy outside. The girls have been having a blast hanging out with their grandmas. My Dad's been quiet. He seems very disturbed by all the news. We all are, but he seems to be taking it much harder."

"This is killing me, not being able to be with you all. I'm so sorry, Hon."

"Frederic, there's nothing to be sorry about. You've been chosen for a huge job, and the country is in the biggest crisis of the century. How's the boss?"

"Angrier by the day. He had these big plans, and now all this has put a wrench into the whole works."

"How bad is it?"

"Bad enough that you guys are not coming home anytime soon. It's just not safe. We've asked the press and social media executives to keep a lid on this, but there's serious unrest all over the place. Even in blue states, especially in the red counties, and there are a lot more of those than you would think.

"I've planned for a massive supply of food and other essentials to be brought up to you. Should be there later today. Listen, there's probably gonna be a bit of a ruckus. There's a truck coming with a large outdoor freezer. There's an MP detail escorting them. The freezer is enormous, and it's solar-powered. It shouldn't take them long to get everything unloaded and set up. I have assurances that the entire crew is trustworthy and that they'll be gone by sunset at the very latest. Call me just as soon as they're done."

"Hon, I don't like the sound of this. They're going to draw unnecessary attention to themselves and us."

"I thought about that. But the truth is, there's military on the move everywhere. I think you'll be okay."

"Are you sure?"

"Yes, I'm sure. But, as a precaution, there'll be four other military convoys traveling in the area as decoys. What with all the fighting up north from there, I don't believe people will give it much thought. Besides, your Secret Service detail is there, and they aren't leaving anytime soon, either. They've got direct access for a helo evac if need be."

1ST ARMORED NEW WAY DIVISION FIELD HQ

Shepherdstown, West Virginia

0800 EDT — 6 Jul 2061

Lieutenant Colonel Jackson King and his unit of the Illinois National Guard troops had been redeployed and attached to the 3rd Battalion, 1st Armored New Way Division for the last ten days. Having seen action in a significant battle already, plus some local skirmishes with irregulars in far downstate and far western Illinois, the Pentagon brass wanted his nascent combat experience on domestic soil for purposes back in the east. He and his troops had arrived by air at the Radford Army Ammunition Plant, at Radford, Virginia, fifteen days ago. Their initial assignment was the northwest defensive perimeter of the base.

Standing watch had been somewhat unsettling for Lieutenant Colonel King's soldiers. Behind them lay a vast labyrinth of underground storage containing unknown quantities of high explosives, along with equally vast amounts of chemicals and compounds needed to produce more. At the outbreak of hostilities, the Pentagon brass had beefed up security in and around the highly sensitive ammunition complexes, which were still under federal control. The loss of control at similar plants in Middleton, Iowa, and Independence, Missouri, during the April rebel attacks had alarmed the Pentagon.

The old 1st Armored Division had originally been based at Ft. Bliss in El Paso, Texas.

The fort had fallen to Texas forces after a pitched battle back in April. Forced to abandon half their tanks, a retreating column of tanks (with no ammunition), APCs, and all manner of other vehicles had left the base in haste, entered El Paso's city streets, and raced south. There, at the southern limits of the city, they had crossed the international border into Ciudad Juárez, Mexico. President Cyrus had personally called President Hernandez of Mexico to request an escape route for the force. Permission was granted.

Once in Mexico, the armored column had rolled westward on Federal Highway 2 to the Douglas, Arizona, border crossing. The column crossed back over into the United States. From there, the survivors and equipment were airlifted out of the Douglas Municipal Airport and were flown to the LIBs' stronghold of Virginia.

In Virginia, the 1st Armored Division, under orders from the president, had been renamed the 1st Armored New Way Division. It regrouped at Ft. Barfoot, near the historic Revolutionary War-era town of Blackston.

While there, it had been reinfused with five thousand fresh troops, along with weapons and materiel, including two hundred new main battle tanks and an additional fifty unmanned drone tanks.

Refreshed, reinforced, and re-equipped, the 1st were given orders to proceed with all haste north to Sharpsburg, Maryland.

There, they encamped within the site of the Antietam National Battlefield, just a few miles north of Sharpsburg. With much of American history erased from the classroom curriculum, most of the troops were unaware of the significance of Antietam in the First American Civil War.

The Battle of Antietam was fought there on 17 September 1862. It had lasted twelve long, savagely bloody hours.

Union casualties were 12,717. Of that number, 2,108 were killed, 9,540 were wounded, and 753 were missing or captured.

Confederate casualties were slightly less, with 10,316 casualties. Of that number, 1,546 were killed, 7,752 were wounded, and 1,018 were missing or captured.

The math was sobering. For every hour of the twelve-hour battle, 1900 souls were being killed, wounded, or so obliterated that there was nothing left to bury (or count).

All that carnage happened with primitive black powder single-shot rifles and first-generation cannons. Now, in 2061, troops armed with weapons of far greater destructive firepower were in movement across the vast spaces of a fractured nation and a rapidly escalating Civil War 2.0. Armed civilians, especially in rural areas, were also now joining the fight.

In the wee predawn hours of 5 July, the 1st Armored New Way Division had left their encampment at Antietam and had raced south on Sharpsburg Pike. Once in Sharpsburg, they hooked right onto Maryland Route 34 and drove southwest. At 0430, having successfully crossed the Potomac River into Shepherdstown, West Virginia, a fierce firefight erupted. After a pitched battle that had lasted the better part of the day, the Army of West Virginia had retreated after having been outmanned and outgunned by the FEDs. Casualties were heavy.

At the field headquarters, Lieutenant Colonel Jackson King sat quietly, listening to General Nathan Pope discuss the planned linkup with the 1619 Division.

The 1619 had crossed the Potomac into Harpers Ferry on 4 July. They entered the outskirts of town unopposed. It was a ruse. An ambush had been set up. It marked the beginning of a long, bitter fight that lasted the better part of the day. After having pushed back the Army of West Virginia, the Shenandoah Militia, and irregular fighters, the 1619's main elements had headed northeast towards Shepherdstown for the planned linkup with the 1st Armored New Way Division.

On the way, they became locked in pitched battles with different irregulars—townspeople, really—along with stragglers from the Army and the Militia. The fighting was reported as fierce. Several tanks had been captured and then re-flagged with the State Flag of West Virginia or the Old Way Stars and Stripes.

As General Pope entered the tent, a palpable air of anxiety filled the air. The resistance of the local populace to the FEDs' uninvited presence on West Virginia soil had been an unexpected and unnerving surprise.

General Nathan Pope was an imposing figure. All of six-foot-five inches tall and 299 pounds, he was a staunch New Way LIB. He had come from poor and humble beginnings. Raised by a single mom, also a LIB, they had become homeless while he was in the sixth grade after the bank had repossessed their home.

The trauma of it all had an indelible effect on Nathan. He could now, even at fifty-two years of age, still vividly recall his mother telling him who had victimized them, "The greedy capitalists." Pope, a West Point Graduate, Class of 2041, had steadily risen in the ranks to his current command.

Pointing to a map, the general continued, "The 1619 is approximately here. They're tied up fighting a large and spread-out force using all sorts of improvised explosive devices, Molotovs, and trenches filled with flaming biodiesel oil. It's a mess, and we're gonna clean it up and quick. West of Kearneysville, forces are gathered about three miles outside the city limits. We expect them to attack us at any time once we enter Kearneysville proper.

"Our objective is twofold. First, the 3rd Brigade Combat Team will form a defensive perimeter to guard our rear and protect the bridge over the Potomac. Both the 1st and 2nd Brigades will drive southwest on Kearneysville Pike to the outskirts of Kearneysville. We'll exit here and go around the town to the west. We'll then turn and head southeast on Route 9 to Shenandoah Junction. The rebels' right flank begins just to the east of the town. We'll drive behind the enemy and attack from their rear.

"Speed is essential. I can't emphasize that enough. We can't get bogged down fighting everyone who shows up with a gun. Roll past as much of that type of resistance as you can. For more organized resistance, shove a shell down their throats and send them all to hell."

Lieutenant Colonel King spoke up, "General, there have been some reports of more sophisticated weaponry being used by some of these irregulars and the militia. Some new IEDs utilize coal dust. RPGs. Even a report of TOW missiles that took out some of our tanks at Harpers Ferry."

"Like I said, Lieutenant, send them all to hell. Our immediate objective is to link up with the 1619. They've had a heck of a twenty-four hours. Any questions?"

From the back of the room, "Sir, we're hearing rumors of an alliance possibly forming out west in the Great Plains. Got anything on that?"

The general looked towards the back of the room. "I've heard those rumors, too. I've got nothing on that right now. Right now, our focus is on the task at hand. The brass has made it clear that the reinforcements we've received up to now are just the tip of the iceberg. The president's plan to state-hop our way across all rebel states and bring them back into line is the highest priority. He's assured the brass they will be given all the resources they need to get the job done. As for air power, expect a shitload of air support today."

Lieutenant Colonel King spoke up again, "General, are there any negotiations going on we're not aware of? I mean, this thing has already gotten out of hand, and it looks like it's going to get a whole lot worse. There must be some way to avoid all the bloodshed that's sure to happen next. I can't get it out of my mind that, at the end of the day, these are our fellow Americans we're shooting at."

General Pope paused, looked around the room, then down at his notepad. He scribbled something, looked up, and focused on King. "Yeah, these are our fellow Americans shooting at us, alright! Listen, you know, and I know that if these rebels would lay down their arms and fall back into line with the president's plans for the New Way, all of this would stop immediately. But they're fixated on the Old Way. So, if it's a fight they want, it's a fight we're gonna give them and one that they won't soon forget. In fact, we'll give'em all a fight they'll remember for generations. There can be no compromise or going back to the Old Way, absolutely none."

Upon hearing the words, Lieutenant Colonel King felt a weight come over him. A weight he'd never felt before.

Indeed, at other times in his life, when burdens would come along from one fiery trial or another, his faith had sustained him through it all. But this felt altogether different. A sense of foreboding seemed to rush in on him. He quietly said a prayer and waited for dismissal.

"Alright, everyone. We leave in thirty minutes. Let's be smart and stay safe!

I'll see you on the battlefield."

GOVERNOR ALAN ROY COMMAND POST

Northwest of Kearneysville, West Virginia

0800 EDT — 6 Jul 2061

West Virginia Governor Alan Roy had spent thirty years in the United States Marine Corps. Upon retirement at age 55, he entered politics. First elected to the West Virginia Senate on the Constitution Party ticket, then ran for governor three years ago and won in a landslide.

He was immensely popular for his no-frills, plain speech and for quickly getting to the point of any matter brought to his attention. He detested political speak and surrounded himself with like-minded populists whenever and wherever he could.

He had a knack for connecting with the common man, especially the ex-coal miners who had all lost their jobs due to the FEDs' ban on all coal mining, production, transport, and consumption decades earlier. The effects on the West Virginia economy had been especially catastrophic.

Inheriting the long-running crises, the governor had fought hard for the coal miners to be well-compensated and retrained, primarily for new careers in the clean-energy, IT, or tourism sectors of the state.

With the state and its citizens still recovering from the total burndown of the nation's coal industry, the consequences had pushed ninety-five percent of West Virginia's populace squarely into the CONs camp ideologically, politically, and socially. West Virginia was a cauldron of anger and resentment, and it was armed to the teeth.

At the outbreak of hostilities, the governor, a decorated veteran, determined he would don his Marine Corps uniform and actively direct the West Virginia response to the escalating conflict, come what may.

His most trusted military confidant was General Steven Sickles. Sickles's official height was listed as six-foot-five. His height may have been slightly exaggerated. It was more believable that he was every bit of 185 pounds of solid muscle. With his hallmark red hair and freckles and a mild temper, his troops had affectionately nicknamed him "Ol' Red Hot."

A West Point graduate, Sickles had been in the same graduating class as General Nathan Pope, Class of 2041. Intel was that Pope was in camp up in Shepherdstown. Soon, they would face off against each other on the battlefield.

Gathered around the governor's makeshift conference table were a gaggle of officers, along with the Chief of Staff and Chief of Security.

A large map of the area was arrayed on the table. The governor studied it one more time. "General Sickles, I'm expecting Pope to lead his armored column to the general area of Kearneysville, then probably east on into Shenandoah Junction. I'm certain their immediate objective is a linkup with the 1619. After that, more reinforcements and then a major drive west to Martinsburg. Intel also has a large force of at least division strength, possibly more, gathering here near Berryville, Virginia. It looks to be for a probable invasion of our state from the south, most likely along U.S. 340. They'll probably head here to Charlestown. From there, a linkup with 1st Armored and the 1619. At that point, they'll have an entire corps. General, any update on our current numbers?"

"Governor, we have approximately twenty-two thousand in uniform. Counting militia and irregulars, add another roughly seven thousand. There are also reports of large numbers of armed men and women streaming into the state from the west, from southern Ohio and eastern Kentucky. Almost everyone is flying one of four flags. Old Glory, the Gadsden, Don't Tread on Me, or An Appeal to Heaven. I guess it's quite a sight."

"I bet it is. Any handle on the numbers coming in through the checkpoints?"

"Don't know yet. I have orders out to have them make camp temporarily until we can sort things out. In the meantime, quite a few have said, 'Sign us up.' We're trying to figure out where to send them."

Chamberlain jumped in. "Hell, general, we'll take as many of 'em as we can get. We lost one-quarter of our force at Harpers Ferry. If they're tough and ready, we'll take 'em all."

The governor, a close friend of Chamberlain, looked at him after a pause. "Awfully green, Wally. Probably a fair number with no training. That could be more of a hindrance than a help."

"Ah, hell, Governor. Give us some good weapons, and they'll fight. Besides, I bet more than half of these patriots are a mix of vets, hunters, retired LEOs, and the like. Probably some ex-coal miners, too. We'll check 'em all out and put the green ones and the older ones way to the rear. Any vets, especially younger combat vets, they know what they're getting themselves into. They know the drill, so into the maelstrom they'll go with all the rest of us."

The governor looked pleased. "That sounds good, Wally."

Turning back to Sickles, "Make it happen, Steven, and quick."

★ ★ ★

1619 ARMORED DIVISION FORWARD POSITION

Two Miles East of Shenandoah Junction, West Virginia

1203 EDT — 6 Jul 2061

DeShawn King was in the fight of his life. Shells were exploding all around him in a ferocious battle between the 1619 and the Army of West Virginia. The rebels appeared to be reinforced and had a resupplied

Shenandoah Militia. Arriving in the nick of time, the 1st Armored New Way Division had joined the fight and was attacking the rebels' left flank. By some miracle, he was still alive, and his tank was virtually untouched. Meanwhile, ahead and behind him were burning hulks that had become flaming death chambers for the dead soldiers inside.

Fighting for over four hours now, a dry creek bed off to his right was now running with blood. *American blood*, the thought had occurred to him. *No*, he thought. *These are vermin. Rebels that must be crushed at all costs.* During a short lull, he had thought of home back in McHenry, Illinois. Thought of his mother and, especially, his father. His last communication with his dad in late June had him and his guard unit just South of Ridgeway, Virginia, near the border of North Carolina.

Though she had remained loyal to the New Way, the western part of North Carolina, from west of Winston-Salem and Charlotte, into the Smokies, was a hornet's nest of Old Way followers. While King was not privy to the exact plans, there was no doubt in his mind that the 501st Corps was preparing to roll south into North Carolina, most likely via U.S. 220. From there, they would probably head southwest, fan out, and then drive further west to push the rebels into the mountains, hoping to starve them out due to the loss of their supply lines.

An explosion ten yards from his tank snapped King back to alert. As he recoiled his head, he screamed into his headset. "Ayanda, get us the hell outta here. Head back towards that tree line! Squad, regroup on me. Move now!"

As King's squad of tanks turned to make a tactical retreat, he could see a large force of newly arrived federal armor inside the tree line. *More reinforcements, probably from the 1st Armored*, he thought. *Fantastic!*

They're getting ready for another push! Just then, an armor-piercing shell hit his number two tank beside him. The explosion immediately blew the turret off, which was instantly followed by a large jet of flames shooting skyward from the gaping hole from whence the turret once was. King had seen tanks go up before, but none that close to him. He had a microsecond thought of his own mortality. *Damn*, he thought. *Delarosa's gone!* He yelled into the mic. "Anybody see who put that shell into Delarosa's tank?! Damn!"

★ ★ ★

AFTERMATH OF THE BATTLE OF SHENANDOAH JUNCTION

East of Town

SUNSET — 6 Jul 2061

The nurses stood in stunned silence as gazing out over the battlefield. It was littered with corpses, burned-out vehicles, and other implements of war. Intermingled in the wreckage of military vehicles were a fair number of obviously civilian vehicles, especially trucks. There were also downed military aircraft, most of them choppers. Nurse Cary, a student of World War II history, thought to himself, *This reminds me of Omaha Beach in 1944.*

The group of twenty nurses had come from a nearby hospital at the end of their shift. None had ever worked in a natural disaster of any significant size. One nurse had worked in Ohio when a local town took a direct hit from an F5 tornado a few years ago. While there had been the loss of life and a fair number of injuries that had filled the ER, what was now in their field of view was another matter entirely. There were simply no words.

Nurse Nancy had vague recollections of old black-and-white photos from the Civil War, dating back to the 1860s, that her grandfather had shown her. Her grandfather had been a Civil War buff most of his life. She couldn't remember much from his collection of old Civil War photos, except for the ones from one particular battle. It held a special significance for her grandfather because the edge of that infamous field of death was very near to his farm up north in Sharpsburg, Maryland—The Battlefield of Antietam. She recalled the morbid photos showing corpses in various positions of death. What she saw now made those photos loom pale in comparison.

With the heat of July above normal, the stench of death was overwhelming. Nurse Cary looked out and estimated the death toll had to be enough to fill a stadium.

Faint cries were heard by the group of nurses. They were coming from the battlefield. Nurse Cary knew for a fact that some of his fellow nurses were CONs, some were MODs, and he himself was LIB. None of that mattered now. The maelstrom of war had arrived with full fury on 6 July 2061.

Just then, turning to his right, he saw the arm of a wounded soldier rise from among a group of the fallen about fifty yards away. Moved to tears, he rushed forward to help.

★ ★ ★

ANN STUDIOS

New York, New York

1830 EDT — 7 Jul 2061

The usual voice of the intro began, but then stunned the audience with a new name. "This is the ANN Nightly News with Marian Moore. *America at War.* Here now, reporting from New York, Marian Moore."

Without warning, Olivia Kinley had disappeared. There were rumors, but none were confirmed. When an at-war America tuned into the evening news, they saw a total stranger. She was wearing a scarf with the New Way flag colors of red, green, and yellow.

Marian said nothing to indicate what had happened to Olivia. She launched into the lead story. "The last forty-eight hours have seen the Second American Civil War escalate dramatically. The full scope of yesterday's major battle in the Shenandoah Valley of West Virginia is coming into clearer focus. Here, with a live report, is Sonny Jenkins near Harpers Ferry, West Virginia."

The scene cut away to an open field littered with smoking debris and bodies, lots of bodies. Soldiers were milling about in the background, tending to the dead and wounded.

Sonny looked disheveled. "We're here at the very rear of the Shenandoah Junction Battlefield. We're roughly midway between Harpers Ferry and the hamlet of Shenandoah Junction here in West Virginia. The pungent smell of death is overwhelming. Yesterday's battle here began a little before eight in the morning with a tank and artillery barrage initiated by the 1619 Armored Division. At its height, around 3 p.m. local time, the fighting was so intense that there was just one continuous roar echoing throughout the valley. We had to retreat from our position three times as the battle expanded exponentially, especially after the 1st Armored New Way Division arrived a little after three this afternoon, after fighting their way all the way here from just outside Shepherdstown.

"Rebel forces, composed of the Army of West Virginia, held their own and were aided by their own armor, cannons, aircraft, and something new that was used by the Shenandoah Militia, IEDs using coal dust.

"The combined forces put up stiff resistance. It appeared that the pitched battle saw momentum shifts from one side to the other throughout the long, bloody day.

"Clearly, the tide turned with the arrival of the 1st Armored New Way Division. Rebel forces are now in full retreat toward the west and are rumored to be regrouping near an airport called the Eastern West Virginia Regional Airport.

"After the guns fell silent, we came across a group of nurses who had driven an hour to get here. They were tending to the wounded as best they could. Locals arrived to help as well. We interviewed one nurse who would only give his first name, Cary. Here's a clip.

The screen cut away to the nurses staring out over the central part of the battlefield in stunned silence. Sonny approached one of the nurses and held out the mic. "Can you tell me what you saw when you first arrived?"

"There are no words that adequately describe the sight. We were so sickened at the scene that we froze in place for a minute or so. It's carnage, absolute carnage. Quite a few of us were crying. I saw a hand go up over there and ran over to see what I could do."

"Were you able to help?"

"Yeah, but she's in bad shape. As more help arrived, I got the attention of a couple of army medics. They came over and took her away to a field hospital."

"Did you note what side she was on?"

Nurse Cary paused and took in the question. He looked down at the ground and slowly began to lift his eyes back up. He looked the reporter in the eye, "No. But what I do know is this: she's a red-blooded American."

"Marian, back to you."

"Thank you, Sonny. Stay safe. Army Chief of Staff General Evelyn Vance held a press conference. Here with a report on that is Matt Sydney."

Matt Sydney, in the White House Press Briefing Room, looked animated. The veteran reporter was obviously fighting a cold. "Things got heated here today with reporters from numerous news outlets demanding answers to questions that have largely gone unanswered at the daily White House Press Briefings. Today, Army Chief of Staff Evelyn Vance read a prepared statement. Let's roll that clip."

"Yesterday was a decisive victory for President Cyrus's plan to reunite the country and end the illegal rebellion against the New Way. Federal land and air forces engaged rebels near Shenandoah Junction, West Virginia, and soundly defeated them.

"The rebels have suffered heavy casualties and have retreated towards the western part of the state. Their wounded are being treated with compassion. Captured officers and soldiers are being interrogated and will be formally charged with treason and then face a military courts-martial. Captured organized militia and civilian insurrectionists will be processed and charged with treason, sedition, and insurrection."

"Matt, do we know any numbers yet for the casualties?"

"I've been trying to track down numbers. Sources at Berkeley Medical Center in Martinsburg, West Virginia, state they are treating 'hundreds of casualties.' There are other urgent care and smaller rural hospitals throughout that region of the state that are also telling us they are treating many, many casualties.

"Pentagon sources state that the ground campaign is now in high gear and that the administration is determined to bring a quick end to the rebellion. With this newest escalation of the Civil War, it's anybody's guess what happens next. This is Matt Sydney reporting from the White House."

THE ALLIANCE

THE OVAL OFFICE

Washington, D.C.

0700 EST — 2 Jan 2062

President Cyrus sat patiently at the Oval Office desk, listening to detailed reports from his inner circle of advisors. In the meeting were Chief of Staff Matt Kensington, Chairman of the Joint Chiefs of Staff Jeffrey Homer, NWBI Secretary Mosby Simmons, and a newcomer to the inner circle, NSA Director Kwame Thomas.

After twenty minutes of listening, Cyrus broke his silence, "These progress reports are encouraging. The Army of the New Way has subdued West Virginia, Indiana, Kentucky, parts of Tennessee, and Southern Illinois. We've got a toehold in Missouri and Arkansas. We're poised to strike the Deep South next. I know the losses have been more than anticipated, but I'm convinced the campaign's next phase will achieve a final victory. I think the Great Plains states will give up sooner rather than later, when we subdue the Deep South, I fully expect them to fold. I fully expect that all this will be over by July. General, when can we invade the South?

"Mr. President, we're finishing up the battle plans as I speak. We're looking at January twenty-second to begin operations. I'll be presenting the finalized battle plan in tomorrow's briefing."

"General, I'd like to talk some more about the situation out West. Things seem stalled out there. How can we break the stalemate?"

"Mr. President, we're doing everything we can. There's an issue with manpower out there."

"Excuse me, what did you say?"

"I meant personnel. We can't recruit enough personnel into the armed forces to fight. We're stretched thin."

"What about a draft?"

"You know how unpopular that is with the young people. Don't forget they're a big part of your constituency."

"They can't have their cake and eat it too. They want the New Way, then it looks like they're gonna have to put down their screens and fight for it. Matt, prepare an executive order for this afternoon. We're going to draft every person in college, whether they like it or not. General, our forces will swell dramatically in the coming weeks and months. Start preparing now for this surge of soldiers. Whatever you need, you'll get it. Also, I want a concall with the West Coast generals. Time to kick some ass if I must and tell them I want Northern California and all of Utah back under full federal control by the end of February."

"Yes, sir, Mr. President."

Cyrus next turned to NSA Director Kwame Thomas. "Kwame, what's the latest?"

"Having a hard time penetrating the inner workings of the rebellion leadership. They're all keeping their cards close to the vest. Encryption doesn't help us at all. We can't listen in on their open systems comm devices. The encryption is unbreakable."

Cyrus erupted. "Damn, Kwame, I don't want to hear 'can't.' I want more intel on these rebel bastards! I wanted it long before yesterday!"

"Yes, Sir, we'll double our efforts."

"Director Mosby, what is the NWBI doing to increase the apprehension of CONs on the wanted list? What about the re-education centers? How many are enrolled?"

"Mr. President, last week we just hired a thousand new agents. There'll be a lag time for their training to complete. In the meantime, our focused efforts have arrests up by thirty-seven percent since December 1. The re-education centers currently have close to two million enrolled students. We're working on expanding capacity as other occupied areas are liberated back into federal control."

"Excellent, Mosby, excellent. Sooner or later, we'll wipe this country clean of these sickos or die trying."

CHADRON MUNICIPAL AIRPORT

Chadron, Nebraska

0200 MST — 15 Feb 2062

The last several months had been grueling ever since the FEDs' victory at Shenandoah Junction, West Virginia, the previous July.

From there, the FEDs fought their way across West Virginia, finally subduing the rebellion there by the end of August. Next, they entered federally controlled Ohio on 11 September. From there, they rested, regrouped, and resupplied.

On 11 October, they swept into Indiana. The rebellion was put down at significant cost to both sides in terms of soldiers and materiel.

Then, on 18 November, they entered the rebel, self-proclaimed state of Southern Illinois. Fierce fighting raged for the rest of the month, with three large CON armies stymying the FEDs' advance. By 15 December, the CONs had been pushed back to Cairo, Illinois. There, they failed in a desperate attempt to keep the FEDs from crossing the Mississippi into Missouri.

Elsewhere, there were three other significant battles. In Kentucky, the Battle of Lexington on 22 September; in eastern Tennessee, the battles of Johnson City and Knoxville took place on 2 and 10 October, respectively. To date, the CONs had not won a major battle.

Throughout the Fall of 2061, local militias won several smaller battles against smaller federal units in various parts of New England, especially in upstate New York, parts of Long Island, Vermont, New Hampshire, and rural Maine. In many instances, notable numbers of LEOs (law enforcement officers) refused to fire on the local citizenry and often would quit on the spot and join up with the militias. After each minor victory, a counterattack by combined federal and loyalist National Guard forces crushed the local militias and rebel LEOs. Those who survived were sent to re-education camps. Leadership was arrested and charged with treason and insurrection. Although there were rumors of summary executions of CON leaders from these minor battles out east, none had been proven.

On the main battle fronts, the CONs continued to fight bravely. They had been reinforced by hundreds of thousands of armed citizens who had joined state militia groups and by irregular forces of local townspeople throughout the battle zones. Combined, they had put up fierce resistance, but to no avail as the FEDs' inexorable march westward ground on.

To the west lay a priceless treasure: the Great Plains—the new American Redoubt. For decades, it had been derogatorily called "flyover country" and branded as the home of the nation's so-called "basket of deplorables," a phrase coined by a politician many decades earlier. Insults aside, it remained the breadbasket of the fractured nation—a prize for any army that could take it—and hold it.

Hampering the CON's efforts was the supply chain. It ebbed and flowed from somewhat reliable to barely functioning. Although trade was limited, it continued with Mexico, Canada, and overseas, but people were going hungry in some places. Ever resourceful, Americans on both sides of the conflict rallied to establish victory gardens. The almost lost art of canning, well-known and still practiced in rural areas, spread like wildfire among suburbanites and city folks.

Cities and towns on the Great Lakes and inland waters organized large fishing fleets almost overnight, using sport fishing and other boats to catch food.

Rural folks had it much better, with grain stockpiles available in many counties. Plus, many rural areas were home to avid hunters who knew where fresh game could be found.

Medicine and biodiesel fuel oil were both becoming an acute issue in some locales. Herbal remedies had become quite popular, as had home brewing of biodiesel for non-electric vehicles. Fortunately, electricity was in adequate supply due to the miracle of the ion-solar panel.

On a cold February night in the middle of the Great Plains, Oklahoma Governor Mary Whitfield had called for a second secret meeting of all the governors and militia leaders in the Great Plains. They had all gathered in a hangar at a small municipal airport in the remote northwest Nebraska town of Chadron.

She had organized the meeting after the disastrous battle of Cairo, Illinois. The loss of the strategic town at the confluence of the Ohio and Mississippi Rivers, at the southernmost tip of Illinois, resulted in significant setbacks for the Army of Southern Illinois, the Army of Kentucky, and the Army of Missouri. The Army of Oklahoma had provided an entire division for the battle. Thankfully, most of them had safely retreated over the Mississippi and had made their way west to Sikeston, Missouri.

Motioning everyone to take their seats, the Governor opened the meeting with a prayer, "Heavenly Father, we come before you during this late hour with anxious hearts. We are hurting, and we ask for your divine wisdom as we meet here to discuss our defense of liberty, liberty that you gave to this nation at its birth nearly three hundred years ago. Lead us now, oh Lord, to victory. In the name of the Father, Son, and Holy Ghost. Amen."

She continued, "Everyone, I'd like to thank each of you for taking the significant risk of coming here at night. I especially want to thank Nebraska Governor Michael Yost for selecting this excellent and remote location for this meeting. I know we could have met over video. Still, I wanted all of us to meet in person to strengthen our resolve with personal assurances to one another, and specifically to sign this historic document.

"In my right ear, I have a comm with an encrypted channel with our military surveillance units. I'm pleased to assure you that all is quiet in the air and on the ground in this neck of the woods.

"We're all painfully aware of the current military situation in our struggle to defend liberty and to make the Union whole again under the banner of Old Glory and guided by the Declaration of Independence, the Constitution of the United States, and our Bill of Rights.

"In addition to continuing their push west, the FEDs are poised to open a separate campaign into the Deep South.

"I know that we've spoken recently about a unified command structure. Although it exists unofficially, I believe it is time to establish an official alliance within our military command and control structure under a single unified command. With our negotiations completed, I believe we're in agreement and can sign the charter for this extraordinary agreement, and introduce our new supreme commander over all our armed forces. "Governors, military leaders, ladies, and gentlemen, I'd like to formally introduce General James Buford, our newly appointed Supreme Allied Commander of all the Continental Army."

Sustained applause was heard as General Buford walked over and stood next to Governor Whitfield and Nebraska Governor Michael Yost. After shaking hands with both Governors, the general approached the microphone and quickly waved his hands to stop the applause.

"Governor Yost, Governor Whitfield, distinguished governors from all the liberty-loving and Constitutionalist states, ladies and gentlemen, I humbly accept this appointment to reorganize and better coordinate our combined military forces to achieve nothing less than full victory over these haters of the American way. Those who have hijacked a storied political party and embedded themselves in it like a tapeworm. Those who have conspired to brainwash millions of Americans, young and old alike, into rejecting our history, our ideals, and our founding documents. More applause was offered up. The general patiently waited a moment and then continued, "I cannot promise you an easy victory. I also cannot promise that loved ones near and dear to all of us will be spared from the maelstrom of Civil War 2.0. Such is the awful nature of armed conflict. But this I can promise you, those who join ranks with us to defend the cause of liberty and to restore the Union whole to a 'Government of the people, by the people and for the people,' a whole Union which is again based on the United States Constitution, such persons join a just, noble, and holy cause. Like the Founding Fathers, I also pledge my life, my fortune, and my sacred honor in defense of liberty."

As the general stepped away from the mic, Governor Whitfield shook hands with him. She approached the mic and spoke again, "This historic document is on the table before me. No one knows this, but I collect fountain pens. In my collection is my most treasured piece, a fountain pen once used by President George Washington. We will use that same pen to sign the agreement."

After a sustained round of applause, the governors, one by one, queued up to sign the historic document forming a new, powerful military alliance. It was one that they all hoped would change the course of the war. As each governor signed according to a predetermined protocol, then was individually ushered back to their awaiting aircraft, which immediately took off to their respective home state.

After the last governor had signed and left, Governor Whitfield stood against a backdrop of a large blowup of the Constitution. She then motioned to the cameraman that she was ready to record an address to the nation that would be broadcast later that evening. Once the recording was completed, Governor Whitfield and her entourage boarded their plane along with General Buford, where a meeting of various military leaders had been called.

In flight, General Buford conducted his first meeting. "Everyone, thank you for coming aboard. Later today, we'll surely get you back where you need to be.

"I've been given full authority to extend commissions to any personnel I believe can bring what we need to the table in this fight. I've privately asked Colonel Eric Adams to officially come out of retirement. His response was immediate and in the affirmative. I have commissioned Colonel Adams to lead all militia groups willing to join the Army of the Republic under a new unit, aptly named the 1776 Division. He and I are in full agreement that no white supremacists or Nazis will be permitted into our ranks. Colonel Adams, you've been promoted to Major General Adams. Congratulations."

Adams reached out and shook hands with Buford. "General, it is a high honor to again step up for the cause of liberty. I will do my duty, and I will not let you down."

Buford took his seat. "I know you will, Adams. It's great to have you back.

"Eric, I need you to get the word out to all the militias that we can't have everyone sign up, leave their posts, and come out west. We need good numbers to stay behind to provide intel and act as a guerrilla force if the war comes to their neck of the woods. Thoughts on that?"

"General, I propose we encourage the single men and women to come out here and form up. The married ones and the seniors can best serve the cause by remaining in their communities to act in whatever capacity is deemed necessary by their local commanders. We've got thousands of CONs that are current or retired county sheriffs, sheriff's deputies, local police chiefs, and local police officers with military backgrounds."

The general tapped his fingers a few times and continued, "I like that idea. Let's talk more about that later this afternoon.

"Next, I'm appointing Captain Lamarcus Washington as my aide-de-Camp under the rank of 1st Lieutenant. Lemarcus comes highly recommended to me by General Adams. Lemarcus was a crucial figure in the assault at Scott Air Force Base.

"Lemarcus—I know your family situation and the apparent contradiction with what General Adams just proposed here with married folks staying in their locales back home. Of course, some exceptions are bound to happen. Adams was insistent that you would be perfect as my aide in your case. Besides, I've never been accused of being a legalist, and it doesn't go well with being a realist."

The moment of levity brought quiet laughter to the meeting room.

General Buford continued, "We can get your family from wherever they are back east, out here, to a place far safer. There's more food out here, too."

"Thank you, general. I'm grateful for the opportunity to serve the cause of liberty. Getting my family out here sounds wonderful. They're currently holed up in a bug-out."

"I anticipated that response, and arrangements are already in the works. Offline, you can provide the information needed to extract your family from the bug-out and bring them safely back here."

"Thank you, general."

"Moving on, I've commissioned Sergeant Major Wallace Chamberlain to serve as brigadier general of a newly renamed Shenandoah Division. Plenty of good soldiers up and down the spine of the Blue Ridge. Wallace, what you did out at Harpers Ferry saving the Founding Documents is going to be in the history books someday. Mark my words."

"Thank you, General Buford. There's not a day that goes by that I don't think of Hancock."

"Eerie connection there, for sure. So, I'm attaching your unit to the newly designated Army of the Potomac under the command of General Steven Sickles."

"Army of the Potomac? Really? That's a name I last read in a history book."

"Well, damn, if some of our history isn't repeating itself. I always loved the name. I'm somewhat of a closet romantic. Anyway, they're forming up rapidly in northwest Georgia.

"Chamberlain, your orders are to conduct a search and confiscate or destroy missions of any federal forces throughout Appalachia from northwest Georgia clear on up into the Alleghenies in Pennsylvania. I've got a woman in mind to lead similar efforts in the Appalachians in New York. To be clear, your mission is to seek out military supplies for confiscation.

Wage war via hit-and-run battles, if possible, with a strict order to avoid civilian casualties. Understood? Additionally, food trucks bound for civilian grocery stores often confiscate half the load and leave the rest on the trucks. Clear?"

"Yes, Sir."

"Alright, now some even bigger stuff. I've chosen General McDowell to lead the newly formed Army of the Southern Great Plains. For starters, he'll be forming up out of Abilene, Kansas, and getting ready for the FEDs' push into Arkansas. After that, General James Lynette is commanding the Army of the Northern Great Plains. He'll be forming up out of Jamestown, North Dakota. Any questions?"

Colonel Patton spoke up, "General, I need a private word with you.

I want to discuss a plan I've been working on."

"Okay, Colonel. Everyone else, that's all. Get some rest. It'll be dawn soon."

|||| **18** ||||

BEING YELLOW

THE KING RESIDENCE

McHenry, Illinois

1645 CDT — 6 Apr 2062

Eleanor King was worried. Her husband, Lieutenant Colonel Jackson King of the Illinois National Guard, had not been heard from for a few days. This had happened before around major battles, but each time it had happened before, she held her breath and dreaded every ring of her comm.

Her best friend, Lyla, had been her frequent go-to since the war began. They spoke daily and often would visit each other's homes for a simple bite to eat. Today, Lyla called Eleanor later than usual after being out and about and looking for food. "How are you doin', friend?"

Eleanor was kneading some dough for a loaf of bread when she answered, "Been better. Every time the comm rings, my heart jumps into my throat. How are you today?"

"Worried about you, Sister. I take it no word from Jackson today?"

Eleanor paused, "Not a one. I've tried calling him twice. I just get an immediate voicemail. Say, have you had any issues calling folks out of the area?"

Lyla gave a hmmm, "Well, now that you mention it, I have. Must be part of the war problems."

"Like we don't have enough problems. The comm lines go down, there's gonna be a whole mess of upset people, me included. You comin' to prayer meetin' tonight? Come early."

Lyla paused to think for a moment, "You know, I think I will. Can I walk with you?

"Of course. Why don't you come over at five? I just picked some lettuce from our greenhouse, along with some tomatoes and cucumbers. I've got some soup left over from last night. Sound good?"

"Oh, Eleanor, that sounds nice. I went shopping today. Had a ration card for bacon and chicken. I finally found a store with some bacon and chicken. I got five strips of bacon and a chicken leg. Do you know that I have lost fifteen pounds since January? I needed to lose it, too. So, I guess this is a blessing in disguise."

"Yeah, well, just so this doesn't keep goin' on into next year. I heard some folks are really in a bad way in Chicago and other big cities. Lots of fighting and stuff."

Lyla sounded surprised, "Where did you hear that? It's not been on the news at all."

"Hey, come on over, and we'll talk more in person."

"Sure, I'll walk on over in ten minutes."

Eleanor made sure the comm call had hung up and then powered it off. Rumors were going around that even if your comm was turned off, it could still be used to listen in on their owners. She wasn't sure what to make of this latest conspiracy talk, but decided it was better to be safe than sorry. She had determined that any introduction of anything remotely political on a comm call would trigger a gracious ending of the call.

Immediately after turning the comm off, she jumped up from her chair and thought to herself, *You dummy—what if Jackson calls!* Startled by the thought, she quickly turned the device back on. She decided the best thing to do would be to have the ringer on full volume but leave the phone in the living room while she went on the front porch and waited for Lyla. At least she'd be out of earshot of any possible eavesdropping.

After about twelve minutes, Lyla walked over and came up onto the porch. Before picking up where they had left off, Eleanor spoke in hushed tones to her friend, "Your comm on you?"

Lyla looked puzzled, "No, I left it in the kitchen."

"Good. Listen carefully. From now on, if you want to talk about anything remotely political, let's talk out here unless the weather is bad. Then, we can go to the basement. No matter what, we can't be talkin' with either of our comms nearby. I got mine in the living room with the volume up in case Jackson calls. Understood?"

Lyla remained puzzled, "Sure, but what's up? What's with the secrecy?"

"There's a rumor goin' 'round that people can hear us over our comms even when we're not using them."

"What people? Who?"

"The New Way."

"But they're on our side."

"I'm not talkin' about sides. I'm talkin' about privacy. My conversations are private, and I have a right to my privacy."

"Girl, you almost sounded like a CON just now. You, okay? You do remember who started this war, right?"

Ellen was taken aback by the question. "What kind of a question is that? My husband's been gone for a year fighting, and at this exact moment I don't even know if he's alive or dead."

Lyla, taken aback by the sharp reply, changed her tone. "I'm sorry, Eleanor. Nerves, I guess. If it makes you feel any better, I'll respect your wishes."

"Thank you."

Lyla continued by bringing up a new subject. "What else did you do today?"

"Well, today I busied myself working the victory garden, bartered for raw food supplies, and did a little fishing in the Fox River at the dam to try and add to my food stocks. I caught some small bass and some crappie."

"Nice. Did you clean them?"

"Sure did. Worked with some of the neighbors behind our house. They've been helping me learn the art of cleaning fish. Also, smoking fish, and smoking meat and poultry, too. With things getting scarcer, this method is a great way to preserve food.

"I know there's still plenty of working farms all over the county, but their supply of food only goes so far."

Eleanor nodded in agreement, "That's right, Lyla. We got to do what we got to do in case food gets even more scarce."

"That's a scary thought, Eleanor. I swear I might die of fright one of these days."

"Don't you do no dyin' on me, Lyla! Don't even jest of it. We just got to keep prayin' that this war will be over by Christmas."

"Wouldn't that be wonderful?

"You know it's time for the nightly news. Sit with me, and we'll have a bite afterward."

"Thank you, Eleanor."

Eleanor grabbed the remote and turned on the TV. They settled into the couch to catch the news. The familiar face of the new anchor, Marian Moore, appeared on the screen right on cue for the voiceover introduction.

"This is the ANN Nightly News with Marian Moore. *America at War.* Here now, reporting from the ANN studios in New York, Marian Moore."

"Good evening. Today, federal forces suffered their third major defeat on the battlefield against CON rebel forces. Here is a live report from Darshan Treyvon from Columbia, South Carolina."

The screen cut away to a stark background of smoke, charred implements of war, and burned-out or pulverized buildings. Reporter Darshan Treyvon spoke, "The five-week Battle of Columbia is over. Federal forces are retreating over the border back into North Carolina. The stunning defeat comes on the heels of New Way losses at the Battle of Fargo in North Dakota last month. Before that, the stunning defeat of federal forces at the Battle of Kansas City.

"In Columbia, South Carolina, there was jubilation that the New Way forces were driven out. CON forces have been emboldened by their recent battlefield successes here in the South and out West. All these recent victories came on the heels of traitor CON General David

Buford's appointment as the so-called Supreme Allied Commander of the Continental Armies.

"The battle here was a fierce fight that saw repeated advances and withdrawals by both sides. Air forces dueled it out in the skies. It looked surreal, like something out of old film footage of World War II dogfights. Tossed into the mix were modern helicopter gunships as well as unmanned drone fighter jets. It was a hellish sight.

"Sources state that casualties are in the many, many thousands. "The recent successes of the rebels are being attributed to the Alliance that was formed earlier this year, in January. Recall that the historic moment saw all the governors of states in rebellion sign over Command and Control of each state's armed forces to the traitor General James Buford of Montana.

"Buford is known as a brilliant military planner and tactician. Buford has revamped the rebels' leadership posts from top to bottom and has brought his military planning prowess to turn the tide against our brave New Way forces. The battlefield results speak for themselves. The New Way forces steady march westward and southward has now been significantly challenged. Marian, back to you." The image cut away back to the studio in New York, where Marian continued, "Hampering the federal forces in the South, many New Way forces are tied up all up and down the Blue Ridge trying to track down and kill or capture the leader of the rebel so-called Shenandoah Division of the Army of Appalachia. His name is Brigadier General Wallace Chamberlain of West Virginia. His band of criminal rebels has been wreaking havoc with supply lines and winning a fair number of minor battles.

The results are tying up thousands of federal troops that could otherwise be redeployed elsewhere to reinforce our brave soldiers here in the South.

"Recall that it was this same Chamberlain who led the daring raid at Harpers Ferry, West Virginia, to steal the disgraced white supremacist documents known as the Declaration of Independence, the Constitution, and the Bill of Rights. The long-discredited documents were scheduled for burning on worldwide television on the former white supremacist holiday, the 4th of July. After they were stolen, President Cyrus officially banned the 4th of July as a holiday throughout lands under New Way control.

"Chamberlain's antics, and those of his soldiers that day, have served to make him somewhat of a legend among white supremacist patriot militia groups from coast to coast.

"Small skirmishes in rural areas have exploded in number. Every state in the New Way has seen a dramatic increase in rebel activity, which has been almost exclusively concentrated in rural areas. Most of them have been small skirmishes with DHS, ATF, and NWBI personnel who have been increasingly pressed into a paramilitary role. Local rural law enforcement has frequently been at odds with these federal law enforcement agencies. It is reported that substantial numbers of local police, county sheriffs, and deputy sheriffs have joined the side of the CONs in these localized clashes.

"At a press conference today, DHS spokesperson Kamala Beatrice stated that efforts to rein in rural areas under federal control are ongoing. Further, she noted that local law enforcement not enforcing emergency decrees are being arrested and held without bail under the provisions of martial law in effect from coast to coast.

"Now, from the Pentagon, Matt Sydney reporting."

Moore looked down at her monitor as the scene cut away to show the face of Matt Sydney, "At the daily press briefing here today, Pentagon spokesperson Rohit Edgar told reporters that the recent setbacks on the battlefield will be reversed soon. He attributed the optimistic statement to the swelling ranks of draftees at boot camps at federal bases on the East and West Coasts. They are soon to graduate and be deployed to shore up the New Way forces' depleted ranks. The surge, the product of President Devin Cyrus's executive order to draft all military-aged college students. "While there has been some unrest among the college draftees, most have complied and are being offered generous financial incentives after the rebellion is finally put down. Marian, back to you."

Cutting back to the studio, Marian Moore had a slight look of concern, "Next, here with us now, our veteran military analyst, General Merla Laylin, with our weekly review of the battle maps. General, it's been a tough go of it lately. What can you tell us?"

General Laylin stood before a large screen and began his delivery, "Marian, the battle map shows federal forces regrouping here in North Carolina, west of Charlotte. The 315th Corps, composed of the May Day Division and the Vinet Division, suffered heavy casualties in the Battle of Columbia. They have made a tactical withdrawal to resupply and await the arrival of the college recruits coming out of boot camp.

"Out west, the Army of the New Way is regrouping near Ozark, Arkansas. Recall the Army of the New Way, which is composed of the 308th and 501st Corps, a total of half a million soldiers. Among them is a growing legend, the 1619 Division.

"Despite recent setbacks by our forces in the field, my sources within the administration and at the Pentagon remain upbeat, with a new offensive being planned."

The scene ended with the general looking stoic, and cut away to Moore continuing the news, "In other war-related news, colleges across New Way states, continue to see massive protests regarding the ongoing military draft. A common theme is the protesters insisting on complete exclusion from the draft since they are 'the country's future leaders and influencers.' The Cyrus administration is threatening arrests for draft dodgers and will be making a statement on the matter at tomorrow's White House Press Briefing.

"In other news, the Cyrus administration is playing down reports of food shortages…"

With tears in her eyes, Eleanor King had heard enough and turned off the TV.

ARMY GROUP WEST FIELD HQ

Ozark, Arkansas

0700 CDT — 10 May 2062

A month earlier, General David Johnston had been handpicked by President Cyrus to take over command of the largest number of federal troops to wage combat on American soil since the First Civil War, two hundred years ago in the 1860s. The combined armies totaled over 600,000 troops under his command. Even so, Johnston was under no illusions about what lay ahead.

Johnston was an imposing figure at six-foot-six and 285 pounds. He had graduated from West Point twenty-five years earlier. He finished fifth in his class. As an officer in the North African War years earlier, Johnston had distinguished himself at the Battle of Sirte.

Today, somewhere out in the west in the vast ocean of amber waves of grain that are the wheat and cornfields of the Great Plains, his old friend from the academy and throughout most of his military career, General James Buford, was undoubtedly trying to outwit Johnston's plans with his own plans to turn back the FEDs' looming attack near Ft. Smith, Arkansas. As Johnston reviewed the final plans for the next big offensive push to the west, he took little comfort in knowing that Buford had been plotting and planning as well.

Johnston was not surprised to hear of Buford's sudden elevation to such a lofty position and responsibility over all the CON Army's. Buford was, without question, a keen military planner and tactician.

His organizational skills, particularly in selecting the right leaders for the right jobs within the right units, had resulted in dramatic reversals of fortune for the Continental Army. His prowess had quietly solicited admiration not only from his old friend Johnston but also from many of Johnston's contemporaries who were just as determined as Johnston was to put down the rebellion and usher in the utopian plans of the New Way. Walking in confidently to the meeting room at the hotel that had been commandeered to serve as his temporary headquarters, General Johnston walked over to the head of the table and returned the salutes of the general staff. "At ease." The general took his seat.

The officers followed his lead and took their seats as well. After a moment, the general stood up and walked over to a large map being projected on the wall of the conference room. "I want to thank each of you for your hard work and long hours that were required to get this battle plan finalized. As you know, the enemy is reorganized and reenergized. In short order, they have become a formidable fighting force, much more so than they were earlier this year. We will need to redouble our efforts to stay on top of the situation as the battle develops. Anything short of that could be disastrous. Questions?"

Brigadier General Sorenson spoke up, "Is Patton in the mix on this one, General?"

"I believe so. Intel reports that the Army of the Central Plains is headed south from the Kansas City area. Look, I know their success up in Kansas City, especially the 101st against us, is on all our minds, but they're coming up against a much larger force down here. We've learned some valuable lessons since then. Lessons that we're going to use today."

"Care to elaborate on that, general?" asked Sorenson.

"We have a better understanding of how Patton operates. He's a maverick of sorts. He takes unnecessary risks. He's arrogant. He's a showoff and loves to do the unorthodox. So far, he's pulled it off. Not gonna have it this time. I've read his book. We're going to bag the entire 101st by battle's end. Follow the plan, everyone, and we'll crush these damn CONs. Dismissed."

ARMY OF THE CENTRAL PLAINS HQ

Near Alma, Arkansas

0647 CDT — 13 May 2062

After the brilliant victory in Kansas City, Colonel Patton had been promoted to brigadier general commanding the CONs 606th Corps.

The Battle of Ft. Smith, Arkansas, had been raging for three long and bloody days. Now, on 13 May, the 101st Corps, part of the CON Army of the Central Plains, was in a jam. The 101st was cut off from the 82nd Corps of the CON Army of the Southern Plains to their west. Patton's 606th Corps was tied up fighting a significant element of the FEDs' 501st Corps between Alma and Dyer, Arkansas.

The 82nd Corps was at risk of being trapped 30 miles to the west in Gans, Oklahoma. From their near entrapment at that location in Gans, Oklahoma, and due South of the Arkansas River, the other half of the CON Army of the Southern Plains, 22nd Corps, was tied up and in a fierce tank and artillery duel with the FED's 308th Corps near Panama, Oklahoma. The FEDs' General Johnston, commander of Army Group West, had ordered an entire division from the westernmost point of the 308th Corps to break off, swing west, and then drive north in an attempt to encircle the CONs' 82nd Corps.

CON General Brandon McDowell of the Army of the Southern Plains had radioed General Patton for help.

On the first day of the battle, the Army of the Central Plains arrived late on the 10th, which enabled the 82nd Corps to regain ground it had lost earlier in the day. The 101st Corps armored divisions had proven their skill and dogged determination once again. A reversal of fortune occurred on day two of the battle, with the FEDs 1619 Division punching a hole in the CON line to the north of Ft. Smith. The line was composed of elements of the 82nd Corps and the 101st Corps. The FEDs' air cover had been superb with the deployment of the FEDs' Combat Air Drones. They had given fits to the CON Air Force.

Federal forces, spearheaded by the 1619 Division, had successfully pushed through Ft. Smith, Arkansas, on the state's shared western border with the state of Oklahoma. The FEDs' hard-fighting drive to the north and South of the CON forces had created a pocket. A pocket that now threatened to quickly devolve into an encirclement of both the CONs 82nd Corps and 22nd Corps and, thus, the near destruction of the Army of the Southern Plains.

The pocket had quickly been named the Gans-Panama Pocket. To save the Army of the Southern Plains from destruction, Supreme Allied Commander of the Continental Armies, General James Buford, was on the verge of ordering General McDowell to have the 22nd Corps and a small part of the 82nd Corps retreat north over the Arkansas River via the U.S. 59 bridge. The tactical withdrawal would enable a linkup with the main body of the 82nd Corps north of the river. From there, a tactical withdrawal to Sallisaw, Oklahoma, to regroup, which would be vital to the defense of the approaches to Oklahoma City, the state capital, straight west on I-40. Over the din of artillery fire, Patton had to yell into the radio set, "Brandon, I'm gonna do all I can to try and help you out, but damned if we're not having a helluva time with the FEDs' Blanc Division on our left over here in Alma. We've got our artillery zeroed in on 'em now, and we're givin' 'em hell!"

General Patton listened to General Brandon McDowell's plea for help. "David, the left flank of the 82nd is in danger of collapse. As of this moment, the 1619 has the upper hand. If our left flank collapses, the whole thing comes crashing down on our heads, and we're done! Can you do anything?"

"What's their position now, Brandon?"

"Sending coordinates now!"

"Brandon, tell your boys to hang on. The cavalry is coming!"

"Get us out of this jam, and I'll be indebted to you!"

"You just tell those boys to hang on! Keep given' 'em hell! I don't care if I have to commandeer one of our tanks and come all alone. We're gonna get those bastards!"

General McDowell hung up and quickly called Brigadier General Theodore Leesman, Commanding General of the 1776 Division of the 82nd Corps. "Teddy, tell your troops to hang on. Patton says he's coming!"

"How long before he gets here?"

"Not sure. Look, if the line collapses there, we lose the whole thing and quite possibly the war. Can you hang on?"

"Shit, yeah! I just had a runner from the 1619 come over under a flag of truce. He hands me some damn letter from General Hood insisting we surrender."

"How did you reply?"

"I grabbed a phrase right out of World War II's Battle of the Bulge lore! 'Nuts!' is all I wrote. When the runner left, he had a dumbfounded look on his face. The poor fellow probably went to a school where they don't teach that stuff anymore. I told my staff that surrender is not an option."

"Good show, Teddy! Listen, we can't lose the 1776! Your call when and if the time comes to make a tactical withdrawal. That's an order! We'll deal with the aftermath later, but win or lose, the 1776 must survive this battle! Clear?"

"Yes, sir. Don't worry, general, we'll hang on. I have an idea. We'll talk soon! Thanks, Buddy!"

"Godspeed, Teddy!"

"Godspeed indeed!"

Within moments of hanging up, a dense fog began to envelop the 1776 Division. The day had started earlier with a light mist. It now grew denser seemingly by the moment. Although the implements of modern warfare had the means to "see" through a thick fog, the fog's presence quickly disoriented the soldiers. Fog or no fog, the 1776 artillery batteries continued to pour fire downrange on the FEDs.

1619 DIVISION FORWARD POSITION

Northwest of Muldrow, Oklahoma

0837 CDT — 13 May 2062

Sergeant DeShawn King was in the thick of it again. He was exactly where he wanted to be, in a tank and fighting hard. He was glad the commander of the 1776 Division had refused to surrender. The 1619 Division was fixing to destroy it today.

A month ago, King had been offered another promotion but had turned it down because it meant he would have been sent to the rear and out of harm's way. King was on a mission to get whatever pounds of flesh he could for the cause of the New Way and to destroy the Old Way once and forever.

Bagging the 1776 Division would lead to the collapse of the 82nd Corps. He had been made aware of the FEDs' successes to his south and west against the CONs' 22nd Corps as well. The thought had come to his mind that this could be the day of the most significant victory of the war. One that could finally pave the way for the full agenda of the New Way. A new era of promise was a fleeting thought.

His squad was using infrared to see through the thick fog that had unexpectedly settled on their position. King's tank squad was in the lead. They had advanced approximately two hundred yards beyond the CON artillery barrage. While many of the tanks of his and five other squads had traversed outside the area where the shells were exploding, the rear echelon of the column had gotten caught right in the thick of the barrage and was being decimated.

King had to put that out of his mind and focus on the task at hand. He knew they were attacking the very end of the CON's defensive line in this sector. He also knew they were up against the 1776 Division, a tough outfit. But, if his tank column could battle its way through and swing left, the 82nd Corps of the CON Army was in danger of encirclement and possibly capture, or preferably, in King's mind, annihilation.

The decision for the 1619 Division to push hard to the northwest and take on the CONs' left flank held by the 1776 Division while leaving behind the rest of the FED's 501st to tie up Patton's 101st and 606th Corps was turning out to be a brilliant tactical decision. Despite losing some of the tanks to the rear, the forward elements that had advanced past the artillery barrage were having a field day in a target-rich environment.

With the line being held by the 1776 Division in imminent danger of collapse, DeShawn King and his squad of tanks were feeling near jubilation. "Hell, boys, I think we're real close to bagging these bastards! New target! Lasing target. Stand by—range—112 meters. Target is stationary! Give me a *HEAT* round and fire when ready!"

CON Tanker Isabel Inez was the platoon leader. With an all-female crew, she and her crew had earned a reputation as a tough bunch of tanker gals that had held their own now through three tank battles. Now, here in their fourth, there was nothing to her squad's left flank except undefended country. She understood that allowing the 1619 to take that ground and outflank her position, then swing down and around to the rear, could spell defeat for the CON forces. "Rachel, we just got lased. Launch countermeasures now!"

Flipping a switch, tanker Rachel Nam activated their AITAC (Artificial Intelligence Tank Countermeasures), which autoloaded a special intercept round into the barrel. Once the AITAC was activated, all operations of the tank were temporarily taken over by the onboard AI.

"Activated! Brace!" yelled Nam.

While bracing and praying, Inez watched for the flash of light from the FEDs tank barrel 112—meters away. She saw the flash and simultaneously heard the telltale sound of the AITAC round fire out of Inez's tank main gun. The AITAC round instantly intercepted and detonated with the incoming HEAT round from the federal tank at a mere fifty yards from Inez's position. While they were pummeled with shrapnel and a fireball that quickly dissipated, there had been no harm done to her, her crew, or their tank. The CONs' secret new weapon had worked flawlessly.

Now it was Inez's turn, "New target! Lasing target! 112—meters! Stationary! Sabot round—fire when ready!"

King had waited expectantly to see the HEAT round destroy another tank filled with holdouts of the Old Way. His squad had destroyed at least ten tanks, and he had delighted in seeing each CON tank go up in flames. He saw the bright flash, followed by the near-instant sound of the concussion and the sight of the plume of smoke. *Another one,* or so he thought. With the smoke clearing, he could see that the CON tank was unscathed. "Shit—that's the third time today I've seen that! What the hell are they using that they can intercept my tank rounds!"

Just then, the lasing alarm went off. King screamed into the headset, "Evasive maneuver now!"

The driver had just floored the gas, causing the tank to lurch barely a meter or two laterally toward the CON tank's position. A millisecond later, King was knocked unconscious as the sabot round grazed his tank. The timing of the driver's small lateral motion was just enough to escape a catastrophic hit. Dazed but alive, his entire crew had survived a normally lethal hit as the round had just missed by a centimeter, not penetrating the turret. Even so, the shock wave momentarily knocked the entire crew unconscious. Coming to, King yelled again into the headset, "Shit, that was close, back the hell up and take cover just below that rise behind us!"

TEMPORARY COMMAND POST

Two Miles Northwest of Bokoshe, Oklahoma

1237 CDT — 13 May 2062

With heavy fighting having raged most of the morning and now into the early afternoon, Lieutenant Colonel Jackson King and his unit had been attached to the main tip of the spear, the FEDs Rainbow Division. The crack elements of the division had been driving hard to encircle the CON's 22nd Corps. The main body of the 22nd was now due east of their position. King's unit was the end of the left flank for the Rainbow Division.

With incoming artillery and tank rounds, King and his officers had taken cover behind a row of armored vehicles. King felt sick to his stomach. He had had his fill of death for one day. Devotion to duty compelled him onward, but inside, he was ripping apart.

In the twinkling of an eye, a 75 mm artillery round landed twenty or so yards away from them. The explosion killed everyone except King. A moment before the blast, he had run to the other side of the armored vehicle to fetch a paper map from the driver's seat because his tablet had malfunctioned. The blast threw him hard to the ground and knocked him out for a moment. Coming to, his ears ringing profusely, he scanned the area. An entire volley had blanketed everything within a hundred yards of where he and his commanders had stood. Noticing no movement anywhere near his position and being momentarily deaf, he walked among his fallen staff, slowly kneeling and checking each one of them for any signs of life. They were all gone. In shock and overcome with emotion, he knelt again and prayed over their bodies. When he was done, he stood up, zombie-like, and started walking towards the northwest.

After walking an hour or so, he came to a farmhouse and slowly walked towards the door. A dog started barking. King stood still. The door opened and out came a man, limping and brandishing an assault rifle pointed right at King's chest.

"Hold it up there, fella. Hands up in the air, nice and high, where I can see them both. Who are you?"

"Lieutenant Colonel Jackson King of the Illinois National Guard of the Army of the New Way. I just walked over an hour away from the battle over there near a town called Bokoshe."

The farmer was a middle-aged white guy. To King, the farmer looked stout, strong as an ox. He had a no-nonsense look about him.

Suntanned and leather-skinned, the farmer looked a little surprised to see King. "Well, you're standing on true U.S. soil, that's for sure. Out East, whatever the hell they call themselves now, as far as I'm concerned, is occupied territory with no resemblance whatsoever to the real United States.

"Out here, we're the ones that support the founding documents that y'all were fixin' to burn to ashes on live TV on the 4th of July last year. Oh, and let's not forget that day of infamy started with y'all blowing up Mount Rushmore. Killed two hundred three people, as I recall. What's the phrase you LIBs like to use? 'Burn it all down,' wasn't that it?"

Convinced the death of another Black man at the hands of a white guy with a gun was but a moment away, King resigned himself to the thought and responded matter-of-factly, "I'm not here to argue about that."

Angry, the farmer yelled, "Well then, what the hell are you here for? Are you being yellow and deserting? If you are, I guess technically, you're my prisoner."

Exhausted, King stood there motionless and speechless. The farmer yelled again, "Well, what do you have to say for yourself?" Still sullen, King kept his hands raised high. He looked down at the ground for a moment. The thought remained with him, *This White guy is about to shoot me down dead. Dear Jesus, please help me!*

Raising his head and making clear eye contact with the farmer over the barrel of his gun, King answered, "Sir, here and now, I completely renounce the New Way. I renew my pledge of allegiance to the flag, the Stars and Stripes of the United States of America. I renew my pledge to uphold now and forever more, the founding documents: the Declaration of Independence, the Constitution of the United States, and the Bill of Rights. I renew my pledge to uphold the republic for which the Stars and Stripes stand for, one nation under God, indivisible, with liberty and justice for all. I pledge to defend the Constitution from all enemies, foreign and domestic. Sir, I would like to defect."

As he was reciting his pledge, King witnessed the farmer's stance and countenance begin to relax. As King continued, the farmer slowly began to lower his weapon. Just as he said the final words, the door behind the farmer opened, and out walked onto the porch an attractive black-as-night woman. Somewhat cowering behind her were two beautiful children, a boy and a girl, of mixed race. Both appeared to be under ten years of age.

The farmer turned his back for a moment, put his weapon down, and leaned it up against the wall. He then turned back to face King again and extended a hand of greeting. "Well, Lieutenant Colonel King, you can put your hands down now. I want to welcome you back to the United States of America. It's a bit smaller than it used to be, but some good patriots are workin' on fixin' that. Meet my wife Cleo, son Nick, and daughter Isabella.

"Isabella, run inside and fetch my comm and a tall glass of lemonade for the Lieutenant here—hurry."

ARMY OF THE SOUTHERN PLAINS FIELD COMMAND HQ

Two Miles Southwest of Gans, Oklahoma

1759 CDT — 13 May 2062

General Brandon McDowell turned and yelled at the radioman, "Get me General Armistead."

After a moment, the radioman handed McDowell the headset. "William, what's the latest?"

"Brandon, I just gave the order to begin an orderly withdrawal to the north over the Rt. 59 bridge. Our right flank is starting to collapse as I speak."

"Okay, I'll do what I can to get you some air cover."

Just then, a radar operator yelled out, "Multiple bogeys coming up low and fast from the South. They just started popping in and out on the returns a moment ago."

"How many?" McDowell yelled.

The radar operator yelled. "Standby."

Five seconds later, the callout: "Hundreds!"

"ETA?" McDowell asked.

"In moments!"

Stunned, McDowell cursed, "Damn. Withers, what air assets can we divert?"

"Not much, Sir. Not if we want to help save the 22nd with what we have left on the scene and still be in the fight in support of the 82nd."

Exasperated, General McDowell looked around the room with the look of a chess player who knew they had just been checkmated. "Ladies and gentlemen, this could be it. If it is, it's been an honor to serve with you all."

Looking over to an MP near him, he calmly gave an order, "Sergeant Rubin, step outside, observe, and report back."

MP Sergeant George Rubin stepped outside the tent and looked to the South. He heard a growing roar and saw a terrifying sight as hundreds of aircraft fast approached. Some others had heard the roar as well and had stopped to look up. Sergeant Rubin closed his eyes and said a quick prayer. Before he was done, the aircraft were right on top of their position. With eyes closed, he waited to hear the explosion that would usher him into eternity. He thought, *"Today, I guess I die."*

Inside the command post, the radio crackled over the loudspeaker, "Attention General Brandon McDowell of the CON Army of the Southern Plains. This is Captain Héctor de Santa Anna of the Republic of Texas Air Force. Sorry, we're late—we're here to help and have immediately started attacking New Way forces. Please pass the word along to avoid friendly fire."

In a moment, the sounds of explosions out towards the FEDs' 308th Corps position immediately grew in intensity.

The personnel in the tent erupted in cheers. After getting a quick confirmation from the front that the 308th was under heavy air assault, a visibly euphoric McDowell yelled into the mic, "General, you just made our day! Remember the Alamo!"

Captain Santa Anna responded, "Remember the Alamo indeed, and also proclaim liberty throughout the land!"

"I'm a soldier, not a singer, but if I could belt out The Yellow Rose of Texas right now, I sure would!" McDowell laughed, as did everyone in the tent.

"General, save that song for later when we meet. I can actually carry that song pretty well. Although my distant relative General Antonio López de Santa Anna would most definitely not approve."

The room erupted in laughter. Just then, the radioman handed a note to General McDowell. He read it out loud. It was from Brigadier General Theodore Leesman, "Miracle! Armored column from Patton's 101st has smashed through the 1619 to relieve the 1776! The 1619 has turned tail and is retreating toward Ft. Smith!"

McDowell looked up and smiled. More cheers erupted, then he yelled out, "Someone get General Buford back on the line! We're not withdrawing!"

IIII **19** IIII

ON AND ON

A videoconference was moments away. All the Constitutionalist state governors and the top military leaders of the Alliance would attend remotely. Governor Whitfield felt encouraged as she picked up the secure line connecting her to the President of the Republic of Texas, Samuel González. After a moment, he was on screen along with the rest of the invited civilian and military leadership of the Alliance.

Feeling a deep sense of gratitude towards Texas, Mary opened with a direct word to the President of Texas, "Mr. President, this is Governor Mary Whitfield of Oklahoma. I think I speak for all the governors and military leaders on this call. We can't even begin to thank you enough for yesterday's decision to join the fight. It was the right one. I am sure you'll not regret it. Our mutual love of liberty and freedom will propel us together towards victory over a common enemy."

"Thank you, Governor. The decision wasn't easy to send our soldiers into harm's way. After long deliberations, we felt it was just a matter of time before Cyrus would turn his sights on us. It just made sense that with our core values identical to the CON states, Texas should choose to ally itself with all of you in this fight to restore the United States to Constitutional rule."

"President González, we couldn't agree more. Welcome to the fight, and I look forward to additional planning sessions with you and your team soon.

"Okay, everyone, let's continue. I want to bring in the Supreme Allied Commander of the Continental Armies, General James Buford. Before starting this call, I asked General Buford to give a complete rundown of our progress on the battlefield. General."

"Governor Whitfield, Mr. President, and to all other freedom-loving governors and leadership, good morning. Today, I have much to report. "First, our Pioneers Army Group, composed of the Army of the Rockies, the Army of Greater Idaho, and the Army of the Southwest, has done a tremendous job keeping all New Way military operations tied up all up and down the West Coast. They are pretty much locked down and unable to come even close to the Continental Divide, much less the Great Plains. We control the airspace from the Rockies clear over to the eastern edges of the Great Plains.

"The Army of the Southwest has liberated large parts of eastern and northern Arizona, as well as all of Southern Nevada. We've liberated several counties along the far southeastern edge of the California border that share a border with those liberated areas of Southern Nevada and Northern Arizona.

"The Army of Greater Idaho has liberated a large chunk of northwestern and northern Nevada along its shared border with the State of Northern California and the State of Greater Idaho.

"General Eric Adams of the Rocky Mountain Militia has done a great job of keeping the patriot militias well-trained, disciplined, and supplied. Their guerrilla tactics have been a significant component in our fight. For instance, the Northern-Cali Patriot Militia scored a major victory last evening by knocking out the largest ammo train to date.

"Moving on. Commander Rachel Cortez, commander of the Arizona Constitutionalist Militia, just received a commission as an attaché to the Army of the Southwest Navajo Division. Cortez is half Navajo and will be a great asset in coordinating our military actions in the Southwest.

"Army Group Southeast, composed of the Army of the Carolinas–Georgia, as well as the Army of the Gulf States, has had recent successes against the FEDs Army Group South.

"With over three-quarters of a million troops, our forces have pushed back the Army of the DSP and the Army of the New Light. The DSP has been pushed back to the north and east out of Atlanta. New Light is just north of Charlotte. It's no secret that the FEDs badly wanted those two cities for retribution measures, considering the Awakening movement occurring in those areas just over four months ago. The movement has energized the populace of the town and suburbs towards Liberty's Light.

"The FEDs have an iron grip control over the eastern portions of the Carolinas and a small bulge here in southeastern Georgia along the coast.

"We cannot allow the FEDs to take Atlanta. It's key to holding the South. We also cannot allow them to take Charlotte. Our positions in both those metro areas are tying up vast numbers of federal troops and materiel in the mid-Atlantic region, which, otherwise, could be diverted out to the fight out West.

"As you know, Army Group Yankee was our most significant fighting force, composed of three field armies: the Army of the Potomac, the Army of Appalachia, and the Army of the Tennessee.

"The Army of the Potomac has seen the worst casualty numbers and has been severely depleted—down about forty percent of their peak strength. They've had a rough go of it. Their losses, of course, were due to the FEDs' successes early on, particularly in West Virginia and Ohio. We have aggressive efforts underway to rebuild its three depleted divisions: the Washington, the Lexington, and the Concord. We expect to have them back in the fight in six to eight weeks.

"We have many fighting-age, single people streaming in from all over the country wanting to sign up for the fight. Many have risked their lives to cross from New Way territory to CON territory. A fair number of converts out of the New Way are greatly disillusioned by what Cyrus and the New Way movement have done to their lives. Word is the converts are rife with patriotic fervor. All the recruits are being boot camped just as fast as we can get them."

Governor Whitfield had patiently waited to ask a painful question. Buford's comments on the high casualty rate of the Army of the Potomac had created the opening she was looking for. "General, it's always on all our minds. What are the latest casualty counts?"

"Yes, Governor. Always a painful topic. Our current totals are as follows: 40,327 KIA; 13,459 injured; 5,001 missing in action. We're still putting the numbers together from the Battle of Ft. Smith. We're also upwardly revising the numbers from Kansas City and some of the smaller action west of the Rockies. On the FEDs' side, we have proof that they have been lying about their casualty numbers. Reliable sources out East provided the following federal casualty numbers: 45,707 KIA; 12,866 injured; 7,512 missing in action. We have reason to believe the MIA count includes somewhere around a five percent desertion rate. Most of them were apparently college kids forcibly conscripted.

"As for the rest of Army Group Yankee, they've fared better. The Army of the Tennessee saw substantial victories in the Volunteer State at the Battles of Knoxville, Cleveland, and Chattanooga. These three victories came on the heels of the failed attempt by the FEDs to acquire, by force of arms, the approaches to Atlanta from the north via Dalton, Georgia, by way of Chattanooga.

"The Army of Appalachia has lately been kicking some serious ass all up and down the Blue Ridge and the Smokies. Chamberlain and his troops have become living legends out there. His Shenandoah Division has retaken large swaths of the lower half of West Virginia. They've also managed to liberate a large chunk of southeastern Ohio.

"Out here in the Great Plains, a great victory at the Battle of Ft. Smith the other day. The three-day battle see-sawed back and forth. On the last day, the 82nd was in the process of losing its right flank and had just received orders to withdraw back to Sallisaw, Oklahoma.

"Up around here near Muldrow, Oklahoma, the 1619 Division had driven hard out of Ft. Smith to the northwest and came within a few tanks of outflanking the 1776 Division. Combined, the success of the

FEDs threatened to encircle and destroy the entire Army of the Southern Plains. I dare say it could have cost us the war.

"Well, we all know what happened. The Texas Air Force flew in and joined the fight here to save 22nd Corps between the town of Panama, Oklahoma and the Arkansas River. I'd like General Weland Happ, Secretary of the Texas Army, to speak on their after-action report."

General Happ appeared on the center screen to address the meeting, "Good morning. As you know, the Texas Air Force and the Texas 1st Armored Cavalry entered the fight as well, racing in from the South along U.S. 59 through Heavener, Oklahoma. From there, they fanned out and began attacking the FEDs' 308th Corps from the rear. That action was decisive. Up here between Muldrow and Liberty, Oklahoma, elements of Patton's 101st Corps broke through the 1619 and sent them into a full retreat into and out of Ft. Smith.

"To sum up, the combined forces of the Texas Army and Air Forces, the Army of the Southern Plains and the Army of the Central Plains, and our allied air forces continue to push federal forces back towards eastern Arkansas. The FEDs are in full retreat throughout the state."

General Buford now appeared on screen, "We also had a great victory at the Battle of Kansas City earlier last month. Although it was smaller in scope, it was strategically important. Up north in the Dakotas, we're on the offensive. The Army of the Northern Plains has pushed federal forces back into Minnesota. Plans are to keep driving the FEDs back to the east into Wisconsin.

"I have every confidence in our armed forces. I believe the tide has turned throughout the theatre of war.

"I know this has been the mother of all briefings. I appreciate your patience. But are there any questions?"

After a brief silence, Kansas Governor Hill spoke up, "Thank you, General Buford. I want to personally congratulate not only you but everyone up and down the line for the great victory here in Kansas City. General Longstreet and I were talking last night. We spoke at length about the dramatic reversal of fortunes the Continental Army has had since you took over as Supreme Commander. Well done. We thank you for the tremendous job you've done since taking command. General Buford, can you tell us what you're hearing regarding armed rebellion in New Way territory at the county level? The New Way press censorship has been quite successful in suppressing adverse news."

General Buford paused and then replied, "First of all, thank you, Governor Hill. We have a great team of senior leadership. Of course, full freedom of the press remains sacrosanct out here in CON-land. As to your question specifically, I'd like to have General Eric Adams of the 1776 Division answer that. He has been digging into those rumors. Eric."

After a bit of shuffling, the focal image of the videoconference switched over to General Adams.

"Good morning, all. Been an excellent briefing with all the encouraging news. Governor, that's an excellent question. Our sources indicate that many counties out East are not complying with the New Way policy changes. Recall that the Federal Firearms Confiscation Act outlawed all guns except over-and-under double-barrel shotguns and the new .22LR dual-shot rifles, both types for hunting only, and only for certain times of the year. Well, the law has backfired and energized the resistance in CON counties and even some MOD counties.

"For example, New York counties Allegany, Chenango, Delaware, Essex, Fulton, Greene, Hamilton, Jefferson, Lewis, Orleans, Oswego, Saratoga, Schoharie, Steuben, Tioga, Warren, Washington, Wayne, and Yates Counties have all voted for secession and are now preparing for armed resistance via local militias and what they call 'County Forces.' We're checking, but we believe 'County Forces' refers to local sheriffs who are in rebellion.

"We're also getting similar reports of unrest from CON counties up and down New England and the Great Lakes. Of note, a particularly strong-armed resistance movement has sprung up in McHenry, Kane, and DuPage Counties, located outside Chicago, Illinois, in the Fox River Valley. Joining them are several other counties along the Illinois side of the Mississippi River, especially outside of Galena.

"In Jo Daviess County in far northwest Illinois, in the town of Galena. New Way supporters have burned down the museum home of President U.S. Grant, recall, the 18th President of the United States and the same Grant who commanded the Army of the Potomac during the First Civil War of the 1860s under President Lincoln."

Governor Whitfield queried, "Any fallout from that, Colonel?"

"Yes, the town is now surrounded and cut off from the outside world by a newly formed militia force called Grants Militia. They're demanding an unconditional surrender of the entire city government and police force. We're hearing that most of the town's citizens gave up their weapons five months ago as part of the New Way mandatory firearms confiscation program. The rural folks, of course, did not comply. The bottom line is that without federal assistance, the town has no chance. Helping our cause further, Jo Daviess County Sheriff Roberta Sanchez and her deputies have sided with the CONs. The Illinois State Police in that district are also fully CON and in mutiny with their superiors at the State Capitol in Springfield. Galena is outnumbered and outgunned. Therefore, we may soon come into possession of a major rail depot that could enhance opportunities for offensive operations into Illinois.

"I know most of you have probably never heard of Galena. I have and spent some time there twenty years or so ago. I became familiar with the area and was surprised to see the extensive rail network that intersected there from all four points of the compass. I can't emphasize this enough: this would be a huge strategic gain if we can liberate Galena."

Iowa Governor Otis Oldenburg entered the conversation, "General Buford, we'd love to help here. We've been building up a rapid reaction force based out of Dubuque. Sort of a home guard unit, if you will. The local force was created if the FEDs ever tried to enter northeast Iowa from the Illinois side of the Mississippi. I've met the commander and the soldiers of this unit. The commander is the mayor of Dyersville. The rest are a mix of farmers and city folk. Among them are about two dozen LEOs and SWAT members. They are as fine a group of part-time soldiers as you'll ever find—fierce patriots, too. Most have combat experience. Dubuque is just across the river from Galena, Illinois. I know they'd help."

"How big is the force, Governor?" Buford asked.

"I thought it was a little over a thousand. Let me check on the exact number and get back to you."

"Okay, we have some assets in Wisconsin that could be added to this. I'll check and contact you offline."

Governor Whitfield chimed in, "General Adams, thank you for your report. Everyone else, I know we've gone long. Let's plan to reconvene again soon. Before we sign off, I'd like to invite South Dakota Governor Jordan Willa to say a few words about a possible restoration effort at Mount Rushmore."

"Thank you, Governor Whitfield. Yes, our team on the ground has made some progress, but it's slow going. The rocks are huge chunks of granite. We're slowly cataloging them one by one by laser imaging each boulder as it's removed from the rubble pile. It's a massive jigsaw puzzle, and it remains unclear if we can accomplish what we're attempting to do. Stay tuned."

"Thank you, Governor Willa. Thank you all. I know it was a long meeting. I'll send an invite for the next meeting. Stay safe."

ANN Studios

Washington, D.C.

0900 EDT — 21 May 2062

Veteran on-air personality Ian Muldrow had been the national host of the most–watched Sunday morning program in the country for a decade. At fifty-five years of age and with a full head of salt-and-pepper colored hair, Muldrow was under no illusion that the popular Meet the Newsmakers show was a critical conduit for New Way thought. Seated on his cushioned chair, Ian awaited the intro to the show. "This is the ANN Meet the Newsmakers show with your host, Ian Muldrow.

Now live from our studios in Washington—here is your host, Ian Muldrow!"

"Good Sunday morning to you all. I'll be your host for the next hour. We have a packed show today, bringing you all the news from across New Way America. To start things off, our first guest is Chairman of the Joint Chiefs of Staff, General Jeffrey Homer. General, good morning."

"Good morning, Ian. Thanks for having me. Great to be on your show again."

"General, it has been a trying time with Old Way rebels responsible for the deaths of thousands of New Way citizens. What can you tell us about the military situation at this time?"

"Since the beginning of the rebellion, our troops have done a tremendous job in fighting them with everything they've got. It's been hard work, and it was not without sacrifice. We've had tremendous success on the battlefield. Although there have been some recent setbacks, we believe our upcoming operations are poised to bring decisive victory in the summer months."

"What can you tell us about those plans?"

"For operational and security reasons, there is not much I can say about that. However, it suffices to say that the Cyrus administration remains committed to bringing the rebellion to an end as soon as possible. I'm in daily strategic meetings with the President, and we remain on the same page regarding the ultimate goals of the President and the New Way. We will never allow the Old Way to return."

"General, what's the latest from Ft. Smith and the sneak attack launched by Texas when we were so close to victory that day?"

"As you know, Texas and the administration had a secret non-aggression pact. Texas broke that pact and will pay dearly for its aggression. Their outrageous actions cost the lives of thousands of brave soldiers that day."

"General, speaking of enemies, the military was recently put in charge of providing security for the Enlightenment Camps. How's that going?"

"Yes, we're using older troops, age fifty and older, to be exact. The younger soldiers are needed for the front lines.

"The job of these older troops is to keep the camps safe and secure from outside agitators and infiltrators and from those inside who have been described as hard-core Old Way people.

"They are not responding to counseling or drug therapy at all. Quite often, they attempt to escape or instigate camp riots. They present quite the challenge to our security personnel and are a clear danger to the stability and goals of the camps and the community at large if they escape."

Ian looked down at his notes and continued, "What happens to the incorrigibles, General?"

"They are removed from the camp and sent elsewhere."

"Where to?"

General Homer was quick to reply, "That, I'm afraid, is classified."

"Has anyone graduated from the Enlightenment Camps yet?"

"Yes. Tens of thousands have been restored to their communities, where they're settling back into their daily lives. Lives which are now enlightened and in full alignment with the New Way ideas, thoughts, and goals."

"General, there have been reports of weapons smuggling into CON holdout areas throughout the New Way states. Any information on that?" Ian asked.

"Yes, we're aware of those reports as well. Thankfully, it's a minor issue. We are coordinating interdiction efforts all the time, working closely with our like-minded federal, state, and local partners."

"General, the most painful part of our segment. What are the latest casualty numbers?"

"Our most recent count does not include the Ft. Smith casualty count. We're still tabulating those numbers. We have 8,000 KIA; 4,000 injured; 100 missing in action. Rebel casualty numbers are 45,000 KIA; 37,000 injured; 3,200 missing in action."

"General, some have questioned the accuracy of the numbers. What do you say to them?

General Homer seemed taken aback by the directness of the question. He looked at his notes and saw that it was not a question that was supposed to be asked. Looking Ian in the eye and giving a cold stare, the General replied, "Come to the Pentagon. We'll sit down and have ourselves a little chat."

"Well said. Well, that wraps up our segment with General Jeffrey Homer. We'll be right back after this commercial break. Next up is President Cyrus's Chief of Staff, Matt Kensington."

THE KING RESIDENCE

McHenry, Illinois

1413 CDT — 21 May 2062

Eleanor King had just returned home from church. There had been a potluck after service, and she had decided to stay. Receiving condolences on the loss of her husband at the Battle of Ft. Smith had been hard to hear but comforting. The word that her husband was missing, and presumed dead, had hit her like a proverbial bolt from the blue. She had received the horrible news two days after the battle had ended.

The nightly dose of war updates had made her weary even before the shocking news. Now, it seemed almost unbearable. She had sobbed until there were no tears left. Adding to the misery of all she knew, the food shortages were a chronic problem. She had found herself hungry more times than she cared to admit. Thankfully, Eleanor and her church family were having a decent spring harvest from their indoor hydroponic gardens. Now, with the arrival of spring, big plans were being made for the outdoor victory gardens at all the congregants' homes, as well as on the church grounds.

Deacon Jones, a farmer, slaughtered a pig on Friday last and had it prepared for the Sunday meal after church. The taste of meat at a meal had been a delight for all who had stayed behind after services.

The war now just seemed to be going on and on with no end in sight. She headed for the bedroom and was about to lie down when her comm rang. She thought of letting it go to voicemail, but figured it could be DeShawn calling. She picked up the comm and saw an unfamiliar prompt. "Incoming encrypted call." She hit accept, waited a moment and said, "Hello."

The voice on the other end was one she had heard a million times before. "Hi, hon. It's me. I'm okay."

"Jackson, you're alive! Glory to God, you're alive! Praise Jesus!" Eleanor screamed.

"Hon, are you okay?" Jackson asked.

With a halting voice filled with emotion, she continued. "Am I okay? I've had the worst week of my life! An Army Chaplain showed up at our door last week to tell me you're missing and presumed dead. Something about an artillery barrage, and that's the last thing I heard before I passed out." She broke down and wept tears of joy.

"I'm so sorry I put you through this. I'm okay, Hon, really. Let me know when you're ready, but I need you to listen very carefully."

Sobbing some more, Eleanor fought to compose herself. After another minute or so, she regained her composure and could speak clearly again, "Okay, I'm calmed down now. So, what happened? Where are you? When can I see you?"

"Listen to me very carefully. Yes, I did get caught in an artillery barrage. By some miracle, I survived a near-direct hit on our position. I was standing at the driver's door of a heavily armored truck. The others were on the opposite side and were killed instantly. I was knocked out. When I came to, I went over to check on the men I was meeting with. They were all dead. I looked around and saw no other soldiers nearby alive.

"I was in shock. I started walking towards the north with the intention of surrendering. Then it hit me. Whom am I surrendering to? I, an American, was looking to surrender to Americans? I found the thought absurd. Then I thought. *No, I'm not surrendering. I'm going to defect. Cyrus is crazy.* Hon, what have we done? What have we let him do? I just couldn't be a part of his plans anymore. I just can't. My values and beliefs are more in line with CONs than with these socialists. I may disagree on some things, but not enough to keep shooting at my fellow Americans. This is madness! The sum of all our anger should not have come to this."

"Oh, hon, I'm with you all the way on this. You've been through so much. I'm so sorry. Were you able to defect?"

"Yes. I came upon a farmhouse. The owner, a white guy, met me at the door with an assault rifle pointed at me. I thought he was gonna shoot me down dead right there on the spot. I said a quick, silent prayer, and then I recited an oath of allegiance I made up right there on the spot. It was a mix of the Pledge of Allegiance, the soldier's oath, and some stuff ad lib. It was tense for a few moments, but when I started talking, the farmer began to relax. The farmer and I talked some more, and when I said I wanted to defect, he lowered his gun, stuck his hand out towards me, and said, 'Welcome back to the United States of America. It's a bit smaller than it used to be, but we Patriots are working on fixin' that.'

"Then his family comes out, a black wife and two mixed-race kids. The next thing I knew, the local sheriff came and picked me up. No cuffs. He brings me to a military camp somewhere, and some MPs stand watch over me while a Native American woman in military intelligence interrogates me. She gathered a bunch of facts and left the room to 'check me out,' she said. She came back with a lieutenant and said I was free to go. I told them I didn't want to leave and that what I wanted was to join their fight to take the country back. They were both surprised, to say the least."

Eleanor was shocked to hear all this, "My word! All that! So, where are you?"

"I'm in Oklahoma. We're getting ready to move out somewhere. Not sure where."

"When can I see you? Will they give you leave at all?"

"I can't take leave right now. Not because they wouldn't let me, but because our home is in Illinois. It's a New Way state. They told me that if the New Way leadership knew I was still alive and had defected and was visiting home, they'd come and arrest me, charge me with desertion, and have me executed. They'd also probably execute you for harboring a traitor."

There was a long pause as the stark words sank in for Eleanor. "Jackson, what about me? Am I in any danger with the local authorities?"

"I don't think so. McHenry County is a strong CON area except for some isolated pockets. But, for the most part, support for the Constitution is strong out by us. But here's the thing. For now, you can't let on that I called. I'm dead as far as anyone else is concerned."

"What about DeShawn? He took the news very hard."

"As much as I hate to say it, even our son can't know right now that I have done this. When the time is right, I'll tell him, but for his safety and yours, he can't know right now. It's simply too dangerous, Hon."

"Hon, I'm supposed to go to a memorial service for your death in three days. What will I tell them?"

"Smile, and shout 'Glory Be', and then tell them the Lord Jesus has planted my feet on Higher Ground."

IIII **20** IIII

45 DAYS

Supreme Allied Commander of the Continental Armies, General James Buford, was in a contemplative mood. The Second American Civil War was now in its third year. The entrance of Texas into the conflict at the Battle of Ft. Smith, Arkansas, in May 2062, on the side of the CONs, had had a dramatic effect on the battlefield throughout the remainder of that year, all of 2063, and on into June of 64.

Buford was keenly aware that the military might of Texas exceeded that of half the world's nations. Now, its anger and might have leveled the playing field by providing the CONs with the capability for large-scale offensive operations against Federal New Way forces. The death toll was staggering, as one would expect, using the modern weapons of 21st-century warfare. He had the thought, *Civil war seems to exact a grotesque toll of malevolence. Such is the sick nature of fratricide against one's own countryman.* His thoughts brought a sudden nausea over him. Without warning, he vomited and quietly wept for the dead.

With over a million dead, the nation's anger continued to boil. The anger did not seem to lessen. If anything, with each passing battle, the desire to avenge the war dead from the previous fighting grew, precisely as it had done in the First American Civil War of the 1860s.

In the First Civil War, the combined Union and Confederate death toll was 620,000. All that carnage occurred from mostly single-shot, black powder rifles and pistols, artillery, and, of course, the bayonet. That number exceeded the nation's war dead in the combined totals of the American Revolution, the War of 1812, the Mexican War, the Spanish-American War, World War I, World War II, and the Korean War. The total was roughly two percent of the total population of 1860s America. Now, Civil War 2.0 was being waged with weapons of far greater destructive force.

Buford knew that if the war continued and the death rate compared to the total population matched that of the First Civil War, then the current death toll for this war was not even close to what it could be. "A frightening thought," he muttered to himself.

Buford looked over at the calendar and paused to take in the date. He was pleased that the Continental Army had made significant progress in the last year. After liberating Arkansas and Missouri, the CONs launched an offensive into Minnesota. They captured most of the state, leaving only the Minneapolis–Saint Paul metro area and a few cities in local hands. The Army of the Northern Plains had been heralded as a liberator throughout most of the state. Southern Illinois was again firmly in control of the CONs and had been recognized as the new State of Southern Illinois by all the CON governors and the Republic of Texas.

All that he had contemplated weighed heavily on his mind as he rose to speak to his general staff.

Behind him, a large paper map of northern Illinois and southern Wisconsin, "Alright, everyone, listen up. Well, we've come a long way, haven't we? We are standing on free Illinois soil. This seemed unimaginable at this time last year. While it's true that many parts of the state remain under New Way rule, we've made significant progress from here in Galena to roughly a third of the way down the state along the Illinois side of the Mississippi River, clear to the Quad Cities area.

"The FEDs retain an iron grip over a large swath of Wisconsin. That swath includes the capital, Madison, and a solid corridor from the Mississippi River, through Madison to Milwaukee and down along the eastern side along Lake Michigan into Northeastern Illinois. We're working on a plan to deal with that. Right now, partisan guerrilla fighters and the Badger Militia activities over there are wreaking havoc with the FEDs' supply lines. They have a solid hold on southwestern Wisconsin. Their strong presence there has given us some protection on our left flank in Illinois.

"We are now at the threshold of two big pushes. From here, we drive further east towards Rockford and then proceed to the approaches to Chicago via the far northwest and west suburbs of the Fox River. The river flows south from Wilmot, Wisconsin, into Illinois, passing Elgin and intersecting I-90 and U.S. Route 20. Our goal is to push eastward to the Fox River. Further plans will be revealed at the appropriate time.

"In the South, the Army of the Gulf States is ready to leave their encampment in Atlanta. From there, they'll drive northeast through South Carolina and link up with the Army of the Carolinas–Georgia in Charlotte. From there, a second link up with the Army of the Tennessee. Together, this combined force is to drive north up into Virginia. Questions?"

General Daniel Forrest, commanding General of the Army of Tennessee, spoke up, "General, my troops are hearing of a high desertion rate among the FEDs. Do you have anything on that?"

"Yes, I'm aware of those rumors as well. Hard to say how much of that is true or not. The New Way has total control of the press, so nothing is being reported about desertions or defections in the media at all.

"It seems like from our perch, we get a steady trickle of FEDs who want to defect at almost every battle. Lately, there's been a slight uptick. For instance, 133 defectors at the Battle of Mankato in April, and about 340 two weeks later at the Battle of Rochester, Minnesota. Our policy remains the same. Defectors are to be interrogated and checked out. If they check out okay and if they take the Pledge of Allegiance and the Oath of a Continental Soldier, they can join our ranks."

"Understood, General. What about the POW camps? Any recruits coming out of there?"

"Not much. Soldiers of the New Way tend to have been heavily indoctrinated against us. The POW camp in Des Moines reported about 45 guards of color. Whenever they get a new batch of prisoners, the FED soldiers are always shocked to see that the guards are not White.

"Personally, I find that weird as hell. It's one thing to hear about some of the weird shit the New Way teaches the kids in the schools. It's another to see the fruits of it. My word, we've got thousands of people of color in our ranks. I count seven in this meeting right now! Take Lemarcus

Washington here; he has been an invaluable asset to me personally and to our planning successes. I would not hesitate to take a bullet for him, or for anyone in this room, for that matter."

Lemarcus spoke up, "Likewise, General."

Buford made a fist with his right hand, tapped his chest, then pointed straight at Lemarcus and nodded.

Lemarcus saw the gesture and commented, "E Pluribus Unum!"

Everyone responded in unison, "E Pluribus Unum!"

THE WHITE HOUSE

Washington, D.C.

0700 EDT — 16 Jun 2064

President Cyrus quietly entered the Situation Room. Having been up half the night studying war maps. He looked tired. He had grown increasingly frustrated with the turn of events over the last 12 months. With another influx of 500,000 new college draftees into the Army, he wanted to hear good news from Joint Chiefs Chairman General Homer. Good news or else.

"Good morning, everyone," Cyrus began. "Please pardon my appearance, a rough night, and no sleep. General Homer, what is the latest?"

The General stood up and quickly walked over to the giant screen on the wall. "Mr. President, things have changed in the last twenty-four hours. Down here in Atlanta, there are lots of signs the CON Army is getting ready to leave in the next twenty-four to thirty-six hours. Up here in Charlotte, there's also a lot of activity. Our sources on the ground tell us the two are to link up here outside of Charlotte. Another force, the Army of Tennessee, has started to push east out of Tennessee slowly. They look to be headed to Asheville, North Carolina, just the other side of the Smokies. After that, probably then down into the Charlotte metro area."

"What's the troop strength?" Cyrus inquired. "Combined, approximately six hundred forty-five thousand."

"What does the AI model show if the rebel armies link up?"

"Mr. President, there's a seventy percent chance the CONs would be at the outskirts of Washington within ninety days or less."

"Yes, I see. What do you propose we do about this, General?" General Homer, usually calm and collected, looked a little nervous.

"Mr. President, there is an additional complication. Two."

"Yes, I'm listening, General."

"Over here in Southern Ohio, it appears that the Army of the Potomac is preparing to head east into West Virginia or possibly cross over here into Southeastern Pennsylvania. If they do, they could pose a threat to the capital from the Maryland side."

"What do we have up there to protect us?"

"We've got four divisions made up of Maryland, Pennsylvania, Ohio, and New York National Guard Troops. All hard-core New Way people."

"And their loyalties to the New Way, General?'

"All vetted and run through intensive AI screening, Mr. President. They're as fanatical as you can get."

"Any MODs in the mix?"

"No, Mr. President. Any MODs were given General Discharge papers and sent to re-education camps."

"Director Mosby, what's the latest on the CON roundups?"

"Mr. President, we do not believe there are any openly CON folks left under New Way jurisdiction. They've either slipped away into rebel areas or have been detained and placed into re-education camps, or they're in hiding. There's a bounty of $10,000 leading to the apprehension of any CONs. So far, the program has netted thousands of them. They've all been sent to the camps."

"Excellent. Report back to me next week. I want to know if our deprogramming curriculum is having the intended results."

"Yes, sir, Mr. President."

"General Homer, getting back to the threat we face from the CONs potentially coming at us from two fronts. What do you propose?"

The moment had arrived. General Homer had been up all night wrestling with the idea that had come to him in the darkness. "Mr. President, the threat is real, and it is severe. The hopes and dreams of the New Way are in real danger. I believe our armed forces can defeat the enemy in the South, but handling this significant threat, combined with the new threat from the Army of the Potomac, is another matter entirely. Our estimates put the troop strength of the Army of the Potomac at 375,000. If the Army of Appalachia abandons their guerrilla tactics and fights us out in the open, the numbers go north of a half-a-million.

"Mr. President, an opportunity has arisen that we need to explore seriously. We can annihilate two whole armies of the rebels in Charlotte and Atlanta. As you know, the entire Charlotte and Atlanta metropolitan areas fell under the spell of the Awakening. Our estimates had upwards of ninety-seven percent of the population of both metro areas firmly in the CON camp. Residents are flying the Old Way Stars and Stripes. They've even taken to flying a flag depicting the disgraced Mount Rushmore on it. In my opinion, both cities are beyond hope of redemption back into the New Way thought."

President Cyrus leaned forward in his chair. "General, what exactly are you getting at? I fail to see the connection between brainwashed civilians and the rebel army that threatens us."

"Mr. President, I propose we sacrifice these two lost cities for the greater good of the New Way. I am recommending the limited use of tactical nuclear weapons to destroy the two whole CON armies in Atlanta and Charlotte before it's too late.

"Once destroyed, issue an ultimatum for all the CON forces to surrender, or else we will use more tactical nukes.

"I'm convinced their destruction will pave the way to certain and final victory and an end to the war. It worked for Truman, why not us?" The room went silent.

Presidential Advisor Matt Kensington looked around the room. Cyrus looked frozen. Jai Perry's eyes bulged slightly. NWBI Director Mosby had a subtle smirk. DHS Secretary Frederic Sheldon looked pale. Several others also seemed frozen in place. General Homer stood motionless, staring directly at the President, awaiting his reply.

Jai Parry rose from his chair. He walked over to Homer and stood face-to-face with him, and yelled, "General, have you lost your damned mind? Millions of people will die—not hundreds or tens of thousands, but millions!"

With a condescending tone, Homer, about six inches taller, looked down at Jai and yelled, "Back off, Jai! Get off your self-righteous pedestal and look at the bigger picture here! We could lose this war! Do you understand me?"

Jai looked to throw a punch, but was held back by Kensington and Sheldon. Both of whom had quickly risen out of their chairs and followed Parry after sensing his rage.

The President yelled, "That's enough! Everyone, sit down!"

The President looked shocked. Neither any members of his cabinet nor any of his advisors had ever mentioned that they could lose the war. Now, General Homer just had. Cyrus thought, *and plunged back into the darkness of the Old Way? Not on my watch.* He then motioned for the MPs to draw near. "Soldiers, we will keep order here, is that clear?!!"

Four MPs took up positions at the four corners of the room. They said nothing.

The President walked over to look at the map on the screen. He studied it for a considerable amount of time. No one spoke. Slowly, he turned around and looked at General Homer squarely in the eyes, "Do it—tomorrow at dawn. MPs, lock this room down. Except for General Homer, no one leaves until I say so."

CHEYENNE MOUNTAIN COMPLEX

Colorado Springs, Colorado

0342 MDT — 17 Jun 2064

General George Winfield was on the night shift. Sipping a coffee at his command desk in the central control room at the joint NORAD/ USNORTHCOM complex. He was quietly chatting with the duty officer when all hell broke loose.

The Klaxon sounded, and red lights started flashing. The giant center screen on the wall zoomed in on the southeastern United States. A live infrared satellite feed showed bright flashes glowing over Charlotte, North Carolina, and Atlanta, Georgia.

The General calmly yelled out, "What just happened here, people? Talk to me now!"

Master Sergeant Kiplinger shouted out, "Sir, sensors show multiple nuclear detonations over Charlotte and Atlanta. Ground motion monitors confirm the shocks are above ground level and not of natural origin. Gamma detectors also confirm nuclear detonation. Standby for origin search."

The General remained calm, "Were these launched from air, land, or sea? Anything on tracking?"

Sergeant Anderson spoke up, "No launch detected from anywhere outside the mainland. We have no inbound detections. Checking for domestic origin."

"Domestic? Advise."

The red phone lit up. He picked it up. "General Winfield here."

"This is the chairman of the Joint Chiefs of Staff, General Jeffrey Homer. General Winfield, you are ordered to stand down. The President of the United States has authorized the use of tactical battlefield nuclear artillery against rebel armies in Charlotte and Atlanta. We had solid intel that they were preparing an invasion of Virginia to fight their way up to the capital."

A stunned Winfield struggled to find the words. "Sir, we just nuked two of our cities. Is that what I just heard you say?"

"Yes, General, you heard correctly. The President will be addressing the nation within the hour. In the meantime, keep our defensive posture unchanged. I have already contacted my counterparts in Russia and China to explain the situation. I'll call you back after the President's address. In the meantime, hold steady."

THE GOVERNOR'S MANSION

Oklahoma City, Oklahoma

0500 CDT — 17 Jun 2064

Governor Mary Whitfield had just started eating breakfast when a military aide rushed in to inform her of the destruction of Charlotte and Atlanta by nuclear weapons. Shocked to the point of almost choking on her food, the Governor coughed it up. She jumped up and rushed out of the kitchen to the secure command center down in the basement to contact General Buford and the rest of the war cabinet.

It took just a few minutes for all the stakeholders, including President González of Texas, to join the call.

Mary opened the meeting, "Everyone, a great tragedy has just occurred. General Buford, what can you tell us?"

"Governor, I can confirm the destruction of Charlotte and Atlanta. We had AWACS in the air over Anderson, South Carolina. That's about midway between the two cities. They were at 38,000 ft. Clear skies with unlimited visibility. They saw the mushroom clouds over both metro areas. Ground observers with a recon unit in Toccoa, Georgia, saw the Atlanta mushroom clouds. Another unit outside of Kings Mountain, North Carolina, saw the clouds rising out of Charlotte."

"Any ideas on civilian casualties?"

"Multiple detonations were observed. Governor, it must be in the millions."

Silence followed for what seemed like an eternity.

Whitfield, fighting back tears, continued, "And the fate of our troops there?"

"I can't reach any of the leadership or command posts in either city. We're still trying, but it looks bad. Governor, it's still too early to say for sure, but based on their last known positions and the indications of where the nukes detonated, in addition to the civilians, we may have lost two whole armies."

"God have mercy on us all."

"Governor, there's something else. We have a very reliable source out east. The intel they've been providing has been quite useful and impeccable for over eighteen months. Cyrus may not be done using nukes. He's desperate to force our surrender. I believe the Army of the Potomac is in grave danger. They're encamped near Caldwell, Ohio, near the West Virginia and Pennsylvania border."

"What do you recommend?"

"As you know, we did come into possession of nuclear-tipped artillery shells in the April 2061 base attacks."

Montana Governor Wayland Emerson spoke up, "Excuse me, everyone. Are we going to consider a nuclear retaliation? I'm not sure that's the correct response. I need some serious convincing. Up here in Montana, we've lived with ICBMs in silos scattered all over our state all our lives. There's always been this quiet tension knowing that the weapons of Armageddon were lying beneath our feet and targeted for some city over in the Eastern Hemisphere. But use nukes here on our own soil? General Buford, what makes you so sure Cyrus is not done using nukes yet?"

"I appreciate your comments, Governor Emerson, I do. Look, everyone, things have gone badly for the New Way on the battlefield lately. They've not won a significant battle in months. Many of their recent draftees and conscripts are turning out to be soldiers not worth a damn. Reports indicate that desertions and Section 8 cases are on the rise.

"Our source tells us that General Homer, Chairman of the Joint Chiefs of Staff, was the one to suggest to Cyrus that Charlotte and Atlanta be nuked. He was going on and on about how both cities were lost and beyond saving anyway after going through the Awakening. He used the 'lesser of two evils' argument.

"He reasoned that destroying two whole armies of ours that were near those cities was a worthwhile sacrifice, especially towards ending the war by forcing us to surrender. I propose we turn the tables and see if we can get Cyrus to surrender. New York City and Chicago are currently the staging areas for a significant buildup of troops and materiel. After massive population declines in the last decade, New York City and Chicago pretty much have the same population as Charlotte and Atlanta.

"I propose we launch a retaliatory strike against New York City and Chicago. If we do not strike, I believe Cyrus will use nukes again. If we counter-attack by using nukes, we will show him that he cannot use any more nukes against us and get away with it. He'll be forced to stop, and the damage will be limited to just four cities."

Texas President González had been waiting to lay down an ace. Now was the time to play it. "Excuse me, everyone. Realistically, nuclear-tipped artillery shells can't be used in time. We have no assets close enough to fire a shell into New York or Chicago. However, Texas is in possession of B61 nukes. We've adapted them onto hypersonic cruise missiles and can launch them towards any target in the continental United States on my authority.

"I'm feeling ill at this very moment at the thought of having to do this, but General Buford is right. Look at what Cyrus has done to date. Millions dead. He destroyed the Alamo, Mount Rushmore, and Stone Mountain, replaced the flag, started a war, canceled the Constitution, declared martial law, and awarded himself dictatorial powers. But for Chamberlain's daring raid at Harpers Ferry, Cyrus had plans to destroy the founding documents on live TV. Now, there are rumors that Cyrus is getting ready to demolish the monuments in Washington. Roughly half the country is living under totalitarian rule. It's clear to me that he's as mad as a hatter.

"I've not shared this with you all until now, but early on after his inauguration, he was on a secure call with me. It was on that call that he privately threatened to nuke Austin here in Texas after the FEDs failed raid here. I advised him we had nukes and that we would not hesitate to destroy Washington if he nuked Austin. So, he backed off in exchange for my agreeing never to disclose that we had nukes. Well, I knew he was a liar, and I also knew he could never be trusted. Here he's gone and killed probably millions in Charlotte and Atlanta. I genuinely believe he will not hesitate to kill millions more. As I see it, we have no choice."

The room went silent. The faces of all the governors were ashen.

Kansas Governor Jonathan Hill broke the silence. His voice, filled with emotion, rang out over the speaker, "Good Lord, how did it come to this? If we do this, can we try to limit casualties?"

Nebraska Governor Michael Yost spoke up, "If we try a surgical or low-yield nuclear strike, Cyrus may take that as a sign that we do not have more powerful nukes. He would see that as a sign of weakness."

President González spoke, "Governors, the survival of your republic and ours hangs in the balance. Recognizing the sovereignty of Texas as its own country outright, we alone possess the nukes needed for this strike. I alone, by the power of the Texas Constitution, have the authority to launch this retaliatory attack against the New Way, which aligns with Article 5 of our treaty arrangement with you. However, as a part of our alliance, I will not makc that decision without unanimous consent from all the governors."

Governor Whitfield knew that President González was right. If they were to opt for the unthinkable, it had to be by unanimous consent. Anything less would probably mean the war was lost. Governor Whitfield took a deep breath and spoke, "Governors, we can do a secret ballot or a voice vote. Which would you prefer?"

One by one, the governors spoke up. They were all in favor of a simple voice vote.

Whitfield continued. "Alright, I will call out the names of each state. For the record and to be clear, all in favor of the unanimous consent to launch a retaliatory nuclear strike against Chicago and New York in response to Cyrus authorizing the atomic destruction of Charlotte and Atlanta, say aye.

"What does the great state of Kansas say?"

"Kansas says aye."

"The great state of Nebraska?"

"Nebraska says aye."

"The great state of North Dakota?"

"North Dakota says aye."

"The great state of South Dakota?"

"South Dakota says aye. May God have mercy on us all."

"The great state of Montana?"

"With a heavy heart, Montana says aye."

"The great state of Wyoming?"

"Wyoming says aye."

"The great state of Greater Idaho?"

"Greater Idaho says aye."

"The great state of Northern California?"

"Northern California says aye."

"The great state of Utah?"

"Utah says aye."

"The great state of New Mexico?

"New Mexico says aye."

"The great state of Western Colorado?"

"Western Colorado says aye."

"The great state of Southern Illinois?"

"Southern Illinois says aye."

Whitfield spoke of Indiana, "Sadly, with the capture of the Governor and all CON members of the state legislature, the great state of Indiana also has no provisional government and is unable to cast a vote."

Whitfield continued, "The great state of Iowa?"

"Iowa says aye."

"The great state of Missouri?"

"Missouri says aye."

"The great state of Arkansas?"

"Arkansas says aye."

"The great state of Louisiana?"

"Louisiana says aye."

 The great state of Mississippi?"

"Mississippi says aye."

"The great state of Kentucky?"

"Kentucky says aye."

"The great state of Tennessee?"

"Tennessee says aye."

"The great state of Alabama?"

"Alabama says aye."

"The great state of Florida?"

"Florida says aye."

"The great state of West Virginia?"

"As the Governor in exile, West Virginia says aye."

"The great state of South Carolina?"

"South Carolina says aye."

"The great state of Hawaii?"

"Hawaii says aye."

"The great state of Alaska?"

"Alaska says aye."

"The great state of North Carolina?"

Governor Whitfield appeared on screen, "I believe I speak on behalf of all of us on this call and many millions of patriots across the nation. The hearts and prayers of all Liberty-loving people, as well as our condolences, go out to everyone in your great state as well as to every one of our friends and citizens in the great state of Georgia."

"Thank you, Governor. As you know, North Carolina, along with Georgia, was one of the 13 original colonies. Today, we've lost a part of the soul of our state. With the eastern portion of our state still occupied by the FEDs, the free part of North Carolina is in mourning. I've personally lost a great many family and friends in Charlotte. With a heavy heart, North Carolina says aye."

"The great state of Georgia?"

"This is Senate President Mbali Yamikani. I'm now the acting Governor. Our hearts and prayers go out to our friends in North Carolina and, obviously, to all Georgians. We believe that Governor Lanre and his entire family are among the casualties in Atlanta—also, Lieutenant Governor Alhaji and her entire family.

"I was at a conference in Dalton, Georgia at the time of the attack. I believe that among the great number of dead, I have lost my entire family as well. Efforts to contact them are still ongoing, but it looks like they're all gone. My heart is heavy, but I have a duty now to protect the rest of Georgia for the cause of liberty. I will mourn later. I do not take this vote lightly, nor is revenge on my heart. I make this vote to preserve, protect, and defend the Constitution of the United States of America and the Georgia Constitution for this and future generations from all enemies foreign and domestic. I am confident we will emerge from this tragedy of war to help rebuild. Georgia also says aye."

Winfield noted Georgia's vote and spoke. "On behalf of the great state of Oklahoma, I, the duly elected Governor, Mary Whitfield, with sorrow, say aye."

After scribbling a note, Governor Whitfield made the formal announcement for the record. "Let the record show that the ayes are unanimous. President González, we have unanimous consent. Please proceed with the retaliatory strike with all haste before Cyrus nukes us again. Governors, we are obviously at the precipice. Take whatever precautions you need to ensure your respective line of succession is not all in the same place at any given moment. May God be with us all in this dark hour."

THE WHITE HOUSE

The Oval Office

0645 EDT — 17 Jun 2064

President Devin Cyrus was seated at his desk. In one minute, all the morning shows on all networks would be cutting away for his address to the nation. The nation was having a heart-stopping moment with the breaking news that two American metropolitan areas, currently in rebellion, had been nuked.

"Mr. President, we are live in ten seconds. Standby."

At the five-second mark, the technician held up one hand, gave the signal for five–four–three–two–one, and pointed to the President just as the red light lit up atop the camera.

"My fellow New Way Americans. Today is a solemn day. Yesterday, we received a reliable intelligence report that the Old Way rebel armies were planning a dastardly invasion of Virginia from the south. The plan had two large armies, one in Atlanta and one in Charlotte, joining forces near Charlotte, along with a third army now on the move in eastern Tennessee. These combined armies constituted—"

DREADNOUGHT TEXAS

Off the Coast of Galveston, Texas

0545 CDT — 17 Jun 2064

Captain Gerard Ellison of the Republic of Texas Navy had been assigned to the restored and modernized World War I/World War II-era Battleship Texas. Formerly the USS Texas (BB-35). She had the unique distinction of having a dual-capable propulsion, navigation, and weapons system that could be operated manually or electronically.

She had a storied history with the United States Navy in the first half of the twentieth century, spanning World War I and World War II. She was decommissioned on 21 April 1947. Then, just nine days later, on 30 April 1948, her name was struck from the Naval Vessel Register. After that, she became a floating museum. Two years ago, with war looming, Governor González had ordered it to undergo extensive restoration. She was refitted, secretly militarized, recommissioned, and renamed *Dreadnought Texas* on 6 June 2061.

The irony of the date of the recommissioning ceremony was not lost to Captain Ellison. It was on that date, 117 years earlier, on 6 June 1944, Battleship U.S.S. Texas had provided extensive fire support off Omaha Beach during the D-Day landings against the Nazis during WWII.

The ship's dimensions were an overall length of 573 feet, a beam of 95 feet 2.5 inches, and a maximum draft of 29 feet 7 inches. Her array of armaments included four torpedo tubes, six 14-inch guns, twenty-one 5-inch guns, and ten Thor-missile tubes.

On station off Galveston for the last forty-five days, Captain Ellison was in daily contact with Admiral Dennis Leonard. Both were United States Naval Academy graduates at Annapolis, Maryland, in 2044.

As loyal sons of Texas and with the disillusionment of the Union, it had been an easy but sad choice for them to resign their commissions with the U.S. Navy in defense of liberty with the rebirthed Republic of Texas. *Dreadnought Texas* cruised at 19 knots in a figure-eight pattern along the entirety of the Texas Gulf coast. The crew held battle-station drills twice daily to stay sharp. Through all those drills, the ship's vast firepower had not fired a shot in anger.

With Civil War 2.0 now in its thirty-eighth month, the news of Charlotte and Atlanta's atomic destruction had, just thirty minutes earlier, reverberated throughout the entire ship. To a person, the ship's complement of 900 sailors were all horrified at the news.

Captain Ellison was staring through his binoculars when the red phone lit up. The Executive Officer on the bridge answered it. With Ellison looking on expectantly, the phone was handed to him.

"This is Captain Gerard Ellison, Commanding Officer of the *Dreadnought Texas*."

A familiar voice was on the line. It was the Admiral.

"Captain Ellison, this is Admiral Leonard. On orders from President González, I have a priority one authentication call. What is today's password?"

Familiar with the routine, Ellison answered. "The password is DELTA TANGO OSCAR MIKE. Please authenticate."

The Admiral responded, "Confirmed. Second authentication is CHARLIE SIERRA WHISKEY LIMA BRAVO JULIET ZULU ROMEO YANKEE. Standing by."

Captain Ellison motioned to the ExO. They took a few steps over to a red box on the bulkhead of the bridge behind them. He pulled on a chain around his neck and pulled up a key. "ExO will retrieve her key—insert and turn at my command."

After a moment, Captain Ellison continued. "Turn."

With that, the door was unlocked and pulled open. Ellison pulled out a red envelope. He walked back over to the phone as he opened the envelope. Studying the contents of the authentication sheet, he compared the code given by the admiral against what was now before him on the heavy stock of laminated card paper he'd just removed. Satisfied that the code matched, he handed the card to his ExO for a secondary comparison. She also confirmed a match and handed it back to the captain.

"Admiral, we have authenticated the code. What are your orders?"

The tension level on the bridge had risen dramatically in a matter of moments. Captain Ellison calmly waited for the Admiral to reply.

"Captain Ellison, targeting coordinates are now in your launch commit system. Launch codes are as follows: QUEBEC PAPA VICTOR JULIET FOXTROT ROMEO DELTA TANGO YANKEE. Confirm."

Captain Ellison looked at the second section of the card. He confirmed the launch codes and repeated the process with his ExO, who also confirmed. "Admiral, launch code is confirmed. Orders?"

Admiral Leonard paused for just a moment. "In response to the atomic destruction of Charlotte and Atlanta, and in keeping with our Alliance agreement, the President has authorized a retaliatory strike against two New Way targets, New York and Chicago. You are to arm six missiles, program them with the target coordinates sent to you, and launch them immediately. I will stand by and await your launch confirmation."

CHEYENNE MOUNTAIN COMPLEX

Colorado Springs, Colorado

0455 MDT — 17 Jun 2064

The Klaxon sounded for the second time that morning. General Winfield wheeled around in his command chair and yelled out. "Talk to me!"

"Sir, missile launch detected."

Winfield jumped out of his chair. "Origin?"

"Off the Texas coast, approximately 27 nautical miles east, southeast of Galveston."

"How many?"

"Six—headed towards the mainland. Already hypersonic."

The General picked up the red phone to contact General Jeffrey Homer.

THE WHITE HOUSE

Press Room

0710 EDT — 17 Jun 2064

White House Chief of Staff Matt Kensington tapped his fingers while watching the President's address to the nation. Sitting with him was the President's entire Cabinet and a myriad of aides.

The news of the destruction of two American cities had cast a pall over the entire room. The Cabinet members had entered in silence and sat stoically.

On the wall were multiple TV screens, each tuned to a different morning news channel. The center screen was the only one with the sound turned on, and it was tuned to the American News Network feed of the President's speech. The Oval Office Address to the nation had interrupted the network's "Morning in America Show", live from their studio in lower Manhattan in New York.

Another screen on the bottom right of the wall was from the ANN affiliate in Chicago, covering the ongoing violent anti-draft protestors destroying a significant part of downtown Chicago.

Everyone's eyes were glued to the center screen. With the volume turned up, they listened intently to the President.

Without warning, the feed from Chicago went black. No one paid much attention to it.

A few moments later, the President had come to the crux of his Oval Office message, "In closing, I now issue an ultimatum to all states in rebellion. You have until 8 a.m. Eastern Time tomorrow to lay down your weapons and to surrender unconditionally. Failure to do so will see the destruction of your respective Capital cities beginning at—"

Without warning, the feed from New York was accompanied by a shrill sound. Simultaneously, the screen turned static. A moment later, the National Emergency Alert tone sounded on every comm in the nation.

COLORADO PATRIOT MILITIA FIELD HQ
Near Eleven Mile Canyon Reservoir, Colorado
1403 MDT — 20 Jun 2064

Sergeant York studied the detailed report of the destruction of four large metropolitan areas that had occurred three days earlier. He was sickened by it all.

Inwardly, he raged against President Cyrus even more. It was Cyrus's decision to nuke Charlotte and Atlanta. That decision had forced the hand of the CON Alliance. At a minimum, the CONs faced the prospect of losing the war. At the extreme, they were now faced with the specter of nuclear annihilation. Could the country survive such a nightmare? *Probably not*, he thought. For York, it was clear that either scenario would mean the end of the American Republic.

Franklin York was a descendant of Founding Father William Floyd of New York, one of the 56 signers of the Declaration of Independence. York had been given a sacred honor of trust. He was one of 56 people, all descendants of the signers, who were members of a secret society created by President Eisenhower in 1956, appropriately named after the Roman numeral for 56, "The LVI." The LVI had been given a singular, but until now, dormant task to save the Republic from destroying itself in a civil war from the use of its nuclear arms.

While York knew he couldn't end the war, he could try to ensure the war wouldn't end them all. He picked up his comm and called his old friend, General George Winfield at the Cheyenne Mountain Complex.

General Winfield had taken a short break and was in the chapel communing with God in silent prayer. There were two dozen other soldiers there. Many with heads bowed. Some holding the Rosary. Some with eyes wide open, staring intently at the altar. Some were quietly weeping. None was speaking.

Winfield felt his comm vibrate. Looking at the display, he could see it was York. Winfield quietly exited the room and stepped into one of the small adjacent reflection rooms. He closed the door and answered, "This is General Winfield."

"George, how are you?"

"Franklin, are you okay?"

"Yeah, I'm okay. You know, it's unbelievable, I haven't gotten a scratch on me this whole war. George, did you lose anyone the other day?"

Feeling grieved, George replied. "Yeah, I did—my sister's entire family in Charlotte. I also lost an aunt and uncle in New York. They were both in a nursing home with Alzheimer's. It's probably better that way. How about you?"

"My condolences, George. I lost two uncles in Chicago. A sister in Atlanta. Two cousins in Charlotte. How's Satie?"

"She's fine. My condolences to you, Franklin. Listen, let me call you back later."

The General hung up and briskly walked to the nearest secure comm room. He called York back immediately on the encrypted line of his comm.

Winfield said, "Hello," paused, and then said, "Listen, I hate to do this, but you know, of course, that because of the AIs, I need to authenticate. What's the passphrase?"

"LEXINGTON CONCORD GETTYSBURG OMAHA BEACH."

"Authenticated. What is the combination?"

"ZERO SEVEN ZERO FOUR ONE SEVEN SEVEN SIX."

"Authenticated. What is the key?"

"ECHO QUEBEC UNIFORM ALFA LIMA."

"Authenticated. Okay, Franklin, what's up?"

"George, given events, I'm activating the Eisenhower Directive. Is that clear?"

The General paused for a moment. "Understood, York, I'll be in touch. Stay safe."

IIII **21** IIII

OH SNAP!

It was Eleanor's turn to serve in the church nursery during the Sunday service. She was paired up with four other volunteers. So far, the headcount in the nursery was sixteen kids aged 4 to 10. Eleanor was delighted by the diversity of the kids present: four Black, four White, four Hispanic, two Asian, and two Indian.

Eleanor recalled the plight of the Patels. Rajesh and Senu Patel were the twin 10-year-old sons of Ravi and Ankita Patel, both of whom had recently converted to Christianity. The Patels had recently moved into the Woodstock area with their parents. Ravi and Ankita Patel were naturalized as U.S. citizens seven years earlier. The Patels had immigrated to Chicago from India in 2050. From 2050 to a year ago, they had lived a comfortable life in Chicago's Gold Coast. With the anarchy, violence, and riots in Chicago showing no signs of abating, they sold their condo for a considerable loss in 2063. They moved to Woodstock precisely one month to the day before Chicago's destruction.

Eleanor surveyed the room once again. Four of the kids had mild coughs, probably from the cold going around. Seven of the kids looked like they had lost some weight, which was not surprising given the food shortages. She thought of her own Victory Garden and was happy with how the crops were growing and looking. The harvest would add valuable and needed food supplies to the church's food pantry.

Working at the check-in counter, Eleanor entered the detailed attendance report and printed out the wristbands required for each child. With the last form filled out, she clicked the mouse button and waited for the confirmation. The hourglass on the screen was doing its thing and then inexplicably froze. A moment later, it turned white. Then a message popped up on the screen:

Welcome to Anarchy, courtesy of the Black Hole virus. We now return you to a simpler time. Bye, 再见, **Adiós**, **अलवदिा**, **Au revoir**, وداعا, **До свидания**, **বিদায়**, **Adeus**, حافظ خدا"

Then the screen went blank. She was not one to swear, so she used her favorite substitute, "Oh snap!"

CHEYENNE MOUNTAIN COMPLEX
Colorado Springs, Colorado
0859 MDT — 20 Jun 2064

With five MPs at his side, General Winfield had ordered the lockdown of the USNORTHCOM Cheyenne Mountain Complex. With the mammoth blast doors closed, no one could get in or out until further notice.

As he went on the PA system, he looked down at his tablet to read the carefully worded message he would deliver to all personnel inside the complex. "May I have your attention, please? This is Commanding Officer General George Winfield. I have an announcement to make." He was about to continue when suddenly his screen locked up. Then a message popped up on the screen:

Welcome to Anarchy, courtesy of the Black Hole virus. We now return you to a simpler time. Bye, 再见, **Adiós**, **अलवदिा**, **Au revoir**, ‏الوداع‎, **До свидания**, **বিদায়**, **Adeus**, ‏خدا حافظ‎"

Then the screen went blank.

THE GOVERNOR'S MANSION
Oklahoma City, Oklahoma
0959 CDT — 20 Jun 2064

Governor Whitfield was reading an encrypted email she had just received from General Buford. It was a detailed after-action report of the 606th Corps victory in the Battle of Belvidere, Illinois. She had read most of the report and was mid-sentence when her screen froze. A moment later, it turned white. Then a message popped up on the screen:

Welcome to Anarchy, courtesy of the Black Hole virus. We now return you to a simpler time. Bye, 再见, **Adiós**, **अलवदिा**, **Au revoir**, وداعا‎, **До свидания**, **বদিায়**, Adeus, حافظ خدا‎"

Then the screen went blank. She immediately hit reset on the computer, but nothing happened.

THE OVAL OFFICE
Washington, D.C.
1059 EDT — 20 Jun 2064

President Cyrus quietly read the latest dispatches from the Western theatre of the war. News of recent successes on the West Coast had buoyed his mood. A New Way rapid reaction force had re-taken a portion of the mammoth Sierra Army Weapons Depot in a remote part of Northern California near the Nevada border. A fierce battle was underway for control of the rest of the base. The report had them gaining the upper hand. He was in the mid-sentence of the last paragraph of the dispatch when his tablet screen froze. A moment later, it turned white. Then a message popped up on the screen:

Welcome to Anarchy, courtesy of the Black Hole virus. We now return you to a simpler time. Bye, 再见, **Adiós**, **अलवदिा**, **Au revoir**, اعادو, **До свидания**, **বিদায়**, **Adeus**, ادخ ظفاح"

Then the screen went blank.

Shocked, Cyrus screamed out an expletive. A secret service agent bolted in through the door with his weapon out. "You okay, Mr. President?"

"Yes! I mean, no, this computer just locked up. Get me someone from Desktop Support in here now!" He yelled.

The agent quickly left the Oval Office and noticed a lot of commotion. He ran into Chief of Staff Matt Kensington at the other end of the hallway. Matt was on his way to see the President. The agent asked Kensington where the IT guy was. Matt pointed him out inside a group of aides huddled together with their laptops open. All of them looked confused.

The IT specialist was in the group, examining one of the laptops. He looked perplexed. He had just been fixing a minor issue for one of the aides when he saw the white screen and red words. He had instantly been swarmed by several people who had just walked out of a staff meeting with Matt Kensington.

The agent walked over and yelled for him to follow him back to the Oval Office. Looking somewhat bewildered, the IT guy put down the laptop and squeezed out of the crowd towards the agent. Together, they all rapidly walked back down the hallway and entered the Oval Office as the crowd of aides yelled and demanded he come back.

The agent saw the IT guy's White House ID badge hanging from the pocket of his shirt. "Mr. President, here's the IT guy, Enrique Donovan."

"Thank you. Enrique, my laptop just froze up. I hit reset, and nothing is happening. I need this fixed now. Can you help me?"

Enrique from Desktop Support picked up the President's laptop and saw the same thing he'd seen not only on his personal screen but also on all the staff's screens in the hallway. He had a sickening feeling, "Mr. President, there's a bunch of aides outside with the same problem." Enrique turned to Matt, "Matt, is your laptop working?"

Matt Kensington opened the lid. He had just used his laptop in a low-level staff meeting not more than ten minutes earlier. He had closed the lid for the short walk to the Oval Office when he ran into the Secret Service agent. "It was working in the meeting a few minutes ago." Kensington fiddled for a moment. "Hold on." After another moment, "Huh, mine's locked up too. What the hell? Enrique, what's going on? Have we been hacked?"

|||| **22** ||||

PULSE

The Secret Service had a fleet of semi-trailer trucks adorned with placards that read "Hazardous Waste." From the outside, they were impossible to tell that these were decoys. Inside the semi-trailer, a well-appointed, heavily armored, and secure communication mobile command post provided a safe and secure place for Department of Homeland Security Secretary Frederic Sheldon. The protective detail had conspicuously driven Sheldon in the stealth semi the two-hour drive from Washington to see Frederic's wife, Samantha, and the family, holed up at their remote cabin near Parker Island, Virginia, in the Shenandoah Valley.

Arriving at 8 p.m. the previous evening, Sheldon had reveled in seeing everyone. It had been six weeks since his last secret foray up to their retreat, and the entire evening had been a welcome respite for them all.

Now, with everyone asleep, he had put on a robe and walked out to the large outdoor freezer that had started life as a shipping container five years earlier. Sheldon had quietly designed and ordered the construction of the freezer as he saw the nation heading for war.

Walking up to the massive freezer, he opened the door and stepped inside. He slowly looked around, checking out the vast array of frozen foodstuffs for Sam, the kids, his parents, and his in-laws. He was delighted to see that the supply was ample, especially considering the worsening food shortages being experienced in all New Way-controlled areas.

Next, he walked to the back of the freezer and pulled the shelf away from the back wall. The shelves were stocked with loaves of bread.

Squeezing in behind, he pulled away the small piece of plastic trim held by a strong magnet at the bottom right corner of the back wall. It revealed a small dime-sized button. He pressed it, and, with a click, the back wall opened from the right. He pulled on the edge and opened it. He walked in and closed the door behind him.

Seeing the secret communication room and the AI robot manning it was surreal. All of it was military grade and hardened against electronic warfare attacks. He sat at the central console and hastily started pushing buttons. In moments, the screen came to life. Pulling up a list of names, he selected the ones for tonight's secretly encrypted video call and hit the "Call" button. One by one, their faces appeared on screen.

"Jai, good early morning. You safe?"

"Yeah, I'm good. You?"

"Good here also. Donna, how are things?"

Secretary of the Interior Donna Sheryll looked weary. "I'm tired, Freddy, but I'm holding up. Been an awful time of late."

"I know, Donna. General Gage, good morning."

General Gage, former Chairman of the Joint Chiefs of Staff, had bloodshot eyes, highlighted by dark circles beneath them. "Good morning, everyone, glad to be on this call."

"General Winfield, good morning."

"Everyone, good morning."

Sheldon paused to pull up some notes. "Thank you all for attending at this late hour. I wanted to update everyone on the package. It's almost ready for delivery. General Gage, status?"

"Shipping and receiving reports are excellent. We're ready."

"Excellent. General Winfield?"

"All good here as well. Do we have a tracking number?"

"Not yet. Got some loose ends, but we're very close to having one."

GULF OF MEXICO

North of the Yucatán Peninsula, Mexico

0444 CDT — 1 Aug 2064

The stealthy submarine was 23 years old. The captain and crew marveled that she had slipped into the Gulf of Mexico undetected. She had maintained radio silence for her entire voyage of 65 days. The silence had included all data connections beyond the hull of the sub. Because of the communications blackout, the captain and crew were unaware of the worldwide chaos that had erupted because of the Black Hole virus a little over a week ago.

Three hours after submerging, the Black Hole virus infiltrated every network and system on the planet, both secure and unsecured.

The sub's long voyage had taken her south down the Pacific Ocean from the northern hemisphere, across the equator, and into the Indian Ocean. There, the Captain had ordered a southwesterly course towards the southernmost tip of the continent of Africa, the Cape of Good Hope. Once she rounded the Cape into the South Atlantic, the Captain set a course on a northwesterly heading. The sub then traveled back over the equator and on into the North Atlantic. From there, on into the Caribbean Sea.

There, she had slowed to a pause and quietly lurked suspended over the depths of the Grand Cayman Trench, located midway between the islands of Jamaica and the Cayman Islands, south of Cuba. The Grand Cayman Trench was indeed an abyss, with a maximum depth of just over 25,000 feet.

For 24 hours, she had sat suspended at maximum depth over the trench, waiting and listening for any signs of detection.

Satisfied they had arrived undetected, the Captain ordered a course that would have the sub ever so slowly and quietly make her way into the Gulf of Mexico on a moonless night. The sub was now on station 200 nautical miles due north of the Yucatán Peninsula.

"Surface!" the Captain ordered.

From 357 feet below, the sub began her ascent to the surface. The ascent stopped with just the conning tower breaking through the calm seas. A quick radar sweep detected no ships clear to the horizon.

The Captain climbed up the ladder of the conning tower. He opened the hatch and climbed up and out of the sub into the moonless and pitch-black night. It was a warm and humid evening, almost stifling.

The Captain's binoculars fogged up for a moment. Taking them out, he scanned the horizon a full 360 degrees.

After the Captain was satisfied that no ships were near them, he turned, climbed down the ladder, and closed the hatch.

"Rig for dive!" A moment later, "Dive! Dive! Dive! Take her down to 50 meters."

CHEYENNE MOUNTAIN COMPLEX
Colorado Springs, Colorado
0354 MDT — 1 Aug 2064

The Klaxon sounded. Fighting a cold and sleep deprivation, General Winfield jumped out of his chair at the command desk. "Talk to me."

"Missile launch. Gulf of Mexico."

"Texas again?"

"Negative. Texas remains off Galveston at thirty-seven nautical miles. Positive marine launch detected 200 nautical miles north of the Yucatán Peninsula."

"How many!? Trajectory?

"Three, approaching hypersonic. Trajectory indicates probable air burst. We have a positive EMP attack profile. Confidence is high. I say again, confidence is high."

"Probable targets?"

"Virginia Beach, Louisville, and Colorado Springs right over our heads. ETA, just under three minutes."

|||| **23** ||||

THE QUIET

SHELDON FAMILY CABIN

Near Parker Island, Virginia

0615 EDT — 1 Aug 2064

Seven-year-old Tabitha Sheldon loved her doll. It was part old-fashioned doll made of plastic, but with a mid-twenty-first-century twist, it was also robotic. Admittedly, it was an older-style robotic doll without an internet connection. It had thus survived the Black Hole virus attack.

Her doll could walk or crawl. It could wave its arms around. Also, it could talk like a little girl of three years of age. Tabitha had named her doll Faith. She loved to talk with Faith. This morning, she was alone in her room with the door closed, playing with Faith.

Tabitha looked inquisitively at the doll and opened the conversation. "Faith, what would you like to do today?" she asked.

Faith looked up at Tabitha and replied, "Swing set, Mommy?"

Tabitha smiled. "Why, of course, child. But first, we must get you dressed and feed you breakfast. Would you like pancakes for breakfast?"

"Yes, Mommy, and when you mak…"

The doll's lips stopped in mid-sentence. Her arms had been slowly moving, but they had also stopped.

"Faith, what were you saying?" Tabitha waited for the response. None came. Tabitha picked up the doll and wiggled it a little, then asked again, "Faith, what were you saying? What's wrong?"

Still no response. She turned the doll over onto her stomach, pulled up the back of her little dress, and looked at the battery light on her back. It was off. Tabitha had never seen it off before, especially after a night of charging. Frightened, she yelled out, "Mommy! Mommy! Come quick!"

Sam Sheldon had been out on the deck reading a book. Frederic was back in D.C., and her folks and in-laws were in their bedrooms. Benjamin was coloring with his youngest sister, Andreanna.

When Sam heard Tabitha scream, it startled her. Her tone was different. Jumping up from her chair, she opened the screen door and yelled out as she ran towards her room. "What's the matter, Baby Girl? Mommy's coming." The hallway was dark. On the way past a light switch, she flipped it. Nothing happened. Annoyed, she ran a few more steps to Tabitha's door and flung it open, "Baby Girl, what's wrong?"

Tabitha sat on the floor next to her bed, quietly crying. "Faith is broken or something. The battery light is out. She won't talk or move or anything. Please fix her, Mommy."

Sam quietly knelt and wiped a tear from her daughter's face. She then turned and picked up Faith. She jiggled it. Nothing. She flipped it on its back and saw that the battery light was off. "Well, Honey, I think she just needs a charge. Let's plug it into the charger, and I bet the light will go back on. You'll have to keep her plugged in while you talk to her, okay?"

"Okay, Mommy."

Sam crawled over to the wall at the foot of the bed, where the charging cable lay underneath the nightstand. She picked it up and plugged it into Faith's back. No charging light came on.

"Did it work, Mommy?"

"Hold on, Sweetie." Annoyed, Sam jiggled the cable at the connection point on the wall, then at the back of the doll. Still no light. She reached up and turned the switch on the bedside lamp. Nothing.

Just then, her dad, Lloyd, burst into the room. "Sam, does your comm work? Mine's dead. Lights aren't working either."

Sam took her comm out of her back pocket. She had taken a quick look at it earlier when she had gotten out of bed at 5:30. She knew it had been totally charged, but now the display was dead. "That's weird. Mine is dead, too. Was there a storm last night?"

"You know me, Honey, light sleeper. I had the window open last night. Heard the critters and the crickets, but no rain or thunder."

"How about mom's phone?"

"She's in the shower. Let me go back into our room and check." As her dad returned to the other side of the house, both in-laws entered Tabitha's room. "What's going on? Both our phones are dead. The power's out, too."

Before Sam could answer, she heard a commotion from the front room.

Protective Detail Lead Agent Haney burst in from the front door, "Mr. Watkins, where's Sam?"

Lloyd looked a little concerned. "She's in Tabitha's room? Why?"

"Are they decent?" the agent asked.

"Yes. Say, what's going on?"

"I need you to get everyone into the front room immediately."

Lloyd walked back toward the hallway to the bedrooms and gathered everyone in the front room. As soon as each one entered the room and saw Haney, they started peppering him with questions. The agent motioned for everyone to quiet down. "Okay, is everyone's comm dead? No display? No power?"

Everyone answered in the affirmative.

Sam spoke up, "Agent Haney, what's wrong? Was there a storm last night, or did rebels sabotage the power lines, or what? When will the power be back on?"

Agent Haney looked Sam right in the eyes, "Mrs. Sheldon, everyone, I need you to listen very carefully to what I am about to say. I'm certain there has been an attack. Probably an electromagnetic pulse attack, or EMP for short. If there was, then everything electronic , everywhere, is broken."

Owen Sheldon grew pale. He knew what this meant. Owen's wife, Cassidy, held her hands up to her mouth.

Sam began recalling some conversations Frederic had with her a few years back about an EMP attack. She had expressed disinterest and laughed it off as more conspiracy talk. Now, she was faced with something unimaginable. She could feel her anxiety level rising. "Agent Haney, when will the power be back on? What about our comms? I need to speak to my husband."

"Mrs. Sheldon, we're all in a bit of a jam here. The power may not be back on anytime soon."

Sam interrupted, "Well, like, when? Later tonight? Tomorrow? When?" Haney continued. "I don't know, maybe months. Maybe longer. As a part of our training, all recruits into the Secret Service are taught about EMP, how to recognize an attack and its lingering effects…"

Sam's mom, Kendra, interrupted, "Lingering effects?! I've never heard of any of this stuff. Would someone tell me just what in the hell is going on!"

Sam looked at her firstborn son, Benjamin. He, Tabitha, and Andreanna had come into the front room and were listening to the adults. Sam looked at their faces. She knew her kids. Andreanna was too young to understand, but Benjamin and Tabitha looked concerned. "Benjamin, I want you to take your sisters out into the backyard to the swing set."

"But, Mom, I don't wanna. I wanna know what's going on, too. I was right in the middle of a game on my console, and then the power cut out."

"I know, Honey. That's what we are trying to figure out. Everything is going to be fine. Please do as you're told."

Agent Haney inwardly cringed at Sam's assurance to calm her children. If this were an EMP attack, he knew what that meant.

Reluctantly, Benjamin began guiding the girls to the back, out the sliding glass doors, toward the deck.

"Agent Haney, do they need an escort?"

"They'll be fine, Mrs. Sheldon. Besides, we can see the backyard clearly from here."

The adults went silent, waiting for the kids to walk out the back door. They waited to see the glass door shut and the kids a good 20 feet or so off the deck and into the yard.

Kendra leaped back into the conversation and yelled, "What is going on, Agent Haney!?"

"Look, an EMP attack is a surge of high energy caused by a high-altitude nuclear blast. The pulse goes through everything, including earth, and fries all electronics."

"Well, how long does it take to fix them?" she asked.

Lloyd was quick to answer, "Kendra, that's just it. They can't be fixed. They're all unrepairable."

Kendra looked scared. "What do you mean 'all'?"

Agent Haney looked her squarely in the eyes, "Everything everywhere has broken all at once. It's as if we have all been placed back into horse-and-buggy days before the age of electricity."

Kendra teetered but was grabbed by Lloyd to keep her from collapsing. He helped her to a chair. Sam went pale. "Dad, we need to pack up the kids and drive back to D.C. I don't feel safe here anymore."

"Oh, Honey, we can't."

"Well, why not?"

Agent Haney interjected, "Let me repeat. If this was an EMP—and it sure seems that way—then everything everywhere that's electronic has broken all at once. So, everything with a printed circuit board has been permanently fried. That includes comms, cars, trucks, trains, planes, radios, television, computers, household appliances, medical devices, and industrial equipment. The entire utility grid is broken because they all rely on electronic switches and stuff."

Lloyd spoke up, "And these cannot be fixed."

Agent Haney turned towards Lloyd. "Correct. Everything everywhere would need to be replaced. It will take years."

Sam started to hyperventilate. Her mom knew what to do and got her to sit down.

Owen Sheldon jumped in, "Agent Haney, how can we verify this was an EMP?"

"Our cars are all dead. I had Agent Adkins walk out to the street to look around and check on your neighbor across the street to see if they are experiencing the same issue as we are. If they—"

At that moment, Agent Adkins burst through the door, yelling, "Haney, I need to talk to you outside right away!"

"No need, Adkins. We're all aware that something significant has happened.

What did you find out?"

"I walked over to the neighbor across the entrance to the Sheldon property. They're experiencing the same thing. Everything is broken. Something else, though. The guy is one of those analog preppers."

Cassidy yelled out, "Oh, dear Lord, we've got white right-wing nuts living across the street from us? Did they greet you at the door with lots of guns pointed at you?"

"Actually, no, they did not. They were very kind and polite. The mom is Black.

"They're a family of seven, not including the two sets of parents. The guy I spoke with is named Kevin. He's a retired U.S. Marine Corps lifer. He and his wife, Kim, are the homeowners. Analog preppers are a special breed. They planned for EMP. Kevin has three old antique vehicles. A 1959 Chevy Apache pickup truck, a 1967 Buick Riviera, and a 1968 Chevy Impala. He showed them to me, and they all ran. Meanwhile, the four EVs in the driveway are as dead as a doornail.

He can't even open the doors to them. Kevin also mentioned he was a member of AmRRON."

Agent Haney looked shocked, "No shit!" Then he looked over to Sam sheepishly, "Sorry, ma'am."

Lloyd spoke up, "Wow, the American Redoubt Radio Operators Network. That's a group of Patri…"

Cassidy interrupted again, "A group of White supremacists!"

Owen jerked his head around and looked at Cassidy with a stern look, "Quit interrupting! Let Lloyd finish!"

Lloyd continued, "As I was saying, it's a group of patriots linked together via ham radios and Morse code. To be clear, Cassidy, they are not even remotely White supremacists. Anyway, many of them bought ancient analog sets decades ago. It's all tube-based, dating back well over 150 years. There's nothing in these old sets that has printed circuit boards. So, they are not affected by an EMP attack.

"Many hard-core operators went a step further and have massive lead-acid battery banks to run their rigs for months if they must. They'll have primitive foot-powered or hand-powered generators to charge up the batteries. Most operators know how to fix these old analog radio sets if needed. Agent, what did Kevin say? I presume he's been on the ham radio." Agent Adkins looked surprised that Lloyd knew so much about AmRRON. "Yes, he did say that. The word on the AmRRON is that it was an EMP attack. The entire nationwide grid is down. Also, parts of the grid in Canada and Mexico are down as well. Thousands of planes have crashed. Fires are burning all over the place from crashes, and shit."

"I need to get over there and talk to him and see if he can find out what's happening in the Capital. Anything else, Owen?" Haney asked.

"Yeah, the quiet."

"The quiet? I don't follow ya."

"Remember the dull sound we could hear from the property's backyard yesterday? I guess it was the valley kind of acting like a megaphone, taking the sounds of cars and trucks from all up and down the valley and amplifying their noises. Go outside and listen now. The quiet is deafening."

DESHAWN KING TANK SQUAD LOCATION

Battle of Minooka, Illinois

0515 CDT — 1 Aug 2064

DeShawn King and his tank squad of the 1619 Division had just moved up into position on day two of the Battle of Minooka, Illinois. The small town was situated southeast of Joliet, both outside the radiation zone of the Chicago metro area.

The 1619 was still attached to the 501st Corps as a part of Army Group West. In a bruising fashion, the entire federal army group had been pushed back to the east to Momence, Illinois, near the Indiana border. Their fighting retreat had continued since the FEDs stunning loss at the Battle of Ft. Smith, Arkansas. It had been a grueling time for everyone. Losses had been staggering for both sides. Morale among the FEDs had plummeted. King's hatred of all things CON had now grown into a rage.

Seven days ago, with the CON army's supply lines stretched thin, the FEDs had scored a significant victory at the Battle of Momence,

Illinois. There, FEDs' air support had changed the tide of battle. The CONs were now in a slow, organized retreat and had established a new defensive line near I-80, north and northwest of Minooka. To the rear of that line, Plainfield, Illinois. Beyond that, the strategic town of Oswego, Illinois, on the banks of the Fox River, had quickly become a central CON staging area.

The Black Hole virus had disabled most of the FEDs' equipment out of service, but the newer tanks had enough manual control to remain effective in combat. The loss of critical systems in the tanks diminished their accuracy considerably.

Just as King was about to give the order to fire their first day's combat round, everything electronic in the tank broke. With the radio dead and zero power in the tank with which to fire and maneuver, King realized they were sitting ducks. He ordered everyone out. The crew was forced to exit via the emergency escape hatch located on the floor of the tank because the electrically activated hydraulic hatches at the top of the turret and another one above the driver's head were both inoperable. When he and his crew emerged unscathed from the tank's backside, they stood up and looked around. What they saw shocked them.

King yelled out, "Shit, guys. What the hell just happened? All the helos have crashed. All the other soldiers are outside of their tanks, too. What the hell?!"

King hollered over to the tank commander next to him. "Andres, what just happened? Your tank dead, too?"

Tanker Andres Meyer was new, having reported for duty just five days ago. He looked a little scared. "I dunno, bro. This is screwed up. What just happened?"

King, senior in rank, barked an order, "Andres, take your squad over to that downed helo behind you and see if there are any survivors. Take any survivors back to the aid station pronto!"

Just as he saw Andres and his troops begin to move, King looked at the sky back toward the east and saw a giant military C-7A jet nosediving into the ground five hundred yards to the rear of their position. Upon impact, King and his men could feel the ground shake. The impact was simultaneously coupled with a tremendous explosion and fireball. King yelled out. "Shit! Shayne, run back to HQ and see if you can determine what the hell is going on. I think there's been an EMP attack."

AMRRON CORPS HQ

Northeast of Henry's Lake, Idaho

1013 MDT — 1 Aug 2064

Drew Norman had been working the comms since the early morning hours. He was inside his ham radio office in his mountaintop bug-out home. Drew and his family of six had bugged out three years earlier, right after the war started.

As the head of the AmRRON Corps, Norman played a central role in supporting the patriots who relied on the various operators across the country for real-time information.

Founded fifty-three years earlier in 2011, the American Redoubt Radio Operators Network mission plan: "We are committed to maintaining a continental network of radio operators for disaster response and civil defense, always ready to serve our communities, our states, our nation, and our fellow countrymen with unconventional communications in times of need."

While the Civil War 2.0 had kept him and his fellow ham radio operators busy, the internet and digital comm channels had remained up and running until the Black Hole virus had struck weeks earlier. That attack had downed everything except real-time comms, which included ham radios, Morse code, CBs, and VHF radios that the prepper crowd had long embraced.

Drew had an entire analog rig to his left. To his right was the modern digital rig he had used daily for the last three years, except on the first day of the month. That day was Analog Day. It was the one day of the month when hard-core analog preppers fired up their generators and ran on analog rigs for the day's comm sessions.

A little before 7 a.m., he had been talking to an operator outside the Atlanta Radiation Zone via his digital ham radio when the EMP occurred. It took just a moment for him to realize what had happened. When he did, he went back to the house and started the ancient analog-wired diesel generator. Next to it is a full 10,000-gallon tank of biodiesel fuel.

With his bug-out power quickly restored, he powered up his analog ham rig, a vintage 1959 Heathkit DX-40, and tuned to the 20-meter band frequency of 14.074 MHz. He then started tapping out Morse code:

CQ CQ CQ DE KB1WRP KB1WRP STOP
AMRRON COMMUNICATIONS CONDITION LEVEL ONE STOP
EMP ATTACK CONFIRMED STOP
GRID DOWN STOP

VOICE BROADCAST 1900 ZULU STOP
SPREAD THE WORD STOP
WILL BE OFFLINE FOR SIXTY AND ON VOICE CALL AT 1900
ZULU SHARP K

With the alert sent, he switched over to the 40-meter band frequency of 7.776 MHz, grabbed the microphone, and tried to reach General Adams.

"KD7CEA, KB1WRP—Kilo Bravo One Whiskey Romeo Papa, KB1WRP—Kilo Bravo One Whiskey Romeo Papa, KB1WRP standing by."

After three additional attempts, Adams responded. "Drew, glad to hear your voice. Are you all okay down there? They just handed me the Morse code alert. Great job!"

"That was good. You guys are really on the ball. Yeah, we're good here. Thanks for asking. I just got the diesel generator fired up. Colonel, how bad is it out there?"

"Real bad. I saw three commercial jets fall out of the sky near me. God rest their souls. We're working on setting up the analog concall with the governors and military leadership. Thankfully, we had a plan for an EMP attack."

"Any idea who the perps are, Colonel?"

"Not a clue yet. If I had to guess, I would say it's probably a foreign actor taking advantage of our current predicament. Whoever it was, I gotta hand it to 'em, they planned and executed it well."

"Roger that. I'll be doing a voice broadcast at 1900 Zulu. Got anything you want me to pass along?"

"Pray, 'cause we're all in a real fix now. All modern comms are dead. The internet is dead. All computers are dead. We need all available analog ham patriots to act as relay stations. I will send you the coded message via Morse later this afternoon. You have the designated list of secure analog operators with the decoders, so you and everyone else with them need to guard them with your lives. How's your horse-riding skills?"

"Not too bad, but I prefer my analog 1968 Chevy. Runs like a champ. I had my wife go out to the shed and make sure she started. By golly, the first turn of the key! Ol' reliable analog 327 gasoline engine."

"Got any carbon credits to offset that beast? Did you get enough gasoline in storage? Just how old is that gasoline you got stored for the apocalypse? The last drop out of the last refinery trickled out in 2061."

"Carbon credits? Ha! I need a little humor right about now. Yeah, the gasoline is a state secret. If I told you how much I had stockpiled, I'd have to kill ya. Just kidding. Seriously, I used that special additive to preserve it. Man, that stuff was expensive but worth it. There's not a hint of the gas going bad at all. Crazy good stuff. I expect all the greenies to be crapping in their pants right about now. Their three-thousand-dollar smartphones are permanently fried. The same goes for all the solar arrays and all modern appliances. All rail, planes, and buses are dead. The EV cars will never run again, and the power is out nationwide indefinitely. Grocery stores are probably seeing riots right about now, too. The death toll from this must be staggering already, and we're not even through day one. God have mercy on us all."

"Yeah, well, let's not forget that the preppers represent a tiny fraction of the overall population in CON territory, or anywhere else for that matter. Your analog capabilities simply don't exist for most folks, no matter where they live. The way I see it, CON, MOD, or LIB, we're all in the same horse and buggy boat now. If you step outside, it's like even the animals are affected. The quiet is deafening."

THE WHITE HOUSE

Washington, D.C.

1313 EDT — 1 Aug 2064

In the Situation Room, President Cyrus sat at the head of the conference table. The room was usually packed for a hastily called emergency meeting of his Cabinet and Joint Chiefs. But today, many were missing, and, with all comms dead, there was no way to reach them.

Cyrus opened the meeting. "Morning, everyone. Obviously, an apparent EMP attack. Director Thomas, what does the NSA have?"

NSA Director Kwame Thomas looked like he had been sucker punched. "Mr. President. We have zero information on this. A blank sheet of paper. Nothing in our view up to the attack occurred."

The President paused for a moment before continuing. "I see. Kwame, keep digging. General Homer, what do you have?"

"Mr. President, NORAD detected a missile launch. Specifically, three were launched. Looks like from a vessel approximately two hundred nautical miles north of the Yucatán Peninsula. I was on the hotline with General Winfield at the Cheyenne Mountain Complex. He had confirmation on the launch and the trajectory. The targets for the air burst were Virginia Beach, Louisville, and Colorado Springs. That sent the pulse out and, wham, we're down."

"General, I want our top technical folks on this right away. We need to address this issue immediately. What is the situation with our fighting forces?"

"Mr. President, communication is spotty to nonexistent. Our analog capabilities and EMP-proof communications are nonexistent in many areas and for almost all our military units. We are having to resort to novel measures to reach our commanders in the field."

"Novel measures? Explain," the President said. "We have couriers out on horseback…"

Cyrus interrupted, "Horseback? You can't be serious."

"I'm very serious. Sir, we are adapting and improvising as we go. There is a car museum nearby, over in Alexandria, with antique gasoline vehicles. The problem is there's no gasoline. Recall your executive order last year shutting down the sole remaining gasoline refinery in 2061 to achieve your net-zero carbon goal. We're checking to see if these antique cars will run on pure alcohol. If we can get them to run, we'll confiscate them and use them."

"General, I need no reminders of any executive orders I issued. Quite frankly, your comment borders on insulting. I need to know the condition of our fighting forces. Can they still fight? What is going on with the CON military units? Can they still fight?" After pausing a moment, the President turned and looked over at Air Force Chief of Staff Aaron David. "General David, what about our aircraft?"

"Mr. President, every air asset we have at Reagan National is dead on the ground. Given the variety of military and commercial assets there, I believe the same situation exists everywhere across the country.

"There were two commercial aircraft that crashed into the Potomac. A third crashed short of a runway. Several columns of smoke from the ground can be seen that coincide with the approach pattern into Reagan. Given that evidence, I believe any military assets in the air at the time of the attack have crashed or crash-landed.

"Normally, at this time of day, we have hundreds of military air assets aloft. We have combat operations underway in Illinois at Minooka, as well as in Cincinnati, Ohio, and out west in California, north of Sacramento, in Oregon near Lake Umatilla, and in Washington state near Moses Lake. Since we can't communicate with any of our assets, we have no accounting of their status."

Cyrus looked and sounded exasperated. "Shit, General, how can this be? I thought our military aircraft were EMP-proof?"

"In basic terms, they are from an EMP weapon attack. But we've never been able to perform a high-altitude test with a high-yield nuclear detonation. It's only been computer-simulated on the ground. Complicating the matter is that the Black Hole virus erased all of our IT systems. We're in a bad way, Sir. Our best people are going to be on this around the clock to see if we can get our systems back up and running."

"What about improvising? Is there anything we can do to get some aircraft aloft and into the fight?

"I've sent couriers to the Air and Space Museum at Dulles. There are plenty of vintage aircraft on static display there without printed circuit boards. In theory, they could run. In practical and technological terms, these are 100-plus-year-old aircraft from the 1960s to the 1920s. Nobody knows if they'll even start up, and, for sure, no one knows exactly how to fly them. Plus, they all run on obsolete fuels, Jet A, Jet B, and AVGAS."

"What is AVGAS?" the President asked.

"AVGAS is short for Aviation Gasoline. It's 100+ octane. It was mainly used by traditional propeller aircraft and small piston-engine airplanes, which is exactly what many planes are at the museum. Refining all these aviation fuels was halted in 2050 when we cut over to hydrogen fuels for aviation. That was all part of a major leap forward towards net-zero carbon emissions."

"Yes, I know that. So, who did you send out to Dulles to see if we can get some of these old birds up in the air?"

"Mr. President, we have our smartest engineering minds and pilots from the Pentagon making their way out to Dulles as I speak."

|||| **24** ||||

THE BATTLE OF MCHENRY

EASTSIDE OF TOWN

McHenry, Illinois

1201 CDT — 15 Aug 2064

After a series of victories in the Great Plains, the CON Army had rolled into far northwestern Illinois via U.S. 20—also named Grant's Highway—using it to cross over the Mississippi River at Dubuque, Iowa, and on into Galena, Illinois.

Victorious in Galena, the CONs had rolled eastward unopposed along U.S. 20 through the small far-northern Illinois hamlets of Elizabeth, Stockton, Lena, and Freeport, until hitting the LIB stronghold of Rockford.

After New Way forces were routed in Rockford, a severely diminished force put up a stand in Belvidere near an abandoned automobile manufacturing plant. At the Battle of Belvidere, the CONs were greatly helped by the Stateline Militia, which was composed of staunch CON irregular militia forces from rural areas all along the Illinois and Wisconsin state line.

The Stateliners, as they referred to themselves, successfully put up fierce resistance east of the old plant and wound up blocking the FEDs' only escape route. With their supply lines cut and ammunition nearly exhausted, the FEDs surrendered with only a third of their numbers still left standing.

The CON army had now split into two. The southern group went southeast and was composed of the 606th Corps. At Momence, Illinois, the 606th was fighting a losing battle and was ordered by General Buford to make a tactical withdrawal to the northwest. In retreat, the 606th fought a rear-guard action before linking back up with the northern group, the 101st Corps.

The 101st Corps had formed a line from Elgin, Illinois, just south of I-90, all the way up to Richmond, Illinois, just south of the Wisconsin state line.

General Buford had initially planned for the 101st to cross the Fox River and push east toward Chicago. At the same time, the 606th would engage the FEDs at Momence—the prize: O'Hare Airport and the two adjacent mammoth rail terminals plus the I-294 interchange with I-90. A logistics delay had held up the 101st by 24 hours. The next day, the nukes hit Chicago. The 101st was then ordered to hold the line, awaiting orders. When the EMP hit, there they remained.

With the CONs vulnerable, Cyrus had ordered the FEDs' army in Wisconsin to cross into Illinois from Wilmot, Wisconsin, and proceed on foot down a five-mile-wide radiation-free corridor on the east side of the Fox River.

It had not gone according to plan. What started as a skirmish east of the city of McHenry three days earlier had mushroomed into the most significant land battle of the war, the Battle of the Fox River Valley.

On Day One, in the early morning hours, FED forces came upon a scouting party of CONs near a small chapel in the Village of Johnsburg, just to the North of McHenry. Fighting erupted within minutes and slowly escalated throughout the day.

On Day Two, FED forces marching up from the south, following their fresh victory at Momence, joined the battle and extended the fighting from McHenry clear down to Elgin. Toward the end of daylight, a FED artillery barrage struck a field hospital in McHenry and killed nearly fifteen hundred people—wounded soldiers and medical staff. As Day Two ended, Buford had nicknamed the battle GB2, short for Gettysburg II. The name stuck and spread like wildfire among the soldiers.

King and his tank unit was now without tanks and on foot and had been reassigned to the infantry of the 1619 Division. On day three of the battle, he found himself in the thick of it again, fighting near a semi-destroyed veterans' hall. He was glad he had been lifting weights and brushing up on his judo skills during downtime between battles for the last few months. It was helping him stay alive amidst the carnage of hand-to-hand combat raging for the better part of three and a half hours. In those hours, he had lost his entire squad of soldiers.

Amidst the sounds, fury, and savagery, his mind and body had gone on autopilot as he bashed and bayoneted his way from one hated CON soldier to another. Slowly, the sounds grew less as he climbed over the dead.

Exhausted and covered with the sickening filth of hand-to-hand combat, he suddenly found himself alone and face-to-face with his next opponent. It was the last CON soldier standing anywhere near him. The CON soldier was also caked in the blood and filth of battle.

"You piece of CON shit! My Dad and my battle buddies are all dead because of the likes of you! I'm gonna slit you wide open and watch you die, you son of a bitch!"

King took his weapon, reared it back, and prepared to lunge his bayonet forward into the CON's belly. Just as he started the lunge, he heard a hoarse voice cry out, "DeShawn?"

King froze. He wondered, *How does this guy know my name?*

Now frozen in place, King peered into the eyes of the CON he was about to kill. He felt oddly out of place. *What is happening to me?* He wondered. He noticed the soldier's eyes and locked onto them intently.

The CON spoke hoarsely again, "DeShawn, it's me, your Dad."

King yelled, "You liar! My Dad is dead! He was killed at the Battle of Ft. Smith, Arkansas! Who the hell are you, and how do you know my name?

The CON then dropped his weapon. "DeShawn, I could never kill you. I know the pain and anger you feel, the rage—all of it. I've had those same feelings myself, but I didn't die at Ft. Smith. All the soldiers around me did when a shell landed near them. I was shielded by a truck. When I came to, I got up and walked away to surrender. Instead, I wound up defecting and fighting to save the republic.

"DeShawn, it really is me, your Dad, Jackson King. Your mother's name is Eleanor. Your mom and I got married in Chicago. You were born on September 17, 2041, in McHenry. She nicknamed you punkin' when you were just two years old."

With recognition came release. DeShawn started to sob. He dropped his weapon, fell to his knees, and held out both hands, all the while crying out, "Daddy," repeatedly.

Jackson King also fell to his knees and embraced his only son. Together, they wept. At 12:59 p.m. on 15 August 2064, in the city of McHenry, Illinois, that section of the battlefield went quiet because the killing had finally stopped.

IIII **25** IIII

COURAGE, VALOR, AND LAW

FORD'S THEATRE

Washington, D.C.

1703 EDT — 13 Sep 2064

Ford's Theatre was President Devin Cyrus's choice for a fundraiser to benefit New Way parents who had lost a soldier in the Great Second American Civil War, which was now in its third year.

The benefit had been hastily planned in early June, before the catastrophic events that occurred afterward, which had set the country and the world back into a horse-and-buggy era. The President had made the short trip from the White House to the theatre in a bulletproof carriage pulled by a team of four horses.

With the nations of the world struggling to take care of their own citizens, there was no one left to come to the aid of other countries, especially one as large as America.

Ford's Theatre was one of Washington, D.C.'s oldest buildings. The site had originally been built in 1833 as a multiracial Baptist church. In 1839, the church split along racial lines. After being purchased by John T. Ford in 1861 and subsequently converted from a church to a theatre, the original structure was destroyed by fire in 1862. Ford had the rubble cleared and started with a clean slate. After erecting a new theater, it quickly became one of the capital's most prestigious theatres during the First Civil War.

On Good Friday, 14 April 1865, President Abraham Lincoln sat quietly high up in the Presidential Booth of Ford's Theatre alongside his bride of 23 years, Mary Todd Lincoln, who was the daughter of a prominent and wealthy slave-owning family in Kentucky. Also seated with the first couple was Major Henry Rathbone and his new fiancée, Miss Clara Harris. Together, the two couples sat and looked down at the stage to enjoy the playbill for the night: *Our American Cousin.*

The night was a welcome break, coming just five days after the end of the First American Civil War on 9 April, with the surrender of the Confederate Army of Northern Virginia under the command of General Robert E. Lee to Union General Ulysses S. Grant at Appomattox Court House, Virginia.

At 10:15 p.m., President Lincoln found himself laughing at a key humorous line in the play. With the crowd of 1,700 theatergoers also laughing, most of them did not hear the single gunshot from a small single-shot Philadelphia Deringer. The gunshot mortally wounded the President, having entered his skull just behind his left ear. The bullet traveled through his brain and came to rest at the front of his skull after having fractured both orbital plates.

The assassin's shot had been fired by a prominent actor at the time, and a known Confederate sympathizer named John Wilkes Booth. His dastardly deed was part of a larger conspiracy to attempt to re-energize the Confederates and continue the War.

Mortally wounded, the unconscious sixteenth president of the United States was carried across the street to a boarding house owned by a tailor named William Petersen. Lincoln was carried into one of the bedrooms upstairs. There, he was placed diagonally on a bed too small for his tall and lanky frame. He remained there after the doctors felt that he was in no condition to be moved any further due to the seriousness of the wound.

The room remained filled with doctors and vigil keepers, great and small, all night. Finally, at 7:22 a.m. the following day, 15 April 1865, President Abraham Lincoln entered eternity. Secretary of War Edwin Stanton uttered the immortal words, "Now he belongs to the ages."

Well-versed in American history, Cyrus had insisted he had no desire to sit in the Presidential Booth. He detested the Lincolns, especially his wife, Mary Todd, because of the story of her family's slaveholdings in Kentucky.

Awaiting the start of the gala, the President organized a quick meeting just off the stage to the right. "Matt, any updates on getting anything working again?"

Matt Kensington was slow to respond, "Mr. President, lots of smart minds are still working on this. I must be frank: it doesn't look good."

"Damnit, Matt, I don't want to hear that. There must be someone who can do something to get us back on our feet. All the money these tech companies have, and we're still burning candles and cooking over carbon-fueled fires weeks after the attack? This is unacceptable. Our war effort has morphed into something out of the history books from the time of Lincoln. No airpower, no drones, no mechanized divisions, no satellite intel. We're having to use First Civil War tactics." Cyrus paused. Frustrated, he let out a laugh. "You know, I find it kind of ironic we're here raising money in the very place where an assassin's bullet cut down that man."

"Mr. President, we're all just as frustrated as you…"

Cyrus snapped back, "Don't patronize me! Let's not forget I have the burden of being President, and you have the much lower burden of being just my Chief of Staff! I can assure you my frustration level dwarfs yours, Matt. It dwarfs it significantly."

Matt was taken aback by the President's usage of the word 'dwarf', a term on the official banned list. He thought of objecting, but decided to let it pass. He figured that, after all, the President was right. "Mr. President, I've got an old friend over in Alexandria. He's a brilliant electrical engineer. I'll send a courier out to him and see if he'd like to join the efforts."

Cyrus seemed buoyed by the offer. "Alright, that's what I like to hear. I'll order a dispatch on horseback to speed up the process. Any word on getting any old gasoline or diesel-powered vehicles up and running? Any updates from Dulles?"

"Nothing. The whole carbon fuel thing is a giant catch-22. No working pipelines or refineries means no production and no fuel."

"Keep on it, Matt. At this point, I feel like you're the only one I can trust. All those other bastards in my Cabinet are not worth a shit."

ABANDONED STOREFRONT
F St. NW, Washington, D.C.
1717 EDT — 13 Sep 2064

Frederic Sheldon sat quietly awaiting the arrival of a courier. It had been a difficult time for the country and himself. Although he was grateful to know his family was safe in the Shenandoah, he missed them terribly. He was weary of war and the constant news of devastation and suffering mounting across the country.

The nuke exchange had cast a pall over everyone. Everyday folks were shocked that the war had reached a nuclear apex.

The latest casualty estimate from the atomic destruction of the four large metropolitan areas was seventy-five million. The horror of it all had led to many suicides at the Pentagon and all around the nation's capital. Sheldon felt a growing anger. It was the feeling one gets when they realize they have been greatly deceived. The anger had been welling up in him even before the nuke exchange. Now it was about to boil over.

A soldier interrupted Sheldon's somber reflections. "Mr. Secretary, the courier is here. She has authenticated correctly."

"Thank you, Joseph. Escort her in and tell the guards to ensure she has not been followed."

"Yes, sir."

A moment later, a female wearing fatigues was silently escorted into the room. Sheldon noted the name on the uniform, which said Harrington. "Mr. Secretary, my instructions are to deliver a message to you and no one else. I beg your pardon. We've never met, and I was never much of a news person. I don't know what Frederic Sheldon looks like. I need to see your government-issued ID. Also, a state-issued ID as well."

Sheldon looked at her stoically. "Under the present circumstances, I fully understand." He retrieved both IDs as requested and handed them over to her. She carefully studied both and looked at Sheldon intently. She repeated her review twice more. She was satisfied. "Mr. Secretary, it's an honor to meet you. An envelope is taped to my back. She turned around, untucked, and lifted the back of her uniform, which revealed a small manila envelope taped to the center of her back over the spine. "I was instructed that only you are to remove this."

"I understand." Sheldon took a step forward and carefully pulled at the tape and envelope to peel it away from her back. Feeling slightly embarrassed, he found himself compelled to speak some words of compassion and humanity, "Excuse me, I want to do this slowly so as not to hurt you."

Responding to this simple gesture, she returned the kindness, "Thank you, Sir. Is your family OK?"

"Yes, they are. Thank you for asking. What's your name? How's your family?"

"Private Harrington. I grew up in the Bronx. I moved away four years ago. I kept in touch regularly, though. Spoke to my mom the day before the nukes. After the war first started, she kept detailed notes about where everyone was at. When we last spoke, she didn't mention that anyone in the family had left or was traveling. She prayed every night for each one of the family by name. Lot of good that did. I believe they're all gone. We were a big family, too. Thanksgiving dinners were always a huge Irish affair. Thirty-plus every year—three turkeys every year. My mom loves…" The emotions suddenly welled up and halted her ability to continue speaking any further.

Sheldon was holding the envelope and could sense the profound loss this soldier had experienced. He thought of his own family and felt a muted sense of joy. They were still alive out west. "I'm so sorry. You know, I walked away from my Christian faith during college. My professors, all atheists, convinced me the whole thing was a fairy tale. Very recently, I came to my Awakening to the truth that they were all wrong. I think malice, anger, war, and all other evils must have a source. A conscious being that is the opposite of God since God is love. Private Harrington, I will pray for you."

Private Harrington was now facing Sheldon. Her face grew angry. "Pray for me? No thanks. If there is a God, where is he in all of this? I mean, c'mon!"

Sheldon paused, searching for a response. "I remember a time when my daughter was about five. Her mom and I knew she had a temper, and we'd been working on her, talking to her. Giving her instructions on what was proper behavior and what was not. We punished her more than a few times. But she mostly hadn't changed. Then, one day, she had the biggest temper tantrum I ever saw. Her mom and I couldn't stop her. We finally had to step back and patiently wait for her to get it out of her system. With all that's happened now, I wonder if God is patiently waiting for this, the sum of all our anger, to be spent out of our system. I know one thing: God didn't send those nukes. In a way, I think we all did."

Her angry face melted away. Somewhat weary-looking, her countenance now appeared contemplative. "Well, if there is a God, then why did he allow all this to happen?"

Sheldon took in the comment and thought about it for a moment. "I certainly don't pretend to know all the answers. But I know we're all given free will. Even at five years old, my daughter exercised it with her tantrum. I think maybe God was telling us all along where our nation was headed. We just weren't listening."

She laughed slightly, "You sound like a MOD."

"Ha! I was one of Cyrus's biggest supporters. That all changed when the nukes went off. I'm still trying to figure things out.

"You know, the other day, I had this memory come back to me from my childhood. We're at church right after the second 9/11. I was seven. The church is packed, and we're all singing, '*Jesus loves me, this I know, for the Bible tells me so, little ones to him belong, they are weak, and he is strong.*' I look up and see tears streaming down my mom's face, and I ask her why she's crying. She leans over, looks me square in the eyes, and says, 'One day, you'll understand that love will triumph over evil.'

"I know one thing," Sheldon continued, "I'm convinced beyond a shadow of a doubt that Cyrus has got to be stopped." Pausing, he stuck out his hand in friendship. Harrington put her hand out, and they shook hands. Trying to sound somewhat fatherly, Sheldon looked her square in the eyes and said, "Private Harrington, I thank you for your service, courage, and time, and I wish you Godspeed."

"Thank you, Mr. Secretary. Likewise. Thank you for taking the time to listen and share your thoughts. You've made me think."

"We all need to do some critical thinking these days. It's a healthy thing."

"Agreed. Bye-bye." She turned and quietly walked out the door. "Joseph," said Sheldon, "make sure she heads in the right direction out the back exit."

"Yes, sir."

Sheldon studied the envelope. Opening it, he carefully read its contents. Satisfied, he took a lighter and set the note alight. He watched the flames quickly devour the flash paper as he dropped it to the floor.

Satisfied there were no remnants left, he turned to his tactical unit commander, Marco Duran. "Commander, are you ready?"

"Yes, sir!"

"OK. We go."

Sheldon turned around and walked towards the door and out into the night. Behind him, 150 soldiers followed in formation at a brisk pace.

Commander Duran kept abreast of Sheldon as they walked west on F Street, then turned left and headed south on 10th Street. As they made the turn, Sheldon saw a large group of soldiers approaching from the south. It had to be Parry and his troops headed toward them, so he hoped.

The Metropolitan Police Department assisted the Secret Service protective detail in keeping the President safe inside Ford's Theatre for the Gala. With all modern communications permanently disrupted, the Secret Service was relegated to relying on human eyes, ears, and couriers. It also quickly developed a signal flag system.

Agent Ferguson was the first to spot the large group of armed soldiers approaching from the north. Almost simultaneously, Agent Roberson spotted an equally large group coming from the south.

Agent Roberson yelled out, "Halt! Who goes there?"

The reply was immediate, "This is Speaker Jai Parry. I have a large contingent of heavily armed soldiers. There are two other groups. One is halted just to your north. You are outnumbered and outgunned.

"We are here to arrest Devin Cyrus for treason and violation of the presidential oath of office to preserve, protect, and defend the Constitution of the United States. I do this pursuant to Section 4 of the Fourteenth Amendment to the United States Constitution.

"By invoking section 4, I am now the acting President and have assumed the full powers and duties of the Office of President of the United States. You are now ordered to lay down your weapons."

Agent Roberson yelled back, "This is Secret Service Agent Roberson. Jai, weren't you one of the ones in favor of banning the Constitution? Seems to me you don't have a leg to stand on. You got a lot of nerve to whip that disgraced document out of the dumpster and try to start a coup."

"Agent Roberson, your point is noted. But it seems I've had a sort of awakening to the truth. I realized I had no authority to support the scrapping of the Constitution. Neither does Cyrus. Therefore, my view has changed, and I believe the Constitution is still in force, and is in fact irrevocable. I don't want any of you to get hurt. So please lay down your weapons and surrender."

"Or what, Jai?"

"We'll be forced to shoot. For the last time, you have sixty seconds to lay down your weapons. If you do not, we will open fire on your position."

Roberson turned to Ferguson, "What do we do?"

Ferguson looked nervous. "I don't know. With our numbers plus the

Metropolitan Police, we have close to a hundred people with weapons. Let me call Bryant." It was pure muscle memory, and a brain lapse that saw Agent Ferguson bring his wrist comm up to his mouth and attempt to call the lead agent with the President. Just as quickly as he got it close to his mouth, he remembered the comm had been rendered into nothing more than a bracelet. "Man, oh man!" he yelled. "Let me run inside."

"It'll be too late! I show 20 seconds left!" Agent Roberson answered.

Sheldon had motioned for his squad to head to the far side of the street to avoid being in the line of fire from Parry's squad. They were now crouched down and had taken cover behind cars, trucks, planters, and whatever else they could find.

Sheldon looked over and saw Parry's squad make a similar move. The police and secret service agents were now in a crossfire. Unknown to them, Parry and Sheldon had put a crack team of snipers on roofs close to the buildings where they were. With the secret service snipers directly above them, they, up to now, were unaware that they were now in the sights of soldiers under Jai Parry and Frederic Sheldon's command. The sniper had a target in his sight and was tracking it. With his other eye open, he saw the red flag go up. It was the signal to use lethal force against an immediate threat to the security perimeter protecting the President of the United States.

Exhaling, he paused his breath and pulled the trigger. Headshot. Clean kill. He raised his right hand to chamber another round. His hand never made it. The sniper himself was now dead.

Down below, mayhem broke out with automatic weapons fire from ground level. Above, three other FED snipers had just been eliminated. Sheldon looked over and saw a group of his men lying wounded twenty feet away. He turned and yelled to Duran and his squad, "Covering fire!" Hunched down, he headed over to the closest downed soldier and pulled him back over towards some cover provided by a large tree planter.

Duran shouted, "You're gonna get yourself killed! Get your ass over here now, Sheldon!"

He looked over at Duran and shook his head no. "I guess I picked a heck of a time to become a patriot! Covering fire!" Sheldon leaped up and ran back over to the group of downed men. He grabbed two more by their collars, one in each hand, and dragged them back to the same spot as the first one.

Duran and his squad shifted positions and moved over to protect the wounded soldiers. He yelled for another team to reposition. "Hutchinson, move your squad over there behind that other planter. Covering fire!"

Meanwhile, a hundred yards away, Parry's team gained the upper hand and slowly crept towards the Secret Service and Metropolitan Police force line. Parry thought he heard automatic weapons fire erupt from his right. He hoped it was General Gage's men covering the rear exit of the theatre. He shouted over the din of the battle to his commander, "Duffy, can you make out how Sheldon's men are doing?"

Ducking down, Duffy looked at Parry. "Sir, they've taken some casualties, but I swear I saw Sheldon running back and forth and grabbing wounded soldiers."

Frederic Sheldon saw one last soldier lying in the prone position. He was breathing but unconscious. Under fire, Sheldon had retrieved eleven wounded soldiers. "Duran, one last man. Covering fire!" He jumped up and ran forward five steps when he was hit in the right leg just above the knee. The round had shattered his femur. He fell to the ground, screaming in pain, "I'm hit!"

FORD'S THEATRE

Washington, D.C.

1803 EDT — 13 Sep 2064

President Devin Cyrus was bruised and had a slight cut over his right eye. He had been slightly injured by shrapnel from a flash-bang grenade. Looking somewhat bewildered, he was shocked to see Jai Parry standing before him. Parry spat in his face.

Visibly angry, Parry raised his voice. "Devin Cyrus, I'm placing you under arrest for treason, sedition, insurrection, and violating the Oath of Office."

Cyrus erupted. "Jai, you've lost your mind. I'll have you shot for this. Besides, the Vice-President is number one in the line of succession. You're out of order here. Someone arrest this man!"

No one moved. The entirety of Cyrus's security detail had either been detained, wounded, or killed. All the guns in the room were brandished by members of the three teams involved in the operation to arrest the President.

Parry continued. "Cyrus, the Vice-President, is also under arrest. As Speaker of the House of Representatives, according to the United States Constitution, I'm number two in the line of succession. Checkmate."

Cyrus's face was red. "Checkmate, my ass! What Congress? We're under martial law, remember? The Constitution is no more."

"Cyrus, I had a lengthy conversation with the Chief Justice of the United States, Douglass Fredericks. In his view, when you canceled the Constitution by executive order, you violated your oath and a shitload of federal statutes."

"The Chief Justice has no authority to make a ruling, and he would need a majority of the court to go through the entire legal process affirming his opinion," Cyrus yelled.

"First of all, it was not a ruling. It was his legal opinion as one of, if not the, preeminent constitutional scholar of our times.

"Second, getting the whole court involved is, for the moment, kind of hard to do since they're all dead. Recall that nine of them were vaporized in New York at a fundraiser. Three others were vaporized in Chicago while delivering a series of lectures.

"Third, it was the Chief Justice's opinion that since you declared martial law under the National Emergencies Act, before your EO was issued to cancel the Constitution, then martial law is still legal and binding. So, I'm keeping martial law in place for now.

"Last, he said it was only after your illegal EO to cancel the Constitution that that order and every other EO issued by you since then is technically null and void since you were operating outside the bounds of the Constitution. In his expert opinion, you surrendered presidential powers at that moment after committing high crimes."

"That's the craziest shit I ever heard, Jai. I'm gonna love seeing you hang. In fact, I know the perfect tree on the West Lawn of the White House. It'll work just fine!"

Parry motioned for Duran to take Cyrus into custody. As he took a step forward, a loud voice yelled out from high up. "Thus, always to tyrants!"

Everyone swung their heads around towards the sound of the voice. They all heard a loud bang and felt warm liquid splatter their faces. Turning to look, they saw Cyrus collapsing to the floor with a fountain of blood from the left side of his neck. Then they heard a second bang from whence the yell had come. They looked up just in time to see Matt Kensington falling to the stage dead. He had fallen from the same booth Lincoln had been assassinated in.

IIII **26** IIII

THE OVERTURE

THE WHITE HOUSE

Washington, D.C.

2011 EDT — 13 Sep 2064

Chief Justice of the United States, Douglass Fredericks, stood with Jai Parry in the Lincoln Bedroom of the White House. As a history buff and one who appreciated symbolism, Fredericks had suggested that Parry consider taking the Presidential Oath of Office in that room to send a powerful message to the nation. Parry had agreed.

Reporters had been brought in to take notes. The newspapers were scrambling to find ancient analog printing presses of any size with which to print a newspaper. They were scouring museums, with no luck so far. The newspapers had been digital-only for decades. For now, newspapers were posting large handwritten posters throughout the town and sending couriers by horseback with duplicate handwritten posters to deliver to nearby cities. It was time-consuming, but the populace was desperate for news.

On hand to witness the swearing-in ceremony was an artist who would sketch the history-making moment, as modern cameras no longer worked, and no one made film anymore for vintage analog cameras.

Also present was the Chief Justice's law clerk, a young lad of twenty-seven. He owned a small collection of antique analog stenographer machines and, more importantly, knew how to use them.

With significant security details in and outside the White House, the time came to make the transfer of power official.

With Parry's wife and four children looking on, along with several aides, the Chief Justice removed Lincoln's Bible from a leather pouch he had brought to the ceremony. It was the Bible he had hoped to use for Cyrus's swearing-in ceremony over three years earlier.

The Chief Justice called for quiet, approached Parry, and held the Bible in his outstretched hand.

"Please place your right hand upon the Bible and repeat after me. 'I, Jai Parry, do solemnly swear…'"

"I, Jai Parry, do solemnly swear…"

"That I will faithfully execute…"

"That I will faithfully execute…"

"The office of President of the United States…"

"The office of President of the United States…"

"And will to the best of my ability…"

"And will to the best of my ability…"

"Preserve, protect, and defend…"

"Preserve, protect, and defend…"

"The Constitution of the United States."

"The Constitution of the United States."

"So, help me God."

"So, help me God."

The Chief Justice stuck out his right hand, "Congratulations, Mr. President."

THE GOVERNOR'S MANSION

Oklahoma City, Oklahoma

1003 CDT — 14 Sep 2064

An aide knocked and quickly entered Governor Whitfield's office. It was Miguel Sánchez. "Governor, we're getting a Morse code from out east. You'd better come and check this out."

Whitfield looked up from her notepad. "A Morse code message? Who is it?"

"That's just it. They're saying they're the President of the United States," Miguel quipped.

"Really. Well, now, this I gotta see." Whitfield followed Sánchez out the door, down the hall, and into the comm room. She walked up to Pvt. Jonathan Waya, the oldest son of the Oklahoma State House Speaker of the House, Chief Billy Waya. "Okay, Jonathan, watcha got?"

"This started coming over a few minutes ago. I'll read it to you, Governor."

FROM US PRESIDENT PARRY STOP
TO GOV WHITFIELD STOP

*SEEK VOICE COMM AT EARLIEST CONVENIENCE STOP
AWAITING RESPONSE K.*

"How do you want to reply, Governor?"

"Tell them to stand by. In the meantime, get on the ham radio and get me Governor Emerson and General Buford. Get Adams, too."

Pvt. Waya replied to the Morse code. He then reached over and keyed the mic for the ham radio. Whitfield stood by, waiting patiently. During the wait, several others in the room had walked over to where she was standing. Without words, they could all sense something was up. After another minute, the ham crackled with the unmistakable voice of Governor Emerson.

"Mary? Emerson here. What's up?"

"Standby, Governor. I'm waiting a moment to see if General Buford and General Adams are joining."

"Understood."

Another moment passed, and both replied and were on the frequency. Whitfield keyed the mic, "Thank you all for responding. Listen, I just received a message in Morse code. Let me read it to you. After that, Governor Emerson, if you could be the first to share your thoughts, General Buford, then General Adams."

Whitfield read the message word for word and awaited feedback.

Governor Emerson responded, "This is bizarre. How do we jump from President Cyrus to President Parry? What happened to the Vice-President? How do we know this is not a trick?"

"Well, we don't, Governor. That's what's concerning me," Whitfield answered. "General, your thoughts?"

"I agree, this is strange. Well, ask them what happened to Cyrus. Can we think of any questions to ask to authenticate if it is Parry? I never met the man myself."

"This is General Adams. I never met him, either. We need to move very slowly here, people. Why don't we do this: send a reply and have them join a voice comm on 14.333 MHz ASAP."

General Buford replied, "Great idea."

The two governors agreed. In five minutes, all parties concerned had acknowledged the radio call on the ham radio 20-meter band frequency 14.333 MHz."

Whitfield started the conversation, "This is Governor Mary Whitfield of Oklahoma. Also on this frequency are Montana Governor Wayland Emerson, Supreme Allied Commander of the Continental Armies, General James Buford, and General Eric Adams. To whom am I speaking?"

"Good morning, everyone. This is Jai Parry, President of the United States."

The aides in the room could see Whitfield's face, showing a slight smirk as she keyed the mic to respond, "I have no way of authenticating that statement. Your voice sounds like the man serving as Speaker of the House of Representatives in Washington. What happened to Cyrus?"

"Governor, I completely understand your doubts. President Cyrus was assassinated as he was being arrested last evening. The Vice-President has also been arrested. Both are charged with multiple charges—serious charges—that I'll not get into currently. Some might view this as a *coup détat*. Others and I are looking at it quite differently. As number two in the presidential line of succession, I was sworn in by Chief Justice Fredericks at a little after 8 p.m. Eastern yesterday."

Whitfield looked stunned and recalled the time she had met Judge Fredericks a decade earlier, before he had become Chief Justice. "Ummm, Okay, where was Cyrus killed?"

Parry continued, "At Ford's Theatre in the Capital, by his top aide, Matt Kensington. Matt then took his own life."

Mary was shocked, paused for a moment, and then continued. "Really. Motive?"

"Matt had just had a note handed to him informing him of the deaths of his parents, his brother, and his family at a re-education camp in upstate New York near Syracuse.

"A few months ago, Matt had reported his family as CONs and requested that they be detained and sent to the camp for re-education. Anyway, after he read the note, he went upstairs to the theatre to have a moment alone. On the way up, it appears he just snapped. He cold-cocked an agent and grabbed his gun. Meanwhile, we were downstairs in the process of arresting Cyrus. We were a moment away from taking him into custody when Matt fired a single shot. It struck Cyrus in the forehead. The irony is that Matt fired the shot from the Presidential Booth, the same place where Lincoln was sitting when he was assassinated."

Mary and everyone in the room went silent for a moment. Then she had an idea, "Is the Chief Justice with you now?"

"As a matter of fact, he is. He's been beside me during this conversation. Also with us is his law clerk. He has an antique analog stenograph machine and has been recording our talk. Let me hand the mic over to the Chief Justice."

"Governor Whitfield, this is the Chief Justice of the United States, Douglass Fredericks. Mary, speaking with you again is an honor and a pleasure."

Whitfield was stunned. She immediately recognized his deep, raspy voice. "Justice Fredericks, it was an honor to meet you years ago. How long has it been? About ten years or so ago, I'd say. You remember me?"

"Do I remember you? Of course I do! As I recall, it was at a lecture at Atlanta's John Marshall Law School in the summer of 2054. The topic was 'Law in the Ancient World.' You asked a lot of great questions and made quite the impression on me that day. I remember thinking you were destined for great things."

Whitfield was flabbergasted. She had never shared that story with anyone. The fact that he recalled it removed any doubts in her mind that it was the Chief Justice on the line. Still, she queried one more time, "Justice Fredericks, are you under duress?"

His reply was immediate, "Certainly not! Mary, I understand your hesitancy, but everything you've heard here today is true. Jai Parry is now the President. I administered the Oath of Office yesterday evening in the Lincoln Bedroom of the White House at a quarter past eight last night. Mary, we need to stop the killing. I beg you to please listen to what the President has to say. I'm handing the mic back over to him now."

"Governor Whitfield and everyone else listening. Given my complicity in this national tragedy, I consider myself an interim President. Along with my fellow co-conspirators last evening, our immediate goal was to remove Cyrus and prepare for the re-establishment of Constitutional law. Not some brand-new charter, but the original one from 1787 with all its amendments fully intact, with not one word changed. At the proper time, sooner rather than later, I will resign from the presidency, remand myself into the custody of the proper authorities, and face what may come. At which time, I will expect nothing less than a peaceful transfer of power. None of this can happen, of course, until the war is ended, and we stop the killing. Governor, what are your terms?"

"Standby." The Governor had another idea pop into her head. She remembered her college years on spring break thirty years earlier, when she toured historic sites in and around Cincinnati, Ohio. Two sites, in particular, left a lasting impression. The first was the boyhood home of the 18th President of the United States, Ulysses S. Grant, who, before he was the President, served as General of the Army for the Union under Lincoln during the First Civil War.

The second site was the childhood home of Harriet Beecher Stowe in Cincinnati. *Perfect*, she thought. She keyed the mic, "Mr. President, I propose we meet in two weeks in Cincinnati at the home of Harriet Beecher Stowe, author of the anti-slavery classic, *Uncle Tom's Cabin*."

|||| **27** ||||

STEAM AND LIBERTY

ILLINOIS RAILWAY MUSEUM

Union, Illinois

0700 CDT — 21 Sep 2064

The AmRRON had carried the news of the ceasefire now in effect. News of it had spread across the nation via the analog ham radio operators of AmRRON, as well as other ham operators not affiliated with them. From the operators, word had spread by word of mouth.

All good soldiers hate war and wish for peace. Buford was no exception and had been delighted at the news of the pause in the fighting.

For the last three weeks, General Buford's headquarters had been set up on the grounds of an antique railroad museum in Union, Illinois— just north of U.S. 20.

Coming upon the museum had been a surprise after rolling into Union. The museum had many 100-plus-year-old analog diesel and even older coal-fired steam locomotives.

The general had assembled a team of mechanically inclined soldiers for a special meeting this morning at 0700. At precisely that time, he entered the room with his protective detail.

Colonel Oswald turned and saluted Buford and yelled, "Ten-hut!" The room went quiet. Seventy-six soldiers stood up at attention. The general took his place in front of the room. "At ease. Good morning, everyone. Regarding the ceasefire news of a week ago, it remains in place until further notice. I currently have no further updates to report. As soon as I do; I'll pass along the news.

"With this pause in the fighting, we now have an opportunity right under our noses. Yesterday, I thoroughly toured the grounds here. With every piece of our modern transport inoperable since the EMP attack, I'd like to explore getting as many of these steam engines fired up and moving as possible. The railroad mainline is conveniently located right next to the museum property. These old dinosaurs could be an absolute godsend if we can get them running on the mainline.

"These iron horses are fully analog and should run. All they need is water and fuel—wood or coal. Coal would be preferable, but since coal can't be found here, we'll use wood. I know it's scarce after much of it has been harvested to supplement heating and cooking needs by the locals here. But there's wood still out there. This is where you folks come in. Your orders are twofold. Acquire a sufficient supply of wood and get these steam engines up and running. There are hundreds of pieces of rolling stock here that could be used to transport supplies for both civilian and military needs. Questions?"

Sergeant Anderson spoke up. "General, any help available from museum staff that could show us how these things operate? These things are 120 years old, or more."

"Great question. I want to hand the conversation over to Jason O'Neil. He's the caretaker here at the museum. Jason."

"Thank you, general. Everyone, I'm glad you're all here. I've been a CON all my life. As to your question, regrettably, most of the staff's knowledge is off to war somewhere. A fair number of staff who were too old to fight are in poor health. We may be able to interview them and gather any information they have that could help us. I know some stuff about steam engines, but sadly, I don't know the important parts, like firing up a boiler and operating a steam locomotive. But, hey, God gave us a brain, and Americans are known for having an indomitable spirit. So, let's give it a shot and see what we can do. General."

"Thank you, Jason. I love your can-do spirit. Questions?"

"General, what about the diesel electrics? Seen several of those locomotives on the grounds here, too."

"Good question, Private. We have some biodiesel, but we need to keep it in reserve in case someone figures out how to get our equipment running again. Maybe later, if it becomes apparent that it won't happen, we could siphon some of our diesel off for one of the diesel electrics. Come to think of it, if anyone here has any old knowledge on diesel, go with this man. What's your name, Private?"

"Private Gary Reyes."

"You're Private Reyes no longer. You're now Sergeant Reyes. Congratulations. Anyone with diesel knowledge should follow Sergeant Reyes. Jason, lead these men to your best candidate diesel-electric. Everyone else, work on a steamer. We'll reconvene here at eighteen-hundred hours and check your progress."

1800 CDT

"Ten-hut!"

General Buford walked in and ordered the men at ease. "Jason, what can you tell us?"

"Thank you, General. I split our group into three. I put four guys over in the library to pore over all the printed manuals on our best chance, the Atchison, Topeka and Santa Fe Steam Locomotive number 2903. She's a 4-8-4 built in 1943 by the Baldwin Locomotive Works out in Eddystone, Pennsylvania.

"She last steamed up seven years ago. Been in inside storage ever since. She's the fastest steamer we've got. She'll do over a hundred miles an hour on a good track. I put a group of ten guys, one per side, to check on the wheels, grease, and other stuff, all under my direction. The rest I sent out to fetch wood all up and down the sides of the tracks. There's still a fair amount of scrub trees out there.

"Sergeant Reyes was a big help. It took his team all of an hour to realize the diesels were not gonna start anytime soon. They came over and joined our work on the 2903. A little later and the library guys came running over after finding the manual on how to fire her up. Reyes started poring over the manual. We just got her running, not more than 30 minutes ago. We decided not to blow the whistle because we wanted to surprise you. Wanna step outside and see it?"

Buford beamed. "Would I!? Hell yeah!"

After stepping outside, everyone waited anxiously as O'Neil walked toward the tracks and gave a hand signal. Down the tracks a hundred yards, the tracks disappeared underneath the door of a mammoth pole barn. A soldier was standing next to the door and saw the hand signal. He disappeared inside via a side door. A moment later, the barn door slid open. As it did, enormous puffs of steam billowed from the inside. A moment later, a sound no one there had ever heard before. It was muffled, sounding like *chuff.* The locomotive slowly emerged from the barn, emitting a plume of steam, and then began making a louder *chuff-chuff* sound. A large crowd gathered to watch the spectacle. As the engine got closer, Buford could see Sergeant Reyes's head sticking out of the locomotive engineer's compartment. Buford smiled and waved at Reyes. Reyes waved back. Then, without warning, Reyes pulled the steam whistle chain, and it let out a loud blast. It was the loudest sound yet to come from the old steam engine. Everyone jumped and whooped and hollered.

Reyes continued slowly moving the locomotive forward until it was parallel to the group. Everyone could feel the ground vibrate. He then braked, slowed, and came to a complete stop. Looking out with a big grin, he looked straight at General Buford, saluted, and yelled over the steam hissing out of the behemoth. "Mission accomplished, sir."

Buford smiled, laughed, went to attention, returned the salute, and yelled back. "Well done, Sergeant!"

Reyes jumped down from the cab and was quickly mobbed by the soldiers.

Buford turned and looked at O'Neil and asked, "Say, is there a nickname associated with this locomotive?"

"Not that I can recall. She's always been known as 2903 for as long as I've volunteered here."

"Well, if it's not too much of a bother, can we paint a name on her? Sort of a nose art kind of thing, as it were. I'd like to name her *The Liberty Special.*"

IIII **28** IIII

CINCINNATI

HARRIET BEECHER STOWE NATIONAL HISTORIC HOME

Cincinnati, Ohio

1207 EDT — 28 Sep 2064

The Harriet Beecher Stowe National Historic Home was declared a national historic site by President Peterson in 2041.

The home—dating back to 1833—was constructed to provide a residence for the Rev. Lyman Beecher, a Presbyterian minister, and his family. He had moved the large family there from out East after accepting a job offer in 1833 to teach and serve as president at the nearby Lane Theological Seminary in the Walnut Hills area of Cincinnati.

The seminary had been founded four years earlier in 1829. Cincinnati was founded in 1788 on the north bank of the Ohio River.

The city had grown into a prosperous and important hub, as well as a hotbed of the abolitionist movement, prior to the First Civil War.

The reverend fathered thirteen children. His daughter, Harriet, would marry and become Harriet Beecher Stowe, a renowned author of the era.

Harriet Beecher Stowe went on to author thirty books, such as *1843's The Mayflower: or Sketches of Scenes and Characters among the Descendants of the Pilgrims*, *1856's Dred, A Tale of the Great Dismal Swamp*, *1874's Woman in Sacred History*, and *1877's Footsteps of the Master*.

Without question, her most famous work, *Uncle Tom's Cabin*, was published in 1852. Its impact further fueled the fire for the growing cause of abolition, more so than any other written work of that era.

Harriet's interest in the abolitionist movement solidified after attending the famous Lane Debates at Lane Seminary in Cincinnati and witnessing a slave auction in Kentucky. She became increasingly stirred to lend her voice to the growing movement calling for the abolition of slavery.

Whitfield's choice of the venue was purposeful. She meant to silently send a signal of respect and love. No more, no less.

Getting here from Oklahoma City had proved a monumental challenge. No planes, no trains, no cars. Finally, her protective detail settled on assembling a small motorcade of biodiesel-powered trucks, accompanied by a follow-up tanker truck to keep the vehicles fueled along the route. Plan B was a series of horse trailers also in the motorcade. In the event of an unforeseen issue, they'd saddle up and go by horseback. Whitfield loved horses, but not that much.

The journey had been a nine-hundred-plus-mile drive that had taken nearly twenty hours. Arriving yesterday afternoon, Whitfield had requested a tour of the home before retiring to her room for the remainder of the day.

Arising early, she and the President had breakfast at 7:30 a.m. At 8:30 a.m., they had convened in the dining room for four hours. After concluding discussions on ending the war, Whitfield had requested that she and President Parry be allowed to sit alone on the front porch of the historic home. An aide had put out two rocking chairs and a small table. It was a sunny and comfortably warm day, with a smattering of puffy white clouds. The breeze was light, and they had just been served some lemonade, although ice was not available.

Parry spoke first, "Governor, it's been a long and terrible road to get to this point. Do you think the other governors will sign off on the terms here today?"

"I can't speak for them. But I do know them quite well by now, and I think they'll all agree to the terms. Maybe a tweak here or there, but nothing major, I expect."

"I must say I was quite shocked at your proposal at the outset, but in a good way," said Parry. "I know I must face charges in due time, as must others."

"I'm certain that you along with Secretary Sheldon, General Gage and others involved in the plan to remove Cyrus will receive consideration for those actions when deciding your fate. I will personally have something to say about that when the time comes."

"What about all the soldiers and FEDs from numerous agencies that turned their backs against the Constitution? What's to become of them?"

Whitfield paused for a good long moment, then spoke, "After this war started, I did some reading on the First Civil War. Regarding your question, I think we have some history to help us.

"Before his death, Lincoln had issued a fair number of pardons as well as spoke about the need to heal up the nation's wounds and that punishing every single Confederate soldier would cause more harm than good. Still, the issue was not fully resolved at the time of his assassination.

"President Andrew Johnson, Lincoln's successor, issued a pardon to all Confederate soldiers on Christmas Day of 1868. I memorized part of it. The President wrote, 'Unconditionally and without reservation, a full pardon and amnesty for the offense of treason against the United States, or of adhering to their enemies during the late Civil War, with restoration of all rights, privileges, and immunities under the Constitution and the laws.'

"President Andrew Johnson articulated his reasons for doing so and revealed his sentiments. What he wrote, I must admit, rings well with my soul. He explained that his pardon would, in his own words, 'renew and fully restore confidence and fraternal feeling among the whole, and their respect for and attachment to the national government, designed by its patriotic founders for the general good.' I read all that and thought to myself, *There it is, right there under my nose.*" A simple, but powerful one-word update written for this current time could say, 'renew and fully restore confidence and fraternal feeling among the whole, and their respect for and attachment to the Constitution, designed by its patriotic founders for the general good.'

"Governor, shame on me for not knowing our nation's history better. That's powerful stuff you just recalled. You memorized all that?"

"Well, just last night."

"Ha, I needed a laugh." President Parry paused, then asked. "Assuming the governors all agree, where do you propose we meet next for the formal surrender?"

"I thought of several candidate venues. I kept coming back to the one that just rings out within me. Inside the Lincoln Memorial, a month from today."

SURRENDER

LINCOLN MEMORIAL

Washington, D.C.

1145 EDT — 28 Oct 2064

The assembled dignitaries and VIPs had filled the interior of the Lincoln Memorial. It was a cool and overcast day. One befitting the somberness of concluding the Second Civil War.

The nation was in tatters. Recovery would take years. But at least the killing had stopped.

The ANN was finally back on the air, courtesy of the AmRRON. General Buford had arranged for a member of the AmRRON to be present with an analog ham radio so that the proceedings could be broadcast live to all ham operators in the nation with analog rigs. The ham operator chosen for the surrender ceremony was Theodore Lee from Harpers Ferry, West Virginia. His technician was Christopher Hyane, also of Harpers Ferry.

Anchoring the broadcast was ANN anchor Olivia Kinley. After

her arrest by the New Way and being sent to a re-education camp, she escaped and had a harrowing journey to the Blue Ridge near Harpers Ferry. She had been fighting the New Way as a soldier in the Army of the Shenandoah for the cause of liberty.

Wounded twice, Buford had heard her story and passed it along to Governor Whitfield, who, in turn, insisted she be here today to add her voice to the ceremony.

There had been some tension between the brass at the Pentagon and Buford over the issue of who would coordinate the broadcast. The Pentagon, now back under Constitutional authority, was rapidly forming up an Analog Communications Department and had asked to solely facilitate the surrender broadcast. But Buford had declined and insisted that the Civilian AmRRON Corps would take the lead, and the military analog radio operators would facilitate the AmRRON. Buford wanted to send a silent message that "We the People" were running the show again, not the military or anyone else. Parry had ordered the brass to stand down on the matter.

At precisely noon, Theodore Lee keyed the mic, "This is KD9THG broadcasting live from Washington. We are covering the surrender ceremony that will officially end the Second American Civil War. My name is Theodore Lee. I'm a member of the American Redoubt Radio Operators Network operating on the 40-meter band. I will now hand the microphone over to Olivia Kinley of the American News Network. Olivia."

"Thank you, Theodore. It's good to be back. It's been three years since I was last on the air bringing you the news. The ANN has been off the air ever since the EMP attack. We're glad to be back on and will continue to use ham radio to bring you the news for the foreseeable future. Once we get our own analog system setup, we'll announce our frequency over the AmRRON."

Olivia continued, "I'd like to describe the scene for you now. We are inside the Lincoln Memorial. Our broadcast equipment and the desk I am sitting at are just a few feet away from the marble statue of our 16th President.

"I have just gotten up and have walked over, so that I am standing right in front of Lincoln. I'm looking out onto the National Mall. I can clearly see the partially demolished Washington Monument. It is surrounded by soldiers of the Army of the Potomac. I'm told they will remain encamped there indefinitely to oversee the restoration of the monument.

"Off to the right, but not visible, the demolished remains of the Jefferson Memorial. Down the National Mall, the still-smoldering remains of the Smithsonian. I'm walking back to our table now. We're situated between the last two columns, towards the back of the memorial, which separates the Central Chamber, housing Lincoln's statue. From here and looking inside the north chamber of the Memorial, we see the immortalized last paragraph of Abraham Lincoln's second inaugural address engraved in marble.

"He delivered these words on March 4th, 1865. Little did Lincoln know that he would live just another forty-one days before his assassination on April 14th. I will now read the marble inscription: 'With malice toward none; with charity for all; with firmness in the right, as God gives us to see the right, let us strive on to finish the work we are in; to bind up the nation's wounds—'"

In a flash, traumatic memories suddenly rushed into Olivia's mind of her perished family as well as fallen soldiers and friends from the war.

She also recalled her own grueling ordeal. Pausing, she began to shed tears. "I'm sorry, give me just a moment," she said.

With tears in her eyes, she was unable to read the engraved words. After another moment, she regained her composure and wiped away her tears. "I'm so sorry. Let me continue: 'to care for him who shall have borne the battle, and for his widow, and his orphan—to do all which may achieve and cherish a just and lasting peace among ourselves, and with all nations.'"

Quiet weeping could be heard throughout the memorial.

After wiping her eyes once more, Olivia cleared her throat and spoke again. "Below the inscription, a long table with black linen. The table edges are adorned with purple bunting, a sign of mourning. Atop the table, the instrument of surrender was to be signed by key leadership of the New Way and key leadership of the Constitutionalists.

"Most dramatically is this: Off to the back left corner and facing somewhat towards the back of the memorial, to avoid even indirect sunlight, the three panels containing The Declaration of Independence, the Constitution of the United States, and the Bill of Rights.

"There is a heavily armed honor guard posted on all sides of each of the three panels of our Founding Documents." Pausing, Kinley walked back over to her desk and continued, "It is now noon and time for the signing of the Instrument of Surrender."

At precisely noon, Governor Whitfield and President Parry met at the black table and signed the Instrument of Surrender. Olivia dutifully described in detail the clothes, the motions, the expressions of everyone who had the duty or the obligation to sign as well.

One by one, the names of the key leaders of the Constitutionalists were called, and they signed. The exact process was repeated for the renegade New Way government leadership as they queued up to sign the surrender document. Then the key leadership of both militaries. It took thirty minutes, and then it was done.

By prior agreement, President Parry would retain his office for thirty days. After which, he would resign and remand himself into custody.

General Chamberlain had been appointed as Military Governor. Over a third of the members of Congress were dead. Martial law would remain in place until new elections could be held and the new Congress sworn in.

With the signing complete, Governor Whitfield walked over toward Olivia. Olivia handed over the mic to the Governor. "Mr. President, members of Congress, Distinguished Governors, Chief Justice Fredericks, ladies and gentlemen of the press, and citizens of the United States of America.

"We have just concluded signing the Instrument of Surrender. A great tragedy has inflicted a grave wound upon us all. It will take time to heal. It will take time to reconstruct. It will take time to get back on our feet. But we will.

"Minute by minute, hour by hour, day by day, month by month, year by year, together in union, we will come back. It will be hard. It will be very hard. However, we Americans are a resilient people.

"A few weeks ago, I became aware of a remarkable story of a father and son who had lost touch during the war. Both fought for the New Way. The father, like millions of Americans, became disillusioned with the New Way and joined the Constitutionalists to fight alongside us. The son believed his father was dead. The son continued fighting against us.

"They met again on the great battlefield that was the Battle of McHenry, which was part of the much larger Battle of the Fox River Valley, now known as GB2, or Gettysburg II. Caked with the filth of hand-to-hand combat, each was unrecognizable from the other. One—the younger— sought to kill the elder. Suddenly, as if by Providence, the veil slowly began to lift from their eyes. First came confusion, then disbelief, and finally, recognition of the truth. Neither would nor could slay the other. Both dropped their weapons, then they wept and embraced.

"Please welcome father and son, now reconciled, Lieutenant Colonel Jackson King of the Illinois National Guard and his son Master Sergeant DeShawn King."

For a full minute, the crowd rose to its feet and offered up sustained applause. Governor Whitfield finally motioned for quiet and spoke, "In peacetime, Jackson King is Bishop King of Christ the King A.M.E. Church back home in McHenry, Illinois. He has a message for us today that we all need to hear. Bishop King."

After another ovation ensued, Bishop King approached the microphone. He turned and motioned for his son to come stand beside him.

Bishop King closed his eyes and appeared to be saying a silent prayer for a moment. When finished, he turned and hugged his son, then turned back to face the crowd.

Taking a deep breath, he started, "Before I begin, I just want to clear one thing up. I've been asked a few times already if I am related to Dr. Martin Luther King Jr. I am not. I merely have the same last name as that great American. I just wanted to get that out of the way.

"My fellow Americans, here we are now, in the year of our Lord,

2064, and a great chasm has nearly swallowed our country whole and destroyed us all.

"Indeed, my heart is heavy today over what has happened to us these last few years. Before going further, let me present two scripture readings. "The first is from 2 Corinthians 3:17. 'Now the Lord is that Spirit: and where the Spirit of the Lord is, there is Liberty.'

"The second is from Galatians 5:13. 'For, brethren, ye have been called unto liberty; only use not liberty for an occasion to the flesh, but by love serve one another.'

"I first delivered this sermon on February 20 of 2061. It has been slightly edited to fit this current time.

"Five years before the war, I had the blessing of being able to take a vacation to the Holy Land and then also a trip to Italy for three days. In preparing this sermon, I was reminded of the Sistine Chapel, which I visited on that trip, and of how that beautiful church of old can serve as a metaphor for a lesson on the United States of America.

"Bear with me, please. Construction on the Sistine Chapel began in 1473 under the auspices of Pope Sixtus IV. Construction was completed in 1481. The Chapel was consecrated two years later, in 1483. Fast forward 28 years, and the record shows that between 1508 and 1512, the famous Renaissance artist Michelangelo created magnificent works of fresco art on the ceiling and walls of the Chapel. The most famous is *The Creation of Adam*. Recall that it depicts God, surrounded by cherubim, reaching out and touching Adam's outstretched fingertips and giving him the gift of life. The last fresco, *The Last Judgment*, was begun in 1535 and completed in 1541.

"I must say, the visit to the Sistine Chapel took my breath away. It is a

UNESCO World Heritage Site. From the laying of its foundation in 1473, it took a long time to get to that state of magnificence in 1541. That's a long time for just one church.

"Construction of the United States of America could not begin without a foundation. The building of that foundation began in the early 1600s with the arrival of the first colonists, notably at Jamestown, Virginia, on 4 May 1607, but that colony failed by 1610.

"On 11 November 1620, the Pilgrims disembarked from the Mayflower and set foot upon North American soil at Plymouth Rock. The Plymouth Colony would later become a part of the British Crown Colony of Massachusetts.

"Construction continued all through the 1600s and into the 1700s. Then, on 4 July 1776, our forefathers signed the Declaration of Independence, which states, 'We hold these truths to be self-evident, that all men are created equal, that they are endowed by their Creator with certain unalienable Rights, that among these are Life, Liberty, and the pursuit of Happiness.'

"After the War of Independence had been won, construction resumed with the signing of the United States Constitution on 17 September 1787 and then, two years later, the Bill of Rights on 2 October 1789. I have goosebumps looking at them over there right now.

"In pondering our current national tragedy, a series of thoughts occurred to me regarding the Sistine Chapel. Consider this: if I had been born in that prior era as opposed to my present station here in this era, and I had visited that church, say, in the year 1484, what would I have seen? A medieval church of no small stature. From a functional form, finished and likely adorned with some statues of the divine, his

Holy Family, and his first followers, the Apostles. Of course, there would also have been candles and a crucifix, but not much else in the way of artwork worthy of future awe and wonder by the world over.

"If truth be told, its interior would sufficiently lack beauty regarding exceptional works of art to glorify God and Christ. To be blunt, it would be a physically finished building, yet an incomplete and flawed edifice to the divine.

"If I had returned to the Chapel in, say, 1509, I of course would have seen some of the early frescoes by Michelangelo and would no doubt have been delighted that the former state of the Chapel, mostly devoid of art, was now coming along and alive in that regard." The Bishop paused here for effect and then added an inflection to his voice, "The flaws were in the process of being remedied!"

After letting that sink in for a moment, he continued. "If perchance, tragedy had taken my life in 1510, I never would have seen the finished works of Michelangelo's first set of frescos, completed, as I stated earlier, in 1512. But, for the illustrative purposes of this sermon, let me reverse my fate, and I do not perish in 1510. I next visit the Chapel on Christmas Eve, 1541. The final completed work of Michelangelo's fresco, *The Last Judgment*, is on the ceiling. Think about that: this World Heritage site, built in 1473 and consecrated that same year, hosted worshipers for nearly 70 years, yet it had shortcomings.

"Only later did those shortcomings become remedied with the last of Michelangelo's frescoes in 1541. In between the start and the finish, the Chapel was a work in progress.

"It is a true statement that upon the founding of this nation, the codified enslavement and deliberate dehumanization of us Black folk led to all manner of evil. This is true. This is an undeniable historical fact.

"Our country was born with flaws. But what happened? Well, white folks, in partnership with free Blacks, formed abolitionist societies. Their purpose was to educate the populace, North and South, regarding the evils of chattel slavery and to persuade all people, great and small, that this evil should be purged from the American fabric.

"It is also a true statement that upon the founding of this nation, insult was added to injury in that hard-coded into the Constitution was the clause which stated that only three out of every five enslaved people would be counted when determining a state's total population for legislative representation and tax levies. All of this was degrading, of course. Said another way, and it was, we were labeled as being three-fifths of a person! The LORD rebuke that! And rebuke it he did.

"The abolitionist's work profoundly affected many people. One, a young lady named Harriet Beecher Stowe, the author of *Uncle Tom's Cabin*. Another, a young man in Illinois named Abraham Lincoln. As early as the 1840s, Lincoln supported the exclusion of slavery in the nation's westward expansion into Missouri, Kansas, and beyond.

"In 1860, Lincoln was the first president elected with less than fifty percent of the popular vote. He won 180 electoral votes. His opponent, Democrat John Breckinridge, received seventy-two electoral votes, followed by John Bell with thirty-nine, and Stephen A. Douglas with twelve.

"Because of Lincoln's strong anti-slavery views, the Southern states rebelled and started a war over it on 12 April 1861.

"Then, in 1864, after three bloody years of Civil War, President Lincoln removed a significant flaw in the fabric of the nation by emancipating all enslaved people. Before that, he had wrongly believed at the beginning of the Civil War that the conflict was solely based on saving the Union. It was only after much blood had been shed that he came under deep conviction that God had allowed the Civil War as a divine judgment for the shed blood of the innocent and enslaved people.

"Lincoln said exactly that when he delivered his Second Inaugural Address on 4 March 1865. Our sister Olivia here just read the last paragraph, which is engraved in marble above me.

"We Praise God that the Confederacy lost that war!

"We Praise God that as our history continued after that war, which then saw more of our nation's flaws remedied in the twentieth and twenty-first centuries.

"We Praise God that this war is over, and that the Constitution and our Bill of Rights have emerged intact!

"We Praise God that the forces of darkness, that tricked so many of us, has been defeated! Those strange voices from before this war saw no beauty in our nation or her founding documents. They saw no redeeming value in keeping this nation together under the ties that have bound us together since the founding in 1776. No, they spoke of 'cancel' or, worse, 'burn it all down' and starting over. If their side had won, what would they have started over with? Marx, Lenin, Alinsky, Soroskaya?

"Washington, Jefferson, Adams, Franklin, Hamilton, and many others who founded our nation did so with reverent fear. Most acknowledged the flaws from the start. Yes, sadly, some of them owned enslaved folks. But they had faith, and they laid the foundations after which this grand experiment we call America would have its sins and shortcomings put through the refiner's fire. Those impurities burned away, leaving behind the purest of gold.

"By God's mercy, this war is now ended. Millions are dead, maimed, homeless, and hungry.

"For the sake of brotherly love, not hate, but for love, it is our moral duty to turn our swords into plowshares. Let us also strive towards the goal of being that city on a hill and that no enemy, foreign or domestic, would prevail to snuff out the light of liberty, now or ever in the future.

"Let us also renew our brotherly love for one another, even when we disagree. I recall the words of a hymn from 1995, '*How Deep the Father's Love for Us*,' by Stuart Townend of the United Kingdom. He wrote: How deep the Father's love for us, how vast beyond all measure, That He should give His only Son, to make a wretch His treasure.'

I ask you, with such a great love Father God has for us; to redeem us wretches, how can we ignore his greatest commandment of all to love our neighbor as ourselves?"

Pointing to the engraved marble high upon the wall, Jackson paused and read the words with all the reverence he could muster. "The hallowed words above me bear repeating yet again: 'With malice toward none; with charity for all; with firmness in the right, as God gives us to see the right, let us strive on to finish the work we are in; to bind up the nation's wounds, to care for him who shall have borne the battle, and for his widow, and his orphan—to do all which may achieve and cherish a just and lasting peace among ourselves, and with all nations.'

"I now close with these eternal words, which even more so, bear repeating, 'Three things will last forever—faith, hope, and love—and the greatest of these is love.'"

At that, Jackson walked a few steps over to his seat and sat down in total silence.

After a moment, Jai Parry stood and began to clap. Then Governor Whitfield, then DeShawn King, then more and more until the whole room of LIBs, MODs, and CONs in unity clapped with fervor.

|||| EPILOGUE ||||

Governor Mary Whitfield sat quietly satisfied in her study. With her was her longtime friend, Chief Billy Waya, Speaker of the Oklahoma House of Representatives. They had just concluded a compromise draft piece of legislation regarding the ongoing recovery efforts in the state.

"Well, Billy, if you get elected today, and I'm sure you will, we're sure gonna miss you around here. But I just know that you'll be a fantastic member of Congress representing our state."

The Chief was wearing his ceremonial headdress today. Holding a glass of water, he had walked over and stood looking out the window of the study on a chilly and mostly overcast day, "Thank you, Mary. If the people of this state send me to Congress, I plan to do my part in the nation's recovery efforts." He turned, looked at her, and smiled, "Say, I heard the good news about some farmers getting their ancient analog tractors running. Should help the planting and harvesting next season."

Whitfield returned the smile at her longtime political rival and friend, "Yeah, that was a bit of good news for a change. Those farmers are ever resourceful. They helped build this country into the breadbasket of the world. Maybe they'll have an even bigger role in our recovery than I imagined."

Waya took a sip of water and asked, "What are you going to do, Mary. You running for re-election?"

"You know, I've been thinking about that. I'm not sure. My husband says I should run for President. I'm actually considering it."

ABOARD THE LIBERTY SPECIAL

Near Cleveland, Ohio

1200 EST — 3 Nov 2065

General Buford was enjoying the ride in the cab of the ancient iron horse. She was having no trouble at all pulling a hundred cars behind her. Half laden with wheat and corn and half filled with relief supplies from government warehouses in the Midwest. It felt good for him and some of his soldiers to be out on a mission of mercy rather than a mission of death from the war.

Getting the old iron horses up and running had been a challenge. Every time he thought of Sergeant Reyes back in Union, Illinois, he would smile. After being promoted, Reyes was put in charge of a program to get other old steamers up and running. It was a challenging and dirty job that so far had netted five fully functional steamers.

Their mission today was a multi-stop tour of Ohio. Stop number one was Cleveland. The citizens there were in dire straits, and he was eager to bring them these much-needed relief supplies. Up in the cab with him was Master Sergeant DeShawn King. They had met at the surrender ceremony at the Lincoln Memorial. They struck up a conversation, and Buford had taken a liking to King. The General offered him a role in the relief efforts, and he accepted.

Over the noise of the behemoth engine, Buford yelled, "King, when we pull into the yard, I need you to stick with me to meet the mayor. I hear he's a likable man."

"Yes, Sir. What do we do then?"

"We'll go over the manifest for the boxcars we're going to decouple and leave behind. Afterward, the mayor wants to have a short and simple fish fry lunch at the railyard with some of the day's catch of walleye. He's aware of our schedule. It's a watering stop here anyway, so we'll be okay timewise."

"Sounds good. I've not eaten much the last day or so."

"Me either. I took in another notch on my belt this morning. Anymore and I'm gonna start looking like Barney Fife."

King gave out a slight laugh, then suddenly grew nervous. Now was as good a time as any. "General, I have a confession to make. It's been gnawing at me since the war ended. I know that I have to come clean. Every fiber of my being is telling me so. Just before the war started, I was involved as the leader of the Chicago Gold Coast one-percenter operation. I'm the one who killed Melvin Barclay."

Buford looked stunned. "Really. Well, we'll need to talk about that at the end of the day."

THE KING RESIDENCE

McHenry, Illinois

1100 CST — 3 Nov 2065

Bishop King was busy using a pencil to write his Sunday sermon on a scarce piece of paper. With a good harvest from all the local gardens in, he was feeling cheerful that they'd make it through the winter okay.

Eleanor was busy cleaning fish and getting ready to put them into the smoker. She looked over to Jackson and inquired, "Hon, what's your sermon on for this Sunday?"

"It's a sermon on faith in lean times. I'm using Isaiah 41:10, which states. 'Fear not, for I am with you; be not dismayed, for I am your God; I will strengthen you, I will help you, I will uphold you with my righteous right hand.' What do you think?"

"You know that's one of my favorite verses. Change of subject. It sure was good to see DeShawn the other day at the train station, ridin' *The Liberty Special.* You suppose they're in Cleveland yet?"

"I expect so. What a sight, seeing him and Buford gettin' along. A proverbial swords into plowshares moment if I ever saw one."

"Amen."

ARLINGTON NATIONAL CEMETERY

Arlington, Virginia

1200 EST — 3 Nov 2065

General Steven Sickles had heard of the unexpected passing of his old friend General Nathan Pope via a courier from a nearby AmRRON station. Chamberlain arranged the courier. Upon receipt of the message, Sickles had determined he would ride on horseback to the funeral at

Arlington National Cemetery. It took three days from his farm near Gettysburg to get to Arlington.

Now graveside, Sickles was moved with emotion. Pope's eldest son Brad was taking his father's passing very hard. Pope had received a Presidential Pardon for violating the soldier's oath to preserve and protect the Constitution of the United States against all enemies, foreign and domestic, and in joining the insurrection. It was Pope's dying wish and an act of contrition that he requested his casket be draped with the Stars and Stripes.

Brad was now holding the tri-folded Stars and Stripes flag. Sickles walked up to him and put his hand on his left shoulder and patted it. "Your Dad was a good friend and an even better father. I will remember him always."

LEAVENWORTH SATELLITE PRISON CAMP (MINIMUM SECURITY)

Leavenworth, Kansas

1100 CST — 3 Nov 2065

Jai Parry, Frederic Sheldon, and General Gage were in month number three of their eighteen-month prison sentence for insurrection against the United States, all three of them having both plead guilty to the charges of sedition and insurrection.

True to her word, Governor Whitfield of Oklahoma had come to Washington on *The Liberty Special* for the express purpose of appearing at the sentencing hearing and arguing the case for leniency for the conspirators in the plot to forcibly remove the rogue President Cyrus from power.

She successfully argued that their bold and decisive action to stop Cyrus most likely prevented the deaths of many more millions of Americans from nuclear annihilation.

EXECUTION DAY

Fort Leavenworth, Kansas

1100 CST — 3 Nov 2065

The disgraced Homer stood motionless against a brick wall. Colonel Williamson approached the mic and read from the death warrant, "Jeffrey Homer, having been found guilty of insurrection against the United States of America—for crimes against humanity, for having violated the soldier's oath, and having planned and convinced the disgraced Devin Cyrus to launch a first-strike nuclear attack against Charlotte, North Carolina and Atlanta, Georgia in the Second Civil War resulting in the deaths of twenty-eight million Americans—having been sentenced by a Military Courts-martial, the sentence of death by military firing squad will now be carried out. Does the prisoner have any last words?"

Homer's voice, muffled by the white hood over his head, rang out in a defiant tone, "My only regret is that we didn't win."

THE WHITE HOUSE

Washington, D.C.

1222 EST — 3 Nov 2065

General Wallace Chamberlain had spent the last year coordinating the military government and overseeing the re-implementation of Constitutional federal operations of the United States Government.

Working with President Johnson and Chief Justice Fredericks, they had developed a special binding referendum as a part of the Special General Election Day 2065. The election was to elect members of Congress to replace those who had perished late in the Civil War.

They all had agreed that their crowning achievement was the Term Limits Amendment Referendum. They were excited to hear that polling data showed it would pass by a large margin. The wording that the three of them had agreed upon was on the ballot. "Shall the Constitution of the United States be amended to set Term Limits as follows: For the Office of Senator of the United States Senate, no person elected on or after November 3, 2065, shall serve more than one six-year term for their natural life. For the Office of Representative of the United States House of Representatives, no person elected on or after November 3, 2065, shall serve more than two two-year terms, even if not consecutive."

By agreement, currently surviving members of Congress (only a third from the Senate and House) were exempt from the term limits.

Also on the ballot, a binding referendum to reinstate the Electoral College.

Sitting on benches in the White House Rose Garden, the two reflected on the past year.

Chamberlain sat in an Adirondack chair in the grass beside the White House Rose Garden. President Johnson sat next to him. After a bit of silence, Chamberlain spoke up, "Mr. President, it's been an honor to work with someone who supports the Constitution with the same fervor that I do. The country is still suffering greatly, but we have a solid foundation for the future. I'm hopeful."

Johnson nodded, "I'm hopeful, too. That said, I can't get that awful day last year out of my mind."

"I don't think anyone ever will. How could we?", Chamberlain said.

Johnson nodded again, "You know, I often think of that speech or sermon Bishop King gave at the surrender ceremony. The words are seared into my heart. I wonder how he's doing back home in Illinois?"

The General took a sip of his coffee, then answered, "I dunno. I'll hop on the AmRRON a bit later and find out."

"That would be great. Pass along my sentiments that his powerful sermon that day is having a positive and lasting impact. It really is."

IIII CIVIL WAR 2.0 STATS IIII

Start date: April 12, 2061.

End date: October 28, 2064.

Belligerents: Socialist/Communist (New Way) forces vs Constitutionalist (Old Way) forces.

Victorious side: Constitutionalists.

Conventional Warfare Military Casualties: New Way Forces 1.5 million. Old Way Forces 900,590.

Civilian Non-Nuclear Casualties (combined both sides): 1.8 million.

Civilian Nuclear Casualties: New Way First Strike, Atlanta, 14 million. Charlotte, 11 million. Old Way Retaliatory Strike: Chicago, 8 million. New York, 8 million.

Number of Major Battles (3 days or longer): 76.

Number of Minor Battles (2-3 days): 467.

Approximate Number of Skirmishes (1 day or less): 5,117.

Has reading *The Sum of All Our Anger: Civil War 2.0* left you disturbed, anxious, or frightened?

The novel was designed to prompt the reader to ask soul-searching questions: How do we avoid the nightmare of a Civil War 2.0? Am I contributing to the widening divisions in America? Have I ceased to show love to those I disagree with? Have I been deceived in some way?

As a husband, father, and grandfather, I took no comfort in imagining what a Second Civil War might look like.

In writing this story, I had a threefold goal in mind:

1. To act as a deterrent towards preventing Civil War 2.0.
2. To defend the Constitution against all enemies, foreign and domestic.
3. To point Americans back to Almighty GOD.

On the first point, for starters, we need to relearn the art of agreeing to disagree and remain family, friends, and citizens in Union.

We as Americans also need to relearn the art of compromise in our political discourse. It is our current no-holds-barred, take-no-prisoners, non-negotiable stance that has put us all in grave peril.

At present, family members, friends, and more are increasingly estranged from one another. This is sad and needs to stop. Reconciliation begins within each of us. Reach out and make amends. Mix all the above with a strong dose of Jesus Christ's *Golden Rule*, and doing all this would go a long way toward preventing a second Civil War on American soil and toward ensuring we remain a free people in a Constitutional Republic.

On the second point, the strange voices in our present day that seek to destroy our American way of life—built upon the Founding Documents of our Republic—must not be allowed to win.

The extremist voices on the far left are a clear and present threat to our Constitutional Republic.

While the extreme right is also a threat, it has no sway in mainstream institutions of higher education. It is in those places—where tomorrow's leaders are being formed—that radicals are emerging in numbers that dwarf those who identify as white nationalists.

The anti-American, anti-Constitution, and anti-God movement in these institutions is alive and well, actively swaying young minds against the bedrock foundations of our Republic.

I believe in my heart that "Burn it all down" is not the answer. Americans essentially are builders, not burn-it-downers.

On point three, I also firmly believe that no politician or political party, current or future, will save this nation. That power alone rests with Almighty GOD.

We the People must return to worship and follow the Ruler of the Universe with humility, contrition, and love, to seek forgiveness and lead in the way forward out of our current crises.

I bid you peace.

William R. Douglas

Stories that tied into the plot.

It was sobering to write this novel and have so many storyline themes emerge in the national news while I was writing.

Some touchpoints were indirect; others were spot-on. Most themes were already typed up, and then a news story would appear that mirrored the theme in part or in whole. It was uncanny and unnerving at the same time.

The list below is by no means exhaustive. There are new stories almost every week that, in small or large ways, touch upon themes in the novel.

To read the whole article, copy-paste the headline below the date into your browser, and you should find it. If not, go to my author page at www. authorwilliamrdouglas.com, click the "News Articles" link, and you'll see a list of news stories, including new ones since the book's publication date.

04/11/2024 – New York Post
Seattle dance squad says they were told American flag shirts made audience members feel 'triggered and unsafe'

04/08/2024 – Detroit News
'Death to America' chants in Dearborn echo across social media, draw local condemnation.

03/13/2024 – ABC News
College Park, Maryland DEI Officer Kayla Aliese Carter "Already planning (BEEN PLANNING) for how we will eat and live and grow after we burn it all down."

07/29/2024 – Air Force Times
Pentagon Developing Combat AI Drone Aircraft.

03/04/2024 – Keith Oberman X Post
Former MSNBC on-air personality Keith Obermann calls to dissolve the United State Supreme Court.

02/07/2024 – New York Post
'Woke Kindergarten' founder Aliea 'Ki' Gross calls for the destruction of the United States and Israel.

01/11/2024 – NBC News
Texas Governor Abbot wields 'Commander in Chief' pen in ordering Texas National Guard to secure the border at Eagle Pass, TX.

01/08/2024 – Associated Press
National Park Service to remove William Penn statue, (Founder of Pennsylvania), from Philadelphia Park. (After a huge outcry, they rescinded the order.)

12/15/2023 – Associated Press
Minnesota edges closer to picking new state flag to replace design offensive to Native Americans.
(Another news organization showed some of the early submitted entries included the hammer and sickle. Thankfully, the final redesign was narrowed down and does NOT include the Hammer and Sickle.)

11/15/2023 – Texas Tribune
Texas secessionists feel more emboldened than ever.

10/20/2023 – UVA Today (University of Virginia)
Americans Say To Meet Political Agendas, Rights May Be Left Behind

10/11/2023 – NBC News
Rep. Shri Thanedar of Michigan renounced his membership in the Democratic Socialists of America over rhetoric at a rally the group promoted a day after the Hamas attack.

10/06/2023 – Newsweek
Hillary Clinton's Cult 'Deprogramming' Comments Spark MAGA Outrage

08/07/2023 – Nation Review
American Library Association Leader Surprised by Pushback after Publicly Identifying as 'Marxist'

06/19/2023 – The Hill
Former NFL star Colin Kaepernick says, 'Black Liberation Isn't Possible Under Capitalism.'

05/22/2023 – Denver Gazette
Colorado teachers' union adopts anti-capitalist polemic.

02/15/2023 – Idaho Capital Sun
Idaho State House calling for formal 'Greater Idaho' talks.

11/14/2022 – The Center Square
Movement to create a new state in southern Illinois gaining momentum.

11/07/2022 – Harvard Politics
The American Flag: A Symbol for Some or All?

08/19/2022 – New York Times
The Constitution Is Broken and Should Not Be Reclaimed
(Authors note: Law Professors Dr. Ryan D. Doerfler of Harvard Law School and Dr. Samuel Moyn of Yale Law School, in a "Guest Essay" in the New York Times write that "The Constitution Is Broken and Should Not Be Reclaimed."

07/07/2022 – RED FAULT, an Austin DSA Publication
Creating a Socialist Vision for Public Libraries: A Conversation with Emily Drabinski. (Author's note: Emily was elected in 2023 as the President of the American Library Association. Their policies and advocacy reach Public libraries in every state in the Union.

06/20/2022 – The College Fix
Student activists seek to remove Lincoln statue at University Wisconsin–Madison.

07/21/2021 – NBC News
Protesters tore down 3 statues of US presidents in Portland last year. What happened to them? (Washington, Lincoln, and Theodore Roosevelt)

01/19/2021 – CBS News
Most Americans don't know what's in the Constitution: "A crisis of Civic education"

07/03/2020 – Lakota Peoples Law Project

Return Mount Rushmore and the Black Hills to the Lakota!

06/26/2020 – Associated Press

Black leader wants Lincoln statue at UW-Madison removed.

06/19/2020 – CNN News

Protesters tore down a George Washington statue and set a fire on its head.

11/09/2017 – ABC News

'Star-Spangled Banner' is racist, must be replaced, California NAACP says

|||| **ABOUT THE AUTHOR** ||||

William R. Douglas is a two-time novelist. After obtaining a Journalism Degree in 1980, his career took a turn toward Information Technology. In the IT Field, he was still able to enjoy writing, whether it was technical documentation, newsletters, or other material.

He has worked for companies such as EDS, IBM, Sears, Walgreens, and The Boeing Company.

He lives in the small town of McHenry, Illinois, with his wife, Laurie, and cat, Peaches. They enjoy spending time with their kids and grandkids and are very active in their local church.

Follow the Author: www.authorwilliamrdouglas.com

|||| OTHER WORKS ||||
BY WILLIAM R. DOUGLAS

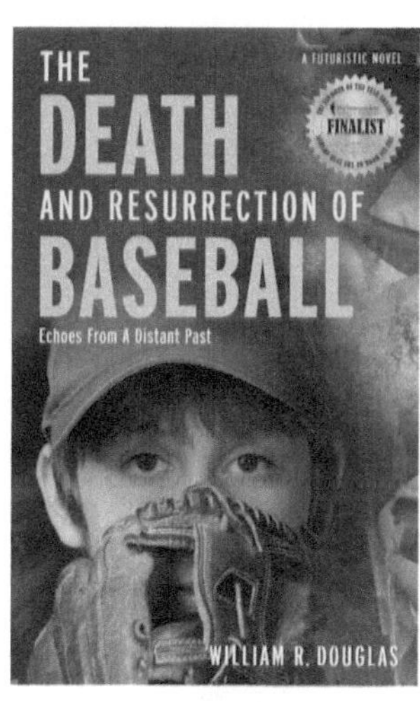

My debut novel, *The Death and Resurrection of Baseball: Echoes from a Distant Past,* is a futuristic "what if" story in which several factors contribute to the extinction of the sport of baseball. One of those factors was a proverbial nail-in-the-coffin event, a Second American Civil War beginning in the year 2061. The baseball book plot starts in the year 2166, a full hundred years after the end of Civil War 2.0

The baseball book is a feel-good story of hope featuring 12-year-old protagonist Joe Scott.

That debut novel has been well-received and was recognized as a Finalist in the Independent Author Networks 2023 Book of the Year Awards. Also, the book was recognized as a Finalist in the Readers' Favorite Book Awards Contest for 2023.

I appreciate your support.

QR CODE FOR THE   QR CODE FOR THE
1ST NOVEL   U.S. CONSTITUTION

www.ingramcontent.com/pod-product-compliance
Lightning Source LLC
Chambersburg PA
CBHW032108310726
48972CB00001B/142